# LOST
# INNOCENTS

Also by Patricia MacDonald

*Mother's Day*
*Secret Admirer*
*No Way Home*
*The Unforgiven*

## MOTHER'S DAY

"Keeps the reader hanging on until the bitter end."
—*Mystery News*

"MacDonald digs with relish into the town's secrets, and its stockpile of hot emotions—betrayal, rejection, anger, jealousy, and unrequited lust—pushes the buttons that titillate readers."
—*Publishers Weekly*

"A thrill-a-minute chiller from the author of *The Unforgiven*."
—*Ocala Star Banner*

## NO WAY HOME

"Patricia MacDonald's novel is that rarity, a thriller that stirs the emotions as well as excites the senses. Her superb tale of life and death and, in the end, life reborn, is one you will not soon forget."
—*San Diego Union*

"A perfect summer's read . . . a mystery of uneasy answers."
—*New York Daily News*

## THE UNFORGIVEN

"Real and immediate . . . almost hypnotic . . . gruesomely effective . . . a scary, engrossing book."
—**Stephen King**

"A terrific psychological thriller. Full of suspense and intensely readable."
—**Mary Higgins Clark**

# PATRICIA MACDONALD

# LOST INNOCENTS

**WARNER BOOKS**

A Time Warner Company

This book is a work of fiction. Names, characters, places, and incidents are either the product of the author's imagination or are used fictitiously, and any resemblance to actual persons, living or dead, events, or locales is entirely coincidental.

If you purchase this book without a cover you should be aware that this book may have been stolen property and reported as "unsold and destroyed" to the publisher. In such case neither the author nor the publisher has received any payment for this "stripped book."

WARNER BOOKS EDITION

Cover design and photo illustration by Tony Greco

Warner Books, Inc.
1271 Avenue of the Americas
New York, NY  10020

Visit our Web site at
www.warnerbooks.com

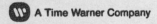 A Time Warner Company

Printed in the United States of America

Originally published in hardcover by Warner Books.
First Paperback Printing:  November 1999

10 9 8 7 6 5 4 3 2 1

*To my nephews, Stephan, Andrew, and Thomas Oliva,*
*with love*

# *Prologue*

## Tuesday Afternoon, Late October

*R*ebecca Starnes tossed her hair back and sat up straight against the park bench, surreptitiously tucking her knit shirt into her jeans so that it would lie more smoothly over the curves of her chest. Out of the corner of her eye, she watched the guy in the parking lot jumping off the wall on his skateboard and landing back on the pavement. It was a daring trick, and she tried not to gasp each time he missed. He was wearing wraparound sunglasses, so it was impossible to tell if he was glancing her way. She definitely did not want him to think she was staring.

Rebecca was pretty sure she had seen him before, probably at basketball games. But she didn't know which school he went to. There were a lot of Catholic high schools in the area, and it was a big league. He could be from any one of them. For sure he didn't go to Perpetual Sorrows, because she would never have missed seeing him around her own school. She draped an arm over the back of the park bench and tossed her hair again.

A woman pushing a baby carriage along the winding

sidewalk stopped in front of Rebecca and smiled. "He's cute," she said. "How old is he?"

"Six months," Rebecca said impatiently. Justin Wallace, seated in his stroller beside Rebecca, was busy examining his round, thick plastic teething ring covered with pictures of Donald Duck and the nephews.

Rebecca craned her neck to try to look around the woman, who was blocking her view of the skateboarder. The woman, absorbed in smiling and waving one finger at Justin, did not seem to realize she was in the way. Rebecca sighed and tried to be polite. "How old's yours?" she asked, indicating the carriage the woman was rocking gently.

"Just an infant," said the woman, giving the netting over the carriage a proprietary pat. "He's sleeping."

"Not Justin," Rebecca said, glancing at the baby beside her, wishing the woman would move on. "I'm just babysitting for him," she explained.

As if realizing that no mother-to-mother camaraderie was to be had here, the woman said good-bye, gave Justin another little wave, and resumed pushing her carriage. Rebecca glanced up from under lowered lids and saw that the skateboarder was still there. She arranged herself again on the bench, hoping to look attractive but not provocative.

Meanwhile Justin shook his teething ring impatiently, gnawed on it a moment, then regarded it with the curiosity of a research scientist formulating an experiment. Silently Justin considered the boomerang effect. He studied the possibilities, then let the teething ring fly. He had no sooner released it from his tiny hand than he realized that he had miscalculated. The teething ring dropped with a tiny thud only a foot away from him, in the dirt under the puffs of crisp brown petals on a dying hydrangea bush. Justin's lively gray eyes, recently alight with anticipation, now clouded over. His face crumpled as he let out a loud, pitiful wail.

Distracted again from her fantasies about the skateboarder, Rebecca turned and frowned irritably at her charge. The temptation to bark at him faded away as she gazed at him. He looked adorable in the little red sweater with the Dalmatian on it that his grandmother had knitted for him. Rebecca loved all kids, but she loved Justin especially. His parents were young and they had to work hard to make ends meet. Usually Donna's mother helped them out, but occasionally they asked Rebecca to fill in. Rebecca enjoyed taking care of Justin. She would have done it for free, just to help them out. But Johnny and Donna always insisted on paying her. Rebecca thought it was kind of romantic, the way they were starting out together, having a family.

Of course, whenever she mentioned this around her mother, Sandi Starnes would have a fit. "Don't think you're gonna go off and get pregnant and have your mother for a ready-made baby-sitter," she would cry. "No way." Over and over she would warn Rebecca that she had no idea how hard it was to be a mother as young as Donna Wallace. And her mother ought to know.

Rebecca's father had left when she was only five. He had another family now, up in Massachusetts. Rebecca saw him three times a year. He wasn't bad as fathers went, but Rebecca knew her mother had to work hard to make ends meet. She'd taken on extra shifts at the restaurant so that Rebecca could go to Catholic school. Rebecca gazed at the baby in the stroller. It seemed as if having a baby to care for would be wonderful, but a lot of mothers, like Donna Wallace and her own mom, ended up having to work all day. A lot of families seemed to just break apart. Still, it didn't have to be that way. Some marriages worked out, she thought defensively. Some people stayed together.

She looked ruefully at Justin. "What's the matter, Justin?" she asked sympathetically.

Justin looked up at her, helpless to explain. Tears brimmed in his eyes and coursed down his round cheeks. Rebecca reached into his stroller for the miniature crocheted afghan, also his grandmother's handiwork, which lay in a wad around his knees, and pulled it up over his denim pants and red sweater. "Are you cold?" she asked kindly. It was getting a little chilly. Autumn had been warm up till now, but it was almost November, and the days had taken a sharply cooler turn.

Justin reacted furiously, feeling the bitter frustration of the supremely misunderstood. He wailed louder and shook the bar in front of him with his dimpled fists. "Justin," Rebecca muttered, wondering if the cute guy on the skateboard was judging her incompetent. "Cut it out. What's the matter? Stop crying. You want your bottle? I'll get it for you. Just stop crying."

These were the moments when Rebecca knew her mother didn't have anything to worry about. Rebecca wasn't about to get herself tied down with a baby. She wanted to go to junior college and maybe train to be a lab technician. She liked science. It was her favorite subject at Perpetual Sorrows. She wanted a condo and her own car, and she wanted to be able to help out her mother with money now and then. Rebecca smiled ruefully to herself as she thought about her mom, worrying over nothing.

Rebecca didn't even have a boyfriend yet, much less plans to have a baby.

She went around the stroller, crouched down, and rummaged around in the pocket for the bottle of apple juice. She felt her cheeks flaming as the baby yowled, and she didn't dare look up to see what the skateboarder's reaction might be.

"I think this is what she's looking for," said a male voice.

Rebecca froze, startled but hopeful. She hadn't heard anyone coming up behind her. Maybe this was him—the skateboarder. Maybe he was taking the opportunity to make a move to talk to her. She took a deep breath and raised an expectant face. Instead of the daredevil skateboarder, a grown-up man stood in front of her. Wearing dull chinos and a windbreaker, he held out the teething ring in one hand.

She glanced over at the parking lot. The skateboarder was gone. Rebecca sighed. "Thanks," she said, reaching for the teething ring. Justin sat up in his stroller and watched the exchange, wide-eyed. "It's a he."

"Really?" the man asked, surprised. "I thought with those curls . . ."

Rebecca ran a fond hand over Justin's head of soft ringlets. "A lot of people think that," she said. She reached out for the teething ring.

"It's kind of dirty," said the man, looking at it. "He threw it under that bush over there. Let me wash it off in the water fountain."

"Okay, thanks," she said. She scrambled up from behind the stroller and resumed her seat on the bench. The man walked over to the water fountain and rinsed off the teething ring. Then he brought it back and handed it to her. He sat down on the same bench, not too close, but Rebecca had a fleeting feeling of unease. She told herself that this was not some weirdo. He was completely normal looking.

"You must be very proud of him," he said pleasantly, in a way that suggested Justin belonged to Rebecca.

"Oh, he's not mine," said Rebecca, marveling to herself at how adults could be so dense. First the other mother, now this guy. Rebecca didn't like to think she might look old enough and boring enough to be a mother. "I'm just baby-sitting for him." Justin had resumed chomping happily on his teething ring. "I'm only fifteen."

"Oh," said the man, nodding. He took a packet of cheese crackers out of the pocket of his windbreaker and opened it. He took a bite out of one of the crackers. "Don't you have school?" he asked.

Rebecca shook her head. "I go to Catholic school," she explained. "It's a Holy Day of Obligation."

"Ah," he said, nodding. He munched on his cracker thoughtfully. Then he seemed to remember something and held out the packet. "I'm sorry. I didn't mean to eat in front of you. You want one?"

Rebecca shrugged. She was a little bit hungry. She hesitated for a moment, though. Like all kids, she'd heard about taking candy from strangers. Parents were forever panicking about things like that. This was not exactly some drooling pervert in a deserted place. A woman with glasses was seated on a bench just down the winding path, reading a book. Rebecca could see her glancing up occasionally from where she sat. Some Chinese guy was doing those Buddhist exercises in a clearing across the pond. A police car had rolled slowly by not ten minutes ago. All these things flashed through her mind as she gazed at the cheese crackers in the cellophane. You had to think of these things. After all, all those stories in the papers gave you the creeps. Not necessarily here in Taylorsville, but you never could tell. . . .

The man gave her a wry smile. "They're not laced with anything," he said. "I just bought them over there at the 7-Eleven."

Rebecca blushed, humiliated that the man had read her thoughts, that he knew she was suspicious of him.

"Don't be embarrassed," he said, reading her mind again. "These days, you can't be too careful. Children are the most precious thing in the world, and they have to be warned to be on their guard. I'm sure your folks have drummed that into your head. I mean, every parent worries about that kind of thing."

Rebecca assumed this meant that he had children and immediately felt a little more at her ease. She smiled, although in truth his words made her feel wistful. She wished she had a dad who would call his child the most precious thing in the world. She couldn't quite picture Bud Starnes saying that about her. "I'm not a child," she said.

"What's this little guy's name?" he asked, gesturing toward the stroller with the half-empty packet.

Rebecca glanced down at the stroller, glad for the change of subject. "Justin," she said. "Justin Mark Wallace. He's my buddy." At the sound of his name, Justin looked up and gave Rebecca a wide, toothless grin. Rebecca smiled back. Then she reached for a cracker.

The man grinned, nonchalantly edging closer to her. He leaned his arm across the back of the bench so that his fingers could ever so slightly graze her flesh.

# Chapter One

$\mathcal{A}$s the car pulled over to the edge of the cobbled, circular driveway, Maddy Blake gazed up at the sprawling, Tudor-style house in the fading twilight. Amber-colored leaves drifted silently down from the stately trees, carpeting the emerald lawn. Thorny branches climbed up the sides of the imposing home, making it look rooted, as if it had stood there forever. "Wow," Maddy said. "This is quite a place. No wonder he charges so much."

"Worth every penny," said Doug defensively.

"Oh, I agree," she said hastily, avoiding her husband's glance. "Absolutely."

Maddy and her husband, Doug, were invited here, to the home of Charles Henson, Doug's attorney, to celebrate. Last week Charles had successfully argued on Doug's behalf against a charge of sexual misconduct with a female student at the high school where Doug was a history teacher. The administrative law judge who heard the case had dismissed all charges, and after five weeks out of work, Doug had his job restored. Nevertheless his reputation was not as easily regained.

"I've heard the wife comes from money," said Doug. "That makes a big difference."

It was Maddy's turn to cast a sidelong glance at her husband, who gazed steadily through the windshield. Was that a barb? she wondered. This ordeal had been exhausting and expensive. All their savings had gone into paying Charles Henson for Doug's defense and to paying the bills while Doug was out of work. Maddy was a stained-glass artist who worked for herself, so her income was sporadic. She certainly did not come from money, but she had worked steadily, trying to keep the money coming in while Doug's job was in limbo.

Doug did not give her time to think about it. He leaned over the seat and smiled his dimpled smile at their three-year-old daughter. "We're here, Amy," he said. "Time to get out of the car."

Amy, who was fair like her father, gave her dad a dazzling grin. "I'm bringing George," she said, waving the stuffed monkey who was her constant companion.

As he leaned over the seat, Maddy studied her husband's soft, sandy blond hair and gentle eyes and thought how handsome he looked in his tweedy sports jacket and tie. She had not been surprised to find that a student had a crush on her husband. A few years ago Maddy herself had fallen for him at first sight. But the way the student had described it—that Doug had blackmailed her, demanding sex for a good grade . . . Fortunately, by the time it got to the courtroom, Doug's accuser twice failed to appear, and finally, when she did testify, Charles Henson's skillful questioning revealed that she was telling three stories at once.

"Can't you leave the monkey here?" Doug said with a frown.

Amy's face crumpled. "I need George," she pleaded.

"Oh, let her bring him," said Maddy in a low voice. "They're the ones who insisted we bring her. Little kids come with stuffed animals."

"Okay, why not," said Doug.

Maddy turned to her daughter. "You can bring George. It's okay."

Maddy and Doug got out of the car, and Doug opened the back door, reached in, and undid his daughter's car seat restraints. Maddy smoothed down the knit dress she was wearing. She hadn't known what to wear for this occasion. "Do I look all right?" she asked.

"You look great," said Doug, holding Amy's hand and coming around the car to where she waited.

"I still don't really understand why they wanted us to come here," Maddy whispered. "And to bring Amy." They had invited Charles and his wife out to dinner to express their gratitude, but Charles Henson had made a counteroffer.

Doug shook his head. "I don't know. He said his wife doesn't like going out. I think she's a little odd. Somebody told me that she had some kind of breakdown and spent a year in a mental hospital."

"Really?" Maddy asked.

"I don't know that for sure," said Doug. "These days I'm a little leery of gossip. And of course it wasn't the kind of thing I would ever have mentioned to Charles."

"No, of course not," Maddy said thoughtfully.

"Anyway, I'm sure the dinner will be fine. I think he said that they have a cook."

"Don't get me wrong. It's all right with me," said Maddy. "I'm happy to have dinner wherever he wants. He saved us from disaster."

Doug smoothed down his hair. "Well, it wasn't as if I'd actually done anything wrong," he said.

"I know. I know," Maddy said hurriedly. "I'm just saying that it could have turned out . . . Innocence doesn't seem to be a guarantee of anything these days."

"I'm underwhelmed by your support," he said dryly.

Maddy took his arm, immediately feeling guilty. "I'm sorry," she said. "I didn't mean for it to sound that way. Of course I believe in you. It's just that . . . I'm tired, too, honey. Tired out from . . . this whole experience."

He nodded and patted her hand, which was tucked in his arm. Maddy did not look at him. It had been surprisingly easy to stand by him when Heather Cameron made her accusations and the school board suspended him. After the initial shock, she had immediately surged to his defense. They were embattled as a couple, as a family, and resistance had been the natural thing. Now that it was over, now that she had time to think, she was ashamed to admit that she found herself wondering.

Doug led the way across the driveway and started up the flagstone walk. The front door of the huge house opened. Charles Henson appeared in the doorway, dressed casually in a polo shirt and a cardigan. His thick, silvery hair was perfectly combed; even in sports clothes he exuded an air of formality. A fragile-looking woman peeped around from behind him. "Come in, come in," Charles called as they walked up to the front door.

Doug extended his hand and the two men shook hands. Doug clasped Charles's hand with both of his, and Maddy pressed her lips together as she watched them. Doug's gratitude seemed slightly obsequious. Don't be so critical, she chided herself. Of course he's grateful.

"Thank you for—for inviting us," Doug stammered.

"Welcome, Maddy. And Amy," said Charles. He knew them all from the courtroom and from strategy sessions at their house. "I want you to meet my wife, Ellen."

Maddy smiled warmly at the lovely, timid-looking woman behind him dressed in jeans and a chambray shirt. She was as slim as a girl, though Maddy judged her to be nearly fifty. She was still beautiful, with masses of gray, dusty-looking curls pinned up in a topknot. Ellen greeted Maddy, but her gaze was fixed on Amy. She crouched down and admired George, speaking gently to Amy. Maddy felt an immediate liking for anyone who paid such careful attention to a child.

"Come in and have a drink," said Charles. "I don't think Paulina has dinner ready quite yet."

As if in answer to his remark, a round woman in an apron appeared in the hallway. "Half an hour to dinner," she said in a middle European accent. "Does the child want a frankfurter and mashed potatoes?"

"Oh yes, that would be fine," Maddy said gratefully. "She loves hot dogs."

They followed Charles into the huge living room filled with expensive leather furniture, thick rugs, and ornately framed artwork. Maddy's eyes were immediately drawn to the painting that hung over the fireplace mantel. It was a portrait in oils of a much younger Ellen with her arm protectively encircling a small boy of perhaps four or five. He must be grown by now, Maddy thought. They probably have grandchildren.

Charles poured flutes of champagne and handed them around. "Let's drink to justice being done," he said.

Doug stared into the tiny golden bubbles in his glass. "Charles, I don't know how I can ever thank you. We had some bad moments in these last few months."

"Don't worry. You'll feel less grateful when the bill arrives."

Everyone laughed nervously.

Maddy sighed. "I'm just so relieved to have this nightmare behind us," she said. "I mean, this girl made these accusations, and suddenly our whole world was in chaos."

Charles Henson frowned and nodded. "It's terrifying. And the fact that she is the daughter of the chief of police didn't make matters any easier. It's the new McCarthyism. That's what I believe. Kids today have a frightening power. They're sophisticated enough to know just what to say so that their accusations sound believable, but they're young enough so that they have no concept of how their malicious whims can destroy a person's life."

"But Charles," his wife interrupted gently, "you know there is a lot of ugliness in this world. Some of them are just innocent children. . . ."

Ellen Henson's words struck Maddy in the pit of her stomach. Does she think that Doug is guilty? Maddy wondered. Is that what she's trying to say?

Charles was unfazed by his wife's objection. "Darling," he went on smoothly, "I am the first one to admit that a lot of children are victimized by adults, and we need to pay more attention to it, but it's mushroomed out of control. It's become a witch-hunt."

"Well, I think Heather Cameron is a very troubled young girl," said Maddy. "But that's not my husband's fault."

Charles tipped his champagne flute in her direction. "The way you supported your husband was admirable, and helped us immensely in court."

Maddy blushed and looked uncomfortable. "I think it

was obvious to the judge that Heather was lying," she said.

Ellen set her crystal flute on a mahogany end table and spoke softly. "I have something I want to show Amy before dinner. Amy, do you want to come outside with me?"

Amy looked up eagerly, always ready for a new distraction. Ellen extended a hand to her. Maddy put her flute on the table. She found the transition a little abrupt, but she was glad to change the tone of the evening. "I'll come along," she said.

"Good. Mommy's coming with us." The two women and the child walked toward the door as Charles indicated a seat to Doug and he sank gratefully into it.

Once outside, Amy began to run, and the two women walked along behind her, their hands in their coat pockets, their shoes crunching on dry leaves.

They walked in awkward silence for a few minutes, and then Maddy said, "We really are very grateful to your husband."

"Charles is very good at what he does," Ellen said evenly.

Maddy nodded, but she had a distinct impression of disapproval from the older woman that made her feel uneasy. Maddy recognized, with a sick feeling in the pit of her stomach, that she was going to meet with lots more of this kind of reaction. This victory in court did not mean she could let down her guard. People loved to believe the worst. . . . Maddy cast about for something else to say. "This is a beautiful place you have here."

"Isn't it," Ellen agreed. "This was my childhood home. I love it here. I do hate to see the winter coming. I'm a great gardener. It's my passion."

"I've got a purple thumb," Maddy admitted.

"I hope you don't mind dining at our home. I don't enjoy going out in public much. I'm a hermit."

"Oh, not at all. It was kind of you to have us," said Maddy, but she could not help thinking of what Doug had said about the rumors of Ellen's breakdown. She cast a sidelong glance at the woman's seemingly untroubled countenance.

"Amy," Ellen called out, "it's back here, in the garage."

Maddy wondered which garage she might be talking about. The house obviously dated back to the days of the horse and carriage. The walkways were lined with gas street lamps, which had illuminated as darkness fell. A series of connected outbuildings bordering the extension of the cobbled drive matched the main house in style. One of the doors was open and light spilled out from within. Ellen pointed in that direction. Amy saw where she was going and barreled toward the open door.

Maddy could hear Amy's squeals of delight before she caught up with her. She came around the corner into the empty garage, and it took a moment to locate the source of Amy's excitement. Inside the doorway, in one corner, was a large cardboard box lined with flannel. Inside the box was a mother cat and a bunch of kittens. They were not newborns, for they were actively exploring the straw-strewn floor of the garage, but they were small and fuzzy, and Amy was clapping her hands at the sight of them. She crouched down to try to pick up the nearest one.

"Don't squeeze it, honey," Maddy said with dismay. She grimaced, knowing it would be difficult to tear Amy away from these adorable creatures.

"Let her play with them," said Ellen. "She won't hurt

them." She led the way out of the garage as Maddy looked worriedly at her daughter.

"I guess it's all right," said Maddy. She followed Ellen up a gentle incline to a wrought-iron bench in a coppice of evergreens. They sat together on the bench. A gas lamp beside the bench threw a mantle of yellow light on their shoulders. The air was damp with the threat of rain. In the distance, surrounded by overgrown bushes, was a small, clapboard-sided house, which looked like a tiny one-room cottage with a carriage light on beside the front door. Despite the lantern's glow, it was impossible to tell what color the building was painted.

"Isn't that darling," Maddy exclaimed. "What is it?"

"It was my son's playhouse," said Ellen. "It's an actual historical building. I think it was once a tinsmith's shop. We had it moved here and restored, years ago."

"It's just adorable. Wait till Amy sees it."

"I don't allow anyone to play in it," Ellen said. Then she added apologetically, "I'm funny about it."

As soon as she said it, Maddy looked closer and saw that the door was padlocked, the windows blocked with drawn curtains. Instantly she felt uneasy again, as if there were something ominous about the cheerful-looking little building. "Oh, it doesn't matter," Maddy said hurriedly, knowing immediately that she had made some sort of faux pas. "I doubt we'll be able to tear her away from the kittens anyway."

Ellen continued as if Maddy had not spoken. Her voice was a dull monotone. "My son's name was Ken. He died when he was five years old. Meningitis. This is his birth-day. He would have been twenty-one years old today."

The tragic confidence struck Maddy like a blow. Somehow she felt as if she had known it, before the words were even out of Ellen's mouth. She had sensed something terrible. She had not even wanted to ask about the boy. But still, it was the worst of all nightmares, and her heart ached for the frail woman seated beside her on the bench. "How awful," she breathed.

"He came home from kindergarten complaining of a stiff neck. In three days he was dead."

"Oh, I'm so very sorry. This must be a very hard day for you. We shouldn't have come today."

Ellen shook her head. "No harder than any other day," she said.

"I can imagine," Maddy said grimly, although she couldn't. Not really. She looked back at the garage, where Amy's blond head was visible.

Ellen nodded calmly, and they sat in silence, each one thinking of her own child.

Finally Ellen spoke. "So, life goes back to normal for you now."

Maddy sighed, feeling the irony of her observation. "I hope so."

"Charles tells me you're an artist?"

"I do stained glass. I have a studio behind my house."

"Really?" said Ellen.

"It started out as a hobby, but I got some orders, and I wasn't really enjoying my job, so . . ."

"So you made it your profession."

"Well, I put some of my work in a local craft shop. But it wasn't a living. Then I got a commission to do a window at the new meditation chapel at the Catholic church. And that led to several others."

Ellen squinted into the darkness, in the direction of the playhouse. "This is fortuitous that I've met you. I've been thinking I wanted to do something with the playhouse. Maybe you could help me."

Maddy felt uncomfortably jolted by the return to the subject of the padlocked playhouse. She tried to keep her expression impassive.

"I was thinking about Peter Rabbit."

"Peter Rabbit?" Maddy asked cautiously.

"You know, that little blue coat he wore," Ellen said. "And Benjamin Bunny. They would make such beautiful windows. I could just imagine it with the light coming through it, making a pattern on the floor. That particular shade of blue in Peter's jacket. Could those drawings be transferred to windows?"

Maddy hesitated. It seemed strange, but then again, that playhouse was probably a shrine to her son's memory. Maddy's work on the chapel windows were all memorials to one person or another, commissioned by loved ones. "It might be possible. Those old windows are very small. And you wouldn't want to replace the original glass," she said carefully. "Maybe something we could hang from a chain. A set of them. . . ."

Charles Henson appeared at the back door of the house. "Paulina's ready for us," he called out.

"We're coming," Ellen called back, getting up abruptly from the bench and brushing off her jeans. "You'll work on it for me, then?"

Maddy stood up, feeling a little disoriented by the conversation. "I'd really need to measure them."

"I'll measure them," Ellen said firmly. "And I'll call you."

Maddy didn't want to say that she needed to do the measuring herself. She wasn't sure anything was going to come of this. There was time to see.

"I want Amy to have one of the kittens," Ellen said.

Maddy wanted to protest, but she had a feeling it would be futile. Despite Ellen's frailty, she was determined. It would not do to argue with her. She and Doug were here to show their gratitude. Still, she felt distinctly uneasy as they headed back to the house. She told herself it was the acquisition of a pet they hadn't planned for. That was all. She picked up Amy and held her tightly as they walked back toward the house.

# Chapter Two

𝕄ary Beth Cameron hefted the huge portfolio of available properties from her file drawer to her desktop, opening it to a prospectus on a handsome brick Colonial that was uncomfortably out of the stated price range of the nervous, neatly dressed couple seated in front of her. She swiveled the book around so that they could examine the photo, lazily caressing the out-of-reach image with one manicured, pale pink fingernail. The two stared down at the grand house like Hansel and Gretel gazing at the candy-covered gingerbread house. "This is a nice one," Mary Beth said, pretending not to notice their anxiety. Mary Beth knew her clientele. Taylorsville had lots of couples like this—not affluent enough to afford the suburbs close to Manhattan, but willing to tie themselves to an inhuman commute in order to have the impressive house. So they came farther north to Taylorsville, figuring to get a bargain. Mary Beth was ready for them. "A little bigger than what you had in mind," Mary Beth admitted, "but with all the amenities a young up-and-coming family could want."

"It's a bit more than we planned to spend," he said.

Mary Beth looked up in mild surprise. "Oh," she said, turning the page with the same pink fingernail. "Well, we have some darling properties in your price range. Let's take a look." She could feel him shriveling at her words, as the wife looked wistfully, perhaps a shade irritably, at the dream house that had disappeared from view. "We can always come back to it," said Mary Beth.

As the pair frowned at the next picture, Mary Beth glanced at her watch. As usual, she was running late. Darkness was falling, and she did have another obligation. As she was always telling her husband, Frank, real estate was not a nine-to-five kind of job. You had to work when you had the clients at hand. This was one of those times.

The bell on the front door of Kessler Realty rang, and the door opened. Mary Beth looked up and saw her daughter, Heather, walk through the front door. She hated that Sue, the receptionist, left promptly at five. A lot of times they were busiest after five, and Mary Beth did not like wearing two hats. She was trying to make some money here. She smiled broadly at Heather, although her eyes remained cold.

"Hello, Heather," she said.

"Hello, Mother," the girl said sullenly.

Mary Beth looked critically at the teenager in front of her. Heather, she thought, took after Frank's side of the family. She had a face as round and white as a plate, with small, pale gray eyes and lank, drab hair that fell to her shoulders. Her figure was good, but not because she did anything to maintain it. If any effort were required, she'd be fat as a house, Mary Beth thought. Heather's clothes did little to enhance her figure; she was wearing baggy overalls with one shoulder unbuttoned over a Henley-style shirt that looked like long underwear. Her unlaced high-top sneakers completed her resemblance to someone who lived in a homeless shelter. No matter how often Mary Beth offered to take her shopping or tried to show her how to use makeup, Heather stubbornly insisted on choosing the most unbecoming outfits. Although she had tried to appear supportive, Mary Beth had not been surprised when the judge dismissed the charges against that teacher. With all the pretty high school girls, why would any man hit on a plain, surly creature like Heather?

"I'll be with you in a minute," Mary Beth said, trying to maintain a semblance of professionalism. "Why don't you take a seat over there?"

Heather regarded her with narrowed eyes. For a fleeting moment, Mary Beth felt a little guilty. She had promised Heather she would be done, but then this couple had come in. Heather just didn't understand that you had to seize the opportunity when it presented itself. "We have some new magazines," Mary Beth suggested, and felt irritated at having to sound like a receptionist. That's how she'd started out in this office, and she had zero interest in going back to it.

Heather shuffled over to the reception area, dropped into one of the tapestry-covered armchairs, and began flipping through a magazine.

"This one looks nice," the young man said hopefully to his disgruntled wife.

Mary Beth turned her head to look at the picture of a newly painted Cape Cod. "Oh yes, that one is adorable. And there's really a lot you could do with it."

"Maybe we should look at it," he said. His wife made a face.

Mary Beth's phone rang. "Take a look at some more while I get this," she said. As she picked up the phone she saw Heather rise from her seat and begin to pace the reception area, glancing up at the clock.

"Mary Beth Cameron," she sang into the phone. "How can I help you?"

"We have to go, Mother," Heather announced. Mary Beth gestured helplessly for Heather to sit back down, but Heather ignored her.

"You told me yourself we have to be there by six," Heather continued in her impassive, foghorn voice. "I'm sick of waiting. We have to go right now."

Mary Beth cupped her hand over the phone's mouthpiece. "I said I'll be right with you," she whispered angrily. She glanced at her clients. Fortunately the young couple was absorbed in the ring binder of properties. They had turned back to the brick Colonial, and the wife was looking much more cheerful. On the phone, Mary Beth's caller rattled on about rentals. Mary Beth nodded and turned away from her daughter's cold gray gaze. Heather returned to the reception area and fell back into the chair with a thud. She glared straight ahead as Mary Beth got down to business.

Frank Cameron, chief of the Taylorsville Police Department, shifted in his chair, looked at his watch, and shook his head in disgust. "I have work to do. I am a busy man. She knows I have a million things to do. She keeps me waiting on purpose."

"Heather?"

"No, her mother," Frank said scornfully.

Dr. Larry Foreman poured himself his tenth cup of coffee for the day and offered one to the chief. He had late office hours two nights a week, and sometimes he ended up skipping dinner altogether. Coffee was his substitute for food.

"Nah, I don't touch it after the morning jolt," said Frank. "One cup a day. That's it for me. That stuff is terrible for your stomach lining. You know that, don't you?"

Dr. Foreman nodded and added sugar.

"Now if you had a beer, I'd take you up on it," said Frank.

Dr. Foreman walked back around behind his desk, pausing to look admiringly at his reflection in the glass doors on the bookcase behind his desk. He looked good—the jogging had taken away that layer of fat. He looked especially good compared with the chief, whose white shirt and tie only drew attention to a stomach that protruded over his belt. Larry resumed his seat in his tufted leather swivel chair. After taking a sip, he placed the coffee carefully on a napkin. "Why do you think your wife would do that?"

"Why does she do anything she does," Frank snorted. "To piss me off." He shook his head. "Are you married, Doc?"

Dr. Foreman nodded, and Frank picked up a framed photograph of the doctor and his wife and daughters that was sitting on the psychologist's leather blotter. Frank gazed at it for a moment and then looked up at the doctor. "You gonna keep on trying for a son? Or did you give up?"

"We were never trying for a son," Larry Foreman said coldly.

"Hmph," Frank muttered. "I have a son. Frank junior. He's married, got a good job, a baby on the way. He never gave me a minute's trouble. Not once. They say boys are more trouble than girls, but that Frankie . . . he was in Little League, honor society, the works. I've always been proud of him. . . ."

"As opposed to Heather," Dr. Foreman said.

"Don't shrink me, Doc. Please, spare me. I have to deal with your kind in court every day." Frank grimaced. "You think you're fooling somebody. Slipping in little remarks. I'm wise to you. So give me a break. I wouldn't be here at all if the judge hadn't insisted we bring her to someone. I guess my wife picked your name out of a hat," Frank mused, trying to be as insulting as possible.

Dr. Foreman avoided the bait. "You were saying you're proud of your son. . . ."

"And I'm proud of Heather. I'm proud of both my kids. They're good kids. But Heather just . . . she's just in those teenage years. A lot of kids run into trouble in those years. I ought to know. I see 'em every day down at the station. Yours aren't there yet, am I right?"

Dr. Foreman shook his head cautiously and glanced at the picture on his blotter.

"Just wait. You'll see," Frank warned him. "Even girls. More of 'em all the time. So you better treat me right so I'll go easy on 'em when they show up down there."

Dr. Foreman ignored the remark about his children. "But this is more than just a little trouble Heather's gotten into, Frank. She could have ruined this teacher's life, his career. That's a serious thing."

Frank Cameron peered at the doctor with a sour expression. "You can call me 'Chief,' " he said.

"You're not the chief in here," Larry said mildly.

This time Frank chuckled. Then he glowered and consulted his watch. "She'll be late to her own funeral," he muttered. "Jesus Christ."

Frank Cameron found the ensuing silence oppressive. He got up from his chair and began to prowl around the office, like a panther in a cage. "Yeah, this is a fancy little office you got here," he said, glancing out the window. "The best neighborhood, plenty of parking. Smells like big bucks around here. No wonder my wife picked you," he snorted. "My Mary Beth's developed a taste for the finer things in life."

Rain had begun to spatter against the pane. Frank peered out the window at the boutique-lined street. "When I was a boy growing up in Taylorsville, this was a nice town. People knew each other. In those days you had your rich people and your working people. Now we got a whole new class of well-heeled social climbers. People like my wife see that and they want it so bad they can taste it." Frank shook his head in disgust and emitted a deep sigh. "In those days, if you had a problem, you told it to the priest or you had a drink and drowned it. Seemed to work out all right. Seemed like we had less crazy people in those days than we do today." He turned away from the window and stared at the doctor. "I think you people make your patients crazy. I never saw one of you who didn't have some kind of mental problem yourselves."

Larry Foreman forced a smile and refused to bristle. He was not about to be cowed by this bully of a cop. Handling people was his business. He was good at it, which was why he was so well paid. "Everybody's got problems, Frank," he replied smoothly. "And you are not alone in your opinion. But we're not here to talk about my profession or my colleagues. We need to talk about Heather and why she is so troubled. Is there a lot of tension at home between you and your wife?"

"Leave my marriage out of this. Heather's the problem. That's what you have to concern yourself with. You just concentrate on Heather. I'll take care of my wife."

"It's possible that problems at home are part of what's troubling Heather."

Frank shook his head sadly, his bluster momentarily deflated. "I don't know what's troubling Heather," he admitted.

"Do you think she was telling the truth about the teacher?" Dr. Foreman asked.

Frank Cameron glowered at the very thought of Douglas Blake. He balled his hands unconsciously into fists and banged one of them on the back of the chair. "I think he's a pervert, and a first-class asshole. He and his fancy lawyer tried to cover up for him by making a monkey out of me. And the judge fell for it. Do you know what that judge said about me? He called the police investigation 'tainted by personal bias.' Tainted! That burns me," said Frank.

"I guess that means you do believe Heather. . . ."

Frank shrugged. "I don't know. She's mixed up. She's just a kid. She gets no kind of help from her mother. Well, you'll see when they get here. If they get here, goddammit," Frank bellowed.

At that moment there was a knock on the office door. Before Dr. Foreman could respond Frank strode over to the door and threw it open. "Where the hell have you two been?" he demanded. "I've got a city to police and I don't have time to wait around—"

Mary Beth edged in past her husband, apologizing to Dr. Foreman, and sat down. Heather walked in behind her mother, flinching at her father's kiss that brushed her forehead, and refused a seat.

"Why are they here?" Heather demanded. "I thought this was for me. I'm not talking in front of them."

"I wanted a chance to meet with your family first," said the doctor.

"Dr. Foreman," Mary Beth began in a confidential tone, "I know you wanted to meet with the family. The reason my son is not here is that I didn't see any reason to involve him in this. He has an important, highly paid position, and a wife who's pregnant with their first child, and they live a good fifty miles from here—"

"Frank junior is perfect," said Heather. "He never got in trouble. He's their hero."

"Heather, keep quiet," said Frank.

"No, it's all right," said Larry. "We're here to talk. To say whatever is on your mind. . . ."

A beeper went off, and everyone looked at Frank, who fumbled with the receiver in the pocket of his leather coat. "May I use your phone, Doctor?"

"There's one outside," Larry said evenly. Frank rose from the chair and left the room.

Mary Beth rolled her eyes. "This is typical," she said. "You'd think he was a brain surgeon."

"Well, Taylorsville may be peaceful, but it's a big town."

"And he likes to be important," said Mary Beth. "He has to be the big boss all the time." Heather walked over to the window and stared out. Rain covered the window-panes by now. In a moment Frank came back into the office.

"I've got to go," he said.

"Frank, you promised me," said Mary Beth in a shrill voice.

"I've got a teenage baby-sitter and the baby she was

watching who didn't come home tonight," Frank said, a warning in his voice.

"Oh," said Mary Beth, sinking back into her chair, chastened by this news.

"Sorry, Doc. If she'd been here on time . . . But this is an emergency. Heather, honey," he said to his daughter, "it's going to have to be another day." Heather stiffened but did not respond.

Larry looked at the girl's face, pale and frozen as an angry moon, and her father, dressed head to toe in the uniform of unquestioned authority, forbidding her to defy him. Larry glanced at the clock. "Heather," he said gently, so as not to startle her, "why don't you sit down and we'll try to sort some things out."

Heather responded to his quiet voice and turned away from her father. Obediently she took her seat.

# Chapter Three

Frank Cameron strode into the chaos of the Taylorsville Police Station, his wary gaze sweeping the room as six people approached him, all clamoring for his attention. Frank's height, his barrel chest, and his iron gray hair gave him an imposing presence. His entrance seemed to calm the room, to give people the impression, however brief, that everything would soon be all right.

Directly in front of him, seated by herself like a quiet island, a fortyish woman in a waitress uniform clutched a school picture of a teenager. She did not look up and appeared to be almost in a trance. "Who's that one?" Frank demanded in a low voice of Len Wickes, one of his officers.

"Mrs. Starnes, mother of the missing girl," Len whispered.

Frank nodded and glanced at the young couple leaning over the desk of Chief of Detectives Pete Millard. They had whirled around as he entered and were looking at him plaintively—the baby's parents. Pete looked up from his desk. "Chief," Pete said, "these are the missing baby's parents, Donna and Johnny Wallace."

Frank shook their hands gravely. Donna's face was red from weeping. Johnny, who was hardly more than a boy himself, was doing his best to comfort his wife. Despite his efforts, he was struggling to maintain his composure. Johnny was dressed in the jeans and flannel shirt he wore on the job as a construction worker for DeBartolo Brothers. Donna was dressed in an ill-fitting flowered dress and pumps, which she had worn to work at the bank and then to the bridal shower for one of her former high school classmates afterward.

"They were just telling me what happened," said Pete.

"He's the third one we've told," Donna protested.

Frank nodded. "Tell me," he said.

"Well," Donna said, exhaling a gust of misery, "usually he stays with my mother, but she had two doctors' appointments today, and since Rebecca was off from school . . ." Donna began to wail and wring her hands. "Why did I ever let her take him? . . ."

Sandi Starnes, the mother of the missing baby-sitter, flinched at the implied accusation. She wanted to shout that Rebecca was a good girl, and they knew it, and that whatever had happened to the baby had happened to Rebecca, too. . . . She forced herself to stop thinking. She just turned off her thoughts. She had decided that the only way to survive this was to sit in stillness and try to let her mind float free from her body. She had seen a show on meditation on the Lifetime Channel, about how you could use it to deal with stress, and now she was trying it. Something like it.

"All right," Frank thundered, pointing to Pete Millard, the middle-aged detective in a gray suit who was taking the Wallaces' statement. "Get to the bottom line, Pete. Sum it up for me."

Pete gave Frank a quick rundown of the situation, or what they knew of it. Rebecca Starnes had kept the baby at her mother's house all morning. At lunchtime, after Sandi went off to work, Rebecca had planned to take the baby out for a walk. They never came back. Donna Wallace, husband in tow, came up close behind the detective and tried to interject details into his account in a voice shrill with fear. Frank, who was not a patient man, nonetheless appreciated the distraught mother's situation and only told her once, in a mild voice, that he was having trouble understanding his officer.

When Pete Millard finished, Frank glanced at the photograph of Justin Wallace that his parents were waving at him. There were so few really innocent things, he thought, looking at the gentle, formless face. In this job he had seen every kind of cruelty visited on the innocents of the world—often by those who claimed to love them most. It was enough to make you sick. He hated the helpless way he felt, looking at the picture. In the pit of his stomach there was a knot of fear that he intended to ignore. He pushed the photo away. "All right, Mr. and Mrs. Wallace. Here's the situation. Normally, with missing persons, we don't begin a search until forty-eight hours have—"

"Forty-eight hours!" Donna shrieked. "You've gotta be . . ."

Frank raised a hand to silence her. "But," he said loudly, "in the case of children—and both of them technically come under that heading—we will begin to search immediately."

He turned to Pete Millard. "I want a tips hot line set up

right away on this one. We need to get the word out to the public. Get the press liaison working on this. We can use the cooperation of the local stations."

"I've already got it in motion," Pete assured him.

"Good," said Frank in a low voice. "It may be premature, but you can't be too careful with missing kids." He turned around and his piercing gaze fell on Sandi, who remained seated. She had ketchup on her white blouse, and she looked dazed, as if she had just awakened. Frank walked over to her and sat in the chair beside her.

"Now," he said. "Rebecca is your daughter."

Sandi stared at the police chief with a bewildered expression on her face. "Something terrible has happened," she whispered.

Frank nodded. "Well, yes, but we just don't know exactly what, right now. Do we? That's what we have to figure out. Could this possibly all be some big misunderstanding? I mean, we've got everybody here screaming about kidnapping and so on—is there any chance Rebecca just decided to take the baby and go visit someone? Can you think of anyone she might have gone to see? Maybe a friend, or a relative?"

"I already asked her that," said Detective Millard.

"Now I'm asking her," Frank barked. Then he turned and spoke quietly to Sandi again. "How about it, Mrs. Starnes?"

Sandi knew what he wanted her to say. He wanted her to give him a list. A list of people an absentminded teenager might have run into, or called up and decided to while away the time with. Someone who might have absorbed her scatterbrained adolescent attention so completely that she would forget to bring the baby back on time, or even to call. Someone like that."

Sandi shook her head. "There is no one," she whispered.

"Are you saying you have no friends or relations? What about her father? Where is he?"

"He's remarried. He lives in Massachusetts."

Frank Cameron shrugged. "Maybe he was in the area. . . . Maybe he came by the house after you left."

Sandi tried to think about this. Bud Starnes was not the worst father in the world. But he was not given to surprise visits. He dutifully fulfilled his responsibilities toward Rebecca. That was all.

"I see you hesitating," the chief said. He twisted around to look at Pete Millard. "Have we got the father's address?"

"I called there already," said Pete. "Nobody home."

"Call again," said Frank. "Now, Mrs. Starnes, did Rebecca mention where she might be taking the baby? Was there anywhere special she liked to take him?"

This was something Sandi could answer. "She liked to take him to the river to see the fishermen," she said. "Or the mall sometimes. To shop. Or the park. She liked to walk in Binney Park. She didn't say."

"I want every man we've got scouring those places," Frank instructed his officers, who were gathered around to listen. "I want anyone who might have seen them questioned. You got me? Anyone. Anyone with a business, or any business, in any of those places. They didn't just disappear. Somebody saw them. We need to establish a time frame—find out where they were last spotted. This is critical.

"Also, I want you to find out who was working at the

train station and the bus stop. I want to know if Rebecca bought any tickets this afternoon. If so, I want to know where she was headed, and with whom. We need all hands on deck. I don't want anybody standing around here."

"Done," said Pete. "We're on it." He spoke in a low, urgent voice to the other officers, who scattered out the door to their various phones.

Frank turned back to Sandi. "Do you know these people well?" he said, indicating the Wallaces. Donna was collapsed against her husband's shoulder, her tears a dark stain on Johnny's plaid shirt.

Sandi looked vaguely at the Wallaces. She would have said yes, this morning. They were neighbors. They lived two doors down and had always been friendly. Johnny shoveled her walk when it snowed because she had no husband to do it for her. She and Donna sometimes had sat on Donna's cement patio together when she was home for maternity leave. Sandi loved seeing the baby. She loved babies anyway, and Donna loved showing him off, as any mother would. She would have said they were friends. That they knew each other well.

Now she knew that wasn't true. Because she heard them, with her own ears, accusing Rebecca. Saying that Rebecca took their baby. No one would ever say that who really knew Rebecca.

"We know each other," Sandi said flatly. "We live on the same street."

"And Rebecca has taken care of Justin before," said the chief.

"Quite a few times," said Sandi, nodding, her gaze beginning to drift again.

"Mrs. Starnes, does your daughter have any history of mental illness?"

Sandi looked at him again. She stared at this strange man, asking her these questions about Rebecca as if she were some kind of nut . . . some kind of criminal.

Sandi tore her gaze from the chief's face and stared down at the picture she was clutching in her damp fingers. She licked her lips, which were incredibly dry, and she tried her best to form her thoughts into a sentence that would make him understand.

She pressed her cracked lips together and peered at him as intensely as she could. She lifted the picture of the beautiful, smiling teenager with a gold heart locket at her throat and held it until he was forced to look at it.

"This . . . is . . . Rebecca," she explained.

She could see from the look in his eyes that he did not understand.

# Chapter Four

Charles Henson opened the front door and frowned at the rain.

Maddy peered past him out at the cobbled drive, now shiny under the gaslit lamps that lined the long driveway, and shivered. "That wind makes it sound like someone is moaning out there," she said. "Doesn't it?"

"It's turned nasty," Charles said. "Do you need some umbrellas? We have extras."

Doug looked out over his wife's shoulder. "No, we don't have far to go," he said. "Just to the car."

Wind lashed the chilly rain against their backs as they said their hasty good-nights on the Hensons' doorstep. "Wait," Ellen cried as they prepared to make a dash for the car. She ran to the hall closet and pulled out a slicker.

"What is it, dear?" Charles Henson asked in an apprehensive tone as his wife darted past him into the terrible night. "Where's she going?"

"I don't know," said Maddy. "Honey, will you carry Amy?"

"Sure," said Doug, crouching down and scooping up

his daughter and her stuffed monkey. Amy laid her head against his shoulder with a little whimper.

"She's tired," Maddy said with a smile. She was killing time, knowing they were all waiting for Ellen to return. "Well, it was a lovely evening," she said, not for the first time.

"We're glad you could come," Charles said politely, peering into the darkness.

"Here I am," Ellen cried, materializing like a yellow vinyl apparition out of the darkness. She was carrying a covered wicker basket. She lifted the lid with a shy smile and held it in front of Amy, who was high enough on her father's shoulder to look down into the basket. The child let out a cry of delight. "Kitty," she exclaimed.

Maddy frowned and looked into the basket. A small black cat was inside, resting on a folded-up newspaper. "Oh," she said, a little dismayed.

"You did want one, didn't you?" asked Ellen.

Doug gave his wife a warning glance. "Of course we do. We've been thinking about getting a cat."

"He's adorable," said Maddy. "It's just that we're not actually prepared . . ."

"Ah, but I thought of that," said Ellen. "Before I came in for dinner, I filled you up a bag of litter, and put that and two cans of cat food in your car. That'll hold you till tomorrow."

"My kitty," Amy exclaimed.

"We can't thank you enough," said Doug. "That was very kind of you."

Chastened by Doug's graciousness, Maddy put on a smile. "Yes, thank you very much for everything."

"We'd better make a run for it," said Doug.

They scurried for the car doors, Maddy carrying the

basket with the kitten in it. She opened the back door and put it on the seat while Doug belted Amy into her car seat. Then they each got into the front seat and slammed the doors.

"Phew," said Maddy, shaking the rain off her hair. She turned and waved at Charles and Ellen. Their blurry silhouettes wavered against the golden light in the doorway.

"I'll put the heat on," said Doug as he pulled away from the edge of the drive.

"Please do."

In the backseat, Amy was crooning to her new pet. "You'll have to think of a name for him, honey," Maddy said.

"His name's Blacky," Amy announced.

"Blacky's a good name," said Maddy. She turned back and stared out through the swishing wipers. "What a miserable night," she said.

"I didn't think it was that bad," Doug said defensively.

"Oh no, not that," said Maddy. "I meant the weather." She was thoughtful for a minute. "I did think giving us that cat was a little strange, though."

"She probably just thought Amy would like it."

"Mmmm," said Maddy. "Oh, I know she meant well. There's just something odd about it. . . ."

"The rich are supposed to be eccentric," Doug said. "God, I wonder what it would be like to live like that."

"It seems kind of lonely."

"I wouldn't mind trying it," said Doug. "Servants, grounds, beautiful cars, expensive things."

"All the happiness money can buy," said Maddy.

"Hey, don't knock it till you've tried it," said Doug. "Although at this rate, I don't think we have anything to worry about. We'll be living like this forever."

"What does that mean?" said Maddy. "What's wrong with the way we live?"

"Nothing, nothing," he said. "It was just . . . pleasant being there. Spending a little time in those surroundings. In all that luxury."

"I think we do all right," she said. She stopped herself from reminding him that any savings they had accrued toward a more comfortable life were now going to be in Charles Henson's pockets. After all, Doug wasn't to blame for that. He'd had to be defended against Heather Cameron's wild accusations no matter what the cost.

"Yeah, we do fine," said Doug. He was hunched forward over the steering wheel, peering out. "God, it's teeming out there. We should have taken those umbrellas they offered us."

"I wanna see Blacky," Amy crooned from the backseat.

"Not now, honey," Maddy said automatically, craning her neck to see the road ahead as the car crawled along. "Daddy's trying to concentrate. You just stay quiet. You'll see Blacky when we get home."

They drove in silence for a few minutes until the rain let up, then Doug sat back against the seat and resumed a normal speed.

Maddy relaxed a little bit and started thinking again about Doug's reaction to the Hensons' wealth. She knew that Doug always felt he had been cheated out of his chance for money and fame. When she met him, an injury to his knee had just ended his baseball career after only one season on a major league team. He had been an angry young man when they met, and she liked to think that her love had helped him get past that disappointment. But sometimes it seemed as if he would never overcome his bitterness.

"You know money isn't everything, Doug."

"Not if you've got a lot of it," he agreed wryly.

"Their only child died," Maddy said. "Did you know that?"

"No, really?" Doug asked.

Maddy nodded. "When he was five years old. Meningitis. Today was his birthday."

"Jesus," Doug exclaimed. "That's horrible. Charles never said anything, but, you know . . . We never discussed anything personal when I saw him. Well, you know, personal about him. . . ."

"I know," said Maddy. "Well, I'm just saying, they have had their share of heartache."

"I guess so," said Doug.

"Compared to that—the idea of losing a child—we don't have a care in the world," she said.

"No, you're right," he said absently.

"Blacky's a good kitty," piped a little voice from the backseat, as if to remind them of their blessings.

Maddy smiled. Their daughter gave her so much pleasure. The first year had been a little tough on them both. They hadn't planned on having a baby so soon after their marriage. Doug was just starting out as a schoolteacher, still smarting from the loss of his sports career. She had encouraged him to go into teaching, in part because she had such respect for her own, late father, who had been a teacher. That she should be married to a teacher seemed so right.

Many times in that first year she wondered if Doug would ever adjust. He seemed overwhelmed by the new job and the responsibilities of fatherhood. Then again, sometimes she hadn't exactly felt equal to being a mother. But they had adjusted. Nothing could fill your life with joy like a small child. She thought, fleetingly, of Ellen and Charles. Those poor people. How they must have suffered. She shook her head and gazed at her own dark reflection in the side window, covered with raindrops. I wouldn't be in their shoes for any amount of money, she thought.

"Goddammit!" Doug cried. Maddy jerked around; a dark blur obscured her husband's face.

"Blacky," Amy cried.

For a moment Maddy could not tell what was going on. Then, twisting around in her seat, she saw the open basket, empty now, the child's arms stretching out toward her father in the front seat, the scratches on his face, the blood black and shiny in the darkness of the car. The cat was squawling. With a sensation of time slowing down, Maddy heard the brakes squeal.

Blacky scrambled off of Doug's neck and onto the dashboard. For an instant the cat's chartreuse eyes stared into hers, his pupils tiny slits. Oncoming headlights illuminated the kitten, his black fur standing on end, bad luck incarnate. Then she was blinded by the oncoming headlights. She heard Doug shouting, "Hold on," as he grabbed desperately for the wheel.

"Amy!" Maddy screamed as the car swerved and spun out of control on the slippery roadway.

# Chapter Five

The hospital lobby was dimly lit but still humming, even late at night. Hospital staff came and went, their rubber soles squeaking on the highly polished floor. A well-modulated voice paged doctors on the PA system. Carrying Amy, Maddy rubbed her daughter's back and walked along beside Ruth Crandall, the mother of one of Amy's playmates, Ginny.

"Ruth, I can't thank you enough for coming out like this," said Maddy.

"Oh, heavens. I'm glad to do it."

"You're gonna go with Miss Ruth, honey," Maddy said softly. "She's gonna take you and George to her house."

"That's right," Ruth said cheerfully. "Ginny is all excited about you coming over. You're gonna sleep in her room with her."

Maddy squeezed her child tightly, her mind filled once again with the sights and sounds of the accident, that moment of utter terror, the noises that seemed to burst in her ear, and then the sick fear when they spun to a halt and she did not know if her daughter was all right. It was only a moment, but she would remember it forever. "I love you more than anything," she said to Amy.

"Come on, little one," Ruth crooned, and the tired child gave up her protest and fell into Ruth's familiar arms, the stuffed monkey still dangling from her pudgy hand.

"I'll come get her in the morning," Maddy promised. "Sleep tight, my angel." She kissed the soft, streaky cheek again, then reluctantly let her go. She stood behind the sliding doors of the entrance and waved as they went out into the night. With a sinking heart, she turned to head back to the emergency room.

"Maddy," a familiar voice cried.

Maddy turned around wearily and then brightened at the sight of the man approaching her, his eyes filled with concern. "Father . . . Nick," she said.

"Just Nick," he said. "How many times must I tell you?"

"It's the collar," she said. "It's automatic."

Nick Rylander sighed and tugged at the collar as if it were tight. "I was doing my weekly visit at the prison today. I always wear the dog collar up there. I don't want anybody mistaking me for an inmate and slamming me into some cell by mistake."

Maddy smiled briefly. "I don't blame you. I'm sure it's tough. Going up there."

"I don't mind it," he said. "Today I was happy to be there. A guy I've counseled for several years got let out. He was kind of a chronic troublemaker, but he'd been doing time for murder and all along he maintained his innocence. Recently, they arrested a guy for a similar crime and he confessed to this murder, too. So, my guy was sprung. It was kind of a joyful day. Never mind about that," he said impatiently. "What in the world are you doing here at this hour?"

"We were in a car accident tonight."

"No," he said, and his vehemence surprised her. "What happened?"

Maddy explained about their visit to the Hensons', the kitten's escape from his basket, and the ensuing accident. "Doug's down in Emergency. I'm on my way back down there."

"Is he badly hurt?"

"I've been trying to find out. I've been bugging them at the nurses' station, but I can't seem to get an answer."

She fiddled anxiously with a delicate silver ID bracelet she wore. Her wrists looked narrow and fragile as matchsticks to him. "And Amy? How is Amy? Where is she?"

"Oh, my neighbor just came to take Amy home. She's okay. Thank God. In all the commotion, the kitten bolted into the woods. We couldn't find him afterward. Amy was more upset about the cat than anything else."

"He'll be okay," said Nick. "You know how cats land on their feet."

"I hope so."

"People, too," he said. "Don't worry."

Maddy shook her head. "I hope you're right."

"I'll walk with you," he said.

"Oh, it's late, Father . . . Nick," she corrected herself. "You go on."

"Not a chance," he said, putting a hand lightly on her elbow.

"I forgot," she said wryly. "This is your job."

Nicholas Rylander did not correct her. He steered her through the corridor, his hand cupping her fragile elbow as they walked, and he stole a glance at her tired, strained face. He knew about the accusations against Doug by that young teenager, even though Maddy had never mentioned it to him. Everyone in town knew. Maddy had held her head high throughout, a faithful, steadfast wife. Yet with her shoulder-length dark hair, bangs, and freckles, she looked hardly more than a teenager herself. "You've been through a lot lately," he said.

Maddy nodded fretfully. "I just keep thinking how stupid I was. This all could have been avoided. I feel terrible about the people in the other car. They left in an ambulance. I don't know how they're doing, either. And it was our fault . . . Nick."

"Oh, come on," he said.

"Really. I mean it was an accident, but if I hadn't put the kitten in the backseat with Amy . . ."

"It was an accident," he said firmly. "That's what an accident is."

"I guess you're right." She sighed. "Here we are."

Maddy hurried up to the nurse's station and inquired after Doug.

"I have no information," said the nurse on duty in exasperation.

"But I need to know something," Maddy pleaded.

"Nurse McCarthy," Nick said gently, leaning over the desk, "we're going to be in the lounge. I would really appreciate it if you could find out about Mr. Blake for me."

The nurse looked up at him in surprise and then blushed. "Certainly, Father Nick," she said piously, welcoming the opportunity to come to the aid of her parish priest.

"Come on," said Nick. "Let's sit down in there."

Reluctantly Maddy let him lead her to a lounge that was more brightly lit than the corridors, with orange and turquoise chairs, a box of toys, and an assortment of magazines scattered on end tables. A television suspended from the ceiling played quietly above them. Maddy sat on a chair, her back to the TV. Nick walked over to the coffee station and dislodged a couple of Styrofoam cups. The lounge contained only a few people. A heavyset, gray-haired man in a buffalo plaid shirt sat with his head leaning back against the wall, eyes closed, his clenched jaw belying his apparent repose. In a corner by the window two women sat knitting, talking in low voices, each possessed of a canvas tote bag that seemed to be brimming with necessities for a long stay in this room. A middle-aged couple sat nervously by the doorway, looking out constantly, obviously waiting for the doctor to appear.

Nick brought the coffee back and handed her a cup.

Maddy looked ruefully at the steaming liquid. "I guess I might as well. I won't be sleeping tonight anyway."

Nick nodded and took a sip. "Me neither."

"What's your excuse?" she said.

"Oh, packing, you know. Tying up loose ends."

"That's right, you're leaving," she exclaimed, noticing that his thoughtful, handsome face was haggard. "When is it? I've been so wrapped up in my own problems . . ."

Your husband's problems, he thought, and in spite of himself, he felt a little bitterness. He knew that Doug had been exonerated in court. That should have been the end of it. After all, hadn't he just witnessed today that an innocent man could be unjustly imprisoned? Yet he wondered about Doug Blake. He had an easygoing manner, but there was something cold in his eyes, Nick thought. Maybe, if he was honest, it was just the thought of leaving Maddy to him that made Nick dislike Doug Blake so much. Yet so often, where there was smoke . . .

"Nick?"

"Oh, actually I'm leaving day after tomorrow," he said. "Or I hope to."

"So soon?" she said sadly. "I was just getting to know you." She had met him when she'd started the stained-glass window commissions for the new chapel at his church. She had found him perceptive and easy to talk to. "Is it a smaller church that you're going to, up in . . . where is it? Nova Scotia."

Nick nodded. "Actually, no, I'm not going to a church. . . ."

"You're not?"

He shifted in his seat as if uncomfortable with the discussion. "I'm going to be supervising some art restoration at an old monastery up there."

Maddy wanted to ask him why, but she could see he didn't really want to talk about it. "I'll miss you," she said.

Nick frowned and then looked around the room. His gaze landed on the television screen. "Did you hear about this?" he asked grimly.

Maddy swiveled around in her chair to see what he was looking at. On the screen was a disheveled woman in a flowered dress, her eyes red with weeping, a stoic young man with a stubbly beard beside her. The woman was explaining how her missing baby was dressed. When she began to describe the red sweater with the Dalmatian on it that his grandmother had knitted, she broke down crying. The number of a tips hot line ran like a ticker tape across the bottom of the screen. Maddy felt her own eyes well up. She shook her head. "What happened?"

"Baby-sitter disappeared with their child today. Right here in town," Nick said.

"Oh, my God, how awful. They look like a couple of children themselves."

At that moment Doug appeared in the doorway of the lounge, trailed by Nurse McCarthy, who beamed at Father Nick.

Maddy's face lit up. She jumped up from her chair and rushed to her husband. "Honey," she said, "are you okay? What did the doctor say?"

Nick also rose and extended a hand to Doug, who declined to shake it, pointing to his shoulder. "I'm a bit stiff," he explained.

"How are you doing?" Nick asked, wondering if it was a snub.

Doug shrugged. "I'm doing fine," he said. "He thinks I just wrenched my shoulder. But they won't let me leave yet. They're waiting for X-rays."

"But nothing's torn or broken?" Maddy asked urgently.

Doug shook his head. "No, it doesn't look that way."

"That's great," said Maddy, weak with relief.

"Well, I'm going to get going," said Nick. "I'll say goodnight to both of you."

"Thanks for everything, Nick," said Maddy. "And if I don't see you . . ."

Nick waved without looking back.

Doug sat down heavily in the seat that Nick had just vacated.

"Can I get you something?" Maddy asked. "Some coffee or a soda?"

"What did he want?" Doug asked.

In spite of herself, Maddy felt defensive. "He was keeping me company. I met him in the lobby when Ruth came to take Amy home."

"What a coincidence," Doug said, staring after the departing clergyman.

Maddy set her jaw. "He's a priest," she said. "He visits the sick."

Doug put a hand over his eyes. "I know," he said wearily. "Never mind. I'm just in a bad mood. I can't believe this happened. On top of everything else. It seems like it's one thing after another."

Maddy nodded. "It does seem that way."

"All because of that damned cat. Blacky," he said, shaking his head.

"They're bad luck. I tried to warn you," she teased him, rubbing his arm consolingly. "But Doug, we really were lucky. I mean, nothing's seriously wrong with you. That's great. Amy's okay. And we'll have the car back tomorrow. The man from the garage said it was just a blowout."

He glanced at her, and for a moment there was a venomous look in his eyes. She recoiled from him as if she had been struck.

The nurse reappeared in the doorway and beckoned.

"I've got to go," he said, getting up out of his seat. "Why don't you head home? I don't know how much longer this is going to take."

"I'll wait," she said in a small voice, avoiding his gaze.

Doug patted her on the shoulder and followed the nurse out of the lounge.

Maddy watched him go, feeling a little shaky. He's just tired, she told herself. She knew that sometimes her optimism got on his nerves. That was all. She picked up an ancient issue of *People* and tried to read. A thin woman with fuzzy brown hair and glasses came in and sat across the aisle of seats, absentmindedly rocking her baby, who was asleep against her chest, a yellow pacifier dangling from his mouth, his little upper body swathed in a pale blue hooded sweatshirt. Even in slumber, the child looked utterly exhausted. She set a battered brown pocketbook and a gaily printed diaper bag against the leg of her chair. Maddy smiled briefly at her and went back to her magazine, trying to read the article she was looking at.

Just then a doctor came into the room, and the middle-aged couple by the door stood up. "Mr. and Mrs. Sobranski?" the doctor asked.

They clutched hands and nodded, looking petrified. "What is it?" asked the man. "How's Cliff doing?"

"He's fine. He's comfortable. I've got him in a cast. He's got two torn ligaments in the ankle."

"That doesn't sound too serious," the woman said hopefully.

"Not serious," bellowed her husband. Everyone in the lounge looked up at them. Maddy watched curiously as the man buried his face in his hands and shook his head. "He's ruined," the man cried.

"Let's step outside," said the doctor. Mrs. Sobranski, looking very confused, urged her husband along, following the doctor into the hall. Maddy peered out at them for a moment, then, with a shrug, returned to her article.

"Bonnie Lewis?"

Maddy looked up at a uniformed police officer who had entered the room and stood beside her chair, holding a pen and pad poised in his hand. He had shiny black hair and a smooth complexion and looked barely old enough to be a recruit.

"No," Maddy said.

"I'm Mrs. Lewis," said the woman with the baby.

The young officer walked over to the other woman.

"Mrs. Lewis, I'm Officer Termini. I'm here to find out about the accident. They tell me your husband is still in surgery. Can you tell me what happened?"

The woman grimaced nervously. "Well, I can't tell you exactly where it happened because we're not from around here."

"You have Maine plates on your car? Is that right?"

The woman nodded. "We just got to town. My husband has a new job lined up. We were on the River Road. It was bad out, you know. Rainy, and the roads were slick." She paused to consider her words, pushing her glasses back up on her nose with the hand that wasn't holding her baby. "All of a sudden . . . out of nowhere, this car that was coming toward us just swerved right into our path. . . ."

"You were driving. . . ."

"Yessir. I was taking a turn 'cause my husband was tired. I tried to avoid 'em as best I could, but my van landed off the road in a ditch. My husband was hurt. . . ."

Maddy listened to the woman's account with growing distress. She had not actually seen the other people involved. They'd ended up on the other side of the road, and before Maddy and Doug had had a chance to collect themselves, a driver in a Land Rover with a cell phone had stopped and phoned for help. With the rain, the emergency vehicles, and all the confusion . . . But it had to be their accident.

"Excuse me," said Maddy, standing up. The officer and the woman with the baby looked at her. She walked over to the woman and sat in the chair beside her. "I'm sorry, but I couldn't help but overhear. I'm Maddy Blake," she said. She bit her lip as Mrs. Lewis looked at her suspiciously. "We were in an accident on the River Road tonight."

The police officer consulted his pad. "Were you driving a gray Ford Taurus station wagon?"

Maddy nodded and looked sadly at the woman beside her. "I'm so sorry," she said to her. "It was our fault. Officer, it was our fault." For a moment she hesitated, wondering if she shouldn't have said that. The way people were with lawsuits these days. You could say it was the slippery road, the leaves . . . If only she hadn't left that basket on the seat, where Amy could open it. . . . But she had, and it had caused an accident, and now this poor woman had a husband in surgery because of it. This was no time to be trying to shift the blame. She loathed that in other people. She wasn't going to do it herself. "We had a kitten in the car, and he got loose and startled my husband," Maddy said.

The other woman blinked at her from behind her glasses and shielded her baby's ears, as if Maddy were saying something obscene.

"Mrs. Blake, I was about to try to hunt you down next," said the officer. "You've saved me the trouble."

"Are you done with me?" Mrs. Lewis asked abruptly. "I think I want to go to the ladies' room. And maybe . . . is there a cafeteria?"

"There's an all-night coffee shop, ma'am. Next to the lobby."

Maddy bent and gathered up the woman's belongings, then handed them to her. "I hope your husband will be all right," she said fervently.

Bonnie Lewis nodded, but her eyes were wary. Clutching her bags and her sleeping son, she hurried for the door.

# Chapter Six

"Are you sure you're all right?" Maddy said to Doug. "Do you need to sit? What did the doctor say?"

"I'm fine," he said. "Really. He gave me a prescription for painkillers, and basically told me to take it easy. I'm going to have this filled at the hospital pharmacy."

"Okay," said Maddy. "If you're sure, I think I'll give Ruth a quick call. She'll be wondering."

"I'm fine. Go ahead," he said. "I'll take care of this and get us a cab."

Maddy walked out to the lobby and looked around until she spotted a phone. She called Ruth, who reassured her that Amy was fast asleep. As she was talking, Maddy could see through the glass walls into the coffee shop. It was nearly deserted at this time of night. Over by the window she spotted Bonnie Lewis and her son seated at a little round table in the corner. The baby was awake and belted into a modular high chair. He was inserting food in and around his mouth with a tiny fist, while Bonnie sat tensely, her face a study in anxiety, nodding as a slim doctor dressed in green surgical scrubs talked to her.

When the doctor stood up and turned around, Maddy saw that it was a woman. She looked tired, but otherwise her attractive features wore the impenetrable mask of the physician. As the surgeon left the cafeteria, Maddy hung up the phone and hesitantly went in.

"Mrs. Lewis?" she asked tentatively. "I don't mean to bother you. But are you okay?"

Bonnie looked at Maddy with a bleary, stunned expression. She was so thin, she looked birdlike. "Yes," she said in a dull voice.

"Was that your husband's doctor?" Maddy asked.

Bonnie nodded. "The surgeon. She said Terry is out of surgery."

"Is he going to be all right?" Maddy asked anxiously.

"I guess so. He had a ruptured spleen. He got jerked forward when we hit the ditch. Anyway, they had to take it out. The doctor said it sounds worse than it is. She said he can live without it okay."

"Thank God for that," said Maddy.

"He'll be in recovery most of the night." Bonnie looked up at the cafeteria clock. "I've lost track of time," she said apologetically.

"It's easy to do in this place," said Maddy, sitting beside her and placing a hand briefly on Bonnie's pale forearm. "Can I get you a fresh cup of tea or something?"

Bonnie gazed at her untouched tray as if she didn't recognize it. "No, I'm fine," she said. Her lower lip started to tremble, but she struggled to regain control. "I'll be able to see him in the morning." She lifted the squat beige cup from the saucer and took a sip. Then she put down the cup, sighed, and looked out the windows of the cafeteria. Maddy could see that she was trying to blink back tears. The baby, who had wrung all the amusement he could out of a peanut-butter sandwich, suddenly began to wail and squirm in the high chair.

"Don't cry, Sean," Bonnie said. "Daddy's gonna be all right."

"It's just so hard to sit around here and wait, isn't it," said Maddy.

Bonnie reached into her diaper bag and pulled out a rattle in the shape of an elephant. Sean stopped wailing and studied it. "It's going to be a long night," Bonnie said grimly.

Maddy frowned at her. "Where are you two going to stay?"

Bonnie did not look at her. She shook the rattle again. "I guess that lounge will work all right for us. It's got a couple of couches. . . ."

"But that would be miserable for you," Maddy exclaimed. "Especially with this little one."

"Well, I haven't got much choice," Bonnie said matter-of-factly. "I can't exactly afford a motel for us. Terry's been out of work for a while, and now, I don't know. This job may not wait for him. . . ."

Maddy hesitated for a moment and was ashamed of her own hesitation. She glanced out into the lobby and saw that Doug had emerged from the pharmacy and was looking around for her. She was exhausted; she wanted to just go home with her husband, crawl into bed, and hide from everything else. She also knew, weary as she was, there was only one right thing to do.

"Now listen," she said. "You'll do no such thing. You'll come home with us. We have plenty of room in our house, and I have a little girl who's three who will be thrilled to see a baby there in the morning."

"Oh, we couldn't do that," Bonnie said hurriedly.

"You absolutely have to," said Maddy. "Because I won't hear of anything else. I wouldn't sleep a wink tonight, thinking of you and Sean being here. No, this is what we have to do. My husband's just calling for a cab now. I'll drive you back here in the morning, to see your husband. You'll stay with us as long as you need to."

"I guess you have your own problems," Bonnie demurred. "Your car was wrecked, too, wasn't it?"

"Ours wasn't too bad," Maddy said apologetically. "Just a flat. We'll have it back in the morning. Besides, we have another car."

Bonnie looked almost embarrassed, as if she hadn't realized a family could have two cars. This made Maddy feel even more guilty.

"We'd be imposing," Bonnie said weakly.

"Nonsense," said Maddy. "You'd be doing me a favor. It would ease my conscience."

"Well, you have no reason to feel that way, but . . . all right. I guess . . . all right. Thank you. . . ."

Despite her insistence, Maddy felt a little niggling sense of anxiety that her offer had been accepted. She wondered how Doug would react, remembering that flash of malice in his eyes earlier. But she was determined not to show her ambivalence. "All right, then," she said. "That's settled."

"Do I have time to run up and look in on Terry for a minute before we go?"

"Of course," said Maddy, wondering if Doug would mind the wait. He must be exhausted himself. "You go ahead. Why don't you let me take Sean while you run up there. I don't think they'll let him into the recovery room."

Bonnie hesitated, and Maddy could see the wariness in

her eyes, mixed with a reluctance to seem rude or un-grateful. Maddy instantly remembered the woman on TV, pleading for the return of her baby, and identified with Bonnie's reluctance.

"He might be scared being left with a stranger," Bonnie said.

"You're right," said Maddy. "Never mind."

Bonnie leaned over and lifted the child from the chair. He was fussing, but his sticky hands clutched the neck of her dress and the ends of her frizzy hair. "I won't be long. We'll just peek in at him."

"You go ahead. We'll be right here in the lobby," Maddy assured her. "There's my husband. We'll meet you back here as soon as you're done," she added as she saw Bonnie hesitate.

Bonnie picked up her bags.

"Do you want me to keep those?" Maddy asked.

Bonnie shook her head.

"Well, give me the diaper bag, at least."

Bonnie looked anxiously at the bag, as if she thought Maddy might just take her bag and walk off with it. "No, I'll keep it," she said. "I might need it."

Maddy felt a little insulted, though she tried not to show it. After all, it was one thing not to trust a stranger with your child. But a diaper bag? She stifled the urge to protest. "Okay, well, go on," said Maddy. "And good luck."

As Bonnie rushed out of the coffee shop, her burdens bobbing in her thin arms, Maddy walked out to the lobby.

Doug turned at her approach and smiled briefly, then glanced at his watch. "Are you ready?" he said.

Maddy sighed. "Prepare yourself," she said. "We're having houseguests."

"Houseguests? Who?"

Maddy glanced over her shoulder, as if to be sure no one was listening. "You know the people in the van?"

Doug frowned at her as if she were speaking a foreign language.

"In the accident," she persisted. "Oh, honey, the man just got out of surgery, their car is in the garage, and they have nowhere to go. They're from Maine somewhere. They don't know a soul here. She's up checking on him right now."

"Why can't they go to a hotel?"

"They haven't got any money," Maddy whispered. "He was headed here to see about a job. He's been out of work. Something we can sympathize with."

Doug frowned. "Well, we can give them enough money for a hotel."

"And how will they get around? They can't afford cabs. This woman has a tiny baby."

Doug sighed.

"It's our fault they're in this mess, Doug," Maddy pleaded. "I can't just leave them here."

"Don't say that, Maddy," he snapped. "Don't go claiming responsibility. You didn't say that to her, did you?" he demanded.

Maddy shook her head, which was a lie, and she knew it.

"It was an accident," he said. "That's all anybody needs to know."

"All right, it was an accident. But can't we do the decent thing?"

"Maddy—" Doug's response was interrupted when he was nearly toppled by an extremely tall young man on crutches far too short for him. He was hobbling across the lobby, his countenance a terrible combination of fury, pain, and sorrow.

Doug looked at him curiously. "That's Cliff Sobranski," he whispered to Maddy.

"Who's he?" Maddy asked. Suddenly she saw the couple from the lounge hurrying to catch up with the young man. The woman called out to him, her voice full of motherly concern, but the father's face was like a thundercloud.

"He's the top basketball prospect at the university. The NBA has been scouting him in his junior year," Doug said.

"I heard the doctor telling his parents he had two torn ligaments in his ankle," Maddy whispered.

"Oh no," said Doug. He looked stricken as he watched the distressed family trail out into the night. "That poor kid. He had the whole world at his feet. He could have had it all. Unbelievable." Maddy watched Doug, and she could see he was thinking of his own injury, his own truncated career. Part of her felt sorry for him, but part of her wanted to say, "So what? There are a lot worse things in life than that." She held her tongue. There was no use trying to discuss it because he always told her that she simply didn't understand.

At that moment Bonnie appeared, looking frantically around the lobby, jiggling her fussing baby to try to quiet him. Her expression relaxed when she saw Maddy and Doug. She hurried over to them. "I thought you'd be gone," she said.

Maddy wondered why she would think that. "I said we'd wait."

Bonnie shrugged as if to express her lack of faith in such promises.

"Bonnie," said Maddy, "this is my husband, Doug Blake. Doug, this is Bonnie Lewis. The one I told you about." She turned to Bonnie. "How's your husband doing? Did you see him?"

"He's out cold. He didn't know I was there." Bonnie turned to Doug. "Your wife invited us to stay," she said anxiously, "but if you don't want us there . . ."

Doug forced a brief smile. "No, no," he said. "It's no problem. Let me just go see if the cab is here."

Maddy gave the other woman an encouraging smile as Doug went over to the door. "Everything will be all right," she said.

Bonnie nodded grimly and patted the back of her baby, whose little sobs echoed off the walls of the quiet lobby.

Maddy led the way up the stairs to the bedrooms. She opened the door to the guest room. There were twin beds and a bureau. In the corner was the crib, which Amy had outgrown. Maddy had put it there so that they would be prepared for visits from friends or family who also had young children. Bonnie looked around the room, and for the first time she brightened. "This'll be great," she said.

Maddy nodded, feeling pleased at the sight of the pale yellow room with its hooked rug and wildflower quilts. She remembered the day last spring when she and Doug had painted this room. Doug had started out griping that he wished they had the money to hire someone to do it, but in the end it had been fun. They had painted while Amy danced happily around with her doll.

"Maybe we can get a house," said Bonnie. "If the job works out. Before this we've lived in apartments. But now that we have Sean . . ."

"How long have you been married?" Maddy asked.

Bonnie frowned. "Oh, not too long. A few years. It took me a while to get pregnant. Then when I did, it was easy as pie. I worked up until the week I had him." She placed the baby into the crib and took off the knitted booties on his feet.

Maddy leaned against the door frame. "Where did you work?" she asked.

"What?" Bonnie asked, turning around. "Oh, at the library. As an assistant."

"Well, you shouldn't have any trouble getting a job around here. Seems like they're always short staffed at the library."

"I'm not going to go back to work," she said. "Not now. Terry wants to support us. Once I get this little one off to school, I'll be able to go back," she said dreamily. "Terry and I have discussed it and we both feel that it's important for the mother to be home with her child."

Maddy smiled and gave her an assessing glance. She wasn't young, probably mid-thirties, and she was not especially attractive. But she had found herself a husband and she had her first child. Having this baby must have been a dream come true to her. No wonder she wanted to stay home. And it would probably work out fine for them, except for this little nightmare glitch of the breadwinner being in the hospital, minus his spleen.

Bonnie walked over to the bed and began to rummage in the diaper bag. She pulled out a pair of pajamas and set them gently on the bed. "Good thing these weren't in the suitcase," she said. She removed a bottle of baby oil, powder, and a plastic soap container.

"I'll drive you around to the garage tomorrow and we'll get your bags," said Maddy.

Bonnie returned to the side of the crib and unsnapped

the baby's little corduroy pants. He began to make fretful noises.

"Maybe you should let him sleep in his clothes," Maddy suggested, "so you don't wake him up."

Bonnie looked up at her indignantly. "And let him go to bed all dirty and sticky like this? I wouldn't think of it."

Mind your own business, Maddy reminded herself. Every mother has her own way of doing things. "Well, I'm going to leave you two. I'll see you at breakfast in the morning."

"No fruit," said Bonnie.

"What?" Maddy asked.

"No fruit for breakfast. Sean is allergic to most fruits."

Maddy smiled. "Well, my Amy won't touch them anyway. Good night." Bonnie resumed undressing the baby as Maddy pulled the door shut quietly.

She went down the hall to her bedroom, tiptoeing so as not to wake Doug. As she approached the door, she thought she heard the murmur of his voice. She opened the door and saw him sitting on the edge of the bed, his shoulders slumped, a pained expression on his face.

"Doug, what's the matter?" she asked. "Are you feeling all right?"

"I'm all right," he said.

"Maybe you better take one of those painkillers."

Doug shook his head.

"That's why the doctor gave you a prescription."

"I don't need it," he said.

Maddy sighed. "Okay. Whatever you think. I guess I got our guests settled in." From down the hall the baby's fussy cry threaded its way to them. Maddy went to the closet and got out her nightgown. "What a night," she said.

"Maddy . . ."

Maddy turned and looked at her husband. "What?"

"There's another little problem. . . ."

Maddy's heart started to race with apprehension. She held her nightgown up in front of her, as if for protection. "What problem?" Then she frowned. "Who were you talking to on the phone just now?"

"You heard me?" he asked.

"I heard your voice as I was coming in. I didn't hear what you were saying."

"Stanley Plank," he said.

"Who in the world is Stanley Plank?"

Doug sighed. "Our insurance man."

"Oh, right," said Maddy. "You told him about the accident." She shook her head in confusion. "So, what's the problem?"

"Maddy, look," said Doug. "You know the last few months have been so crazy. I mean with this court business. And being out of work . . ."

"Yes," she said, conscious that she was holding her breath.

"Last month, I was paying the bills and there just wasn't enough money to go around."

"Enough money for what?" she said.

"I had to let a few things slide. I had no choice." He was avoiding her gaze, explaining himself to the carpet by the bed.

"Don't tell me," she said. "Not the car insurance."

"It probably won't matter," he said. "It's a no-fault state."

Maddy turned away from him, her jaw clenched. "The car insurance, Doug?"

"It was a judgment call," he said irritably. "Anyway, maybe it'll all go away. . . ."

Maddy shook her head. She felt numb. "I can't believe this," she said. "What could you have been thinking? What if they decide to sue us or something?"

Doug sprang up from the edge of the bed and turned on her, his eyes blazing. "Well, if they do sue us, it's because you have acted as if we were to blame. Inviting them here . . . you might as well have admitted it was our fault."

Maddy's face reddened, for she knew she had said exactly that to the police.

All of a sudden, they heard a noise in the hallway. Doug looked toward the door. "Who's there?" he demanded.

Maddy jerked around and saw a shadow on the half-open door of their bedroom. Amy was not home. It could be only one person. She felt her face flush with shame at the thought that their argument might have been overheard.

Doug strode to the door and pulled it open. Bonnie was standing there, holding an empty baby bottle.

"What are you doing here?" he demanded.

"Pardon me," Bonnie said indignantly. "I only wanted to know if I could get Sean some milk. I didn't mean to interrupt."

"Of course," Maddy said humbly. "Downstairs. In the fridge."

Bonnie raised her chin and turned away. As she turned, Maddy saw something chilling in her eyes—an unmistakable little glint of satisfaction.

# Chapter Seven

$\mathcal{F}$rank Cameron poured a cup of coffee, yawned, and wiped a large hand over his wide, sagging face. He'd spent most of the night at the police station, and out on the search with his officers, and his complexion was nearly as gray as his hair. He had come home, managed two hours of sleep on the sofa in the den, and now was getting ready to go back to the station.

Mary Beth sat at the kitchen table, her laptop open beside her plate of dry toast, studying the screen and picking away at the keys with one polished fingernail. She was groomed and coiffed for the office, her makeup flawless, her fitted red suit at once tailored and seductive. Frank remembered when she'd first returned to work. Heather had just started third grade, and Mary Beth had complained that there wasn't enough for her to do at home. Back then her entire professional wardrobe consisted of two skirts, one gray and one navy blue, and a couple of cardigan twin sets. Although her transformation had been gradual, he felt as if he had completely missed it—as if one day, the wife he knew had disappeared and been replaced by this sharp-eyed real estate mini-mogul.

"What time did you get in?" Mary Beth asked, her gaze not wavering from the little screen.

"Oh, Jesus, I don't know. Five. Six."

"Did you find them?"

"Not yet, Mary Beth," he said caustically. She did not seem to notice.

Heather shuffled into the kitchen and opened the refrigerator door.

"Hello, Heather," Frank said.

"Hi, Dad." She gave him a brief smile and went back to examining the contents of the refrigerator. Frank thought how strange it was for them to all be in the same room at the same time. Usually he left the house before they got up, and when he got home, Heather was in her room with the door shut and his dinner was in the microwave. Meanwhile Mary Beth would be busy making appointments on her cell phone or logging on to the Internet, to share her grievances with some other frustrated female.

He thought back to the time when Frank junior and Heather were children, and they always seemed to eat together. A lot of nights he had kept them waiting, but still, those had been better days. He gazed at his daughter, who was sitting down with a juice box and a Pop-Tart on a paper plate. He felt a sudden, overwhelming affection for her, probably because he had spent the night worrying about Rebecca Starnes, who was about the same age as Heather. She looked vulnerable and kind of sweet to him in those baggy overalls she liked to wear. Impulsively he walked over to her and stroked her soft hair.

Mary Beth pushed her chair back from the table and examined her daughter critically. "Heather," she said, "what in the world inspired you to wear those two items of clothing together?"

Heather looked down at her dull green shirt and her lavender overalls and gazed wearily at her mother. "They look okay," she said.

Mary Beth shook her head. "They look completely ridiculous, Heather. You wonder why you have no friends."

Frank sipped his coffee and closed his eyes. He had a sudden image of Sandi Starnes in that ketchup-stained blouse, clutching a photo of her daughter. Promising God any extravagant thing, if only she could just set eyes on Rebecca again. "She looks fine," he said through clenched teeth.

Mary Beth stood up and walked over to the coffeepot, high heels clicking against the linoleum. "What do you know about it, Frank?" she said.

A knock on the back door precluded his reply. Mary Beth opened the door, prepared to excoriate the person who dared intrude on her family breakfast. But her stiffness vanished at the sight of the two young people in the doorway.

"Karla," she exclaimed with a broad smile. "What a nice surprise. Come on in."

Heather blanched when she saw the visitors. Karla Needham lived two streets over and was one of the most popular girls at school. She was a cheerleader, had perfect looks, perfect clothes, and a boyfriend. A boyfriend who made Heather swoon every time she thought of him. A boyfriend who was standing in her doorway.

"Who's your friend?" Mary Beth asked.

"This is Richie Talbot. Hi, Heather."

Heather gulped down the corner of a Pop-Tart. As she mumbled, "Hi," some crumbs escaped and sprayed out on the table. Heather had known Karla Needham all her life.

As little girls, they had played together. But once they hit fifth grade, Karla had moved on to other things. Not that she wasn't nice. She always said hi and asked how Heather's parents were. But that was all. Until now. This morning. This moment. Heather suddenly felt sick to her stomach.

"We were passing by and we thought you might want to walk to school with us," Karla said pleasantly.

"Why?" asked Heather.

"Hea-ther," Mary Beth scolded, sensing a golden opportunity for her daughter to be seen, for once, in the right company. "Can't you be friendly?" Mary Beth turned back to the couple crowded in the doorway. "Heather was just about to leave for school, weren't you, honey? I'm sure she'd love to walk with you."

The phone rang. Frank reached over and picked it up, glad for any distraction from his daughter's discomfiture and his wife's transparent machinations. He listened for a moment, then nodded. "Okay," he said. "I'll be right there."

He reached for his keys and wallet on the counter. "I've got to go," he said.

"Did you find that girl and the baby, Chief Cameron?" Karla asked politely.

"Not yet." Frank sighed. "Maybe this will be the break we need. Excuse me, everyone." As the door shut behind him, he heard Mary Beth oozing charm to the visitors and ordering Heather to ready herself for the march to school.

"What's up, Pete?" Frank asked as he banged back the door of the station house.

Pete Millard's tie hung loose around his open collar, his normally well-groomed hair was disheveled, raked through by nervous fingers. He jerked his head in the direction of the sergeant's desk. A pudgy woman with steel-rimmed glasses and strawberry blond hair in a messy ponytail, wearing a SUNY warm-up jacket and Reebok running shoes, was looking around the station house disdainfully.

"A witness," Pete explained.

Frank raised his eyebrows and regarded the woman with interest.

"She says she read about it in the paper this morning," said Pete.

"What? She doesn't watch television? It was on the tube all night."

"She doesn't own a television," Pete said. "She made a point of telling me."

"An intellectual," Frank snorted.

"Anyway, she's here now," said Pete.

"Fine. Let's talk to her. Bring her down to room one."

Frank headed down the corridor to one of the interview rooms and turned on the overhead lights. They illuminated every corner of the sickly green room. Frank sat down heavily on one of the molded plastic seats and looked at his watch. Fifteen hours had elapsed since the girl and the baby had been reported missing, and with each passing hour, their prospects grew more ominous.

The door opened, and Pete Millard led the woman into the room. "Chief Cameron, this is Miss Julia Sewell."

"Miz," she corrected him.

"Thank you for coming in, Ms. Sewell," Frank said politely. He knew better than to alienate this alien creature. She appeared to be in her thirties, not a college student, as her jacket might indicate. "Detective Millard says you saw the news of the disappearance of Rebecca Starnes and Justin Wallace in the paper."

"That's right," she said.

"And you recognized them from the pictures?"

"The girl. I saw her yesterday."

"You saw her by herself?"

"No. She had a baby with her. I couldn't swear it was the same baby. They all look alike to me."

"Where did you see them?"

"I was in the park, reading."

Frank's heart began to race. "What park was that, Ms. Sewell?"

"Binney Park," she said. "I was sitting on a bench, near the duck pond. Across from the parking lot. I was reading."

Something was familiar about her, but Frank could not quite put his finger on it. He was just too tired. "What time was this?" he asked, making a note.

"About two o'clock."

"What were they doing?"

"They were just sitting there. The kid was in a stroller. She was sitting on a bench."

"Any . . . anything unusual? Any reason why you noticed them?"

"A man came up to them and started talking to her." The woman disclosed this news with grim satisfaction.

Frank felt the hairs standing up on the back of his neck. Perverts. I knew it, he thought. What is it with these bastards that makes them need to mess with children? His thoughts strayed to his own daughter and her recent experience with her schoolteacher. Kids weren't safe anywhere these days. Even in school. "Did you think it was someone she knew?"

The woman squinted and shook her head. "No," she said. "A stranger."

"Do you mind my asking how you know that?" Frank

asked mildly. He was always wary of witnesses who noticed too much.

"Body language," she said flatly.

Frank nodded and made a note on the paper in front of him, not satisfied with her answer. Something about her was setting off warning bells in him. Most witnesses who came forward voluntarily were eager, not hostile. They were filled with the pure zeal of the innocent bystander, and they were definitely on the side of the police. "Can you describe the man?" he asked.

"Sure," she said.

"Height, weight, age?"

The woman exhaled noisily. "I couldn't tell his exact age. I wasn't that close to him. I would say in his thirties. Blondish brown hair, medium build."

An image came to Frank Cameron's mind of a man who perfectly fit that description. The man who had sat in the courtroom and denied coercing Frank's teenage daughter into having sex with him. Thirties, sandy hair, medium build. Douglas Blake. Frank's curiosity suddenly became personal.

"Wearing?"

"Those chino-type pants. And a dark jacket."

"Color?"

She shrugged. "I'm not sure. Might have been blue."

Frank studied her through narrowed eyes, and suddenly it came back to him—how he knew her. Now he remembered. It was a while ago. She had reported that a guy had grabbed her, tried and failed to rape her. She'd scared him off by screaming. They never found the guy. "Miss Sewell," he said.

"Miz," she corrected him.

"I've been thinking that you looked familiar to me. Didn't you report an assault a while back? . . ."

Julia Sewell blushed but didn't flinch. "Yeah," she said. "Two years ago. And a fat lot you guys did about it. Anyway, what difference does that make?"

Frank looked over his notes and shrugged. "No real difference," he said slowly. "I'm a little concerned that you may not have perceived the situation clearly because of your own experience. We aren't interested in wasting precious hours trying to hunt down some fellow who stopped to ask Rebecca Starnes for the time."

Julia Sewell regarded him with a combination of scorn and outrage. She started to retort, then stopped herself. Her first reaction was to lash out at him. But something more important was at stake here, and even these cops, she reminded herself, were trying, in their own blundering, overbearing way, to do something about it. Besides, she felt guilty. Definitely guilty. She should have intervened. She should have walked up and confronted the man, told him to leave the girl alone.

Julia thought carefully and composed herself before she replied. "He spoke to her, then he sat down next to her on the bench. Then he offered her something. I don't know what. After a minute she seemed to take whatever it was. Then he began to get closer to her. You're right. I was suspicious of him, although my own experience was a little bit different. In my experience, I was walking along and a guy grabbed me from behind and pulled me down into the bushes."

There was a brief silence in the interview room. After a moment she continued. "She had a funny look on her face. Like she was uncomfortable. Then she got up and walked away."

"She got up and walked away?" Frank asked.

"Yes."

"And what did the man do?"

"He sat on the bench for a while. Just long enough to pretend that he had some reason for being there. Then he got up and walked away, too."

"In the same direction?"

"Yes."

Frank and Pete Millard exchanged a solemn, apprehensive glance.

"Did you see what happened after that?"

"No," she said in a low voice, lowering her eyes. "I should have followed them. I wish I had."

"You had no way of knowing, Ms. Sewell. All right," he said briskly. "We'd like to try and get a composite sketch from your description. It may give us a picture of the suspect. You may remember this procedure from your own experience. Do you think you could work with our artist on this?"

"Yes, sure," she said.

"Now," said Frank, peering down at his notes. "What about other people that might have seen this man? Did you notice anyone else in the park? Anyone who might be able to ID him for us?"

Julia sighed and looked at the imitation stuccoed surface of the dropped ceiling. "There were a couple of women with kids. One woman walking her baby in a carriage. A couple of joggers, I think. . . ." She shook her head. "Wait, a guy doing tai chi . . . that's a series of exercises . . . a martial art, I believe."

"I know what it is," Frank said irritably. "What did he look like?"

"He was Asian. Young—late twenties, probably. He was wearing warm-up clothes."

"That's a good place for us to start," said Frank, standing up. "Thank you for coming forward. If you remember anything else . . ."

"I'll call you," she promised.

He hesitated, then added, "I only wish someone had done the same for you."

Julia stopped at the door. "I hope it's not too late," she said sincerely.

"So do I," said Frank in an edgy voice. "So do I."

# Chapter Eight

The banner headline on the *Taylorsville Tribune* proclaimed MISSING over the photos of a pretty high school girl and a laughing, curly-haired baby. Ellen Henson stared at the photos and read the caption: "Six-month-old Justin Wallace and fifteen-year-old Rebecca Starnes. . . ."

"What'll it be, lady?" asked the man in the kiosk.

Ellen looked up at him, startled by his abruptness, then held up a pack of mints. "These . . . and the paper," she said.

The man toted up the price indifferently, and Ellen stuffed both the paper and the mints into her purse. She walked down the block, gazing into windows as she passed by. She was so preoccupied that she scarcely registered what she saw. Finally she found herself standing still, staring into one window for a long time. She read the name of the shop on the window and felt disoriented. How long had this store been here? she wondered. She rarely came to town, but still . . . It was not there when she . . . when Ken was a baby. She was sure of it.

She pushed open the door to the Precious Littles Shop and took a cautious step inside. The walls were painted a creamy yellow, and a wallpaper border of ducks, daisies, and dancing letters of the alphabet substituted for a molding around the ceiling. Ellen looked around, wide-eyed, at the racks of frilly dresses, footed sleepers, and tiny pastel sweaters. She was reluctant to touch anything. She walked around the store, gripping her purse as if it were likely to be stolen, although there was no one else in the store except for the young salesgirl, who was sitting behind a glass case, full of baby bonnets and silver rattles.

The salesgirl was folding hooded terrycloth bath towels into neat piles. She smiled at the gaunt, graying woman who stood helplessly in the middle of the shop.

"Is there something I can help you with?" she asked.

"I've just come to get a few things," Ellen said.

"Grandchild?" the girl asked pleasantly.

Ellen stared at her as if the question were somehow confusing. "No," she finally said. "No . . . just a baby."

If the salesgirl was surprised by Ellen's response, she didn't show it. "How old is the baby?" she asked smoothly.

Ellen looked at her blankly for a moment. Then she unconsciously glanced at the newspaper sticking out of her purse and said, "Uh . . . around six months."

"Boy or girl?"

"Boy," said Ellen.

The salesgirl came out from behind the counter and led Ellen over to the rack of crayon-bright outfits appliquéd with fire trucks or puppies or baseballs. The assortment was both dazzling and daunting. Gently Ellen parted the hangers, her eyes alight at the various cunning outfits.

"Does he like giraffes?" the girl asked, pulling out a pale green sweatsuit adorned with jungle animals.

Ellen gazed at the little suit. "He loves all animals," she said.

"What about cars? Is he into cars yet?" the girl queried, liberating a royal blue and canary yellow combination with a race car motif.

"He'd like that one, too," Ellen said.

The girl went down the row, selecting a half dozen outfits, all of which Ellen agreed to purchase. Pleased but a little surprised by the malleability of her customer, the salesgirl brought them back to the counter to tote up the prices.

"His mother's going to be thrilled with all these," the salesgirl said.

Ellen looked at the girl warily. "What do you mean?"

"Well, I mean you've got a whole wardrobe here, practically. And all very nice outfits. If there's anything she already has, or wants to exchange, just tell her to bring it in. We will cheerfully exchange it."

"That's nice. I'll . . . tell her," said Ellen.

"What's his name?" the salesgirl asked.

Ellen squared her shoulders. "Ken," she said. "His name is Ken."

"That's a nice name," the girl said placidly, laying the clothes on the counter. She removed the tags from each outfit with a tiny nail scissors. "Which card will you be using?"

"Cash," Ellen said hurriedly, digging through her purse for her wallet. She took out the newspaper and laid it on the counter, the headline and pictures facing up. At last she found her wallet, while the girl carefully folded her purchases and placed them in a pale blue shopping bag festooned with curling white ribbons.

The salesgirl glanced down at the paper. "Terrible, isn't it?" she said, shaking her head. "About that missing baby. . . ."

Ellen looked up at her, startled. "What?" she asked. "Oh yes," and she handed the girl a wad of bills, knocking the paper to the floor in her nervous haste. She bent over to pick it up.

"Who would do such a thing?" the girl said, shaking her head as she took the bills over to the register. "It's unbelievable. Those parents must be beside themselves. I don't know what this world is coming to." She spoke in the world-weary tones of the elderly. "I don't understand it," she went on absently as she entered the prices from the tags in her hand into the register.

The girl finished her transaction and turned to give Ellen the receipt. The customer and the package were gone. The salesgirl frowned and shook her head. She knew what would happen. Sometime next week the mother would come in, looking to exchange four of the outfits without the receipt. "Why are people so careless?" she asked aloud to the empty store. Shaking her head, she picked up her feather duster from behind the counter and started to flick it over the display of photo frames. As she dusted, she suddenly noticed the expensive-looking, cognac-colored wallet lying on the counter. The doorbell jingled and the salesgirl looked up, expecting to see the woman, who had surely realized her mistake and returned. A pretty young blond woman came into the store, pushing a stroller, and began to browse as the salesgirl picked up the wallet and looked inside.

# Chapter Nine

$\mathcal{M}$addy walked down the hospital corridor, looking at the numbers above the rooms. She had dropped off Bonnie and Sean at the hospital this morning and now she had come back, as promised, to pick them up. Maddy stifled a yawn. It had been a long night, with Sean fussing and Maddy hardly able to sleep for worrying about the insurance situation. She felt completely exhausted by the events of the last few days, and she wished she could just go away somewhere and hide from the world. Unfortunately, she did not see any hope for escape on the horizon.

At room 304 she stopped, craning her neck to look inside. There were no visitors in the room. The man in the first bed was sitting up, reading a newspaper. He was balding and pudgy and looked to be about forty. His roommate was lying in the other bed, his head turned toward the window. All she could see of him was longish black hair and a tattoo on his upper arm. She turned to the man reading the paper. "Mr. Lewis?" she asked.

The man with the paper inclined his head to the other

bed, with a slightly bemused expression on his face, and went back to his reading. Surprised, Maddy tiptoed over to the other bed. "Mr. Lewis?"

When he turned his face to her, Maddy could scarcely conceal her surprise. Bonnie's husband was not at all what she had expected. He had a broad, high-cheekboned face that would have been handsome had it not been pitted with acne scars. He had a thick, black mustache, peppered, like his hair, with gray, and the bandages across his forehead completed the look of a pirate. A silver crucifix hung from a chain around his wide neck and rested on the flimsy cotton of his hospital gown. His eyes were unfocused, heavy lidded from painkillers. He shifted around in the bed, and Maddy could not fail to notice the well-defined, almost cartoonishly large muscles of his upper body.

"Are you Mr. Lewis?" Maddy asked. She heard, with a shade of embarrassment, the incredulity in her own voice.

"That's me," he said, attempting a smile that revealed small, crooked teeth.

Maddy could not keep herself from staring at him. She would never have imagined that plain, prim Bonnie had a husband who looked like a Hell's Angel. She realized he was waiting for her reply. "Um . . . My name is Maddy Blake. Your wife and son . . . are staying with me."

"Oh, yeah," he said. "Hi there."

"I'm terribly sorry about all this," she said helplessly.

"That was real decent of you to take in my family," he said.

"Well, it seemed the least I could do." She thought of the insurance problem and added quickly, "I was glad to do it. Really."

He shifted his weight in the bed and winced.

"How are you feeling?" Maddy asked anxiously.

The man laid a hand gingerly on his abdomen. "I'm hurtin' a bit, I have to say. Doc says I need to take it easy. But my spirit is strong."

Maddy nodded uncertainly. "Well, I'm sure with that good outlook you'll make a quick recovery."

"I hope so," he said with a sigh. "Did Bonnie tell you about . . . us . . . our situation?"

"She said you'd just arrived here to see about a new job."

A vague look of sadness crossed his face. He nodded, looking away. "That's right," he said.

"I feel just terrible about this," said Maddy. "Will they hold the job for you? I mean, I'd be happy to call your prospective employer and explain what happened. Are you going to be able to work? Did the doctor say?"

Terry shrugged, then winced again. "He said no liftin'. That's gonna be tough, 'cause I'm a laborin' man."

A wave of guilt passed over Maddy at the thought of the Lewises' predicament. A man in between jobs, a new baby. It seemed so overwhelming. "I'm so sorry," she said.

"Don't be sorry for me," he said. "I'm a lucky man. The good Lord looks out for me. The rest of it'll work itself out somehow."

Maddy forced herself to smile. "Do you happen to know where I can find Bonnie and Sean?"

Terry's glazed eyes achieved a sparkle. "I think she was takin' him out to feed him. Whadda ya think of my boy?" he asked proudly.

Maddy was able to smile back without reservation. "He's a fine boy."

Terry smiled at a picture of Sean, just newborn, his tiny

eyes not even open. The photo was propped against the water carafe on the tray table across his bed. "I never tire of lookin' at that picture. Proudest day of my life—the day my son was born." He looked up at Maddy. "You have any children?"

"We have a daughter—Amy," Maddy said, a little surprised that Bonnie hadn't mentioned her. "She's three. She's at preschool right now."

"God's greatest gift, ain't they? No matter what happens to you, you just keep them always in your heart. . . ." He reached out and stroked the baby's face in the picture with a stubby forefinger.

"I couldn't agree more," said Maddy. This macho man, so unabashedly in love with his child, made her feel wistful. Doug never talked that way about Amy. Maybe if Amy had been a boy, she thought. She knew that some men felt a special bond with their sons. . . .

"I hope we'll have a little girl one of these days, too," Terry commented. "A little princess I can carry around on my shoulders. If the Lords wills it. . . ."

His words pierced her rationalization. "Well," said Maddy, squaring her shoulders, "I'm going to go hunt up Bonnie and Sean and take them home."

"Could you hand me my Bible before you go?" he asked, pointing in the direction of his bedside table. "I can't really reach it."

"Sure," she said.

She scanned the surface of the table, then opened the drawer and saw the book sitting there. She took it out and handed it to him. The skin of his fingers felt rough and cracked.

"Oh, here they are now," said Terry with satisfaction.

Maddy looked up and saw that Bonnie had appeared at the foot of the bed, holding Sean against her shoulder.

"Madonna and child . . ." He sighed.

Bonnie flushed furiously, avoiding Maddy's curious gaze, and came to his side to kiss him.

Maddy drove home with Bonnie sitting silently beside her, staring out the window at the gloomy October day. In the backseat, Amy sat next to Sean, pretending to read to him from a picture book she had brought home from preschool, while Sean squirmed in her old infant car seat and made little noises of protest.

Every so often Maddy stole a glance at her passenger. Bonnie was wearing a long gray-pleated skirt and a shapeless purple turtleneck that looked as if it had been washed a hundred times. She had on running shoes and sweat socks, and her curly, dull hair looked as if it could never be tamed into any kind of style. Although her hands lay in her lap, they were not at rest. She folded and unfolded her thin fingers in a constant, restless motion. Her gray eyes darted from side to side as if she were perpetually assessing her surroundings. Maddy thought about Bonnie's placid, tattooed, Bible-reading husband and wondered how in the world these two had ever gotten together.

"Your husband seems to be doing pretty well," Maddy offered.

Bonnie started, as if awakened from a disturbing dream. Then her face settled into a worried frown. "Better, yes," she said.

"Did the doctor say how long he had to stay in the hospital?"

"Probably another day or two," said Bonnie. "Do you want us to leave?"

"No," said Maddy, a little put off by the abruptness in her tone. "Stay as long as you need to."

"We'll be going soon," Bonnie said firmly. "We're anxious to get started on our new plans."

"I'm sure you are," said Maddy. "But this will give you a little chance to rest up. You must be tired," she added. "Sean had a pretty tough night."

"What do you mean?" Bonnie asked.

Maddy heard the defensiveness in her tone and tried to backpedal. "Well, the poor baby had a hard day—the accident, the hospital, a strange house. It didn't sound like you two got much sleep."

"He's fine. We're both fine," said Bonnie.

Maddy sighed. She wasn't being critical, but Bonnie seemed to take offense anyway. "That was good news about the van," she said, trying another subject. They had stopped at the garage and learned that the only damage was that the oil pan had been ripped off. The mechanic promised it would be replaced, probably by the end of the day.

Bonnie nodded and stared out the windshield. "Yes," she said. "All things considered."

"Your husband will be relieved to hear it, I'm sure. He seemed very nice," said Maddy. "I enjoyed talking to him."

Bonnie looked at her through narrowed eyes. "Talking about what?"

Maddy shrugged, aware of the suspicion in the other woman's voice. "He mainly talked about Sean. He's a very doting dad."

Bonnie nodded, and the harsh lines of her face seemed

to soften. "I know," she said. "Having a son was his fondest dream."

"Mommy," Amy wailed from the backseat, "Sean is pulling my hair."

"He's just playing with you, honey. He wants to know what your hair feels like."

Bonnie swiveled around and reached over the back of the seat. She saw Sean holding a tiny fistful of Amy's hair in his sticky hand. She reached over and pried open his fist, and Amy jerked her hair away. Then Bonnie smacked the baby twice on his tiny hand and wagged a finger at him. "Bad boy," she said. "Bad, bad boy."

Amy looked at her wide-eyed as Sean started to wail.

Bonnie settled back down in her seat and gave a sharp little nod of her head. "I'm a firm believer in discipline," she said proudly. "You've got to teach them the right way to act."

Maddy did her best to conceal her dismay. She wanted to protest that a baby Sean's age didn't know good behavior from bad. She forced herself not to criticize. Everyone had their own way of handling their children. Still, she wondered how Bonnie could stand to listen to the baby's sobs. It probably was the way she herself was raised, Maddy reflected. Amy was crooning, "It's all right, Sean," trying to soothe him and obviously feeling guilty for having gotten him into trouble.

"Almost home," Maddy said with a forced cheerfulness. As they rounded the corner of their street, Maddy saw the flashing red lights atop a black-and-white police car and heard the squawk of the police radio. Bonnie sat up and looked anxiously out the window.

"What the heck is that?" she asked.

"I don't know," said Maddy, instantly fearful. "They're at our house."

"What are they doing there?" Bonnie cried.

"It's probably something about the accident," Maddy said with a confidence she did not feel. She recognized Charles Henson's gray Mercedes in the driveway and felt her stomach turn over with anxiety.

"Policeman," Amy exclaimed as she craned her neck to peer out the window.

# Chapter Ten

*M*addy pulled up into the driveway and jumped out of the car. A patrolman was standing by one of the two squad cars. "What's going on here?" she asked. The patrolman shook his head, as if he were unwilling to answer. Maddy returned to the car and opened the back door, unbuckled Amy's seat belt, and lifted her out.

"What do they want?" Bonnie demanded, her eyes wide.

Maddy shook her head. "I don't know. I'm going to go find out." She carried Amy toward the front door. Amy huddled against her mother, intimidated by the strange sights and sounds of the police. The weight of the child against her helped to keep Maddy from trembling.

Maddy opened the front door and walked in. Doug was sitting on a chair in the hallway, his head in his hands. She saw Charles Henson in the living room, talking to three men. One of them was an officer in uniform, one a detective she recognized in a rumpled suit, and the third was Chief Cameron. "What in the world is going on here?" she asked.

Doug looked up at her grimly. He glanced in at the men in the living room and shook his head. He spoke in a distracted mumble. "He's after me. It's a vendetta because of Heather. I swear it. He won't be satisfied until he has my head. You're not going to believe this."

"Doug, what are they doing here?" Maddy asked frantically. Amy was still clutching her around the neck.

Chief Frank Cameron emerged from the living room and regarded her with a cold eye. "Well, Mrs. Blake. We meet again."

"Why are you here?" she said in a barely civil tone. Charles Henson followed him out of the living room.

Chief Cameron held out a piece of paper with a man's picture drawn on it. "Do you recognize this man?" he asked.

"Don't answer him," said Charles.

Maddy clutched Amy tightly in her arms and looked at the picture. The face was clean shaven and even featured, with light-colored hair, combed back the way Doug often liked to comb his hair. She glanced up at her husband, and instantly she knew that they were in danger.

"Doesn't he look familiar?" Chief Cameron asked mildly, with a hint of cruelty in his eyes.

"Not particularly," Maddy said.

"Don't talk to him," Charles said sharply. "Doug, I think the best thing for us to do is to cooperate with their investigation."

Amy craned her head and looked at the picture. "Dada," she cried happily.

Chief Cameron's eyes narrowed. "From the mouths of babes," he said.

"Take her out of here," Doug said angrily.

"I will," said Maddy. She walked back toward the

kitchen. Her heart was pounding. What in the world were they here for now? How long was Frank Cameron going to hound them because of Heather's lies? Maddy didn't know whether to feel fear or outrage. Her anger over Doug's mishap with the insurance had evaporated in the anxiety of the moment. How many more ways could their life go wrong? She was clutching Amy tightly—too tightly.

"Mama, let me go," Amy cried. Maddy put her down and tried to think. Amy was beginning to take off her jacket.

"Wait," said Maddy. "Leave your jacket on. Come with Mommy." She opened the door that led to the garage and went outside. Her car was sitting in the driveway behind Doug's car, and as she approached it, she could see that Bonnie was still inside. Maddy pulled out the stroller and dragged it down the driveway toward the car. She opened the passenger door.

Bonnie gripped the door handle and would not relinquish it. "What are they doing here?"

"The police chief has a vendetta against my husband," Maddy said grimly. "Look, I'll explain it to you later. Would you mind taking Amy for a short walk with Sean until they leave? I want to be here, but I don't want Amy . . ."

Bonnie ducked her head as she got out of the car and mumbled, "All right, all right."

"There's a little park right down there. You can see it from here," said Maddy, pointing. "They've got swings."

Bonnie nodded without looking. "Okay, I get it."

"Just until they leave."

Bonnie turned away from Maddy. She opened the back door of the car, leaned in, and tied the hood of Sean's sweatshirt until only a small disk of his face was visible. Then she lifted him out of the seat. He kicked his dangling feet as he rose.

Maddy looked fretfully at Amy. "You should have a hat on, too," she said. "It is getting chilly. Wait a minute." She went around to the hatchback, lifted it, and pulled out a red knitted watch cap. "We could live out of the back of this thing," she said. She crouched down and put the cap on Amy's head. "Now you go with Sean and Miss Bonnie down to the swings, and I'll see you in a few minutes."

Amy was already helping to secure Sean in the stroller.

"Thanks, Bonnie," said Maddy.

"No problem," Bonnie muttered.

Maddy turned and hurried back into the house. Doug was rummaging in the hall closet. "What are you doing?" Maddy cried. "Where are you going?"

"Why don't you wear your blue jacket?" the chief asked sarcastically.

"He doesn't have a blue jacket," Maddy said.

Charles Henson came over to her and took her arm. He spoke quietly but firmly into her ear. "They are investigating that disappearance of the baby-sitter and the little boy. A witness described a man talking to them in the park, and Chief Cameron seems to think this sketch resembles Doug."

"That could be anybody," Maddy cried. Through the window she could see Amy's red hat as she clambered up on a swing across the street. Bonnie sat on a bench under the bare branches of a tree with the stroller beside her.

"Of course it could," Charles said smoothly.

Doug pulled his dark green jacket out of the closet and put it on.

"Now where are you going?" Maddy cried. She looked at the grim expression on her husband's face.

"I have to play his little game," said Doug. "Don't pay any attention to it. He's desperate. He'll try anything."

Chief Cameron's face turned red, but he did not respond to the accusation. "Let's get this show on the road. We've got a witness waiting down at the station for a lineup."

"A lineup?" Maddy cried. "Are you arresting him?"

"Not till after the lineup," the chief said ominously.

Charles put a soothing hand on Maddy's arm. "We're going to cooperate with their investigation, regardless of their motives, and we'll be back in no time."

"I'm coming with you," said Maddy.

"No," Charles said sternly. "You stay here. I'll bring him home to you as soon as possible."

Doug was apologetic. "I'm sorry, honey," he said. "I hate for you to have to go through this. You've had enough to cope with these last few months."

Maddy reached out and squeezed his hand. "It's not your fault. I'll be all right," she said fiercely. She felt her heart thudding as she watched them go.

The ringing of the phone startled her.

"Mrs. Blake," said a high, nervous voice.

"Yes." Maddy steeled herself against the intrusion. She prayed it wasn't the newspapers again.

"This is Ellen Henson."

"Oh, hi," said Maddy, feeling somewhat relieved. "Are you looking for your husband? He just left."

"Really? No. I just . . . I read about the accident in the newspaper. Are you all right? Is your family all right?"

Maddy looked out the window at the police cars

pulling out of her driveway and gave a shuddering sigh. "I guess so," she said.

"What about the kitten?" said Ellen.

Maddy frowned, then remembered. "Oh, the kitten. I'm afraid in all the confusion last night, the cat got away. He must have taken off into the woods. Amy was terribly upset about it."

"Didn't you find him?"

"Well, it was a chaotic scene," said Maddy. "My husband was injured. . . . I looked around, but it was dark."

"He could die out there," Ellen cried. "He's only a baby."

Maddy felt tears well in her eyes. "I know," she said. "I'm sorry." She had a sudden image of the kitten lost in the woods, his little life suddenly turned upside-down, through no fault of his own. A victim of circumstance. "You're right," she said. "I'm so sorry."

"No," Ellen said fretfully. "It's my fault. I shouldn't have given him to you. I saw the child and I . . . I just acted impulsively. You didn't ask for that cat. I just wanted the child to have it. Why do we do things when we know we shouldn't?"

"I'm sorry," Maddy repeated helplessly. "I should have looked harder."

"Never mind," Ellen said grimly. "I'm to blame."

Before Maddy could reply, the phone went dead in her hand.

# Chapter Eleven

Father Nicholas Rylander reached up and pulled an armload of books off the shelves that lined his living room, packing them into the boxes on the floor. He had three rooms in the parish house—this living room, which looked out over Binney Park, a galley kitchen, and a cell-like bedroom. There wasn't much left to pack, but it was a dreary chore and he had put it off as long as possible. Every so often he would stop and close his eyes against the headache that throbbed behind his left eyebrow. He felt as if he had a brutal hangover, even though he hadn't had a drink. There was grit beneath his eyelids, and the muscles in his neck were tensely coiled. He lifted down a large art book, and it fell open on the desk. Nick stared down at Botticelli's *Martyrdom of St. Sebastian*. In the painting, the saint patiently looked to heaven as arrows pierced him from every direction. The mortification of the flesh—it was an ideal to which a priest aspired. It was God's will. Nick closed the book and rubbed his forehead. Then he shoved it beside the others in a box. Tomorrow, he thought. Tomorrow you'll be gone, and far away from here. It couldn't happen too soon.

He had not been raised to be devout. On the contrary, his parents fought bitterly and nearly drowned in alcohol. Watching their torturous union had hardened him against the idea of ever marrying. While studying art at a university as far away from them as possible, he had found himself marveling at the inspiration of the artists of the Renaissance. Gradually he had felt drawn to Catholicism: his study had led to faith. The priesthood had seemed a natural extension of that faith.

Now he tried to picture himself back in Canada. The monastery was out in the woods, far removed from the kinds of problems he faced here. He would work on the art restoration and regain control of his life. He would start over and try to make the right choices. Choices that God would want him to make. He would not become confused by lust. Try not to make any more mistakes.

"Nick?" said a soft voice.

It was as if his thoughts had conjured her. Her voice reverberated through him; he felt as if he were falling into a bottomless hole. He hated the adolescent way his senses responded to her presence—sight, smell, and sound. He tried not to imagine touch. He felt his cheeks redden. What made him think he would ever be able to overcome it?

He looked up and saw Maddy Blake holding her daughter by the hand, tapping tentatively on his door. She peered into the gloomy interior of the dark paneled room. He realized that although he could see her, she could not see him. He took the moment to gaze at her. Her dark hair glistened under the dim light of the sconce in the hallway. What would make hair gleam like that? he wondered. Her skin also seemed to glow, despite the dark circles he could see under her eyes. "Nick?" she called again, and her voice tolled inside him.

"In here," he said. "Come on in."

Maddy led Amy into the dark room. The walls were lined with bookshelves, most of which were now empty. A silver crucifix was affixed to the dark paneled wall over the fireplace mantel. The room revealed little about the man who occupied it. "Oh, hi. I'm so glad you're still here. Am I disturbing you?" she asked.

Nick suppressed a bitter smile. She had no idea of how she disturbed him—invaded his prayers, disrupted his dreams. "No," he said. "Come on in. I'm glad for an excuse to stop. To what do I owe the pleasure?"

"I can see you're busy," she said, fretting. She too looked as if she hadn't slept, but he doubted it was for the same reason that he had lain awake.

"No, I'm glad you came," he said. "I'm tired of this job."

Maddy shrugged helplessly. "I tried your office and the sextant sent me up here."

"It's fine," he said, clearing a half-filled box off the sofa. "Sit down. You too, Amy. You're both welcome."

Maddy reached into her large handbag and pulled out a talking book. Amy took it eagerly and began pushing the various buttons. Maddy perched on the edge of the sofa cushion. She shivered and looked around. "Brrr . . . it's cold in here."

"I'm practicing for Canada," he said with a smile, indicating the gray pullover sweater he was wearing.

"You look like you're almost done," she said sadly.

"I'm the world's slowest man to get organized," he said. He could tell that his answer did not even register.

Maddy gazed around the room with troubled eyes. "It must feel good to live simply, without a million complications," she murmured.

He smiled ruefully to himself. "It's all in how you look at it," he said. "Maddy, I know you didn't come here to talk about my moving arrangements. What is it? You said everything was all right last night at the hospital. . . . Has something happened?"

Maddy shook her head miserably. "Not about that," she said.

"Then what?"

Maddy stood up and began to pace around the tiny room. "I don't know why I came here," she said. "I'm not very religious. I mean, I'm sure you've noticed I'm not the most faithful churchgoer."

Nick put up a hand as if to stop her, but Maddy seemed to be unable to stop. "I'm not here to talk to you as a priest. I guess I need a friend—someone I can trust."

He blushed and was grateful for the gloom.

"It's probably just from seeing you last night, and you know, you and I have been working together. On the windows. I feel like you know me. You have things to do and I'm taking up your time. I'm really not entitled to your time."

Nick leaned forward and tried to catch her eye. "Maddy, stop."

"In your mind, you've probably already left this place behind. I know how that is when you're leaving a place. The last few days you're just on automatic pilot."

"Not about everything," he said. He wondered at her obtuseness. Was it deliberate? How could she be unaware of the effect she had on him? He reminded himself that she was here for counsel or consolation. No matter what she said, she had picked him because he was a priest, and she could rely on his discretion.

"Maybe it's because you're leaving," she said as if she were thinking aloud. "And I know you'll go away and take all the terrible things I'm saying with you. And I won't have to face you after saying them."

Nick used all his will not to let her see how her remark pained him. "Maddy," he said, "what has happened since last night? I thought everything was okay. Tell me what's going on."

Maddy sighed. "All right," she said. She took a deep breath. "We took the people who were in the accident home with us, because they had nowhere to stay."

"How's the fellow doing who was in the other car?" he asked.

"He was doing pretty well this morning," said Maddy. "You know the hospital these days. Surgery one day, and they're kicking you out the next. It's the insurance companies. They don't want to pay for it," she said, and then she grimaced, as if a pain had shot through her.

"It was good of you to take the family in," said Nick.

"I had to," said Maddy, absently twisting the silver chain on her wrist. "I felt so guilty about them."

Nick gave her a knowing smile. "Guilt," he mused. "How would we manage without it?"

"Well, I'd like to say it was the holy spirit," Maddy said bluntly, "but in truth, it was guilt."

"You're an honest person, Maddy Blake."

Maddy shook her head. "No, that's not it. Last night, when we got home, after I got them settled, Doug told me . . . that he had not paid our auto insurance premium, and that if they decided to sue us, we are not protected."

Nick winced. Fool, he thought. He knew a lot more

about the problems of day-to-day life than most of his parishioners suspected. He had seen people stay with jobs they hated just to maintain their insurance coverage. He had seen people ruined for the lack of it. Douglas Blake had let that protection lapse and left his family vulnerable. He felt his dislike of the man rise to his throat.

"It was stupid," Maddy said fiercely.

"You took the words right out of my mouth," he said.

She hurried on. "I was so angry at him. After all we'd just been through with Heather Cameron." She looked up at him. "Don't pretend you don't know about that."

He avoided her challenging stare. "Well, yes. We never talked about it."

"I know," said Maddy. "I never discussed it with anybody. But I felt . . ." She waved a hand hopelessly. "Never mind. I can't go into it all now. The thing is, today the police came, just an hour ago, and took him in for questioning. About that missing baby-sitter and the baby."

"What?" Nick cried, genuinely shocked.

Maddy looked at him pleadingly. "Nick, I don't know what to think. I mean, Doug would never . . . I mean, he's . . . irresponsible sometimes. Lately he's even been cruel at times and very angry. But this . . ."

Nick shook his head. "I'm sure not," he said.

"But I can't help wondering," she cried.

"No. No, of course you can't."

Amy, who was seated on the floor with her legs straight out in front of her, let out a whoop when she came to the page where a bird whistled.

Maddy reached out and ran a hand gently over her daughter's blond head. Her delicate hand caressed Amy's silken hair, the silver bracelet gleaming among the child's platinum curls. Maddy lifted her hand and fingered the bracelet pensively. "You don't really know my husband," she said.

"No," Nick agreed. He had a feeling that she was going to defend him, and he was not sure he wanted to hear it.

Maddy tilted her head thoughtfully and sighed. "He . . . Before I got to know him I thought he was just a spoiled, self-centered guy. He was handsome, and in those days he had money that he used to flash around. He used to be a professional baseball player. Did you know that?"

Nick shook his head. "I'm not much of a sports fan."

"Well, me neither. I guess I had the usual prejudices about jocks being stupid and all. But he's not. Doug's really very intelligent, and he's a good teacher. His heart is in the right place." She hesitated.

"But . . . ?" Nick nudged her.

Maddy shook her head. "No, I don't mean it that way. I mean, he looks like a golden boy, but his life was nothing like that. It wasn't easy for him, growing up. His parents . . . his mother is a very cold person. She never calls him. Even on his birthday. She's never sent him so much as a birthday card. Can you imagine that? And his father is very passive. He just went about his business and let Doug fend for himself. It wasn't easy, living like that, you know?"

Nick nodded, remembering his own warring parents, who competed for his allegiance, each one wanting him to renounce the other. "It's amazing what children have to go through," he said. "It's amazing that people survive childhood traumas without irreparable damage."

"I know," Maddy said fervently. "I had it so easy. My parents doted on me and my brother. I don't know what it's like to be so neglected. So, I always think, when he's cold or impatient, that it's understandable. His behavior doesn't mean he doesn't love us, or that he would do . . . that he could be guilty of something terrible like the Heather thing. Or this missing girl. It's just his way of coping."

Nick nodded, as if he agreed, but in his heart he could not understand it. How could Doug Blake squander this gift, take for granted this love that was given to him? Even before he had become a priest, Nick had lived alone and never minded it. The silence had been a blessing after the shouting wars of his family home. Once he found his faith, he was never lonely. He felt peaceful, communing with the Lord, the silence once again a blessing after the demands of his parish life. Then he met Maddy, and he had begun to feel the longing for a particular human presence. It had ruined his peace of mind. He had begun to experience loneliness because she was not with him. He looked into her dark, worried eyes, which were waiting for his answer. "And now you want to know if you should keep on believing in him, Maddy. That's what you're asking me, isn't it?"

Maddy nodded numbly.

"Well, I think you already know the answer. From what you've said, you still do believe in him. Right now, he needs you to stand by him."

"I know the police chief hates him because of Heather," said Maddy.

"People will do irrational things when they want revenge," Nick said.

"Right," she said. "That's what this is all about, isn't it? Revenge."

"Well, I don't know. It could be."

"It has nothing to do with what really happened. How could I even think such a thing of Doug?" she cried.

Nick looked straight at her, but his mind felt as if it were ricocheting around the room. It wasn't that hard to think ill of Doug Blake. Nick didn't trust him, and he thought he might well have been guilty of seducing Heather Cameron. He knew in his heart that he envied and resented Doug Blake, because Doug Blake was married to a woman he loved. So it was impossible for him to be fair to the man. All his judgments were suspect.

If he told her now that she should heed her worst suspicions, he might be able to drive a wedge into this marriage with just a word. That would be a sin. He had decided to choose his vocation, to leave behind his misguided passion for her. He could not be the agent of destruction in her marriage. Not if he wanted to save his own soul. "If you don't believe in him," Nick said slowly, "who can he turn to? He has a right to expect your loyalty."

Maddy sighed and then smiled at him. "You're right," she said. "I have to keep the faith." She stood up. "You won't tell anyone I thought these things. . . ." Immediately she realized how insulting that sounded. "I'm sorry," she said. "I know you won't. I came here because I knew I could trust you."

"And you knew I was leaving," he said, rising to his feet.

Maddy crossed the room to him and extended her hand. His face was so sad that it hurt her to look at him. He's sad about leaving, she thought. It has nothing to do with me. As their eyes met, she knew better. She understood that it did indeed have to do with her. She felt possessed of a frightening, strangely exhilarating secret.

Impulsively she embraced him. He wrapped his arms around her and breathed her in. Endearments rose to his throat, but not a murmur or a groan escaped.

Maddy sighed and then felt something inside of her threaten to give way in his arms. She told herself it was normal to hug a friend at a time of parting. But it wasn't friendship she felt as she closed her eyes in his enfolding arms. She longed to touch his hair, to rub her cheek against his and seek his mouth. No, she told herself. It was weariness, and the comfort of his strength. It was alarming all the same. Abruptly she pushed him away.

"I'd better go," she said, avoiding his gaze. "Maybe Doug's home by now. Thank you . . . Nick. Come on, honey," she said, bending and scooping Amy off the floor. "We won't bother Father Nick any longer. He's got packing to do."

"Is he going on a vacation?" Amy asked.

Maddy looked up at him and saw a stricken look on his face. "I'm afraid he's moving, honey."

"Will he move back?" she asked.

"No, honey. He's going away."

Amy turned and waved. "Bye-bye," she said gravely, unconvinced by her mother's explanation. "I'll see you when you move back."

Maddy did not look at him as she hustled the child ahead of her out the door.

# Chapter Twelve

Ernest Unger sensed, more than saw, a movement in the distant clump of trees, and he felt the familiar rush of excitement that such a movement always brought. Moving with the smooth stealth of years of practice, he pivoted, almost silently, and saw his quarry. The buck stood at a distance, quivering within range of Ernest's rifle, his huge rack practically spanning the space between two trees. Oh, he was handsome, Ernest thought, gazing in admiration on his prey as he planned his movements. He could picture that proud head mounted on the wall of his den. Marie didn't allow them anywhere else in the house. Ernest mounted only the very finest ones that he landed. But this fellow—he was worthy. He was one you could talk about for years. Ernest felt a thrill of anticipation. Don't count your chickens, he warned himself. Many a shot went awry, many a fine specimen got away.

He positioned himself silently; the buck did not stir. Now, if only that dim-witted son-in-law of his would just stay put wherever it was he had hunkered down. Ernest hated taking Dan along on these trips. Although Marie and Susie had outfitted him with all the latest gear, and Dan professed a willingness to learn, he didn't know the first thing about hunting. He was clumsy and noisy and had spoiled any number of opportunities when Ernest was so close he could taste it. He knew he was supposed to be bonding with the boy—that's what they called it. Bonding. Ernest missed the good old days when guys just went out together for the hell of it, and all this touchy-feely stuff was left to the girls. Hunting was a man's sport. One of the few activities that a man could still do and not find a bunch of women there trying to join in. Having Dan along was almost as bad as taking the ladies with you.

To tell the truth, Ernest suspected that Dan was a tiny bit squeamish and that he wasn't really trying to learn how to hunt at all. He wasn't a bad shot. Ernest had seen him hit a target with a pretty fair accuracy. It was the blood that seemed to get to him. Susie had grown up around hunters, and she had tried to explain to Dan how it was an ecological thing—keeping the deer population down—and how they could eat venison all winter after hunting season was over. Dan paid lip service to it, but when Marie cooked up venison steak, Ernest had seen him pushing it around on his plate. Well, Ernest wasn't going to be the one to call it off. If Dan wasn't up to it, he'd just have to speak up. Meanwhile he was a positive handicap on a hunting trip.

The buck raised his head and sniffed the air warily, his muscles taut. Likewise, Ernest tightened every sinew and fiber of his compact body, carefully, slowly, lifting his gun and taking aim. For a moment they were as one, hunter and hunted, bound together as if by destiny. Ernest curved his finger softly around the trigger and began to pull.

A terrible shout rent the air. Ernest, poised for the kill, started to fire and nearly fell backward. The buck swung round his magnificent rack, met Ernest's gaze, and leapt away, crashing through the brittle branches at a gallop.

Son of a bitch, Ernest thought. That does it. I don't care if they beg me. I am never taking that ignorant, no-good . . . He recognized Danny's voice, shouting his name in a loud, hoarse cry. Ernest shouldered his gun, his face aflame with rage. He always considered himself a peaceable, sensible man who would never use a weapon in anger or frustration, but for one moment, as he trudged through the underbrush in his camouflage fatigues, he understood how things sometimes got out of hand between people with guns.

"What in the hell is it?" said Ernest as he approached his son-in-law. Dan was leaning against a tree, his face as gray as a pigeon's belly.

"Dad," he whispered in a voice so childlike, so full of dread, that Ernest felt his rage disappear, his paternal instinct rose up in him fierce as a bear on its hind legs.

"Look," said Dan, pointing into a copse of scraggly trees with a shaking hand.

Ernest walked up beside him and looked. "Oh, God," he breathed. "Oh, my God."

Beside him, Dan bent over and retched. Ernest stared in horror at the bruised, mottled body of the girl, her shirt ripped open, her pants yanked down. Bugs and worms had already begun to inhabit this strange being in their midst. Her eyes were open, and unseeing.

Ernest did not speak. Never taking his eyes from her face, he reached out and patted Dan absently on the back.

Then he rested his gun against a tree trunk, removed his jacket, and walked slowly to where she lay. Kneeling beside her, he placed the jacket over her and arranged it around her gently, like a father in the night come to cover his sleeping child.

Half an hour later the silent woods had been transformed into a ghoulish fairground. Police, photographers, and newspeople trampled through the brush, videocams rolled from behind the bright yellow police tape encircling the actual spot where the body was found. Radios squawked, and the assistant DA conferred with police and his office on a cellular phone.

Ernest Unger, now gray in the face, sat on an overturned spackle bucket Dan had found in his car and was sipping on a flat Coke his son-in-law had located and poured into a Thermos cup. Dan stood beside the old man, his hand resting protectively on his shoulder as they patiently repeated, to the several officers who asked, how they had come to stumble over the corpse.

Frank Cameron looked away from the pathetic sight of Rebecca Starnes's body as men from the coroner's office carefully covered it and placed it on a stretcher to remove it from its resting place on the forest floor. He turned to the county coroner, Dr. Simon Tillis, who was replacing his medical instruments in his bag.

"How did she die, Doc?" Frank asked.

"She was shot, actually. In the head, at close range. Judging from the entry wound, I'd guess a small handgun, although we need the slug to say for sure," said the doctor.

"She was awful bruised," said Frank.

"She'd been dragged here. She didn't die right away."

"Nice," said Frank, thinking about the girl's mother clutching her daughter's school picture. "Sexual assault?"

The coroner shrugged. "It looks likely. But we won't know for sure until we get the lab results."

"Those sickos are usually more fond of knives, or better yet, strangulation," Frank observed.

Dr. Tillis sighed. "True, but judging from the condition in which we found her . . ."

"Right," said Frank. "How long till we know?"

"Tomorrow, I'd say."

"Well, light a fire under these people. I want them yesterday," Frank snarled.

Dr. Tillis did not take the chief's anger personally. "Will do," he said.

Pete Millard walked up beside Frank, and together they watched the shrouded body being placed in the back of the county coroner's van. "So, what have we got?" Pete asked. "Was it a sex crime, or were they just trying to get the baby?"

"Can't call it yet. Looks like a sex thing, but we have to wait for the lab."

"But if it was sex . . . ," said Pete.

"Right. Any sign . . . ?" Frank asked.

Pete understood his boss's shorthand. He was referring to Justin. "They're combing this place," he said.

"We were too late," said Frank.

Pete nodded.

"Shit," said Frank. "That poor woman." He was dreading it. The moment that lay just ahead, when he would knock on Sandi Starnes's door and have to find the words to explain what had happened to her beloved, smiling girl.

"Maybe we'll find the kid," Pete said hopefully. "If he's not right here, that could be a good sign."

"Yeah," Frank snorted, his gaze roving restlessly over the trees in the quiet woods. "Great."

# Chapter Thirteen

*H*eather Cameron sat alone at a table for six, her lunch tray in front of her, pretending to read a book. She tried to appear oblivious of the fact that the other kids were avoiding her. She imagined that there was a murmur running through the noisy lunchroom, with her name discernible through the din. She did not intend to look up, not even once. She would not give them the satisfaction. Her heart began to hammer with fear when she saw, out of the corner of her eye, two people approaching her table. She fixed her eyes on the book and prayed that they would veer off in another direction. Instead two trays were set down, one across from her and one beside her. Feeling ambushed, she tried to hide her stinging tears. She ducked her head as if to avoid a blow.

A voice above her said kindly, "Hi, Heather."

Heather looked up warily. Karla and Richie, who had walked to school with her this morning and chattered along as if unaware of Heather's disgrace at being officially branded a liar, were now surrounding her at the empty table. Richie faced her, and Karla stood beside her.

"Hi," Heather mumbled. She regarded the pair suspiciously. This morning she had just figured they were being nice. After all, she and Karla had grown up in the same neighborhood. Since Karla had always been pretty and had boyfriends, it was easy for her to be nice, Heather thought. This, however, seemed a bit too nice. As if Heather were being set up for something. She saw them exchange a collusive glance.

"Can we sit with you?" asked Karla.

"Sure, if you want to," said Heather. But she didn't smile.

Karla settled herself into the seat, tamping her straw on the tabletop to unwrap it. "Did you hear about that girl from Perpetual Sorrows?" she asked.

Heather frowned. "What girl?"

"The one that was missing with the baby."

"Oh, yeah," said Heather.

"They found her. Your father was on TV."

"Is she okay?" Heather asked.

"No," said Richie. "She's dead."

"Oh, God," said Heather, closing her book. The three sat in silence for a moment, stunned at the idea of someone their own age, in their own town, meeting such a fate.

"I heard they questioned Mr. Blake about it," said Richie. "Your dad brought him in."

Heather's face flamed. She wished that the cafeteria floor would open up and swallow her. "That's stupid," she said.

"Why? He's a perv," said Richie. "You said so yourself."

Karla gave Richie a warning glance. Heather picked up her book and opened it again.

"What are you reading?" Karla asked pleasantly.

Heather had to look at the book to be able to answer the question. "Algebra," she said. She peered at Richie, who was popping the top of his soda can, avoiding her gaze. Then she looked at Karla. "How come you two are being nice to me?" she said.

Richie looked up innocently, as if hurt by her question. But Karla did not bother to feign innocence. She slipped her straw into her milk carton and swished it around.

"You must have some reason," Heather said stubbornly.

"Can't we just be nice?" Richie protested.

Heather made a face. "Don't try to jerk me around. I've been jerked around enough. First you walk me to school. Now you're sitting with me. Everybody knows I'm some kind of leper because of this thing with Mr. Blake."

"Okay, Heather. You're right. Well, we are being nice," said Karla. "I mean, we don't mean you any harm. I promise."

"But you want something."

Richie sighed and began to eat his pizza.

"Sort of," said Karla.

Heather felt her heart sink. Even as she insisted to herself that she knew it, she had entertained a secret hope that maybe, maybe these two beautiful people wanted, for some reason, to be friends with her. It wasn't a big letdown, because she'd only had the morning to hope for it. Still . . .

Karla placed a small, perfectly formed hand on her forearm. "Look, Heather. I've known you for most of your life, right?"

Heather nodded, temporarily unable to circumvent the lump of disappointment that was lodged in her throat.

"I believe you, Heather. Well, I mean, sort of."

Heather shrugged, as if this were what she'd expected.

Richie leaned across the table. His fine green eyes regarded her earnestly, and Heather felt her stomach swoop. What must it be like to have a guy like this really like you? she wondered.

"Look, Heather, I know everybody thinks Mr. Blake is a cool guy and all, but I don't think so. He gave me a D last term and it kept me off the football team."

"Did you deserve it?" Heather said sarcastically.

"I missed a test because I was out with an injury from practice. He wouldn't let me make it up. He said it was an automatic F."

"Why didn't you just bring a note?" Heather said dully.

"I did bring a note. But he said if I was that weak, I didn't belong on the team anyway. He's a bastard."

"Why didn't you tell your mother or the principal?"

"Yeah, like you did," said Richie.

Heather sighed. "But why? Why did he do it?"

Richie made a face and squeezed his Coke can until it started to dent. "I think he was trying to get to Karla," he said.

"Oh, come on," said Heather.

"Really. He asked me all these questions about her. He said how she'd probably want to help me make the team."

"He wouldn't do that," Heather protested. "He doesn't . . ."

"Doesn't what? I thought he forced you into it for a grade."

Heather shrugged. "I don't want to talk about it," she said.

"We were really hoping he was going to get fired for what he did to you," said Karla.

"Yeah, well, me too," said Heather.

"He probably would have if you hadn't kept changing your story," Karla said severely. "Why did you do that? Why didn't you show up in court and all?"

Heather stuck her jaw out and stared at the tray. She felt her face flaming, and she wished that they would just go away. "Never mind," she said.

"You liked him, didn't you?" said Karla.

"No," Heather whispered.

Karla and Richie exchanged a glance. "The thing is, Heather, I've heard rumors about him before," said Karla. "Nothing definite. Just talk, you know. . . ."

Heather snorted derisively. "Try and prove it."

Karla leaned toward her and gripped her arm. "That's what we want to do," she said. "We want to get him, and we think we know a way. We have an idea, anyhow."

Heather's heart suddenly hammered with excitement and something weird. A kind of hopefulness. She hadn't realized, even all during the court thing, how much she really wanted to get back at him. The decision to accuse him out loud, in public, had been more like a moment of madness than anything else. She had never realized that it would go so far. But now that she had made such a total muck of it, and everybody else looked at her like a fool—now she realized her mistake. She gazed in wonderment at these promising new allies. "You do?" she said.

"Yes," said Karla. "Would you like to help?"

# *Chapter Fourteen*

*P*aulina Tomczuk looked at her watch and frowned. She had been hunting for Ellen for over an hour now, but she'd had no luck. It was frustrating. She could be anywhere. Paulina had already tried a few of the places she thought she might find her—the greenhouse where she got her plants, the few stores where she infrequently shopped. She had slowly trolled through the busy streets and parking lots of Taylorsville, but there was no sign of Ellen's red Jeep.

I'm a cook, not a detective, she thought irritably as she turned into the gates of the cemetery where Kenny had been laid to rest. The gloomy, windswept expanse was silent and empty. Dry leaves drifted across the still green lawn, coming to rest against the stark, gray markers for the dead. Paulina drove through the winding roads of the graveyard, stopping for a moment to look down the row to the plot where the child was buried. They had chosen a spot beneath a dogwood tree, which was lovely in the spring. Now, in the October gloom, its bare branches reached out plaintively, protectively, over the headstones, like a mother's arms.

This time of year Mr. H was always the most worried about his wife. Right around the birthday. The birthday was always the toughest. Paulina thought that Ellen had seemed all right on the birthday. Almost as if she weren't thinking about it. She had been preoccupied and jumpy, which seemed to worry Mr. H more than if she had been weepy. Paulina was beginning to agree with him.

Not that she was any expert on mental problems. Paulina had raised four children who were all healthy and normal, thank God; likewise her grandchildren. But they had never had to suffer what Ellen had. It was not something a woman just got over. Anyway, when she got to work this afternoon, and Mr. H called, there was no sign of Ellen anywhere. He said he'd been calling on and off all day, to no answer, and he sounded just about frantic. She knew why—Ellen hardly ever went out, and when she did, it was usually after hours of deliberation and she was back in no time. Paulina had agreed to drive around and look for her. She had removed her apron, climbed into the car, and here she was, an hour later, and no luck.

"I'm not a mind reader," she said aloud. She was annoyed. Annoyed that she had been sent on this assignment and annoyed that she had failed. "I'm not a detective," she declared to the inside of her car.

Maybe she's back home by now, Paulina reasoned. Maybe I just missed her. And I have a pie to finish for supper, she thought ruefully. I'm going to head back, she decided.

Just as she was turning out of the cemetery exit, Paulina had an inspiration. The vet. Ellen was so concerned about those new kittens—perhaps she had gone to the vet for something. One more try, she thought, swinging the car in the direction of the River Road. A few minutes later, a glance at the parking lot of the vet's clinic told her that this was not the answer, either.

"I've got to start my pie," she said aloud. She couldn't just drive around all day. Paulina glanced at the statue of the blessed Virgin that rode on the dashboard. "You're going to have to look out for her, Holy Mother," she said as she drove along the winding River Road. No sooner were the words out of her mouth than she spotted a flash of red alongside the shoulder. She slowed down and pulled up behind the red Jeep, which was parked at a lopsided angle. Paulina pressed her lips together anxiously as she got out of her car. There was no one anywhere in sight. The car was empty.

"Mrs. H," she cried. "Ellen." Except for the crackle of leaves and the plaintive cry of birds, the woods were quiet. Black skid marks were visible on the road, and a curl of rubber from a tire rested in the brown grass up ahead. "Ellen," Paulina cried again. She whirled around when she heard rustling in the bushes behind her.

When she didn't see anyone, she assumed it must be an animal. Then, from the trees, she heard the crunching sounds of someone moving through the ground cover and a soft, muffled sob. Paulina was not an exceptionally brave person, but she felt a sudden, fierce determination on Ellen's behalf. She started into the mass of evergreens that bordered the road. She had taken only a few steps into the trees when she saw her.

Ellen was on her hands and knees, crawling along the ground.

"Mrs. H," Paulina cried. She ran toward her, branches and vines catching at the ankles of the half stockings beneath her double-knit pants. Her low-heeled, navy blue shoes were not meant for trudging through the woods, but she plunged on toward the frail woman on the ground ahead of her.

Ellen looked up, and Paulina could see that she was frantic. She raised her arms like a child, and Paulina reached for her with her large hands, still powdery white with traces of flour. "What in the world?" Paulina cried.

"I've been looking for the kitten," Ellen said, grasping Paulina's hand.

Paulina looked at her in complete confusion. "What kitten?"

"The one I gave to the little girl," Ellen said earnestly.

It took Paulina a few moments to realize what her employer was talking about. "Well, what makes you think it would be here? Don't they still have it?"

Ellen clutched at the sleeves of Paulina's car coat. "The kitten ran away. Nobody looked for him. He's too little. I was the one who gave him away. I should never have given him away. I've been looking and looking. I have to find him. . . ."

Paulina knelt down in the leaves, ignoring the brown bits of leaves that clung to her pants, the mud that stuck to her shoes. She could not make much sense of what Ellen was saying, and it frightened her. What was she doing out here, crawling around in the woods? Mr. H had been right to be worried. Paulina put her arms around the narrow shoulders of the fragile woman and stroked her wild, graying curls. "It's all right," she said. "The cat will be all right. You have to come home now."

"You don't understand," said Ellen, shaking her head. "This happening right now. It's a sign. I'm being punished."

"That's nonsense," said Paulina. "Come along now. We'd better get back."

Ellen nodded. Paulina tried to think how she was going to tell this to Mr. H. It was not hard to see this as some kind of mental . . . crisis. She dreaded to see the look on his face when he heard about it. Not for the first time, Paulina wished that her employers had a strong faith to turn to for comfort. She had always found refuge in her prayers, the beads of the rosary like a lifeline in her arthritic fingers. Paulina began to pray now as she took Ellen's arm and pulled her up, supporting her weight as they headed back through the evergreens.

Although Donna and Johnny Wallace's neatly kept bungalow was filled with people, there was little noise above the sound of the TV, which was running continuously. The kitchen counters were laden with food, wrapped in foil and Saran Wrap, and every available seat was filled with an aunt, an uncle, or a cousin. Johnny Wallace was having a beer, because it was the only way he could think of to calm his nerves. Johnny leaned against a kitchen counter and stared vacantly ahead while his older brother sat at the kitchen table and talked at him, trying to analyze the situation optimistically.

In her bedroom, Donna Wallace sat on a bed piled high with stuffed animals, still wearing one of Johnny's shirts over her nightgown, Pound Puppy slippers on her feet, clutching a fist full of soggy tissues in her right hand. She gazed at a photo of Justin on the bedside table. The picture had been taken as Justin was being nuzzled by his grandmother's dog. The child was crowing with delight.

Donna Wallace knew what she had to do. They had heard the news about Rebecca almost simultaneously on the phone and on the television. In the days and hours since Justin's disappearance, the crowd at her house had not thinned. Her angry relatives had shouted the reporters away and refused to let anyone get near her. But there was no way Donna could shake off her duty now. Depositing the tissues in the bedside wastebasket, she stood up on shaky legs. She took off the flannel shirt, pulled the nightgown over her head, and dressed carefully—a clean blouse and dark slacks. Then she put on trouser socks and real shoes. Not running shoes. Not for this.

When she was dressed she looked in the mirror. Her face was white, with patches of gray under her eyes. She brushed a streak of blush across each cheek. Carefully she applied lipstick. Her hair was hopeless. She did not even bother. When she opened the door to her room a crack, her cousin Rose, who was standing outside like a sentry, looked in at her suspiciously.

"What is it, hon?" Rose asked.

"Tell Johnny I'm ready to go," she said.

"Do you really think—"

"Just tell him, Rose," said Donna.

Rose lumbered away from the door and returned in a few minutes with Johnny. He slipped into the room, holding Donna's parka. "You'll need this," he said.

Donna looked at him and saw that he had shaved. She nodded approvingly and touched her hand to the skin on his face.

"We'll go out the back," he said as she pulled on her parka. Her arms and shoulders seemed to ache, as if she had a fever.

"Okay," she whispered.

"Ready?" he asked, meeting her gaze with his own

strong gaze, and she was glad, once again, that she had married him. She nodded.

Johnny took her hand, and they sneaked out the back door. Behind them, they could hear people arguing in the living room. The day was raw, and Donna shivered, even in her parka. Johnny gripped her hand tightly, and they walked across the small backyard, through the two backyards adjacent to it, passing rusty barbecue grills and plastic children's riding toys. Fortunately no one on their block had a chain-link fence. They arrived at the familiar patio of Sandi Starnes's little house, the green-and-white webbed lawn furniture still sitting outside, many of the webs frayed and broken. The patio umbrella in the middle of the white table was down and looked gray and moldy.

Johnny and Donna exchanged a glance, and Donna nodded. Johnny tapped on the sliding doors of the patio, which had the curtains drawn from inside.

A large, surly man came to the sliders, pulled back the curtain, and glared at them. Then he looked slightly confused as he recognized the Wallaces. "Could we come in?" Johnny asked.

The man turned from the sliders, dropped the curtain, and spoke gruffly to someone inside. Donna and Johnny stood shivering on the patio, looking up at the gray sky.

There was movement near the windows, and then Sandi Starnes pushed back the curtains. She opened the sliders. Her whole face was red from weeping.

Donna felt her heart turn over in her chest. "Sandi," she said.

"Hello, Donna," said Sandi.

For a moment Donna thought that she would not be able to speak, that she would just stand there, frozen on that patio, like some cement statue. Then, suddenly, the words came tumbling out. "Sandi, you may not even want to speak to us ever again and I wouldn't blame you if you didn't, but we just heard about Rebecca and we had to come . . . and say . . . and say . . ." The end of her sentence was lost in sobs.

Johnny cleared his throat manfully and took up where his wife had faltered. "And say how we are really sorry and really . . . ashamed that we thought . . . or ever said that maybe Rebecca . . ." He swallowed hard. "Who was always such a good girl."

Donna turned away from the door, hiding her face in her hands, but Sandi, wearing only a little gray cardigan sweater for warmth, stepped out on the patio and put a hand on Donna's shoulder.

Donna turned and looked at the older woman, her eyes fearful but willing to take whatever blows might come her way. "You must hate me," she said miserably. "I hate myself."

Sandi shook her head. She felt a strange stillness inside. Compassion, even, for these two. Who's to say, she wondered, what I might have thought if that baby had been my Rebecca? You think crazy things. You think the worst thoughts in the world. Usually it doesn't turn out to be anything. Someone stopped for an ice-cream cone. Someone forgot to call. There was a flat tire. Usually all those fears were for nothing. You made up all these horrible scenarios in your head, and then all at once the door opened and your precious child was standing there, bright and heart lifting as a rainbow. And then you started hollering because they made you worry so.

Sandi gazed at Donna and Johnny. They looked so vulnerable standing there, like children themselves. But they were not children. They were the terrified parents of a missing baby.

Sandi reached out and squeezed Donna's trembling fingers. Donna grasped Sandi's hand, and awkwardly, gratefully she pressed it to her lips.

"At least my waiting is over," Sandi said.

# Chapter Fifteen

Paulina shook the hand of the priest, who stood in the foyer of the Henson mansion. "Thank you for coming, Father. I know you're trying to get ready to leave. . . ."

Nick shook his head. "It's all right, Paulina. I wasn't getting much accomplished anyway." He thought of Maddy in his arms, their brief embrace that had made him feverish with anxiety. After she left, he had tried to continue his packing, but it was hopeless. "I welcomed your call," he said truthfully. He had been grateful for an opportunity to get out of his own head, to get away from his shameful thoughts and try to minister to others as he had promised to do when he took his vows.

"I haven't been able to reach her husband. He's a lawyer and he's out of the office. So I thought of you. She's not a Catholic, Father. But she's a soul in torment if ever I saw one. I thought maybe you could talk to her. You have a good way with people. I've come to you with my problems often enough."

Nick smiled. "I'll be happy to try. You say she lost her son?"

"It was many years ago, and she had a breakdown afterward. It's always been difficult, but this time . . . It seems like there's a burden that's crushing her. I've found so much help in my faith. I'm not trying to force her to believe anything, but I don't know any other way to comfort her. I told her I was going to call you, but she didn't seem to hear me. When she sees you she may just tell you to get out and leave her alone."

"She won't be the first one," he said with a smile. "All we can do is offer our help." He gestured for her to lead the way, and Paulina started up the wide staircase ahead of him.

"That went pretty well," Doug said cheerfully, loosening his tie. He was seated in a leather chair, next to a mahogany desk in Charles Henson's office at Henson, Newman and Pierce. The offices were in a handsomely renovated Queen Anne–style house across from the public library; Charles's private office boasted a fireplace with an ornate mantel, Persian carpets, and Tiffany-style lamps scattered around.

Charles, who was in the process of opening his briefcase, stopped and stared at his client, who had one arm tossed comfortably over the back of the leather chair. Of course he understood Doug's relief. Julia Sewell had been unable to identify him in the lineup, and though the police had threatened to produce other witnesses, apparently they did not have any at hand. After Charles threatened a lawsuit for harassment, the police had let him go.

"I'd keep that tie tight if I were you," Charles said coolly. "We're not out of the woods yet."

Doug's self-satisfied expression vanished as he straightened in the chair and fixed his tie. Charles chided himself for sounding so harsh. The young man had every reason to be relieved. Charles wondered if maybe his own anxiety was coloring his attitude. He heard the phone ring in the outer office and wondered if his secretary was back to pick it up. She had not been at her desk when they'd come in. Automatically Charles tensed up, wondering if Paulina was calling. But the light went out on the phone line after a moment, and Charles resumed the hunt through his briefcase.

"What do you mean, not out of the woods?" Doug asked warily.

"Well, when we went down there earlier, we had a missing persons situation. Now it's murder," he said, referring to the fact that Rebecca's body had been found. "Chief Cameron would like nothing better than to drag you down there again. He's got his sights set on you."

"Did you mean what you said about filing the harassment lawsuit?" Doug asked.

Charles tapped his Mont Blanc pen absently on the curving leather arm of his chair. "I think we may have to. As sort of a preemptive strike. Just so he knows he can't keep dragging you down there for whatever develops."

"Are we talking a lot of money?" Doug asked eagerly. "Do you think we can win?"

Charles could practically see dollar signs lighting up in Doug's eyes. "Doug, we're not talking about winning the lottery here. These suits can drag on through the courts for years. So far, we haven't got a strong case."

"But that picture was so vague it could have been anybody," Doug said indignantly.

"On the other hand, it could have been you. It did look

like you. It's not as if the witness described a short, bald, swarthy man. . . ."

"She didn't recognize me," Doug protested.

"No, she didn't. Let's hope that's an end to it."

"Well, then why did you say that about the lawsuit?" Doug asked, disappointment in his tone.

"You have just been exonerated from some extremely serious charges, and you are trying to rehabilitate your reputation. We all know how the papers will trumpet a man's disgrace and give only the slightest lip service to his exoneration."

"That's the truth," Doug said.

"Now, you suddenly find yourself back in the headlines, back on the TV news, and if it's merely because this chief of police is having trouble accepting the fact that his daughter lied about you . . ."

"That's how I see it," Doug said.

"Well, a lawsuit may be the only recourse we have to fight back. I mean, if he intends to pillory you."

"So we probably should go for it," Doug said.

"No. Actually I'm hoping that the threat of it will be enough to bring the man to his senses. I'm hoping that from now on he will leave you alone. You don't want to drag your family through any more of this, do you?"

Doug chewed his lip absently. "No . . ."

Charles glanced at his watch and then at the telephone.

Doug spread his hands wide apart. "But I don't see what else I can do. How else am I going to stop him from hauling me in there every time some teenage girl thinks she hears a noise on her front porch? I'm like the bogeyman now. I want to put a stop to this. I can't imagine how a lawsuit could be any worse for my wife than this."

Charles sighed. "Well, as I said, I'm hoping that a word

to the wise will be sufficient. If not, we have to weigh our options. You have to realize that if we get involved in a lawsuit against the police department, you're going to find yourselves under a microscope for the foreseeable future. I know that Maddy was looking forward to everything getting back to normal."

"But it isn't normal," Doug insisted. "It isn't normal to be dragged down to the police station at the chief's whim. Maddy will understand that."

"Agreed," said Charles, feeling a little exasperated. "But threatening the lawsuit is a tactic that may prevent that from happening. So far, the chief is not out of bounds on this." He leaned toward Doug. "A girl is dead. A baby is still missing. He has to try everything, do everything he possibly can, no matter whose feelings get hurt. You file a lawsuit right now just because you had to answer some questions and I guarantee you, you're going to look like Public Enemy Number One."

Doug slumped back in his chair. "All right," he grumbled. "I suppose you're right. For now."

The phone buzzed on Charles's desk and the attorney jumped. "Excuse me a second," he said. When he picked up the phone his secretary told him that Paulina was calling. "Put her through," he said.

Doug peered at a broken fingernail on his right hand and seemed lost in thought as Charles listened to the shrill voice of his housekeeper.

"How is she?" Charles asked. "Is she all right?" He listened for a moment and then said, "I'm on my way." He put down the receiver carefully in the cradle and stood up. "Doug, you'll have to excuse me. I have to go. Right now."

Doug stood up awkwardly and extended his hand. "I just want to thank you again, Charles."

Charles shook his hand briefly and pushed past him toward the door. "I'll talk to you later," he said. Doug took the hint and hurriedly preceded him out of the office.

Charles raced for home, dodging the sluggish rush-hour traffic, risking a speeding ticket whenever he found a straightaway. He did not put on the radio or his CD system. His nerves could not stand the extra input. He concentrated on driving the quiet car and tried not to give in to panic. He tried to tell himself that nothing was wrong, but a little niggling voice inside of him knew better.

Last night he'd noticed that the old rusty padlock on the playhouse door was in the trash and had been replaced with a shiny new one. Flakes of paint on the walkway indicated she had been scraping the clapboards in the front. She'd said everything was fine. He knew she wasn't fine. He'd known it for days.

Charles reached home and pulled the Mercedes behind Ellen's red Jeep and a black Buick that he didn't recognize in the drive. He threw open the front door and called for Paulina as he tossed his briefcase on the marquetry-inlaid hall chest. The homey smell of cinnamon and apples baking filled the elegant house.

Paulina emerged from the kitchen, wiping her hands on a towel and shaking her head. "I'm glad you're home," she said. "Father Rylander's up there with her right now."

"Father Rylander? Who's that?"

Paulina motioned for him to come into the study. He followed her into the darkly formal room. Heavy silk drapes and custom-made bookshelves lined the walls. An arrangement of mums, day lilies, and asters on the library table provided a burst of color against the mullioned windows. "Father Rylander is my priest," Paulina explained.

"Is she all right?" Charles demanded. "Why is there a priest here?"

"I couldn't reach you at first. I didn't know what else to do."

"What happened?"

"I had a heck of a time finding her. I drove all over looking for her. You know, the places she goes. There aren't too many."

Charles understood what she meant and nodded. He briefly laid a hand on the housekeeper's sturdy shoulder. "Thank God for you, Paulina."

"When I couldn't find her, I was about to give up and head for home. Then I spotted her car on the River Road. Parked on the shoulder."

"What was she doing on the River Road?" Charles asked.

Paulina frowned. "She said she was looking for that cat. The one she gave the people the other night. I found her in the woods there, down on her hands and knees. She's all scraped up."

"They were in an accident and the cat ran away," Charles explained.

"She said something about that," said Paulina.

"What was this you said on the phone about the children's shop?" he asked.

"When we got back, someone called from the children's shop and said she left her wallet there this morning," said Paulina.

Charles shrugged impatiently. "I'll pick it up tomorrow," he said. "Maybe she had to buy a shower gift or something."

Paulina shook her head. "The girl at the shop told me that she bought about five outfits."

"Sometimes she's extravagant," he protested, casting about in his mind for someone they knew who might be needing such a gift.

"She told the girl that the clothes were for a baby—named Ken."

Charles felt as if something icy had been poured down his back.

"I found this in her car," said Paulina. She held up a shopping bag with "Precious Littles" written on it in florid script and white curling ribbon cascading from the handles. "It was empty. She had it hidden under the seat of the car. When I asked her about it, she got angry and said she didn't know what I was talking about. Then she went upstairs."

Charles turned away from the housekeeper and stared through the mullioned windows out at the property behind his house. Ellen's gardens were dead now. Only the occasional burst of pink or scarlet showed through the brown leaves where a bunch of impatiens persisted or an errant rose still clung to the bare branches of its bush. In the midst of her gardens stood the playhouse, dark and still, with its empty windowboxes, its peaked roof, and its peeling clapboard sides, large enough for a covey of children to play in. Empty, sad, going to ruin. Charles felt his eyes well up as he looked out and saw a briefly shining past darken in front of his eyes.

"Oh, Paulina," he whispered. "What is happening to her?"

Paulina stood up and briskly wiped her hands on the

tea towel. "You'd better go up to her. I thought she might get mad that I'd called the priest, but he's been up there with her for a while."

Charles nodded as he went out into the foyer and looked up the staircase. Religion. That was Paulina's answer to everything. And it seemed to have worked well enough for her and her family. But Ellen had not been to church since the day of Kenny's funeral. He sighed as he climbed up toward the second floor where their bedroom was.

He accepted his wife's foibles. He knew better than anyone else how she had suffered. He had suffered, too. But he had gone back out into the world, into the fray, because he had to. They had a house and a life to support, and he had work to do. Ellen had made her life here, around this house, with their son, and so here she had stayed. After a while he had tried to nudge her out, but she'd insisted that she was all right as she was. After a long while it began to seem that she was all right. Not perfectly normal. But who among us is perfectly normal? he said to himself.

As Charles reached their bedroom door, it opened, and Father Rylander emerged.

"Father?"

"Mr. Henson?" said Nick, extending his hand. "It's nice to meet you. I've been talking to Ellen. She sings your praises."

Charles frowned. "Did she say . . . did you get any idea of what's troubling her?"

Nick hesitated. "I'm a stranger to her, of course. We talked a little bit about how God gives and God takes away, and how difficult it all is to understand. I don't know if it was any help to her."

"Thank you for coming, Father," said Charles.

"I was glad to come." Nick squeezed Charles's arm encouragingly as he passed him in the hallway. Then he started down the stairs.

Charles hesitated outside the bedroom door. In this room they had lived much of their life together. In the beginning they had laughed and loved, then mourned, and often escaped. Now he was filled with fear. There was no denying the turn she had taken. He could manage everything else, except that. . . . He didn't even allow himself to think it. He pushed open the door and looked in.

She was lying on the bed, curled up in a fetal position beneath the satin comforter. He tiptoed in. She turned her head and looked at him. Her eyes looked dark and fearful.

"Sweetheart?" he asked. "Are you okay? I just met Father Rylander in the hall."

"He was very kind," she said.

"Yes, he seemed so."

"I couldn't find the kitten," she said.

He came over to the bed and sat on the edge beside her. He reached out and ran his hand gently over her mass of luxuriant, graying curls. He remembered when they were golden. "It's all right," he said reassuringly. "It will be all right."

He knew he had to bring up the children's shop. He tried to phrase it delicately. "I'll go pick up your wallet tomorrow at the children's shop," he said.

Ellen turned her head away. "They must have found it on the street," she insisted. "I stopped at a newsstand outside the store. Paulina thought I was in the children's shop. What would I be doing in a children's shop?"

What about the bag? he wanted to cry out. Where are

the clothes? Why would the salesgirl lie? He kept silent. A relentless interrogator in the courtroom, he sat still on the bed and said nothing. He did not want to eviscerate what was left of his hope by forcing her to answer.

Ellen turned back and gazed at his gray head, his troubled countenance. She grabbed his large, strong hand in her own fragile, weathered one. "I'm sorry, Charles," she whispered. "It's just that I'm afraid. I've never been so afraid in all my life."

Charles stroked her hair with his free hand. His own heart shrank from the meaning of her words. "Why are you afraid?"

She hesitated, then decided not to speak. She lay there, shivering under the warm quilt.

"There's nothing to be afraid of," he crooned. "Try and rest. Nothing at all." His voice was calm and soothing. His heart, however, was saying, Please God, not this. Haven't you taken enough from me? Please, oh, please. Not this, too.

# Chapter Sixteen

The following morning Doug and Maddy stood in their driveway, shivering in the day's early chill, watching Amy gather up a bouquet of autumn leaves. Doug sighed. "What a long night," he said.

Maddy sipped from her coffee mug and stared out over the rim at their peaceful neighborhood. Another night of lying awake, listening to Sean's fussing and wailing, had left dark circles under her eyes. She and Doug had lain side by side, neither one sleeping nor acknowledging the other's wakefulness. She knew he blamed her for the miserable night. She didn't want to discuss it.

"So where are you off to?" she asked.

"I'm going over to the garage," he said, "and see if their car is ready. They said they'd have it this morning."

Maddy nodded. "They got ours back to us right away. Let's hope they do the same with theirs."

"I'm going to stand over them until it's done," Doug said grimly. "I can't take another night of this. I have to start work again tomorrow, Maddy. We need to get them out of here so I can get some rest."

"I know," said Maddy.

"It's going to be hard enough walking back into that school. Trying to ignore the stares and the whispers. As if things weren't bad enough, now they haul me in and grill me about that missing kid and the baby-sitter. You think the whole school's not going to be talking about that?" Doug shook his head. "I'll tell you, Maddy, I look forward to bringing that lawsuit against the police. I am sick and tired of being their whipping boy."

"You were vindicated," Maddy said tonelessly.

"That doesn't make any difference to the gossipmongers. You are living in an ivory tower if you think . . . Oh, forget it. All I know is, I need some sleep before I go back to work."

"I know," she said. "I know you need rest. We both do."

"While I'm gone, you better talk to her and let her know they have got to get out of here today."

"All right, all right," said Maddy. She called to Amy, "Come on, honey. Let's go in and see Sean."

Amy toddled over and handed her the bouquet. Maddy took it with a distracted smile and kissed her as Doug got in the car and drove off in the direction of the auto repair shop. Maddy opened the front door and Amy went in. Maddy looked around the house in dismay. There seemed to be clutter everywhere she looked. Not that Bonnie was messy. On the contrary, she was punctilious in her habits. But two extra people in the already chaotic conditions of the last two days added up to disorder. Maddy could see that Bonnie and Sean were not downstairs.

She got Amy settled down with a puzzle and began to tidy up. The familiar routine of housework had a sooth-ing effect. As she threw laundry into the washing machine she realized that her guests probably had things that needed washing. If she was going to put them out on the street, a load of laundry seemed like the least she could do.

She climbed the stairs and started down the hall to the guest room. As she approached the door she could hear Sean's familiar fussy cry. She tapped gently on the door and Bonnie said gruffly, "What do you want?"

Maddy pushed open the door and stepped into the room. The room was very neat. All of Bonnie's belongings were clustered close by her suitcase, as if she did not intend to get comfortable here. She was sitting on the bed, reading a book. Maddy glanced at the cover and saw that it was a historical romance novel. Sean was propped up on the floor against a chair, fussing and gnawing on his fingers. Beside him on the floor was Amy's stuffed Big Bird.

"I was just going to do some laundry," Maddy said. "I wondered if you had anything you'd like me to throw in."

Bonnie looked reluctantly at the little pile of clothes by her suitcase.

"Maybe some of Sean's things?" Maddy asked.

Bonnie swung her legs off the bed and went over to pick up the suitcase. In contrast with his mother's worn and shabby wardrobe, all of Sean's clothes had the cheerful freshness of new clothes. Typical, Maddy thought. We always care more about how the kids are dressed than ourselves.

Bonnie weighed a couple of pants and shirts in her hand and then, reluctantly, handed them to Maddy. "I guess if you're washing . . . ," she said.

Maddy took the clothes and wadded them up in her hands. She knew she had to tell Bonnie now about leaving. She had told Doug she would, but now that the moment was at hand, the words were difficult to say. She wondered how much of that conversation about the insurance Bonnie had overheard. No one had mentioned it again, but Maddy wondered if Bonnie would bring it up now. Threaten her, even, when Maddy asked them to leave. There was a volatile quality about Bonnie, as if something unpredictable could set her off. Don't avoid it, Maddy told herself. Go ahead and say it and let her react however she's going to.

"Umm, Bonnie, there's something I have to talk to you about."

Bonnie zippered the little suitcase and looked up warily.

"I know I said you could stay as long as you need to . . . and I feel bad about this, but . . ."

"You want us to go," Bonnie said flatly.

Maddy grimaced apologetically. "Doug's gone to see about getting your car for you."

Bonnie replaced the suitcase carefully on the floor as if it were potentially explosive. Maddy could not see the expression on her face.

"I don't want you to go, really," Maddy said hastily. "It's just that with the baby crying at night . . . My husband has been out of work for a while, and he has to start back tomorrow, and he's kind of . . . worried about not getting any sleep."

Bonnie straightened up but did not look at Maddy. For a moment Maddy had the panicky feeling that the woman was going to turn on her in a rage.

"I'm really sorry, Bonnie," said Maddy.

Bonnie sat back down on the bed and regarded Sean

coldly. He was still whimpering. "That's all right. I can hardly stand it myself," she said.

There was no resentment toward Maddy in her tone. In fact, it was the most agreeable she had seemed. It made Maddy feel even more guilty about forcing them out. "It's tough when they cry a lot," Maddy agreed.

Bonnie studied her child with a frown. "It's hard to figure out what they want sometimes."

"That's certainly true," said Maddy, hesitating in the doorway. "It gets easier when they can talk."

Bonnie spoke in a dull voice. "My mother always said I would be a terrible mother. She warned me. Of course, she never thought I was good at anything. She said no one would marry me, either. That no one would want me." She gave a brief bark of a laugh. "She didn't know everything."

Maddy saw the expression of a wounded child surface briefly in the other woman's face. Why would a mother undermine a child that way? she wondered. No wonder Bonnie seemed so defensive.

"Well, the first year of a baby's life is the hardest, I think. At least it was for me," Maddy said.

"It was hard for you?"

"Oh gosh, yes," said Maddy. "It's so confusing, and so hard to know what to do."

"When they cry all the time it makes you feel like a failure," said Bonnie. Her shoulders slumped, and Maddy had the urge to put an arm around her.

"It's just a phase," said Maddy. "I think the best thing you can do for them is hold them a lot."

Bonnie looked at Sean as if this idea had not occurred to her. I'll bet nobody held you a lot, Maddy thought, looking sadly at Bonnie. "He might be teething," Maddy said carefully. "Amy used to cry like that. Sometimes it helps if you give them a wet washcloth to chew."

Bonnie tensed up, as if she were about to bristle, but then she nodded. "Maybe," she said.

"Let me get one," Maddy said. Before Bonnie could protest, she walked across the hall, got a clean white washcloth out of the linen closet, and wet it under the bathroom faucet. She brought it in and handed it to Bonnie.

"Here you go, Sean," Bonnie cooed, but the child did not look up. Maddy wondered, not for the first time, if the boy might be deaf. He never seemed to respond when anyone called him. And it would account for his frustration. She decided not to say anything; Bonnie would surely take it as a criticism. If he was hard of hearing, they would find out soon enough.

Bonnie bent down and started to lift him. Startled, Sean let out an angry wail. Bonnie raised a hand as if to smack him, then immediately set him back down on the floor. "He doesn't want it," she said brusquely.

Maddy felt both sorry for her embarrassment and worried about the baby. Through no fault of his own, Sean made Bonnie feel rejected.

"He's got a mind of his own," Maddy said lamely.

"He doesn't like me," Bonnie said, her eyes welling with tears.

"Of course he likes you," Maddy protested. "He loves you. You're his mother."

Bonnie lifted her glasses and wiped her eyes impatiently. "Excuse me. It's just that I'm a little . . . worn out," she said.

Maddy nodded. She could see the fatigue etched in Bonnie's face, her dejected posture. She recognized the feeling. It was hard to cope with a fretful baby, harder still with your husband in the hospital. And now Bonnie had to try to find them a place to stay as well. That kind of fatigue could pose a danger to the baby—he didn't know enough to give his strung-out mother some breathing room.

Maddy hesitated in the doorway, thinking about what Doug had said—that they had to leave today. What was the big hurry? she thought. What did it matter if they stayed another day? What about simple human kindness? You had to think about that, too. "Look," said Maddy. "Why don't you take a little nap? I'll watch Sean for a while. Amy would love to play with him. I'll take you over to the hospital later."

"I have to get us a room," Bonnie said tiredly.

"That can wait till later," Maddy insisted. "Your car isn't even back yet."

Bonnie looked longingly at the pillow. "I am tired," she said.

"Here," Maddy said firmly, reaching out and taking the wet washcloth from Bonnie's limp hand. "You lie down for a while."

At Maddy's insistence, Bonnie put her feet up on the bed and turned over. "Thanks," she mumbled. "You've been nice to me." She said it in a way that indicated few people had ever taken the trouble.

"No problem," said Maddy. She bent and picked up Sean from the floor. He seemed feather light compared to Amy. Sean reached for the white washcloth, still in Maddy's hand. Maddy gave it to him, and he examined it curiously for a moment. Then he put it in his mouth and began to gnaw furiously on the cold terry cloth. Maddy turned him away, so that if Bonnie looked up, she would not notice. In her weary state of mind, she might take it as a betrayal. Although there seemed little danger of that. She lay slumped on the bed facing the wall as if she were already asleep.

"You just rest," Maddy said to Bonnie's back, pulling the door shut behind her. "We'll be fine."

# *Chapter Seventeen*

$\mathcal{M}$addy turned on the TV in her studio to cartoons and gave Amy, who seemed a little listless this morning, a couple of oatmeal cookies. Sean was seated in an old rocking seat of Amy's, still chewing on the wet rag. Maddy hoisted herself onto the stool behind the huge Formica counter that was her work space. She had a lot of glass to wrap, and this seemed as good a time as any to do it. It was a process that didn't involve a lot of concentration, which was good, considering how tired she was this morning. The kids were both pretty quiet, and the studio was peaceful. Maddy had sipped her second mug of coffee as she folded the copper wiring around the perimeter of the glass pieces she had cut for the window she was working on. Each piece of glass had to be surrounded by wire; the wire-bound pieces were then soldered together. She regarded wrapping glass as the same sort of chore that carding wool was to a weaver—one of the tedious but necessary chores of her craft.

Amy giggled as her favorite TV cartoon cat chased a mouse for whom he was no match. Chewing and rocking energetically in the chair, Sean seemed utterly disinterested in the television. Maddy wondered, once again, if there was something wrong with his hearing. It was difficult to engage his attention. She took another sip from her coffee mug and picked up a peacock blue piece of glass. The design for this window was beautiful, and she felt it might turn out to be the handsomest piece she had done. She felt a momentary regret that Father . . . that Nick would not be here to see it.

The thought of Nick brought to mind their brief embrace yesterday as they parted. She blushed, recalling her reaction to being in his arms. Maddy wasn't naive—she could sense a sexual current between people. She wondered only why she had never noticed it before. Perhaps she had noticed it but hadn't wanted to admit it. After all, he was a priest. She had always assumed that priests, who had chosen to be celibate, had some sort of mental block they used to avoid feeling attraction.

Now, as she thought about it, she admitted to herself that no one could avoid temptation. It was simply that taking a vow—whether it was a vow of celibacy or a vow of marriage—meant that you did not succumb to temptation. When you made a vow, you honored it. It was that simple.

Still, as she thought of their conversation yesterday, she admitted to herself how much she was going to miss him. His friendship and his conversation had grown very important to her over the last year that they had worked together. There were many times when she thought of things she wanted to tell him. Now, she realized with an undeniable sadness, there was no use in saving up those observations. Nick would be gone, and there was no use in pretending they would keep in touch. Especially now that she admitted to herself she felt some desire for him. It was probably good that he was going—good for both of them. Theirs was a friendship that threatened to become too important in her life. Although Doug was wrong to suspect anything improper between them, perhaps he'd felt the current before she had even been aware of it.

The important thing, she reminded herself, was Nick's advice; she had to support her husband and maintain a belief in his innocence. No matter how disappointed she was in Doug, there was a huge difference between carelessness and evil. Besides, she had to get her marriage back on track—for Amy's sake as well as her own. She had put a lot into this marriage, and she had to try to get the trust back between them. Yesterday everything had seemed bleak, but today she felt better. Still shaky, but with the hope a new day brought.

The cartoon show ended, and a newscast interrupted the flow of programming. There was a recap of information about the death of Rebecca Starnes. Maddy shook her head sadly at the thought of that poor child, so young, her life cut off. She felt suddenly furious at Chief Cameron; regardless of his anger about his daughter, it was monstrous that he could suspect her husband of such a crime. The announcer intoned that the station would rebroadcast the plea made by the parents of Justin Wallace for their child's safe return. The tape of Donna and Johnny Wallace was heartrending. Donna Wallace held up a Polaroid photo of her son, which looked, unfortunately, like a milk bottle with red eyes and a mop of curly hair.

"Whoever you might be, if you have our son, please give him back to us. We won't be angry. We don't want

to prosecute you. We just want our Justin back again."
Donna Wallace began to weep, and Johnny Wallace put
his arm around her and leaned over the microphone.

"We want our son, back, please," he said, his deep,
gruff voice cracking.

Maddy, who had been watching with one sympathetic eye while she worked, suddenly heard a noise
from Sean's chair. He was sitting up, as straight as a
wobbly baby could manage, apparently galvanized by
what he saw on the screen. His little eyes were wide,
and he was making a grunting noise that sounded like
"Da . . . da . . ."

Maddy felt the hair on the back of her neck stand up.
The child became agitated, rocking madly in his little seat
and repeating the sound. "Da . . . da . . ."

Amy turned to her mother. "What is he saying, Mom?"

Maddy stared at the baby in the chair. "I don't know,"
she whispered.

"It sounds like Dada," said Amy.

"I know," said Maddy.

A game show came on, and Amy said, "I don't want to
watch this."

Sean began to wail disconsolately and jab his tiny finger in the direction of the TV screen.

Maddy came numbly around the corner, changed the
channel to *Sesame Street,* bent, and took the washcloth
from Sean's little hands. She walked over to the sink and
started to run the water. Don't be stupid, she thought.
She thought about Terry Lewis in the hospital. He was
dark haired, just like Johnny Wallace. And Johnny Wallace, in his distraught state, was certainly unkempt, like
Terry Lewis. That was probably all it was. Sean saw that

man on TV and it reminded him of his father. If . . . if . . . that was what he was trying to say.

She soaked the washcloth, wrung it out, and then wet it again. She turned back to the children. Sean was pointing at the TV again. "Brr . . . ," he cried.

"He's trying to say 'Big Bird,' " Amy informed her mother. "Sean can talk."

Maddy walked slowly over to where the child sat. He wouldn't be trying to talk if he had hearing problems, she thought. It doesn't mean anything, she told herself. You couldn't know what babies thought. She peered at the baby with a new and critical eye. He didn't look like the missing baby. Well, the same general coloring, but the baby in the picture had curly hair. Long, corkscrew curls. She tilted her head and gazed at the soft, close, cropped hair. It was the same color hair, but so what. That didn't mean anything. Lots of babies had hair that color. What a crazy idea, she thought. Don't be stupid. This is Bonnie's baby. Bonnie and Terry's baby. Sean.

He was still rocking in the little chair, tears of frustration coursing down his cheeks as if he were bereft of the images on the screen. Maddy came up behind him and held out the wet washcloth. "Justin," she whispered.

Sean swiveled around and looked up at her in surprise. Then he smiled a toothless grin and reached out for the washcloth.

# Chapter Eighteen

$\mathcal{D}$r. Larry Foreman rode the elevator up the three floors of the building to his office suite, holding a paper bag containing a cup of coffee and a sweet roll. He chided himself for starting off his morning on such an unhealthy note, but some days he didn't feel like fighting the good fight. It was a cold, miserable morning, with nothing but gray skies, and Larry suffered from a sunshine deficit disorder. Right now all he could do was dream of a winter vacation at his in-laws' condo in Florida. If it weren't for a hefty mortgage and three girls who needed braces, college educations, and, eventually, weddings, he would spend a few weeks at some luxury resort in the Caribbean. Right now, however, he knew that the only way he was going to live long enough to ever see the Caribbean again was to walk up the stairs and eat half a dry bagel for breakfast, but there was such a thing as too much self-denial.

The door to his suite was open and the lights on, which meant his receptionist was already at work. Since he didn't have an appointment for forty minutes, he would have ample time to eat his sweet roll and catch up on some paperwork. He greeted Arlene and saw her incline her head toward the chairs in the waiting area. Larry turned around with a frown and saw Charles Henson, sitting on the edge of a seat, his briefcase on his lap.

"Charles," he said, surprised to find the attorney here in person. He had testified a few times as an expert witness for Charles Henson, but that was usually arranged on the phone, between their secretaries, long before they ever met face-to-face.

Long ago, when his practice was new and he had very few clients, he had encountered Charles Henson in a very different capacity. He had treated Ellen Henson for depression following the death of their son. It had been a late intervention—Ellen was already deeply depressed when Charles finally convinced her to come and see him—too late, as it turned out. At his recommendation Ellen had entered a hospital, where, with constant therapy and some effective drug treatment, she had started to improve.

Charles Henson stood up. His face was ashen and drawn. "Larry," he said, "I need to talk to you."

At the sight of Charles's face, Larry suspected that the business he was here on had nothing to do with a client. Larry realized ruefully that he wasn't going to get his paperwork done this morning, but he gestured for the attorney to come in.

"Why don't we sit over by the window. Do you mind if I have a cup of coffee while we talk?" he asked.

Charles obediently assumed a seat next to the window and gestured to Larry that he did not mind if Larry had his coffee.

Larry had seen a lot of people who were depressed or

overwhelmed by despair, and he recognized the signs. He stowed his uneaten breakfast in the top drawer of his desk, came over to the window, and took a seat. He looked compassionately at the attorney.

"What is it, Charles? What can I do for you?"

Charles Henson sighed. "It's Ellen."

Larry nodded. "I thought perhaps. You seem very distressed. What seems to be the problem?"

Charles opened his mouth to speak, hesitated, and then tried again. "I've been trying to ignore certain signs, Larry. But I remember what happened when I did that before. Told myself everything would be all right. Just to let matters take their course. . . ."

"Well, we know that doesn't always work with people who are under a lot of strain," Larry said diplomatically.

"I'm afraid that there's something drastically wrong. . . ."

"Tell me about it," said Larry.

Charles described the events of the past few days as succinctly, as unemotionally, as he could. His recitation was disturbing, and Larry sat very still until Charles was finished.

"This is around the time of Ken's birthday, isn't it?" he asked.

Charles nodded. "He would have been twenty-one this week."

"Well, as you know, birthdays, anniversaries—they can be difficult."

"She's always suffered a depression in the fall," said Charles. "But this year, this behavior . . ." His voice trailed away.

Larry sighed and said, "Charles, I am not about to make any kind of diagnosis based on what you're telling me, but if you're asking me if she needs to see someone, I'd say the answer is yes. . . ."

"Will you see her again, if I can talk her into it?" Charles asked.

"I'd be glad to," said Larry.

Charles stood up abruptly. "All right, then," he said. "I know what I have to do."

Larry accompanied him out the door and through the waiting room. As they passed by, a well-dressed woman stood up abruptly from the chair where she was perched and accosted him.

"Dr. Foreman."

Larry glanced over and saw the limp-haired, moon-faced figure of Heather Cameron, his first client of the day, bent over one of his magazines. The woman approaching them was Mary Beth Cameron, her shiny red lips parted in an apologetic but demanding pout.

"Could you wait for me in the hallway?" Larry said to Charles. Then he turned and smiled blandly at Mary Beth.

"Mrs. Cameron, what can I do for you?"

"I'm dropping Heather off a little early because I have three appointments this morning and I figured you two could get started a little early."

"That's fine," said Larry, thinking ruefully of his breakfast.

"Do you think you can help her, Doctor?" Mary Beth asked in a confidential tone. Heather let out a loud sigh, but Mary Beth persisted. "I think if you could just work on improving her self-image a little bit, she wouldn't need to . . . you know, live in a fantasy world. She needs friends her own age and a social life, like other girls."

"If you want to discuss your daughter, why don't you

make an appointment for yourself. Meanwhile, Heather is welcome to wait here," Larry said firmly. "Please excuse me now."

Mary Beth drew herself up indignantly and then turned and blew Heather a kiss. "I'm going to dash, Heather." She didn't wait for a reply.

Larry met Charles out in the hallway as Mary Beth swept past them without a glance of acknowledgment.

"Isn't that Heather Cameron in there?" Charles asked quietly.

Larry nodded. "The court ordered her to get counseling."

"Well, she can't do better than you," Charles said kindly.

Larry raised his eyebrows. "I'm not at all sure that she's the one who needs the counseling," he said.

"Her family, you mean?" Charles asked.

Larry sighed. "For starters. Her mother thinks she fantasized the whole thing," he said, shaking his head, and then suddenly remembered that Charles had represented Douglas Blake.

Charles looked at him in surprise. "Don't you?" he asked.

Larry frowned. "I . . . mustn't talk about this."

"But she changed her story half a dozen times," Charles protested.

"Charles. Have Ellen call me. And don't worry. I know we can help her." He clapped the lawyer gently on the back and turned back to his office before Charles could ask him any more difficult questions.

# Chapter Nineteen

Maddy paced the living room, looking out the window every two minutes to see if Doug had returned from the garage. A nurse had called from the hospital to say that Terry was ready to be released. Maddy was hoping Doug would return before Bonnie was ready to go to the hospital to pick up her husband.

Finally a cavalcade of cars appeared in their driveway—Doug first, then Bonnie's van, and then the car from the garage, sent along to drive back the van driver. Doug thanked everybody and watched as the mechanics pulled out of the driveway. Then he started up the walkway. Maddy rushed out onto the front steps to meet him. She glanced back into the living room, where Amy and Sean were playing quietly.

"Mission accomplished," he said. "Their van is as good as new. They have no excuse for staying now."

Maddy gripped the sleeve of his jacket and spoke in a low voice. "Doug, listen. I'm going to tell Bonnie that Amy is sick and has to stay home. They called from the hospital to say that Terry is ready to be released. I'll need you to drive Bonnie to the hospital and help her pick up Terry. And wait there with her."

"What?" he protested, running his hands through his hair. "Why? I have a lot of things to do. I have to start back teaching tomorrow. I need to work on my lesson plans."

"You can bring your papers with you and work on them at the hospital."

"Why do we have to help her, anyway? Let Bonnie go get him and they can ride off into the sunset together. Here's their car. Why can't they just leave now?"

"Doug, could you just trust me on this? I need you to get them out of here. Listen, this is important. I mean it."

Doug jerked his sleeve away from her grip. "Maddy, what are you all worked up about?"

Maddy took a deep breath. "Doug, I don't want you to think I'm crazy. Just hear me out." She glanced back through the window into the living room. There was still no sign of Bonnie. "I think Sean may be the kidnapped child."

Doug rolled his eyes. "Oh, for God's sake."

"Listen to me, will you? They were watching TV this morning, and when the kidnapped child's parents came on, Sean went bananas, making noises and pointing to the TV."

Despite her request, Doug did look at her as though she were crazy. "He's a baby. That's what babies do. They make noises and point to the TV."

"He doesn't respond to his name. I was beginning to think he was deaf. But when I called him Justin, he looked right at me."

Doug gave her a long-suffering look. "Maddy . . . this

is ridiculous. They're from Maine. They weren't even in town. . . ."

"We don't know how long they were in town. Besides, she doesn't . . . act like his mother," Maddy insisted.

"Your idea of how a mother should act," he corrected her. "Mothers act different ways. My mother always treated me like I belonged to the people next door. That doesn't mean she wasn't my mother—"

"Look, all right, I know it sounds far-out, but just indulge me. I want to get her out of the house so I can take a look through her stuff. Can't you please do that much for me?"

"I told you to get rid of them. To tell them to leave."

"But they're still here," she said in a low voice, "and I want you to do this for me. It's not just for me, you know. If this is the missing baby, then that exonerates you once and for all. I mean, Chief Cameron would still like to believe that you were the one who killed Rebecca Starnes."

"Look, if you want to play Nancy Drew, don't try to pretend that you're doing it for my sake," he said.

"And what if I'm right, Doug? What if Sean is the missing child? Don't you think that would be worth a few minutes of your time? To find out?"

"You're saying you think Terry Lewis killed her?"

Maddy thought of Terry, with his brigand's appearance, his religious streak, and his unfeigned pride in his son. "I don't know," she said. "I don't know. Maybe I'm imagining things, but I just have to try to find out."

Doug raised his hands in surrender. "All right, fine, whatever you want. I'm too tired to argue about it."

"Argue about what?" said a voice.

Bonnie was standing in the doorway, looking at them suspiciously.

Maddy smiled brightly at her. "I was just asking Doug if he would take you to the hospital to get Terry, because Amy is feeling feverish and I want to keep her at home here with me."

Bonnie looked back at the children in the living room. "She looks all right to me."

"Well, I am concerned about her," Maddy said in a tight voice.

"I'll drive you," said Doug. "Get your stuff together."

"If you want to leave Sean here, I can watch him," said Maddy.

"I'm not going to leave him with her if she's sick," said Bonnie, and Maddy wondered if the reason she was thinking the worst of this woman was that she disliked her so much. "Fine," she said, "whatever you wish."

Without another word Bonnie returned to the house and began gathering up stuff to take to the hospital. She put Sean in his hat and hooded sweatshirt, took her purse and the diaper bag. Maddy could hardly wait until they were gone. Doug put together some work to do at the hospital and followed Bonnie and Sean to the door. He looked back at Maddy as if to say "You owe me one." Maddy felt a stab of anger at him for acting like a martyr. Hadn't she stood by him through all that ugliness without complaint? Gone into debt so great they might never emerge from it, just to defend his reputation? Was it so much to ask that he drive this woman to the hospital?

Nonetheless she waved dutifully from the doorway, so that everything would seem as normal as possible.

She turned away from the door as soon as the car was out of the driveway and went over to where Amy was seated on the floor. "Amy, you want to come upstairs with Mommy and play in your room?"

Amy reached over and pulled out her favorite book, an oversize book of fairy tales, from a pile under the coffee table. "Read to me. Read 'Ugly Duckling.' "

"I can't right now, honey," said Maddy. "There's something I have to do upstairs. Why don't you come up."

"I want 'Ugly Duckling,' " she wailed.

Maddy sighed and looked at her watch. She had plenty of time. It would take a while to get Terry released. "Okay, okay. I'll read 'Ugly Duckling,' and then you come upstairs with Mommy, okay?"

Amy nodded happily and settled herself comfortably against her mother. Trying not to rush the story, Maddy read about the ugly duckling, giving Amy a chance to comment, as she always did, on the mean ducks and to commiserate with the duckling as he shivered through the winter, alone and afraid.

"All right," said Maddy, closing the book. "Let's go on upstairs and see what's in Amy's room to play with."

Maddy replaced the book in the pile, and Amy scrambled to her feet. "I wanna juice box, Mommy."

Maddy put her hands on her hips and looked down at the innocent face looking up at her. "What do we say?"

"Please?" Amy said.

"All right," said Maddy with a sigh. "A juice box, then we're going. You can take it to your room if you're careful not to spill it." Amy followed her mother to the kitchen and picked out her favorite flavor from the refrigerator.

"I'll put the straw in upstairs, okay?" said Maddy. "Now come on, let's hurry."

Amy took this as a cue to tear through the house and start up the stairs way ahead of Maddy. As Maddy came down the hallway to the staircase, there was a knock at the door.

Her heart jumped. What now? she thought. She went to the door and pulled it open. Heather Cameron stood on the doorstep, looking up at her from behind her curtain of lank hair.

Maddy felt her face redden at the sight of Doug's accuser boldly standing on the threshold of their home. She was wearing a tight poor-boy T-shirt, a pair of baggy jeans, and unlaced green sneakers. "I would like to speak to Doug, please," Heather said. A worn plaid backpack hung from her left hand.

Maddy regained her voice, but her tone was icy. "Mr. Blake isn't here right now."

"Do you know when he'll be back?"

"He drove a . . . friend of ours to the hospital. He could be gone quite a while."

Heather stood on the doorstep, chewing her lip. Then she looked up at Maddy. "Which hospital?" she said.

Maddy felt herself start to shake. "How dare you come here, Heather? Aren't you ashamed to show up here after what you did to us?"

Heather held the backpack up against her chest. "I didn't do anything wrong," she said stubbornly.

"What are you trying to do?" Maddy cried. "Haven't you caused us enough heartache? Do you think we have forgotten the things you said. . . ."

"I'm not here to bother you. I just want to know about him and Karla," Heather said defiantly. "Karla is telling everybody that she and D—Mr. Blake are hot for each other, and I want to know if it's true."

Maddy's heart was hammering, but she tried to keep her expression impassive. "What are you talking about?"

"Karla Needham," said Heather, lifting her chin. "She's really cool, she's a cheerleader, and she gets every guy she wants. She's telling everybody that there is chemistry between them."

"Why are you talking this way to me, Heather? I'm not a school chum of yours. My husband is not some boy in your class. Don't you realize that you're talking about my marriage here? My husband?"

"Well, you probably feel the same way I do. You can tell him for me that he better not do it with her. Because if he does, that would be very unfair to me," said Heather. "And I will find out, because I'll make sure to find out."

Maddy didn't know whether she was more shocked by this suggestion or by the fact that Heather would come to their house and speak to her this way. It was as if the girl had learned nothing at all from her whole sordid experience with the investigation and the court. "I thought you were going to go to a psychologist to get some help, Heather," Maddy said. "I'm going to have to call your parents and tell them that you came here looking for my husband."

"No, don't," Heather said. "I only wanted to know. I'm sorry. I didn't mean . . ."

"There's something seriously wrong with you, Heather," said Maddy.

"Just tell him I was here," Heather said. She turned and hopped off the front step as if she were playing a game of hopscotch. Maddy watched, stunned, as Heather skipped down the path and crossed the street. Half a block away she got into a little Ford Escort. Maddy could see that someone else was in the car.

What in the world would possess her to come here and suggest that Doug was involved with another schoolgirl?

Maddy wondered. Something is very wrong with that child, she thought. Maybe this is one of those obsessive things. Maybe she has really gone around the bend. Despite the scariness of having an obsessed teenage stalker on the doorstep, Maddy found the idea oddly comforting. This proved that Heather really was disturbed. No one in their right mind would behave the way she had. The encounter made Maddy feel shaky, but she was determined to put it out of her mind. She had other business to attend to.

"Mommy," Amy called from the top of the stairs.

"I'm on my way," Maddy said grimly.

# Chapter Twenty

Doug dutifully escorted Bonnie and the sleeping Sean up to the floor where Terry was recovering. An attractive young nurse seated at the nurse's station was engaged in conversation with a flirtatious intern. Bonnie waited until he was gone and then stepped up to the Formica-topped counter. "I'm Mrs. Lewis," she said tersely in answer to the nurse's greeting. "I'm here to take my husband . . . home. He's in room 304. Terry Lewis."

"Oh, yes," said the nurse. "The doctor is with him right now. You have to sign these papers and then we'll send a wheelchair down there for him."

Bonnie shifted Sean, her pocketbook, and the diaper bag to her other shoulder so she could sign the papers. She signed in all the appropriate spots and slid them back across the counter. The nurse picked up the papers and examined them. Then she looked up at Bonnie.

"You know, ma'am, we don't generally allow babies on this floor."

Bonnie glared at her. "I've brought him here before."

The nurse shrugged. "It's really for the child's sake. We don't want him exposed to infections."

Bonnie pulled herself up to her full height. "My baby's father is injured, not sick."

"Maybe your friend could take him," the nurse said, nodding at Doug. "There's a very nice waiting room just off the lobby."

Doug sighed in exasperation. He should have known he would get no work done here. "All right. Whatever," he said.

Reluctantly Bonnie started to pass the baby over to Doug.

"Can I see him?" the nurse asked sweetly, coming around from behind the desk and craning her neck to get a look at Sean. "I love babies."

"No," Bonnie barked defiantly. "There's too many germs around here as it is. You're the one who said so."

The nurse made a face and went back behind the desk. Doug rearranged the baby on his shoulder. "You better give me that bag with his stuff," Doug said.

"You don't need it," Bonnie said, clutching her belongings. "You're not going to be changing him. You just hold on to him. That's all you need to do. We'll find you when we're ready."

Doug set his jaw and headed for the elevator. He pushed the button and waited for the doors to open, rubbing the baby's back absently, watching Bonnie's rolling gait as she marched toward her husband's room. "Bitch," he whispered.

He was infuriated that he had to spend this last precious day before he returned to his job playing chauffeur to these creeps. But he could tell by the look in Maddy's eyes that there was no use in arguing about it. She had this notion that Bonnie was not the baby's mother because Bonnie didn't act all warm and fuzzy about the kid the way Maddy did about Amy. Maddy didn't realize that plenty of mothers were like Bonnie. "I feel sorry for you, slugger," he whispered. "But you're stuck with her."

Doug stepped inside the elevator and pushed the button for the ground floor. As the doors began to close, he thought he saw a familiar figure hurrying by in the hallway. It was that wild tangle of gray curls. How many people had hair like that? he thought. "Ellen," he started to call out, but the space between the doors was disappearing, and the other people in the elevator looked at him suspiciously. Even if it was her, she might not remember him from the other night. After all, everybody said she wasn't playing with a full deck. He swallowed the name and assumed the impassive expression of the elevator passenger.

Without another look back, Bonnie started down the hallway to Terry's room. At the doorway of room 304, she pulled a compact out of her purse. The hospital corridor was dim, but she did her best to examine her face critically. She ran a lipstick carefully over her lips and forced a comb through her dry, unruly hair, trying her best to get it to look right. It was hard. Her hair had always had a mind of its own. You got your father's hair, her mother would say in disgust, and shake her head whenever she barged into Bonnie's room and found her trying to tame the frizz with gels and rollers. Her mother had beautiful, soft blond hair. She always looked perfect. Right up to the very end.

Bonnie replaced the comb in her purse, straightened out her glasses on her nose, and took a deep breath. He loves you just the way you are, she reminded herself. He is your devoted, loving husband, and you are beautiful to him. "Beautiful to him," she murmured as if to give herself courage. "You are the most beautiful thing in the world to him."

She pushed open the door to the room and walked in. She ignored the man in the first bed. Dr. Tipton, the surgeon, looking attractive and efficient in her white coat, stood beside Terry, who was dressed and sitting on the edge of his bed. Now that he was in his clothes, Terry looked weaker than before. And pale. Bonnie's heart did a flip-flop and seemed to melt at the sight of him, as it always did. He looked up as she came in. She gave him a brilliant smile.

"Hey, babe," he said, giving her a weak wave. "Where's my boy today?"

Bonnie's smile faded. "The nurse wouldn't let him come in. That Mr. Blake took him downstairs."

Terry nodded. "Too bad. I was telling the doc about him."

"Mrs. Lewis," the doctor interrupted, "I was just telling your husband he is not to overdo it. He needs a lot of rest, and no lifting and no driving for two weeks. If he's careful now, there will be no long-term repercussions from this. As I've told you, he can manage perfectly well without his spleen. We just don't want those stitches to break. I want to see him back here in two weeks."

"Maybe, maybe not," said Bonnie.

"Well, you need to see a doctor where you are, to have the incision checked. If you like, I can refer you."

"I'll take care of it. I think I can take care of my own husband, thank you."

"All right." The doctor sighed. "Good luck, Mr. Lewis." She shook Terry's hand.

"I'll let you go, Doc. You have to be about the business of healing the sick. I want to thank you for all you've done for me."

"You're welcome," said the doctor as she turned to leave. Bonnie sat on the bed beside her husband, and Terry let out a groan.

"What is it?" she cried.

"Oh," he said, "it was just when the bed dipped. It hurt a little bit."

Bonnie jumped up off the bed, and he groaned again. "I'm sorry, I'm sorry," she pleaded.

"It's okay, don't worry about it," he said, but he was grimacing.

There was a silence between them for a moment, and then they both started to speak at once.

"What—"

"How—"

Bonnie looked stricken to have stepped on his words. "You go first," she said.

"How's our boy today?" he asked. "Did he sleep okay?"

"He's fine," said Bonnie.

There was a silence again.

"What were you going to say?" Terry asked.

"I was thinking we should leave today."

"Leave?"

"From those people. The Blakes," she said, her face sour. "I can't wait to get away from them."

"But they've been kind," said Terry.

"Believe me," Bonnie said, "they didn't do it to be kind. I overheard them talking and they were just worried we were going to sue them. I didn't tell them we have insurance. Let them worry. By the way, we got the car back. So we can leave any time we want."

Terry frowned. "Well, I'll try. I can't go far."

"Just so we get away from them," she said. "We'll get a room."

Terry sighed, and they were silent again. "Well, I'll be glad to be out of this place," Terry said after a while, looking around the room.

"The nurse is bringing a wheelchair," said Bonnie.

Almost as if her words had summoned her, the nurse appeared. "Okay, Mr. Lewis, let's get you into this thing."

Terry started to push himself off the bed. Bonnie rushed to his side and reached around him, carefully encircling his broad back with her arms. "Here, lean on me," she said. The nurse came near and tried to help, but Bonnie glared at her, and she stepped back.

"I can do this," Bonnie said.

"I'm all right," said Terry. He shuffled to the chair and sat in it, with Bonnie letting him slip from her arms with a look of regret. She felt as if her arms were glowing where they had touched him.

The nurse walked around behind the chair.

"I can push him," Bonnie said.

"Hospital regulations," said the nurse. "You can carry his things." There was a small plastic carrier bag with Terry's photo of Sean, his Bible, and a few personal items in it on the radiator cover beneath the window. Bonnie picked it up and then tried to wedge herself in between the moving chair and the wall, but she was forced to drop back behind the nurse.

Terry waved to his roommate as he passed by his bed. "God bless you, brother," he said.

"Take it easy, preacher," the man in the bed said wryly, looking at him over the top of his half glasses.

"He calls me that. Preacher," Terry confided proudly to his wife as they reached the corridor and she was able to move up beside him.

"That's nice," she said.

When they reached the third-floor lounge she pushed the button for the elevator. The doors opened and they got inside. None of them spoke inside the elevator. At the lobby, the nurse pushed Terry's wheelchair out of the elevator.

"I'll go find Sean and that Mr. Blake," said Bonnie. "He can bring the car up."

"If you don't mind, I'm going to get back up to my floor," said the nurse. "We're short-handed today."

Terry beamed at her. "No problem. I'm blessed. I have a wife who will take good care of me."

Bonnie gazed down at him tenderly. "That's right, my darling," she said.

# Chapter Twenty-one

$\mathcal{M}$addy stood with her hands on her hips, staring curiously at the assortment of clothes on the bed. She had gone through all of Bonnie's possessions except for those she'd taken with her to the hospital. Maddy was feeling guilty but told herself that if her hunch about Sean was right, it was justified. If not, she rationalized, she wasn't doing any real harm. Snooping through others' belongings made her uneasy. After all, she had invited these people into her home. That didn't give her the right to invade their privacy. While she found their belongings odd, she hadn't yet come across anything that indicated something criminally amiss.

The two suitcases were old and battered. Bonnie's entire wardrobe consisted of worn, shapeless tops, a couple of sweaters with pills all over them, two synthetic wool skirts, some shabby underwear, and one shiny blue nightgown with scratchy lace and spaghetti straps that still had the tag on it. Maddy felt almost cruel, looking through Bonnie's meager belongings. The clothes for Sean, on the other hand, were mostly new. That wasn't surprising for a baby. People gave a new baby lots of clothes, and even the most financially pressed mother always managed to buy her baby new things.

No, only Terry's clothes were puzzling. They were all brand new. The white sweat socks were still in wrappers. Two pairs of new jeans still retained their price tags, and three new plaid shirts still had pins in the collar. Even the underwear was new and still folded in its plastic three-packs. Oh sure, she thought, it was natural to get some new clothes to start a new job with, but there weren't any clothes here that had ever been worn. Curious . . . She rummaged through the pockets of the suitcase but found only a zippered bag with toiletries, a lipstick for Bonnie, and a couple of paperback novels. There was nothing personal in any of it. Nothing that would tell you much about the people who were traveling with those bags.

Maddy sighed in frustration. Suddenly she thought she heard a door slamming. Startled, she straightened up and listened. From Amy's room came the singsong sounds of her nursery rhyme tape and Amy banging out an accompaniment on the top of a cookie tin. That's it. It's just Amy, she told herself. I'm jumpy because I'm afraid of getting caught doing this. Even as she thought that, she had to admit to herself that the brief visit from Heather had depressed her and made her feel anxious, like a shadow falling over her life.

Stop it, she thought. Stop ruminating about Heather and get back to what you're doing. I guess I better put this stuff back, she thought to herself. Nothing in here that told her any more than she already knew. She opened the suitcases and tried to remember exactly where each item of clothing had come from. Maddy was concentrating on her task, putting things away neatly, when suddenly she sensed that someone was behind her.

The hair stood up on the back of her neck, and she felt her heart begin to hammer. For a terrible moment she froze; why were they back so soon? Why hadn't Doug warned her? How was she ever going to explain? She tried to concoct a lie, to compose her face, as she turned around.

"Maddy?" said Father Nick, looking at her curiously. "I knocked, but I guess you didn't hear me."

"Oh, Nick, you scared me."

"I'm sorry. I called out, but you must have been absorbed in what you were doing. What are you doing?" he asked, glancing at the suitcases. "Are you going on a trip?"

Maddy shook her head. "No. No. I'm glad you're here. Give me a minute. I have to finish this." Hurriedly but carefully, she replaced every item and put the suitcases back where they went. When she was done he was still standing in the doorway, watching her.

"Come downstairs. I'll make you some tea. Let me just check on Amy," she said. She went down the hall and peeked in Amy's room. The little girl was playing happily. Maddy went back to the staircase, gesturing for Nick to follow her.

When they got to the kitchen, she went to the stove and put on the teakettle. Her hands shook as she lit the old gas burner.

"What's the matter?" he asked. "You seem like a nervous wreck."

Maddy sat on a kitchen chair at the table with him and shook her head. "I am. If I tell you, you'll probably think I'm crazy."

Nick shrugged. "Try me."

"I told you about the people in the accident. How they're staying here?"

"Yes," he said.

"Well, I started to get this idea in my head that they're the ones who took the baby. You know, the missing Wallace baby."

"Did you call the police?" he asked.

Maddy sighed. "And say what? These people have a baby, and the mother doesn't treat him normally? The baby made noises when he saw the Wallaces on TV?"

"They've showed pictures of the baby on TV, haven't they? Couldn't you recognize him?"

Maddy shook her head. "They had Polaroids of a curly-headed little boy; it could be any baby. You can't tell from that. I've taken these people in, and now what am I going to do? Call the police on them? The Good Samaritan, that's me."

Nick nodded. "Yeah. I see."

His understanding warmed her, and for a minute she caught his eye and a complex message passed instantly between them. They both looked hurriedly away.

"Besides," she continued briskly, "we've had enough to do with the police. I told you what happened with Doug. You know, that they picked up Doug and questioned him just because the girl who disappeared was a teenager."

"Right. How did that go?" said Nick.

"You were right to encourage me to trust him. It didn't amount to anything. The witness didn't identify him. Our lawyer is threatening to sue the police department for harassment."

Nick nodded. "So, everything's all right now," he said carefully.

For a moment Maddy thought again of Heather on the doorstep and sighed. Then she got up to pour the tea. Nick studied her as she moved around the kitchen.

"Maddy?"

"Yes, it's fine," she said. "Except for me snooping through the belongings of my houseguests, thinking they're kidnappers."

"Who are these people, anyway?" Nick asked. "You said they weren't from around here."

Maddy poured the steaming water into the cup. "Their name is Lewis. They're from Maine. They're a very strange couple. He looks like a motorcycle biker and she's a frumpy-looking librarian. He seems very religious, though."

Nick looked surprised. "Terry Lewis."

Maddy turned and stared at him. "That's right. Terry is his name."

"And Bonnie. And Sean," said Nick.

"You know them," Maddy said incredulously.

"Yes, I know them. I know them very well. Terry just got out the other day."

"Out?" Maddy asked. "Out of what?"

"Out of prison," Nick said calmly.

"Prison," Maddy cried.

"Do you remember my telling you about the man who was in prison for murder and then the real killer confessed? And he was let out?"

Maddy's mouth fell open. "You said the other night you'd been up at the prison."

Nick nodded and smiled. "I was up saying good-bye to

Terry. I saw Bonnie and Sean when they came to get him."

"No," Maddy cried. "No, it can't be. No. This can't be right. They're from Maine. Their license plate . . ." She felt as if she were drowning in confusion.

"Bonnie is from Maine. I'm sure that was her car they were driving. Terry has been serving a life sentence. It was one of those gas station holdups and some customer identified Terry. He'd already done five years when the real killer confessed. They'd gotten him for another, similar holdup, and he admitted he was the one who'd done the crime Terry was convicted of."

"I can't believe it," said Maddy, thinking of the man she'd met in the hospital bed. He certainly looked like a man who'd spent years in prison.

"I've seen him every week when I make my pastoral visits. He handled the whole thing with amazing fortitude. Forgave the guy for letting him take the rap. I'm not sure I could have been as generous as he was. It was very emotional. Anyway, he was released the day before yesterday. . . ."

"That explains the new clothes," Maddy said.

"What new clothes?"

"In their suitcase. All of his clothes are brand new. She must have bought them for him."

"He told me he had a job interview lined up when he got out. Yeah. That's him."

"Oh, my God, Nick. But a guy who's been in prison all that time . . . He must have had a record or something to be convicted in the first place. All those years in that violent atmosphere . . . And I went and asked them to stay here."

Nick raised a hand to stop her. "Remember, he didn't

belong there, any more than you or I would. He'd had a pretty rough life before he went to prison. I'm not going to tell you it was his first brush with the law. But I think this experience really changed him. I really believe Terry is going to be able to turn his life around."

"Wait till Doug hears this," Maddy mumbled, shaking her head.

"Doug, of all people, should be willing to give others the benefit of the doubt," Nick said, unable to keep a chiding tone out of his voice.

Maddy looked at him across the table and felt a spark jump between them. She lowered her eyes and took a sip of tea.

"So they really are married?" she asked.

"I married them," Nick said simply.

"At the prison?"

"The prison chapel. It was a modest affair," he said.

"How in the world did those two ever get together?"

"It was one of those penpal romances. A lot of the prisoners have them. This one led to marriage."

"I had a feeling she led kind of a lonely life," said Maddy.

"I'm sure you're right about that," said Nick. "It started out with her sending him books, and one thing led to another."

"And Sean?" Maddy asked.

"Oh, he's theirs all right."

"I thought prisoners didn't . . . I mean . . . you know . . ."

"Have sex?" he asked, recognizing her discomfort.

Maddy nodded.

"Oh, they have sex," he said, smiling wryly. "In fact, theirs was something of a shotgun wedding. Not that

there was anyone holding a gun to Terry's head. He was
perfectly willing. And nobody in her life really seemed to
care that much about Bonnie. But yes. He's theirs. I baptized him myself. Only a couple of months ago."

"Oh," said Maddy, surprised, relieved, and at the same
time oddly disappointed.

Nick noted her reaction. "You were hoping perhaps
that you were harboring kidnappers?"

"No,"said Maddy, frowning. "No, of course not.
Maybe . . . I guess I'm just feeling for that mother. Wishing she could have her baby back safe and sound. It tears
your heart out to see that young couple on TV."

"It's terribly sad," he agreed.

They sat in silence for a moment, sipping their tea.
"I'm awfully glad you came by," Maddy said. "You've
really eased my mind." Then she cocked her head to one
side. "Why did you come by? Weren't you leaving
today?"

"Yes," he admitted. "Yes, I'm afraid so." He fished
around in the pocket of his jacket. He was wearing his
civilian clothes, and Maddy thought for a moment how
much less severe he looked in a blue oxford shirt than in
his black cassock.

"Here," he said, taking out a thin silver bracelet and
laying it on the table between them. "I found this hooked
on my gray sweater."

"But how . . . ?" Then Maddy blushed furiously, remembering their brief embrace in his office. "I can't believe it. I didn't even miss it." She picked up the bracelet
and looked at it.

"I figured you would want it," he said.

Another silence fell between them, and this time they

both knew that it was a reluctance to face their final good-bye.

"Well, I've still got to load up my car, before I get on the road," he said, standing up.

Maddy stood as well, wiping her hands on the front of her jeans. "Will you get there tonight?" she asked.

"No, I'm . . . getting kind of a late start. I'll stop and spend the night somewhere. I'll be there tomorrow."

Maddy suddenly did not trust her voice.

Nick forced himself to smile. "Walk me to my car?" he asked.

"Okay," Maddy whispered. She was overcome with a sudden, keen sorrow for the loss of him. When they got outside, she was glad that it was too chilly to linger. They faced each other without smiling.

"I'm sorry, Nick," she said.

He didn't mean to touch her, but he didn't want her to see his eyes, so he reached out and pulled her to him, and she pressed against him fiercely. The smell of her hair and the feel of her slight body in his arms made him hold her too long. He heard the sound of a car pulling into the driveway, and he let go of her as if she were red hot.

Doug pulled up beside Nick's car and got out. Bonnie clambered out behind him. In the front seat on the passenger side, Terry Lewis rested one huge tattooed forearm across the window and leaned out.

"Father Nick," he cried.

Nick's face lit up at the sight of him. He strode over to the car and gently shook the other man's hand. "Hello, my friend. I heard you were in an accident."

"Out of the frying pan into the fire," Terry joked, showing his crooked teeth when he smiled.

"Let me help you out of there," said Nick. He opened

the door and reached in, half lifting the bulky man out of the seat.

"Thanks, Father," said Terry, straightening. "No more trouble. I promise."

Nick smiled and turned to Bonnie. "Hello, Bonnie. I was told you and Sean were staying here."

"Father Rylander," she said, surprised.

"You better take care of this guy."

"I will," she said with her customary abruptness. She looked down shyly at her shoes.

Nick leaned over and planted a kiss on the fussing baby. "And take good care of Sean. He's a fine boy."

"Terry has to go in now," said Bonnie.

Doug caught Maddy's eye questioningly. "I'll tell you in a minute," Maddy whispered.

"Well, I have to be going, too." Nick gave Doug a false smile and extended his hand. "Just stopped to say goodbye."

Doug reached out and shook his hand. His face was grim.

Bonnie put an arm around Terry and began to help him toward the walkway. Nick climbed into his car without looking back. Maddy felt Doug encircle her waist with his arm. Maddy concentrated as hard as she could to keep back tears.

# Chapter Twenty-two

$\mathcal{M}$addy turned away from the sight of Nick's departure and sighed. Doug looked at her suspiciously. Just then there was wailing from the direction of the car. "Will you get Sean?" Maddy said, disengaging herself from Doug's possessive arm. "I'll go open the door." She saw that Bonnie and Terry were slowly approaching the house, and she realized that she had not seen Terry standing up before. She noted that he was not a tall man—not much taller than his wife.

As they approached the steps, Maddy rushed up to the front door and opened it. Terry's face was pale from the exertion. "Come on in," she said. "I'll bet you're glad to be out of that hospital."

Terry nodded and carefully hoisted himself up on the front steps. Bonnie hovered beside him anxiously. Terry stepped into the foyer and looked around.

"Are you all right?" Bonnie asked.

"I'm fine," he said. His eyes surveyed the Blakes' modest house. "This is a palace," he said sincerely.

"Thank you," said Maddy. "Come in and sit down."

"I want to hug my boy. That's the first thing I want to do."

"He's right in here," said Maddy, pointing to the living room. Doug had removed Sean from the car and brought him inside.

Terry seemed to straighten up at the prospect of holding Sean. He limped toward the door of the living room and looked inside. "There he is," he cried.

"Don't you dare try to pick him up!" Bonnie warned. She rushed past her husband and swooped down on Sean, lifting the startled baby off the floor. Sean started to wail.

"Why don't you sit down here and we can put him beside you," Maddy said.

Terry frowned but did as she suggested, falling heavily onto the couch and rubbing his stomach as he got himself settled. "Okay," he said. "I'm ready for him. Bring him over here."

Maddy watched curiously as Bonnie brought the child to his father. A father he scarcely knew, she thought, yet Sean stopped crying as he sank into the sofa beside Terry. He looked up wide-eyed at the pitted, swarthy face, and with one little hand he reached up and tugged at Terry's mustache. Terry let out a cry of delight and began to play peek-a-boo games with the child. Maddy glanced at Bonnie, expecting to see an indulgent smile on her face. Bonnie, who stood back with her arms crossed over her chest, looked on instead with stormy eyes.

Maddy approached her tentatively. "Listen, Bonnie, I've been thinking . . . Terry really shouldn't be climbing the stairs. There's a foldout bed in the playroom you could use. I didn't want to move your stuff until I spoke to you about it."

"We won't need it," Bonnie said bluntly. "We're leaving."

"Today?" Maddy asked. She felt a combination of surprise and relief. But at the same time, she was concerned about Terry, who had had such recent surgery. He seemed frail and in pain. "Are you sure that's wise?" she asked. "Is your husband able to travel?"

"We'll be all right," said Bonnie.

"But where will you stay?"

"What difference does it make to you?"

"Bonnie . . . I'm concerned about you, all right? I promised Ni . . . Father Rylander that I would look out for you."

"Look, I know why you took us in," said Bonnie. "It wasn't to be nice. You were worried about the accident. That we might take you to court."

"That is totally unfair," said Maddy, wounded at the baldness of the accusation but acknowledging the partial truth of it.

Bonnie made a face as if she smelled something rotten.

"All right," said Maddy. "All right. I was a little worried. But I was concerned about you, too. Everyone has their reasons. I'm no better than the next guy."

Bonnie relented. "You don't have to worry. We have insurance. I put Terry on my plan when we got married. The car is insured in my name. You won't hear from us after we leave."

Maddy thought about Doug, who had disappeared into the kitchen, and about how relieved he would be. He had been so nervous lately. This would certainly make him feel better, although she knew he wouldn't trust the news. He'd be certain that the Lewises would change their mind. Nevertheless it was bound to cheer him up, no matter how much he might doubt their reassurances.

"What are you two gals talkin' about?" Terry asked. Sean was grasping his thumb, and Terry was moving it up and down.

"About leaving," said Bonnie.

"I was saying that you don't look like you're in any shape to move," Maddy said.

Terry sighed. "I've had better days," he admitted.

"Would you like anything to drink? A cup of tea?"

"I could use a cup of coffee if you've got it."

"Sure," Maddy said brightly. "Bonnie, do you want anything?"

Bonnie shook her head and sat on the sofa, on the other side of Sean. They made a touching picture there, Maddy thought. They had been through a lot. She thought of all that Nick had told her about them. Terry had lived through a nightmare the likes of which . . . Maddy thought about Doug. The likes of which we could understand, she thought. It was possible for an innocent man to end up disgraced, unjustly imprisoned. Not only had Bonnie stood by him, she had even married him. Clearly she believed in her husband, Maddy thought. There was something admirable about it, really. One more day, she thought. Surely we can manage that. They deserve a break.

Maddy went into the kitchen and put the water on. Doug was sitting at the kitchen table. He looked up at her, an antagonistic expression on his face. She could feel him watching her as she moved around the kitchen, automatically scooping out the coffee, placing the mugs on the counter. Maddy knew something was brewing beneath his silence and his steady gaze. She pretended not to notice.

"What was he doing here?" Doug demanded.

# Chapter Twenty-three

𝕄addy looked out into the hallway and closed the kitchen door, gesturing for Doug to whisper. "He came to return my bracelet," she said, indicating the delicate silver-linked chain encircling her wrist.

Doug frowned at the bracelet, a gift he had given Maddy on their first anniversary. "How did he come to have your bracelet?"

Maddy could not avoid thinking of how the bracelet had gotten caught on Nick's sweater. She recalled the impulsive embrace, the surprising depth of feeling between them, and her face reddened. "It got snagged on something in his . . . office when I went to see him."

"Went to see him about what?" he asked.

"I went to talk to him," Maddy said irritably.

"Is that why these people are still here? Because he is so chummy with them?"

"No. They are still here because that man got out of the hospital not an hour ago."

"I asked you to get rid of them but, hey, whatever Father Nick wants . . ."

"Leave him out of this. He has nothing to do with it."

"Pardon me," said Doug. "It seems like what I need is last on your list. . . ."

"Oh, for heaven's sake," said Maddy.

"Don't tell me I'm imagining this. I've seen how that priest looks at you. He gazes at you like a sick pup. Do you think that was just a friendly squeeze he was giving you in the driveway?"

She felt both guilty and resentful of his accusation. The fact was that nothing illicit had happened between herself and Nick. She had to remind herself that she had nothing for which to apologize. "Don't be disgusting, Doug. We're close friends. He's leaving today, and he was saying good-bye."

"Well, maybe that's how you see it," he snapped.

Maddy shook her head. "Do you want coffee?" she asked evenly.

"What, are you waiting on them, too?"

"Never mind," said Maddy.

"If he's so damn fond of these people, why didn't he take them in? No, he expects you to do it. Why should you do what he wants? I mean, what claim has he got on you? Unless there's something I don't know about."

Maddy glared at him. "Even if that were true of Nick, which it's not, how could you show so little faith in me? How could you even think, for a minute . . ."

"Hey, sometimes things happen," said Doug with a shrug.

Maddy looked at him through narrowed eyes. There was something altogether too fluid about his idea of morality. "No, they don't just happen," she said bitterly. "Not if you don't let them happen. I'm your wife. I made a promise to be faithful to you, if you'll recall. I don't take my promises lightly."

He lowered his eyes. "Let's just drop it," he said.

She stared at him, and the memory of Heather on the doorstep returned. For a moment she wondered. Did he really believe that things could just happen, and he was helpless to prevent it? Could something have just happened between him and Heather? She tried to stop herself from saying it, but she couldn't. "Heather Cameron was here today," she said.

"What the hell did she want?" Doug asked uneasily.

Maddy sighed. She reminded herself that it was not fair to torment him. He had been cleared of those charges. She recalled Heather's odd behavior and how reassuring she had actually found it. "I think she's mentally deranged. She said she was jealous because she thought you were involved with some other girl named Karla."

"Karla?"

"Another girl from school who has a crush on you or something. She was all bent out of shape, as if you were being unfaithful to her. Can you imagine coming here and saying that to me? It was loony. Kind of scary, really. I thought about calling the cops. I really did. But she left without making a scene."

"Karla . . . Needham?" he asked incredulously. "Has a crush on me?"

"That's not really the point, Doug," Maddy said coldly.

"No, of course not," he said, shaking his head. "That Heather is a sick kid. She needs help."

Maddy felt certain that he was saying the words but thinking of something else.

"So," he said abruptly. "What did you find when you

were playing Nancy Drew? Anything interesting? The map to the hidden treasure?"

"Don't patronize me," she said.

"I'm not." He came around the counter and put his hands on her arms. "I'm sorry. I mean it. I'm sorry about Heather coming here and upsetting you. I wish I'd been here. I would have read her the riot act. And . . . I am curious. About our guests. Did you find anything?"

Maddy looked at him ruefully.

"Really, Maddy. I'm sorry. I was out of line."

"Yes, you were," she said bitterly.

"Okay, so . . . ?"

Maddy shook her head. "I didn't find anything. Nick had the interesting information."

"Ah," he said, clearly wanting to make a sarcastic remark but restraining himself.

"It seems that Mr. Lewis was released the day before yesterday from the state prison."

Doug jumped up from the chair. "My God. And you're just telling me this! What were you waiting for? How could you just let me go on without knowing this? Without mentioning it?"

"It's not the way it sounds. He was in for a crime he didn't commit. The real killer confessed, and Terry was released."

"Killer? Killer? Oh, great. You mean he was in for murder?" said Doug.

"That he didn't do," whispered Maddy, gesturing for him to keep his voice down.

Doug threw up his hands. "They're in our living room."

"Well, they can spend one more night."

"Spend the night? You think I'm going to have a violent criminal in the same house with my family?"

"Stop shouting," said Maddy. "Look, I told you. He didn't do it. He was released because he did not commit the crime. Nick told me all about it. He has been meeting with him in the prison these last few years. He said that Terry was amazingly strong about the whole thing."

"Oh, sure," Doug cried. "One hypocrite endorsing another. You can't really believe that, Maddy. I mean, use your brain."

"What is that supposed to mean? Nick is not a hypocrite."

"He's the worst kind. Going around spouting Bible passages and lusting after my wife. Why should we take his word that this convict can be trusted? Oh, sure. . . . Let me tell you something, Maddy. That ex-con is not staying in this house. Do you understand me?"

"Don't you dare talk to me like that. It's not just your house."

The kitchen door banged open and Bonnie stood there. "Terry needs his coffee," she said.

Maddy and Doug exchanged a stony glance, and then Doug threw open the kitchen door and started down the hallway to the stairs.

"It's almost ready," said Maddy, lifting the kettle off the stove with a shaky hand.

"What was he yelling about?" said Bonnie.

"I just told him about Terry being in jail. Father Nick explained everything to me. Doug was a little bit surprised."

"Did Father Rylander tell you that Terry didn't do it?"

"Yes," said Maddy.

"So it's nobody's business where he's been. It wasn't his fault he was in there."

"I know," said Maddy. "I was just trying to explain that to my husband."

Bonnie glared at her. "We don't want to be here. I can't wait to get away from here. And from you, with your perfect little life. All we want is to be left alone, get a nice place to live, and be a family. The less people know about the past, the better."

Maddy sighed, thinking how her life was not the perfect picture it seemed. "I can understand that," she conceded.

"People don't want to give somebody who's been in jail a chance. No matter what the truth was in the end," said Bonnie.

"I think it's great the way you champion your husband. He's lucky to have a wife like you," Maddy said.

Bonnie squinted at Maddy. "Do you really think that?" she asked suspiciously.

"Absolutely," said Maddy. "And I really hope everything works out for you. Nick told me how you met. That you were writing letters and sending him books."

"We corresponded for two years before we actually met," she admitted. "I never had a boyfriend before Terry."

"That's sort of romantic," said Maddy.

"When he sent me his picture and I saw how handsome he was, I didn't want to send him a picture back. I kept telling him I didn't have one to send. I didn't think he'd like me when he saw me. But he did." Bonnie's plain face glowed with the memory. "He said I was a sight for sore eyes."

There was a wail from the front of the house. "Honey, Sean's crying," Terry called out.

His voice startled Bonnie out of her romantic reverie; her face crumpled, and her glow seemed to fade away, like Cinderella's finery at the stroke of midnight.

"Kids," Maddy said ruefully. "They're tough on a romance."

"I have to go," Bonnie muttered, and headed back out the door without another word.

# Chapter Twenty-four

$\mathcal{T}$his just came in from the coroner's office," said Delilah Jones, a pretty young black girl who was a cadet fresh out of the Academy.

"I'll take it to the chief," said Officer Len Wickes. He was very curious about the contents of the report. He and the other men had hardly set foot inside the station since the discovery of Rebecca Starnes's body. They had been busy knocking on doors, looking for the people who had been in the park the day Rebecca and Justin disappeared. They had interviewed every skateboarder, every mother they found in the park, and every man with an Asian surname they had been able to locate in town. When they weren't doing that, they were in the state forest, overturning every rock and leaf, dragging every stream, and generally crawling around on their hands and knees, looking for signs of the missing baby. But nothing. Nothing. Len felt it like a sickness in his own stomach—that they still had not found baby Justin. Of course, in a way, you didn't want to find him. As long as you didn't find him, there was some hope that he was still alive. Len made his way to Chief Cameron's office and knocked on the door.

"Come on in," the chief growled.

Len opened the door and saw that the chief was studying some photographs at his desk. "Coroner's report, sir."

Frank Cameron jumped up from his seat. "Let me see that, Wickes."

Len handed over the report and stood at attention, hoping he would be allowed to know what the report contained. Frank tore it open and scanned the form, skipping over the information he was already sure of.

"Well, well, well," said Frank. "How about that? No sexual assault. Somebody sure wanted us to think there was."

Len cleared his throat loudly, and Frank Cameron looked up.

"Sir?"

Frank always found himself slightly amused by Len Wickes's military bearing.

"Yes, Officer Wickes?"

"Maybe the killer tried, sir, but he wasn't able," offered Len.

Frank nodded thoughtfully. "It's been known to happen. Sometimes they kill the victim to make sure that no one ever learns of their humiliation."

"It's just an idea, sir," said Len, pleased at the chief's receptiveness to his suggestion.

"Go out and call Pete in here, and Rocky Belmont," said the chief.

Len snapped to attention, all but saluted, and went briskly around the station, informing Detective Millard and Officer Belmont that the chief wished to see them.

Pete and Rocky exchanged a glance and followed Len Wickes back to Chief Cameron's office.

As they walked in, Frank Cameron lifted the report in his hand and waved it at them. He didn't even offer them a seat. "Gentlemen," he said, "the coroner's report. No evidence of sexual assault on Rebecca Starnes."

Pete and Rocky both murmured their surprise.

"Now," said Frank, "as Officer Wickes here was quick to point out, that doesn't mean it wasn't a failed assault." Len beamed.

"We all know these perverts are most enraged when they fail. However, this victim seemed to have been dispatched without a lot of extra violence. No mutilation. It wasn't as if she was stabbed forty times or something. No, while we have to consider every possibility, we also have to deal with the facts that we have. And the facts we have indicate that it wasn't a sex crime. So if it wasn't a sex crime, then it must have been about the baby. But there's been no ransom demand. Thus, it might mean that someone wanted the baby for themselves. Who wants babies for themselves?"

"Women," Pete said emphatically.

Frank Cameron nodded. "So we could be looking for a woman, couldn't we?"

Len Wickes raised one finger and wagged it, seeking the chief's attention. Frank Cameron nodded in his direction.

"But you can't rule out the possibility of the black market, sir," said Len. "There's a huge demand for little white babies out there, sir. You don't need to ask for ransom to profit from a kidnapping these days. All you need to do is find a willing buyer."

"He's right about that," Rocky Belmont agreed.

Frank Cameron looked skeptically at the young officer.

This was the early bird who caught the worm. This was the kind of guy who lived for his work. Right now he was raw and inexperienced, but you couldn't fault his eagerness. Frank remembered when he was eager like that, and every case was an exciting challenge. Maybe someday Len Wickes would inherit this job from him. The thought didn't bother Frank. Actually, today it seemed as if it would almost be a relief.

"It's a possibility to be considered," admitted Frank. "It could be a total stranger to the area. It could be a group of guys with masks and a getaway car and a pipeline to unscrupulous lawyers with wealthy clients. Let's be honest. We need to tap into national agencies, the FBI files, for that kind of information. Have we come up with any correlations so far?"

Pete shook his head. "We're plugged in to the computers for all the national agencies. But up till now our information has been too vague—we haven't had any specific characteristics of the crime to feed them. This autopsy report will help. Now we can narrow down the database and key it in to similar cases—murdered caretaker, abducted child. It's a lot more specific now."

"That's good," said Frank. He didn't know too much about computers, but he was properly respectful of the results they could produce. Meanwhile he felt more comfortable in the realm of old-fashioned police work. "Let's work the local angle. How about this idea of the woman. Now what kind of woman takes a baby? We've got a woman who probably can't get pregnant or her baby died and she's not really operating on all her burners, if you get my drift. Maybe she's tried to adopt and hasn't had any luck. Whatever. Pete, I want you to get on the adoption agencies. Rocky, check up on recent deaths of babies in the area."

"I've already got calls out for that information," said Pete.

"Good," said the chief. "Do I need to tell you guys that we are dealing with a very touchy subject here? We need to get this information, but let's try not to step on any toes while we're at it."

The detectives nodded.

Len felt his heart sinking as his ideas seemed relegated to obscurity. "What do you want me to do, sir?"

At that moment Delilah Jones knocked on the open door. "Chief," she said, "it's time for a press briefing."

Frank exhaled noisily. "Shit. I hate this. I've got nothing to tell them, and I have to pretend we're making progress."

"Sir?" asked Len Wickes.

"Man the phones, Wickes. Until further notice. Pete, Rocky, come with me."

Len looked stricken. "Answer the phones?" he asked. He could hardly believe his ears. There was a kidnapping and a murder investigation going on.

"You heard me," Frank snapped, striding past him toward the door. He nearly knocked over Delilah Jones as he passed by her. She glanced at Len and shrugged.

Len prowled around the station house. Every cop in town was out gathering information, and he was stuck answering the phone. As if to mock his misery, the phone rang on Pete Millard's desk. Len walked over and picked it up.

"Detective Millard's desk," he said.

"Hello," said a sweet voice on the other end. "This is Caitlin Markus from the Rainbow Adoption Agency. I have some information Detective Millard asked for, and I wanted to send it directly to his computer."

"No problem," said Len Wickes, sitting at Pete Millard's desk and switching on the detective's computer. "Fire away." As Len waited for the information about couples seeking adoptions to come up on Pete Millard's screen, he picked up a printout that was lying on the desktop. There was a list from the county bureau of records of children who had died in Taylorsville for the last twenty-five years, as well as their dates of birth. As he perused the list, he had an idea. He looked down the list of death dates for the month of November and then for the day. It was worth a glance. Why not? There were two matches on the list. He cross-checked them with this adoption agency's records. One of them was on the list but had successfully completed the adoption. The other had not been seeking an adoption. He made a note of both names. Now, what about the other agencies? he thought. This could be a very time-consuming task. He'd better start collecting lists. A phone rang on Rocco Belmont's desk. He looked around the room and caught the eye of Delilah Jones. "Can you get that, Delilah?" he asked. "I'm busy looking something up here."

Delilah gave him a skeptical look. She wasn't about to let any of these guys treat her like a gal Friday. She had made the grade through exactly the same kind of training they had. But she understood that Len was trying to act important, to save face after being stuck on the phones. She felt a little sorry for him. He was an eager beaver, but there was something endearing about him. It was as if he were a little kid who wanted so badly to be allowed to play with the big guys. She walked over to the phone and picked it up.

Len went back to the printout. As he was studying the

list, his eye was caught by the birthdates. He decided to cross-reference those, too. Why not? he thought. It didn't hurt to be thorough. He poised his fingers over the computer keyboard and licked his lips nervously. What if I make the big break in this case? he thought. Laurie will be so proud of me. Thoughts of his wife's admiration were distracting. He forced his fantasies to the back of his mind as his fingers began to play over the keyboard.

# *Chapter Twenty-five*

*W*hen Doug didn't come down for dinner, Maddy made excuses for him. He was busy preparing for his first day back at school, she said. The Lewis family seemed completely uninterested, absorbed as they were in their reunion. He did not reappear at Amy's bedtime, so she put the child to sleep with promises that Daddy would kiss her good night when he was done with his work. Finally she couldn't stand it any longer. Maddy's mother had once confided that she and her father never went to bed angry. Maddy had always admired her parents' marriage, and she tried to adhere to that rule with Doug, although she didn't always succeed.

She hated arguments that went on and on. They were bad for the marriage and bad for Amy to be caught in the middle of them. Kids could tell when their parents were arguing. They didn't have to know what it was about. They just could sense the conflict in the atmosphere. Better to just clear the air and get it over with. Maddy put her dish towel on the counter, then walked through the house and up the staircase with a heavy tread. Why do I always have to be the one to make up? she thought.

She sighed and told herself it was because it was harder for Doug. He had come from a loveless home. His father was henpecked by his domineering, distant wife, and Doug was always caught in the middle of it. Doug would look to his father for support, but it was no use. He was too meek to come to his son's defense. Maddy had met Doug shortly before his father died. They had virtually no contact with Frances Blake. She had her own life to live, as she told them on the rare occasions when they phoned her. Maddy reminded herself of all this as she climbed the stairs, so that she would be able to confront him without too much rancor. That never helped anything. But she felt a weariness as she approached the door to his office. There were patterns in every relationship. In theirs, she always was the one who apologized first. It would be nice if once, just once, he would make the overture to reconciliation, but in every marriage, she reminded herself, there were things you just had to live with.

Maddy tapped on the door to Doug's office. When there was no response, she turned the doorknob and opened it. It was dark in the office; only a little desk lamp illuminated the space. Doug sat at his desk, holding a photograph. His face seemed to have crumpled, and there were tears on his cheeks.

Maddy's anger evaporated at the sight of him. "Honey," she said, "what's the matter?" She walked over to the desk and saw that the picture he was holding was a photograph of himself in his Philadelphia Phillies uniform, before his knee injury put him out of the game. When they met, he had been on the rebound from that disappointment. Sometimes Maddy thought he still was. She looked over his shoulder at the picture. He looked timeless in his uniform, and ageless. On his face was the joyous smile of victory, of untroubled exultation.

Doug turned the framed photo over, facedown, on his desk and tried to wipe his tears away surreptitiously. "What do you want?" he said.

Maddy put a gentle hand on his shoulder, but he jerked away from her. "I was concerned when you didn't come down to dinner. Why are you so upset?" she said.

"I'm sorry," he said. "It's everything. I'm dreading going back to school tomorrow."

Maddy pulled up the little hassock from the wing chair in the corner and sat beside him, so that she was looking up at him. "You don't have to pretend to be cheerful for my sake. I know it's been rough for you."

He gazed at her for a few moments with an unreadable expression on his face. "You're so loyal," he said. The words sounded cold and almost critical, though she was sure he meant them to be kind.

"I'm your wife. We're partners. Of course I'm loyal to you," she said. "I know it's going to be tough walking back into the classroom after all this. You just have to remember that the court said you were innocent, and it's Heather that's in the wrong." She remembered Heather's visit to the house. "I hope she doesn't start hounding you at school tomorrow."

"I'll take care of Heather," he said grimly.

"I think you'd better just steer clear of her," Maddy suggested.

"I can handle it," he said through clenched teeth. "I don't want your advice."

Maddy clammed up, wounded by his reaction.

He made a halfhearted effort to explain himself. "It's not just that."

"Well, what, then?" she snapped. "Is it this business about having the Lewises here?"

"I don't care," said Doug. "They can stay here. One more night is not going to matter one way or the other."

"Then what?" Maddy cried. She reached up and put her hand on his. He did not take his hand away, but he did not respond, either. His hand felt as cold as a piece of stone. "Is it because I've been hounding you, about the insurance and all? . . ."

"No, Maddy, no," he said wearily.

"Look, I know what a nightmare you've been through, and maybe I haven't always been as supportive as I should have been. . . ."

Doug snatched his hand away from her and picked up the photo again. "You were perfect, all right? You did everything right. This isn't about you." He gazed at the photo with longing in his eyes. "I look at the boy in this picture and wonder what happened to him. What became of the boy who had the world at his feet, for whom everything was easy? This boy who was happy and successful and everybody admired him. Girls fell all over him, and men asked for his autograph. Why did it have to all go up in smoke? Why did I have to lose everything?"

Maddy stood up from the hassock unsteadily and took a step away from the desk, reeling from the insult to their marriage and their life together. She tried to tell herself that that was not what he meant. People got depressed sometimes and said things they didn't mean. But it stung. It really stung her, and he didn't even seem to notice. "I'm sorry we don't make you happy," she said bitterly.

"Oh, it's not that you don't make me happy," he said

absently, staring at the photograph. "But I mean, look at the boy in this picture. He has everything he could ever want. What could ever compare to that?"

Maddy felt as if she wanted to be sick. "Thanks a lot," she said.

Doug looked up at her in surprise and then frowned. "Oh, don't take it so personally, Maddy."

"Don't take it personally? How am I supposed to take it? Amy and I do everything we can to make you happy. Obviously that doesn't amount to much in your eyes."

"If you came up here to pick a fight with me, I really don't need it," he said.

"No, you're too busy thinking about yourself," she sputtered. "God, I'm sick of your whining."

He turned in a flash and grabbed her wrist, his eyes fierce. She was so startled by his action that for a moment it took her breath away. He had never raised a hand to her in anger before. She stared right back at him, determined not to cry out from the searing pain where his hand gripped her arm.

"Let go of me," she breathed. Her voice sounded firm, but in her heart she was anything but confident. For a terrifying moment she wondered if he was going to release her wrist or snap it.

In the next minute he dropped her hand as if it were slimy. "I knew you wouldn't understand," he said. "You never did." He buried his head in his hands.

Maddy felt a sudden weariness wash over her and the desire to close her eyes and sleep for days. She wanted to turn away from him, and his words, and everything they signified.

Rubbing her wrist, she stood up on shaky legs and walked out of his office. Once in the hallway, she leaned against the wall with her eyes closed. He was wrong about her, she thought. It was not that she didn't understand. What worried her was that she was beginning to think she did.

# Chapter Twenty-six

Responding to the sharp rap, Paulina opened the door a crack and looked suspiciously at the cop standing at the front door. "Yes?" she said.

Len Wickes stood on the doorstep, breathing in the crisp autumn morning, his hat pulled low over his brow. He had spent the night doing his own detective work. Way beyond the call of duty. While his wife, Laurie, kept him supplied with cups of coffee, Len had studied his printouts and made his calls. Today he had just a few pertinent questions that needed answering. "May I speak to Mr. and Mrs. Henson, please?"

"Mr. Henson is not here. He's at work."

Len had figured as much. He had heard of Charles Henson. Everyone in the police department had heard of the formidable attorney. It wasn't Charles Henson he wanted to see. "Mrs. Henson, then?" he asked politely.

"Come in," said Paulina. She opened the door and Len stepped into the foyer of the magnificent Tudor house. He took off his hat and held it in his hands. "Wait in there," she said, pointing to the living room. "I'll see if she's here." Paulina started for the staircase and then turned back. "What is this about?" she asked.

"Just a routine inquiry," said Len, trying to sound extremely casual.

Paulina was not in the habit of questioning the police. In her experience, the police were people you could trust, people who protected you. Although Ellen's nerves had been so bad lately, there was a limit to how far Paulina would go to protect her. Clashing with the police was past the limit. She looked back at the policeman anxiously and started up the stairs.

Len went into the living room and looked around. It was a glimpse into another life, one that was foreign to him. He wondered how much a place like this would cost. More money than he would ever see. But Len was not a greedy man. He was curious, not envious. Besides, he thought, looking up at the oil portrait over the mantel of the mother and her long dead son, money truly did not buy happiness. No amount of money could bring that boy back. According to the records of the several agencies, the Hensons' attempts at adoption had been unsuccessful. Len thought for a moment of Laurie and their hopes for the future. Two or three kids, and he had no doubt that they would be able to have them when they were ready. Yes, there were things money couldn't buy.

He turned as he heard someone softly clearing her throat. Ellen Henson had come into the room in her stocking feet. She was a delicate-looking woman in her late forties, maybe early fifties, he judged. She had amazing hair, long, curly, and rather wild, a mass of blond and gray. She looked at him worriedly.

"What is it, Officer? What can I do for you?"

"Mrs. Henson," he said, wondering, as he studied her,

if she was the kind of person capable of violence, unhinged by her desire for a child. She didn't look crazy—maybe a little anxious, but not crazy. But you could never tell just by looking. He had collected the lists from every agency, as well as the town's birth and death statistics for years back, had taken them home last night and pored over them until he'd found the correlations he was looking for. He had already checked the three other names on his list. He was pretty well convinced that nothing was amiss with the others. He had kept the information to himself, not informed his colleagues as he knew he should. But there was the possibility of a coup here that would finally earn him the respect he deserved. "We are, as you know, investigating the disappearance of little Justin Wallace."

"Yes," she said. "I saw it in the paper. Would you like to sit down?"

Len followed her lead and sat poised on the edge of a chair. He hoped he could phrase this delicately enough. "We're pursuing every avenue, talking to people who might, for one reason or another, be trying to get a baby by any means possible."

"I don't understand," Ellen said.

"Mrs. Henson, I'm sure this is just a coincidence, but we noticed from the county clerk's records that your late son's birthdate was the same day that Justin Wallace disappeared. We also know that you have unsuccessfully tried to adopt a child."

Ellen's eyes blazed at him, but he blundered on. "Now, I did a little further checking. I learned that you spent some time in the psychiatric wing of the Shady Groves Hospital, and I wonder if you could tell me what condition you were suffering from."

"I was suffering from depression," said Ellen. "It was brought on by the death of my only child." Her voice was even, but her whole body had begun to tremble. "Does that seem strange to you, Officer Wickes?"

"No, ma'am, not necessarily," he said doggedly. "Now, could you give me an account of your whereabouts on the day Justin Wallace disappeared?"

Ellen sat absolutely still. Len thought perhaps he had hit pay dirt. He watched her contorted face with a fleeting sense of triumph, that he had figured it out. This woman was hiding something. He could tell. He could feel it. If she wasn't able to respond in a minute, he was going to ask to search the house. She probably knew about warrants, what with her husband being a lawyer, but sometimes people just cracked and spilled their guts. And she looked so brittle, so pent up, sitting there, that he had a distinct feeling the breaking point was near at hand. . . .

"Mrs. Henson," he said in a stern but sympathetic tone.

Finally she took a deep breath. "Young man," she said, "I realize you are only doing your job, and whatever pain you are causing me is insignificant compared to the torment of those parents." She paused for a moment, as if struggling to maintain her composure. Then she continued. "Those poor young people who are suffering so, wondering . . ." She closed her eyes, her face tragic. "I can't think about it," she said. "I cannot think about it," and she said it not to him, but to herself. Like a warning.

"Mrs. Henson, would you please answer the question."

She stared at him, as if there were so much she wanted to say but couldn't bring herself to blurt it out. "I was here all day," she said finally. "I never left my house. My housekeeper can tell you. If you have any other questions, you may refer them to my husband." She stood up. "Now, get out of my house."

"I would like to take a look around," he said. "If you don't mind."

"I do mind. You may not take another step into this house without getting a warrant. You may not," she said. "Now, go. Before I start screaming."

Len found her behavior very suspicious. He didn't think he'd have any trouble convincing the chief to get a warrant. Not when he told him about this. "All right," he said. "But I expect we'll be back."

Ellen walked woodenly to the door and closed it after him without a word. Paulina tiptoed down the stairs and saw her standing there, like a little broken doll, her face pressed against the front door. "Are you all right?" she asked worriedly.

Ellen nodded.

"What did he want?" Paulina asked.

"He wanted to know if I kidnapped the Wallace child. The baby who is missing."

"God in heaven," Paulina exclaimed, grasping her chest as if to shield herself from such a horrifying thought. "Is he crazy? Oh, my Lord. Why in the world would he come to you?"

"The child disappeared on Ken's birthday."

"So what?" said Paulina.

"And they know we've been unsuccessful in adopting."

"Lots of people have trouble adopting," Paulina said staunchly.

"He checked up on me. He found out I'd spent some time in a psychiatric hospital after Kenny died." Ellen turned and smiled at Paulina, but her eyes were filled with tears. "He thinks I'm crazy. Maybe he's right."

"Don't go on like that," Paulina said sharply.

The phone began to ring. "I'll get it," Ellen said. She walked over to the phone and picked it up. Paulina could not hear what she was saying, but she could see Ellen's narrow body tense up when she heard the voice on the phone, and then she saw Ellen sag and curl in on herself.

Paulina went to the front door. She watched as the police car pulled away, shaking her head and thinking how Charles Henson would make the police department pay for this when he found out.

Ellen hung up the phone. For a moment she stood very still. Then she stepped away from the phone carefully, as if the floor were made of glass. "I'm going outside . . . to the playhouse," she said.

"Why?" asked Paulina. "There's nothing out there."

Ellen did not reply.

"Wait," Paulina pleaded, hurrying after her. "Come and have something to eat."

Ellen continued to walk, as if she heard nothing. Paulina followed her through the house and watched as she opened the back door. "Wear a jacket," she called after her.

Ellen did not respond. She crossed the yard and unlocked the padlock to the playhouse. Paulina hesitated for a minute, watching her anxiously as she disappeared inside the little building. Then she turned back and hurried to the phone.

# Chapter Twenty-seven

$\mathcal{N}$ick awoke in the dark of the motel room, turned over, and looked at the clock. He was surprised at the hour. He hardly ever slept this late. Freedom, he thought wistfully, and his heart hurt again. He looked toward the windows, shrouded by heavy drapes, and saw a crack of gray light where they met. Rubbing his face with his hands, he got up and walked over to the window to get his first look in daylight at the place where he had stopped. He pulled the curtains open a crack and gazed out. The parking lot of the motel was almost empty. Not too many road travelers midweek at this time of year. In a few weeks it would be Thanksgiving, and there would probably be more people on the road, but right now the place looked deserted. All there was to see was the bleak sky and the deep blue green of spruce trees that formed a jagged horizon on the hillsides. He was only a few hours from Taylorsville, but it certainly looked like the country.

He had not gotten far yesterday. After he'd left Maddy's he had gone home, figuring he was packed and could just load up the car and go. But it was not that simple, of course. People kept stopping in to say good-bye, and Jim Warren, his replacement, had a lot of questions for him. Besides, Nick kept finding things in the parish house that he'd forgotten to pack or dispose of. It seemed to take forever. It was almost five by the time he got going, and he drove until past dark, when hunger and a lot of yawning at the wheel convinced him it was time to stop. After all, there was no hurry. No one was waiting for him. He was not expected at the monastery until the end of the week. Nobody was waiting for him anywhere.

Nick dropped the curtain and decided to take a shower. As he passed by the phone he glanced at it, wondering automatically if it would ring while he was in the shower, as it usually did, then realizing that no one knew where he was. No one would call him here. He tried to tell himself how great that was—just the freedom and anonymity he was seeking.

But as he ran the water, climbed into the tub, and pulled the curtain, he found himself listening anyway. It was a habit. He had become used to the constant demands of his job: the way people were always looking to him for hope, for a miracle, for something he just couldn't give. He took his time lathering himself, feeling the sting of the water on his body, trying to enjoy the privacy of this motel, this liberation from the needs of others. But there was not much pleasure in it. He found himself wishing, imagining, that he was not alone here. That he was in this dark, anonymous place, far from everywhere and everyone he knew, with the one person . . .

The ache of it was almost unbearable. Deliberately, out of long habit, Nick put the thought out of his mind. He knew he didn't have to pretend he didn't love her anymore. He could shout it to the world, here in this lonely motel. After all, she was part of the past now. She would never know the misery she had put him through with her gaze and her smile and the odd, unfinished conversation. He pictured her yesterday, in her kitchen, making him tea as if they belonged together. He could run the picture of it in his mind, like a video. She moved restlessly about the kitchen, thinking of other things, absolutely unaware of him as a man. He was just Father Nick, there to answer a few questions, ease a troubled mind. And then he recalled her words as they parted. Not good-bye, but "I'm sorry." Why had she said she was sorry? Sorry for what? Sorry, as he was, that they had met each other a lifetime too late? No, he told himself. You are indulging the fantasies of a schoolboy. You are building castles in the air, based on two innocuous words from a woman who never gave you a second thought.

But he didn't really believe it. He was not a complete novice with women. Before he'd entered the priesthood, he'd had limited, unsatisfactory encounters with a number of women. Enough to know the difference between indifference and possibility. That was partly why he'd had to leave Taylorsville. If he'd stayed much longer, he might have been compelled to find out. He was afraid that sooner or later he would brush against her, look for her response, say something he shouldn't. She was a married woman, and he was still a priest. Whatever sins he may have committed in his mind and heart, he wasn't about to try to woo her into adultery. Flawed as he was, he would not surrender to temptation, betray his collar willingly.

Nick got out of the shower, toweled himself off, and got dressed. He looked at a yellow, two-sided card perched on top of the television set, announcing there was a free Continental breakfast in the lounge. He figured he'd better load up the car and stop in to have a cup of coffee before he hit the road. He packed up his overnight bag and carried it out to the car. As he unlocked the trunk and rearranged his belongings, he noticed, with a complete sense of his own stupidity, that his briefcase was not among them.

"How could I have done that?" he said aloud. He'd been so preoccupied, so . . . accompanied, when he'd tried to get out that he must not have noticed. And last night he was too tired. He stood, jingling his car keys for a moment, then locked the trunk and went back into the room.

He sat on the edge of the one still made bed and dialed the number of his office. The phone rang and rang until a familiar voice answered. "Parish House . . ."

"Marge?" Nick asked, recognizing the voice of the housekeeper.

"Father Nick?"

"That's me."

"You calling from Canada?" Marge Sheehan asked.

"Hardly. I'm only upstate a ways. Listen, is Jim there? I think I left my briefcase in the office."

"Oh no," Marge said somberly. "He's got services today for the girl who was killed."

"Rebecca Starnes? I didn't realize they were Catholic."

"Well, she didn't go to church here. But she was baptized Catholic. She went to Perpetual Sorrows. Her father was a Catholic, and he insisted they have the funeral in a Catholic church. Monsignor Hathaway didn't want to do it because they were divorced, so they called Father Warren. To tell you the truth, the mother seems to be too bereaved to care. Oh, it's a sad thing," said Marge.

"Yes, it is," said Nick, feeling guilty that he wasn't there for the family, even though he didn't know them.

No, he thought. Forget it, that part of your life is over. "Did they find the baby yet?"

"That poor wee thing is with the angels, Father. Mark my words."

"You may be right, Marge."

"Anyhoo," said Marge. "Do you want me to have Father Warren give you a call?"

"Well, I'm on the road," said Nick. "If he finds it, just have him send it to the monastery, will you? I left the address. . . ."

"I'll do it," said Marge.

"I'll call him when I get to Canada."

"We miss you already, Father Nick," Marge said sincerely.

"Thanks, Marge," said Nick. "I miss all of you." He hung up the phone after a brief good-bye and sat on the edge of the bed, thinking about Rebecca Starnes. What happened to that girl in the park that day? He thought about Douglas Blake. He had advised Maddy to trust her husband, to be loyal. Was it the right advice? Or had he just said it because it would make it easier for him to leave, if she were still loyal to her husband and not looking to him for comfort? Had he advised her to remain loyal to an evil man, a man capable of murder?

A knock on the open door behind him made him jump. He turned around. A wiry woman with a graying ponytail wearing a white apron over jeans stood in the doorway. "Housekeeping," she said. "Can we clean the room?"

Nick stood up. "Yes, I suppose so." He took a last look around to make sure he didn't leave anything else behind. Then he went out to his car as the chambermaid began hauling her cart of linens toward his door. He hesitated for a moment at the door of the car. There's no turning back

now, he told himself, getting behind the wheel and turning
on the engine. You gave her the advice she wanted to hear.
She was with Doug Blake because she wanted to be. You
have done the honorable thing. Now forget her and get on
with your life.

# Chapter Twenty-eight

*D*oug drew the eraser in an arc across the blackboard and sighed. If only all of life's mistakes could be this easy to eradicate. If only you could draw a soft, dense little brick of fabric over them and make them disappear. He stood back and looked at the green board. He could see where the chalk had been. There was still an ivory haze veiling the bright green field, leaving it dull.

This was going to be harder than he had anticipated, he thought. He saw it in everyone's eyes. They all shook his hand and smiled and said congratulations, but that doubt lingered there, tainting him. He had attended the faculty meeting first thing in the morning and taught three classes. No one had said anything to him. Nothing that could even be faintly construed as derogatory. Yet it was there, dogging him. Beneath that layer of worry was another layer. Many other layers, he corrected himself. All concerned with the death of Rebecca Starnes. Though it seemed that he was safe enough. If they didn't know by now . . .

Doug replaced the eraser on the tray beneath the board,

brushed off his hands, and walked over to his desk. He put some papers in his briefcase and snapped it shut. Even as he did it, he wondered why he was bothering to bring this stuff home. He wouldn't be able to concentrate, yet he felt compelled to go through the motions. He pulled on his dark green jacket, picked up his briefcase, and steeled himself to go out into the hallway. Students rushed by, clanging their lockers and shouting at one another. They're not thinking about you, he reminded himself. They have their own concerns. He decided to take a shortcut to the parking lot, out the side door and across the grass. The fewer people he had to talk to, the better.

As the fresh air hit him, he felt a little bit relieved. He stopped at the stone wall that ran along the perimeter of the school and gazed out for a moment at the girls' field hockey team that was practicing down on the field. They looked so angelic, so carefree, hair flying, long legs pumping. Blissful, really. It made him hungry just to look at them. He reached absently into the pocket of his jacket and pulled out an open packet of cheese crackers. He put one in his mouth and began to chew. The cracker was stale and crumbled tastelessly on his tongue.

"Mr. Blake," came a soft voice behind him.

He swallowed the lump in his mouth and stuffed the wrapper back into his pocket. Then he turned around and saw Karla Needham. She was wrapped in a large blue-and-gray Taylorsville warm-up jacket. Her shiny, dark brown hair was a cloud around her shoulders. She was smiling at him—sad eyes, lips—the works.

"Hey, Karla," he said softly. She had one of the best figures of any girl in the school, although you could hardly see it, swaddled as she was in that duffel-type coat. He scanned her quickly, searchingly, from head to toe as she came up beside him and leaned against the wall, clutching her books to her chest and staring out at the field. Their elbows were close, resting side by side on the fieldstone. He felt his heart begin to hammer a little in spite of himself. He could not help but think about what Maddy had reported. That Heather had come by the house and accused him of having a relationship with Karla. She'd said that Karla had a crush on him.

"I'm glad you're back," Karla said.

He smiled to himself. He'd always suspected she liked him. She lit up when he came around. It was that look they gave you, cocking her head to one side. He'd seen that look on lots of girls. They were young, but they knew what they wanted. People acted as if these girls were naive, when actually their hormones were in a constant state of alert. They walked around all day, brushing up against guys, eyeing the crotch of their pants to see if they could provoke a reaction.

"Thanks," he said. "It's good to be back."

She turned around and leaned back against the wall so that she was facing him. "I don't think it was fair, what happened to you," she said.

He glanced over at her. Her dark eyes were glistening, almost as if she were going to weep.

"It's all right," he murmured. "These things happen."

"No, really," she said, and she ran the toe of her perfectly white tennis shoe around in the sooty gravel beneath their feet. The gravel seemed to sparkle like mica. She shook her thick hair over her narrow shoulders. "Everybody knew that Heather Cameron had a crush on you. We all used to tease her about it last year."

"She's a mixed-up kid," he said gently. "She has a lot

of problems and . . . I'm afraid she took out her troubles on me. . . ."

Karla gazed up at him through eyelashes that were long and curved. He could hardly take his eyes off them. "I'm glad it wasn't really true," she said.

"No," he scoffed. "It was just a fantasy she had. . . ."

"I'd hate to think about you, being with her," Karla said softly.

Doug closed his eyes and felt the familiar, dangerous need course through him. Are you crazy? he thought. How can you even let yourself think of this? You're standing here in the shadow of the school. Your enemies are waiting for you to slip, and your life seems to be crumbling around you. You can't even think about it.

But he was thinking about it. And as he thought about it, he felt the heady nectar flowing into his veins, telling him he was alive again, a hero again, a conqueror. It was as if the gods had dropped this beautiful gift in his path, and he couldn't turn away from it, no matter what.

"You want to walk with me?" he asked hoarsely.

She nodded, as if she were too overcome to speak.

He placed a hand on the small of her back, believing he could feel her skin beneath the folds of that coat. Gently, with his burning fingertips, he guided her. He looked both ways as they crossed the street, pretending to check for traffic but actually scanning the area for faculty, for students he knew. They seemed to be alone. He pressed against her gently, as if urging her to hurry, as if he couldn't wait. Actually he couldn't wait to be out of sight. After that, he would take his time. Young girls needed time, and a certain . . . finesse.

He steered her down a quiet block, lined with old houses, and toward the public garden across from a savings bank that was closed for the day. Hesitating at a pair of low fieldstone pillars, she looked up at him. He gazed into the warm liquid of her eyes and nodded, and together they entered the garden. In spring and summer this arboretum was a popular spot for visitors, but now, in the fall, it was quiet, with crisscrossing paths and lots of gaslights, bushes, and trees. It was the kind of place young girls loved to stroll, imagining romantic encounters. He had walked here with Heather at one time. He had walked here with other girls, too. It was always a good place to begin.

"This is a beautiful spot," she said.

They all said the same thing, he thought. They are all exactly alike, at once timid and excited, trembling, and waiting to be taken, unable to gather their thoughts into anything more coherent than a comment on the day or the place.

"Then it suits you," he said. They strolled down one of the pathways, one that was almost a tunnel thanks to the overhang of a bridal bower that would bloom lacy white in the spring. Beneath one of the trees was a small cement bench with scrolled sides. He pointed to it, and she walked over and sat down without speaking. He sat beside her, allowing his trousered knee to fall against her bare leg.

She looked down shyly. Her hands were crossed over her books, small and soft. He stared at them as if they were glowing. "I feel nervous," she said with a soft giggle.

"Why?" he asked. When she shook her head, he reached over and touched her hand gently, as if rubbing some sort of glowing, mystical opal that was miraculously warm to his touch.

She looked up at him, her eyes wide and melting. "I always hoped that maybe . . . that you might see me in a . . . different way."

"I think you're a beautiful girl," he said softly.

"You do?" she asked.

"Of course I do," he said. The need to have her was upon him like a wave, lifting him up, filling him with rapture. She was his for the asking. He knew he should stop, get up and walk away, but it was always the same. His very recklessness, the danger of his actions, filled him with incredible excitement. It made him high. His senses were flooded with sight and smell, like a child's. And not just the sight and smell of her. No, it was everything. The bright air, the crackling leaves, the beauty all around him that seemed drab and superfluous in his everyday life. Suddenly he was new again. For a moment he was young, a hero. He was innocent, and it was all about to start. The fulfillment of every dream danced before him. Unending pleasure and no responsibility.

When he closed his eyes, however, he saw Maddy's face, insisting on explanations and commitments. A never-ending treadmill of demands. He forced her from his mind and opened his eyes to gaze at Karla, fresh faced and adoring. It was like being transported in time. Back to a golden time. His spirits soared, and he felt the weight of his misery lifting. He reveled in pure sensual delight. If he were honest with himself, of course, youth had never been idyllic. High school romances had been fumbling and disappointing. Young manhood had brought an aching body and a lonely life on the road. The golden time he sought had never really existed for him. It was a dream of infancy, of pure bliss, of reveling in the love of an adoring woman who lived only to hold you. He had never known it. Never ever. But he sought it all the same. He had to try to know it, to seize it, or what was the use of living?

Doug reached over, feeling the shadow of the day lengthening behind him, almost touching him, and he slid his hand under the warm fleecy jacket, cupping his hand around the perfect, yielding softness of Karla's breast. At the same time he bent toward her adoring, uplifted face and sought the same yielding softness from her lips.

From the darkness of his car, parked in the quiet roadway that wound through the garden, Richie Talbot held the lens of his father's videocamera steady on the edge of the open window. "He took the bait," Richie said softly. "Good work, Heather."

"He said that was our special place," Heather said dully, sitting in the bucket seat beside Richie. She had believed all his lies, all his talk about how pretty she was and how special. She had ratted on him only because he'd told her it was over when school started this year. Now here he was, trying to do it with Karla, just like Richie said he would. Tears formed in Heather's eyes as she realized, finally, that she'd never mattered to him at all.

"We got him now," said Richie, smiling. He knew their words would be on the tape. He didn't care. One picture was worth a thousand words.

# Chapter Twenty-nine

*P*aulina stood at the well-worn oak refectory table in the kitchen, kneading bread dough on the floured surface of her bread board. She pushed and pulled at the sticky mass under her fingers, trying to turn it into something smooth and satiny, as she had been taught, as she had done a thousand times before. When she put her weight onto the heels of her hands and they sank into the dough, some of the heaviness from her heart seemed to lift.

The door to the kitchen swung open, and Charles Henson stood in the doorway, his face as pale as the flour on her fingers.

"I got away as fast as I could," he said. "Is she still out there?"

Paulina nodded and glanced out the window again.

"I called the chief after I spoke to you. I let them know exactly what I thought of his tactics. I promised him that they are going to be sorry they messed with me. How could they even think . . . ? The girl was murdered, you know."

Paulina nodded. "I heard."

"As if she would ever hurt anyone, or anything. It's outrageous."

They were both silent for a few minutes. Then he said, "How did she take it?"

"She was upset. Then she answered the phone, and she went out there," said Paulina, inclining her head toward the playhouse.

Charles's shoulders sank, his indignation seeping away. "I've spoken to a psychiatrist, you know," he said. "The same doctor she saw years ago. She liked him at the time. He has a very good reputation," Charles said earnestly. "I told him all about it, and he thinks he can help her."

"She won't go," Paulina said.

"She's going to have to, Paulina. I don't know what else to do."

Paulina sank her hands farther into the dough. "That's between you and her," she said.

"Do you blame me? I only want to help her. You know that."

"I know," she said. "It's nobody's fault."

Charles walked over to the window and looked out at the playhouse. "I guess I'll go out and try to talk to her."

Paulina didn't look up. She didn't want to see the expression on his face.

Charles opened the back door to the kitchen and let himself out, pulling it shut behind him. On leaden feet he walked down the little garden path to the playhouse. He could remember when the carpenters were finished with the playhouse, when they put the last daub of paint on the door and declared it done. Kenny had been over the moon with delight at his new hideout. It was a man's kind of hideout, Charles had explained to his son as they had walked hand in hand between banks of flowers down this very path. Kenny had suggested that it was like Pooh's house in the hundred-acre wood, and Charles had agreed that that was the very thing.

Though the day was gray, Charles could almost feel that warm little hand in his again, feel the sun on his shoulders, blessing his head. He'd been thirty-five years old when Ken was born, and he had not taken his son for granted— not a moment of his son's short life had Charles been too distracted, too busy, to savor the joy of it. Charles had loved being a father. That had been some comfort to him in the years since. He tried to think of that time as a gift that had been given to them. A gift that they had truly appreciated.

When he reached the door to the playhouse, he did the only thing that seemed appropriate. He knocked.

"Who is it?" she called out from inside.

She sounded normal, almost gay, and even that filled him with dread. What did it all mean? Was this the manic prelude to the next breakdown? He did not want her to have to go away again. He wasn't certain she would ever come back to him. He remembered those days when she was in the hospital as some of the worst of his life. When he went to see her, she would just stare at him as if she didn't recognize him. When he got home, no one was there to greet him. "It's me, darling," said Charles, and his love for her reverberated in his anxious voice.

"Come in," she said.

He opened the door and ducked down so that he could enter the little house. It took his eyes a moment to adjust. She was seated on the floor, on a quilt, her knees pulled up to her chest. A little candle lantern cast a faint glow. She patted the quilt beside her.

"Come and sit down," she said.

"Why don't you come back to the house, darling," he said. "It's chilly out here."

"No," she said. "I wouldn't have thought of it, but this is perfect. Come and sit here with me."

She looked almost young in the candlelight, he thought. Her curls were tipped with gold, and her face also seemed to glow. She looked strangely peaceful. It frightened him more than if she had been raving.

"I know you have a good suit on," she said.

"I don't care about that," he said, pulling up the knife-sharp pleat on his fine worsted wool trousers and crossing his glossy wing-tip shoes beneath him, Indian style. "I only care about you," he said. "Paulina told me about the police coming here."

Ellen nodded sadly. "They are trying to find the baby," she said.

"I'm so sorry that they harassed you, darling, that I wasn't here to throw them out."

"It's all right," she said, taking his hand. "I don't blame them."

"Why don't you come in the house," he said gently. "We'll have some sherry. Take the chill off."

She smiled at him and reached out, running her fingers over his perfectly combed white hair. "You're still so handsome," she said.

He looked at her, puzzled. "You're still my beauty," he said.

"We're not young," she said.

"No."

"Charles, I have to tell you something. I have been

keeping something from you," she said. "I've suspected it for a while, but yesterday, at the hospital, I saw the doctor . . ."

His palms broke out in a sweat as he panicked. Of course she was acting strange. She said she was afraid. How could I be so dense? he thought. She's sick. Not mentally sick. Physically sick. Of course. It all made sense to him now. Cancer, he thought. It ran in her family. Cancer. "Oh no," he groaned.

She shook her head. "No," she said, reading his mind. "I'm not sick. I'm . . . pregnant."

His mind careened back to the mentally unbalanced diagnosis. He stared at her, trying to make his expression unreadable so she wouldn't know what he was thinking.

"I know," she said. "That's what I thought. When I first had the symptoms I thought it must be some terrible sickness. Or that I was imagining it. You know, my mind playing tricks on me. Then I started to suspect. It was as if it were a cruel trick of the universe. You know, one last turn of the screw to torture me."

"But you're too . . ."

"Old," she said, smiling. "You can say it. I thought the same thing."

"All these years . . . we never were able . . ."

"I know," she said. "I know." She grabbed his hands and squeezed them so hard that he felt the pain, marveled at her strength. "But it's true. Do you understand what I'm telling you?" she said. "Despite everything, we're going to have a baby."

"Oh, my God," he said. He struggled to unfold his aching legs to get near her. It seemed appropriate to be sitting here, in this playhouse, for he felt as terrified as a child. A tiny child all over again. "Oh, my God. Ellen."

She laughed. A bright, uncomplicated laugh.

"But . . . at your . . . age. The odds. So much could go wrong." He didn't want to start imagining it. All he could feel was terror.

Indulgently she grasped his hands. "I know how you feel. I've been feeling it for weeks. But I'm past all that now," she said. "I've had every fear that there is to have. But you know," she whispered, "all of a sudden it's gone. The doctor called this morning, just after the policeman left. He said everything looks good. I need to take extra hormones. Can you imagine? As simple as that? Just some hormones. And vitamins, of course. It's amazing. Isn't it amazing? I've been sitting in this playhouse since then. Remembering. Remembering everything. And making plans. You know what, Charles? I'm not afraid anymore. I feel at peace. I'm certain. This is our miracle, darling."

"Ellen, what if . . . we can't know."

"What is there to know?" she said sensibly. "All will be revealed to us in time. We have to go forward and see what God has in store for us. I have to have all those tests they give to women my age. To find out if the baby is all right. I know in my heart the baby is all right. In no time at all we'll be able to watch on a screen. They have this machine called a sonogram. The doctor said he could tell us whether it was a boy or a girl. I said I wouldn't want to know. Is that okay?" she asked him gently. "I said it didn't matter at all to us."

For a moment Charles sat there, feeling stunned, disembodied almost. If she had told him she was going to die, he doubted he would feel any stranger. He crawled into her arms and let her hold him as his fears and hopes began to flash through him, shaking him like a fever.

They came in waves, crests and troughs, one after another, rolling over him. Through it all she held him, and rocked him, and crooned to him that she understood, and promised him that everything would be all right.

# *Chapter Thirty*

*L*en Wickes, still in uniform, zippered up his leather jacket and began to walk down the winding pathways of Binney Park. The park was a study in deep green and gray, quiet except for the occasional cry of a bird and the thud of runners' feet as a couple jogged by. Len did not meet their eyes. He felt as if they might look at him and shake their heads sadly. He felt as if the whole world knew of his humiliation.

He had returned to the station house, all set to communicate his suspicions about Ellen Henson, only to find Chief Cameron having an apoplectic fit. Not only Charles Henson but some of the other women he had interviewed had called to complain to the chief. Instead of kudos for his extra effort, he had received a blistering condemnation and a week's suspension without pay.

How am I ever going to tell Laurie? Len thought. She was still at work at the beauty shop, but when she got home and found him there . . . Len sighed. She had been so excited when he'd brought home copies of the lists and started working on them. She thought it was admirable the way he did that extra bit that wasn't actually required. She looked up to him for being a cop, and a good cop at that. It pained him to think how she'd feel when she found out. She was always so proud of him.

He still couldn't understand why what he had done was so wrong. He was not used to being reprimanded. If anything, people teased him for being something of a Boy Scout, but he didn't mind. He had joined the police force to help people. When something happened, like the death of Rebecca Starnes and the disappearance of the Wallace baby, it upset him more than it did some people. It was an insult to everything he was trying to do with his life. All he wanted to do, with every fiber of his being, was solve this case.

Len walked aimlessly beside the duck pond, not knowing where else to go. He saw a green-headed mallard gliding lazily across the surface. A mother sat on a park bench, watching her little son play with a sailboat at the edge of the pond. Len and the woman smiled at each other, and Len stopped for a minute to gaze at the boy. Someday, he thought, I hope I have a son. He and Laurie would be good parents. Len was sure of that. Thinking of Laurie made him feel sad and frustrated again. God, he hated to have to tell her this.

The kid was having a little trouble keeping the boat from turning over. Len crouched beside him, showed him how to right the boat and keep it from tipping, then straightened up again. He nodded to the woman on the bench and walked on. Maybe I'll go over to the 7-Eleven, he thought, and get a cup of coffee. He didn't feel like going home. He was a cop. What was there to do at home?

He started to cut across the clearing on the other side

of the pond, his head down, his hands stuffed in his pants pockets, and nearly collided with a man who was standing on one foot, his hands and arms creating the shape of an L in the air.

" 'Scuse me," Len mumbled, moving to skirt the man. He stopped dead in his tracks and turned around. The man had shifted to another, less precarious posture. Len watched him in amazement, as if he were a phantom. The police had scoured this park at all hours and looked up every person of Asian extraction in the town of Taylorsville, to no avail. Every person they spoke to had heard about the abduction, the death of Rebecca Starnes, and some even acknowledged an interest in tai chi, but not one had ever done exercises in Binney Park at all, much less on the day in question.

It's him, Len thought, and the excitement hit him like an electric shock. He's the one. He's here. Carefully Len turned back and walked up to the man. "Excuse me," he said, trying to keep his voice casual. "Could I talk to you for a minute?"

The man's broad, calm face crinkled into a frown, and his black eyes looked suspicious. He stood up very straight, but his hands and arms were slightly bent in a stance of readiness. "Yes," he said in a deep voice.

"My name is Officer Leonard Wickes of the Taylorsville Police Department," said Len, crossing his fingers since technically he was off the force as of this moment. "I'd like to ask you a few questions that concern the death of Rebecca Starnes and the abduction of Justin Wallace."

"I don't know anything about that," protested the man.

"Is that tai chi you're doing?" Len asked.

"That's right."

"Do you do these exercises in this park very often?"

The man nodded. "When I'm in town. I travel a lot on business."

"Well, Mr. um . . ."

"Ishikawa," the man said a trifle reluctantly.

"Mr. Ishikawa . . . is that a Chinese name?"

"Japanese. My parents are Japanese. I am an American," the man said pointedly with just a hint of impatience.

"Japanese, then," said Len. "Do you live here in Taylorsville?"

"Yes," he said. "I live in those apartments over there."

"So you must have heard about what happened here Tuesday."

"No, I'm sorry, I don't know much about what's been going on in town lately. I've been away. What happened?"

Out of town, Len exulted to himself. That explains it. No wonder he didn't come forward. He's been out of town. Len felt his heart lifting, soaring. He'd found the missing witness. He could hardly wait to tell the chief. They'd put him back on the force right away. They'd have to. "So you've been away on business," Len said in a friendly manner.

"No, actually," the man said, "I had tickets to the last game of the Series."

Len's mouth dropped open, his problems and his purpose for the moment forgotten in his amazement at this piece of news. "The World Series? You got tickets? You went?"

Mr. Ishikawa nodded a little sheepishly, acknowledging the admiration in the other man's tone. "I'm a big baseball fan," he said.

"Wow," Len said solemnly. "Wow."

Donna and Johnny Wallace sat stolidly in the chairs in front of Frank Cameron's desk and stared at the police chief with angry, bleary eyes. Frank, who had had almost as little sleep as the distraught parents, tried to reassure them that he was doing everything that could be done.

Johnny Wallace jumped up in the middle of Frank's reassurances and started screaming. "We don't want excuses," he cried. "We want our baby back!"

"I understand," said Frank. "We want the same thing. But all we can do, unless we hear from the kidnapper, is to proceed as we are doing. Checking out every possible suspect. Every possible lead. Now, my question is, what are both of you doing here? What if the kidnapper should call with a ransom demand while you are both here?"

"I couldn't stand to sit there anymore," Donna said apologetically.

"Don't try to make out like this is our fault," Johnny cried.

"It's not my fault, either, sir," said Frank, just barely keeping a lid on his hostility.

"He's right," Donna said wearily to her husband. "One of us should be at home." She got up from her seat, fresh tears running in well-formed tracks down her cheeks. "You'll call us, right, Chief?" she asked in a dull voice.

"If there's anything . . . anything at all," Frank said, putting a gentle hand on her shoulder. He really did feel for her. For both of them, whether they knew it or not.

The phone on his desk rang, and Frank looked at it warily. In between busting his butt trying to get a lead on

the fate of Justin Wallace, he had been wasting his precious time on damage control as one irate citizen after another had called to complain about Len Wickes's
outrageous interrogations. Frank was half waiting to hear
from Charles Henson again. Frank had chewed out Len
Wickes sixteen ways from Sunday when he'd found out
about how Len had taken it upon himself to correlate the
adoption data and use strong-arm techniques on the people who had tried hardest, and with the least success, to
adopt a baby. As much as Frank needed every available
officer, he could not let that kind of hot-dog behavior go
unpunished. Len had slunk out of the station house, almost slope shouldered in disgrace.

Frank picked up the phone as if it were a hand grenade
minus the pin and barked out his name and rank. To his
relief, he heard the voice of Pete Millard on the other end.
Pete had been out checking up on the efforts of the div-
ing team that was searching the lake in the state forest,
looking for the little body of Justin Wallace. So far, nothing. Frank didn't know whether he wanted to convey this
information to the Wallaces or not. As long as there was
no body, there was still hope. But the image of a baby
drowned and tangled in the muddy grass of a lakebed
might be more than Donna Wallace wanted to contemplate right now.

"When are we ever going to get a break on this?"
Frank demanded irritably.

Pete knew it wasn't an actual question. "I'm going to
get back to it," he said.

"Keep me posted," said Frank, hanging up as Delilah
Jones stuck her head in the door.

"What is it?" he growled at the cadet.

Delilah smiled like the Cheshire cat. "Len's here," she said.

Frank pushed himself up from his chair. "I told that ignorant—"

"You're going to like it," she said, beckoning to him with one polished fingernail.

Frank never could get used to those red nails with the severe blue uniform. He scowled, but his heart lifted. Delilah would never dare to announce that Len Wickes was back in the station house unless she was absolutely sure this was good news. Frank assumed his steeliest expression and strode out of his office.

Len Wickes was standing next to Rocco Belmont's desk. He winced slightly at the sight of the scowling chief but held his ground. Seated next to him, in Detective Belmont's chair, was a good-looking Asian man in his late twenties, wearing a warm-up suit. Frank glared at Len.

"What do you want?" he said.

"Chief, I'd like you to meet Mr. Tom Ishikawa. I found him in Binney Park doing his tai chi exercises."

"You're suspended," Frank reminded him. Then he turned to Mr. Ishikawa, who had risen politely from the chair, and said gruffly, "How do you do?"

"Mr. Ishikawa was in the park the day Rebecca Starnes and Justin Wallace disappeared," said Len. "He saw them."

Frank turned his laser gaze on the witness. "Is that right?"

"I saw them."

"We've been looking for you. Don't you read the papers?"

"He's been away," Len said apologetically.

"So, did you see them talking to anyone?" Frank demanded.

Mr. Ishikawa nodded. "A man."

"Can you describe the man?"

Len and Delilah exchanged a glance. Len took a deep breath, and Delilah smiled broadly, ready for the pièce de résistance.

"Well, actually, I know him," said Tom.

Frank stared at him in disbelief.

"Well, I don't exactly know him. But I know who he is. He played two years on a farm team and one full season at first base for the Philadelphia Phillies. His name is Doug Blake."

Frank felt the blood drain from his face as he leaned over against the desk. "Are you sure about this?" he said quietly.

"Positive," said the baseball fan.

"Son of a bitch," Frank muttered.

"He told us he wasn't there," Len said proudly.

Frank straightened up and nodded. "Thank you for coming forward, Mr. Ishikawa. Please be sure and leave a number where we can reach you."

Tom looked uncertainly at Len, as if to say, "Is that all?" Len nodded, and Frank went back into his office, barking orders out the door. "Jones, get me Pete Millard on the phone. Now. Wickes, you're back on duty. Don't fuck up again. You come with me. We're going to go out and pay a call on Mr. Douglas Blake." His voice dripped venom at the suspect's name.

"Dad, Dad," cried Heather.

Frank, who was pulling on his jacket, looked up to see his daughter in the doorway, flanked by two other teenagers.

"Not now, Heather," he said. "I've got something important to do."

Heather's face fell at being dismissed without even a word of greeting, but Richie Talbot had no emotional hangups about Chief Cameron. "I think you're going to be interested in this, sir," he said.

Frank frowned at the videotape in the boy's hand. "What is that?" he demanded suspiciously.

Richie Talbot waved the videotape in the air as if Frank were about to grab at it. "It's a special feature," he said.

"I don't have time for games, boy," Frank said menacingly.

"It's Mr. Douglas Blake. Caught in the act."

Frank looked greedily at the black plastic box. "What exactly do you mean by that?" he asked.

"Have you got a VCR?" Richie said with a broad smile. "I think you'll find it very interesting."

Frank Cameron rubbed his jaw and looked at Delilah and Len, who were crowded behind the teenagers in the doorway. "I think we have time for this," he said.

# Chapter Thirty-one

Maddy opened the back door to the house and walked in. It was no use trying to work. She had been out in her studio, staring at the templates, trying in vain to concentrate. She and Doug had gone to bed at separate times last night, without speaking. This morning he had seemed contrite and asked her to wish him well as he headed back to school. She had tried to summon up some sincere good wishes for his difficult reentry, but all she could think about was his fingers tightening on her wrist, the malevolence in his eyes when he'd turned on her.

"Mrs. Blake?"

Maddy jumped at the sound of the voice behind her as she hung up her jacket. It was Terry Lewis. Bonnie had gone off to buy diapers and baby food at the grocery store and to check out some nearby motels for a possible place to stay. Maddy looked anxiously at Terry. The man was an ex-con after all, and Maddy did not feel entirely comfortable being alone with him. "What?" she asked defensively.

"Sean fell asleep on the couch," he said. "And I can't

really lift him. Would you mind carrying him up to his crib?"

Maddy felt a huge sense of relief at the normalcy of his request. "Sure," she said. "I'll be happy to."

She went into the living room, Terry creeping slowly down the hall behind her. Sean was fast asleep on the couch, his mouth open as he breathed through his rosebud lips. His long eyelashes fluttered on his cheeks. His short, soft hair was damp and curly. When she reached down and picked him up, he fell heavily against her.

"I thought I would rest awhile, while he's sleeping," said Terry.

Maddy rubbed Sean gently on the back and started for the stairs. "That's a good idea," she said. She carried Sean up to the guest room and laid him down gently in the crib. The room was tidy, the bags were packed. Bonnie had seen to that before she went out. Sean grasped a wad of quilt in his tiny hand and slept on peacefully.

Maddy closed the door on him and started back down the hallway. Suddenly she heard Terry calling her name again, this time in an urgent whisper from the foot of the stairs. "What is it?" she asked, hurrying, responding to the anxiety in his voice.

"The police are here," he said. "What are they here for?"

Maddy came down the stairs, her face drawn and angry. "I don't know," she said, although she was filled with apprehension.

"I don't really want to tangle with the police anymore," said Terry.

Maddy nodded. "It's probably about the accident," she said, trying to reassure him and herself.

"I'll go in there," he said, pointing to the little TV room down the hall.

Maddy didn't care where he went. All her attention was focused on the banging at her door, the black-and-white car she could see in her driveway. She composed herself as best she could and opened the door. Chief Cameron stood there, accompanied by a detective in a rumpled suit and a uniformed officer.

"Chief Cameron," Maddy said coldly. "Not again."

"Oh yes, again," he said, pushing his way into the foyer.

"Hey," Maddy protested. "I didn't ask you in."

"Where is your husband?" the chief demanded.

"I don't know," said Maddy. "Probably working late at school. But I think I'm going to call my lawyer, because you cannot keep on harassing us like this." She sounded defiant, but she felt a hard little knot in her stomach. Where the hell was Doug? she wondered. Why didn't he come home right after school?

"You better call a lawyer, 'cause you're going to need one," said the chief with grim satisfaction.

"What's this all about?" Maddy asked.

"About the murder of Rebecca Starnes, for starters. We have a witness who saw your husband engaged in an intense discussion with Ms. Starnes in the park shortly before she died. You know, when he said he hadn't been anywhere near her or the park that day?"

Maddy's heart was pounding. Maybe it was another bluff. "So what," she said, sticking out her chin. "Maybe your witness is mistaken. The last one was, as I recall."

Chief Cameron squinted down at her. "Look, Mrs. Blake. You don't know this yet, but you are about to find out. You believed all his lies about my daughter. I don't blame you for that. But I'm warning you to prepare yourself. The bad news is about to hit the fan." He could hardly contain his glee, and his certainty was terrifying.

The detective in the suit was scrutinizing the house as if he were planning to rent it. The uniformed officer was looking at her with a combination of scorn and pity. Maddy felt a rising panic. "My husband is not here," she said through clenched teeth. "Now will you please leave?"

At that moment the phone rang. "Maybe that's your hubby now," Frank Cameron said unkindly.

Maddy walked to the phone and picked it up stiffly. "Hello?" she said.

"Hello, Maddy. I'm on my way home and I thought I'd pick up a movie for us at the video place. Is there something you'd like to see?"

Maddy flinched at the sound of his voice. Warm and cajoling. Eager to make amends. "Hello, Ruth," she said. "Do you want me to come and get Amy?"

"What's the matter?" Doug asked in alarm. Then he said, "Are the police there?"

How does he know? she thought. Why would he expect the police to be here? What is happening? "Yes," she said.

"Oh Jesus," he cried.

"Where are you?" she said.

There was a silence at his end.

"I'll come and get her right now if you'll tell me where to meet you," Maddy said.

He was silent, thinking.

"Oh no, Ruth, I insist," said Maddy.

"All right. At the fort. By the guardhouse."

Fort Wynadot. It was a historical site that attracted lots

of summer visitors. The scene of some battles between Indians and local settlers in colonial days. It would be pretty deserted now. "Okay," she said. "At St. Anne's. Say, fifteen minutes."

He hung up the phone without replying. Bastard, she thought. I want some answers before the police whisk you away, before Charles Henson starts telling you what to say. She hung up the phone and returned to the foyer. "I have to go and pick up my daughter," she said.

"Someone's smoking in there," said Frank Cameron.

"We have a guest," said Maddy.

"Pete," said the chief, indicating for the detective to go and look in the room down the hall.

Pete Millard walked down the hall and pushed open the door to the TV room. Terry Lewis sat hunched forward on the couch, puffing nervously on an unfiltered cigarette. Pete frowned at the man with the rugged, outlaw appearance.

"How ya doin', brother," Terry said anxiously, glancing up and meeting the detective's eyes for a moment.

Pete did not answer. He contemplated Terry suspiciously, then returned to the foyer. "It's not him," he said.

"I have to go," said Maddy. "My daughter is waiting for me."

"All right, go," said Frank, spreading his arms wide as if making a pathway for her. "Don't let us stop you."

She got her jacket, thinking that the first thing she had to do, when she got out of their sight, was to call Ruth Crandall and actually arrange to pick up Amy. She didn't want Ruth coming by with her while the cops were here, catching her in a lie. She tried to think. There was a phone booth at the convenience store around the corner. She could stop on her way to the fort. She wondered if Doug would be at the fort. She wondered what would happen if the police did catch her in a lie. They couldn't arrest her for that, could they? What did they really know? What was the truth?

Frank Cameron watched her get ready suspiciously. "I'm using your phone," he announced as she checked her purse carefully for her wallet and her keys.

"Help yourself," she said unnecessarily, for he was already punching in the number. He looked down at her, standing by the door, jingling her keys. Waiting for them to leave.

"I feel sorry for you, lady," he said. "Take my advice and cut him loose. That way the crud won't get all over you and the kid."

Maddy called back to Terry in what she hoped was a normal voice, "Terry, I have to go out for a while. To get Amy. I'll be back."

She ignored his muttered reply. She stepped out onto the front steps, where the three officers were conferring. Just then another officer came tearing up the street in a black-and-white, his siren wailing.

Great, Maddy thought. Let the whole neighborhood know. Then she shuddered. It sounded as if they would know soon enough anyway. She got into her car, reminding herself of her plan, her route. First the convenience store, to call Ruth. She had her address book in her purse. Then, the fort. She looked at her watch. She would be there in fifteen minutes. No longer. In fifteen minutes he was going to have to tell her. She was going to make him tell her everything.

# Chapter Thirty-two

*F*ort Wynadot, or what remained of it, sat on a hill-top in the middle of a nature preserve on the outskirts of Taylorsville. From its ramparts you could see the Hudson River, and many a fantasy game of Davy Crockett and the Deerslayer had been played out atop its timbered walls. There were old cannons, small, dense, and unwieldy, that small children loved to sit astride or pretend to fire, although they were inoperable now.

For those with a more strictly historical perspective, there were tours in the summer, with student guides dressed in buckskin outfits to lend an air of authenticity. The grounds and woods were popular with picnickers whenever the weather was good. Today, late on a gloomy fall afternoon, the fort and the park were deserted. Maddy drove slowly through the wooded roads of the preserve and pulled into the lot nearest the foot of the hill, parking her car beside Doug's. She got out and looked around. No sign of him. He had said he would be at the fort, but he did not hail her, so she trudged up the hill.

When she reached the top, she looked around. From

this distance the Hudson looked like a tiny stream, threading its silver way through a dusty green-and-brown valley. She walked around the perimeter of the fort, wondering where in the world he was and feeling more and more angry at the hide-and-seek game he seemed to be playing.

"Doug," she called out sharply.

The third time she called, he answered. "Up here." She looked up and saw him in one of the corners of the fort, leaning against one of those long-distance viewers that cost a quarter and inevitably snapped off as soon as you located what you wanted to look at.

"Come down here," Maddy demanded.

"Why don't you come up," he said. "The view's great from up here. The stairs are right inside."

"I'm in no mood for a view," she said icily.

He took a last, longing look at the landscape, and then, with an expression of resignation on his face, temporarily disappeared from sight. He emerged a minute later from the gate of the fort. She stood waiting for him, her arms folded over her chest.

He came over to her and gave her a dutiful peck on the cheek. Then he pointed to a bench on the nearby path. "Shall we sit?" he said.

"No," said Maddy.

"So that's how it's going to be," he said wearily. "Okay."

"Okay?" she demanded. "Okay? I had to ditch the chief of police to come up here."

"What do the police want?"

"They want to talk to you," she said.

"Really? Why?" he asked ingenuously.

"You know why. Don't pretend you don't."

"No. I don't," he said. "All right? I don't."

"It's about Rebecca Starnes. They have a witness who saw you talking to her just before she was killed."

Doug snorted. "That's what they said before. Remember? I better get on the phone to Henson. More hoops to jump through. This is ridiculous."

"If it's so ridiculous, why are you hiding out here?" said Maddy.

"Hey, you were the one who pretended I was Ruth Crandall when I called. I don't know what you're up to. Don't get me wrong. I think it was nice of you to try to protect me. Very wifely of you." He tried to pat her on the shoulder, but she jerked away from him.

"Don't flatter yourself. I'm not trying to protect you. I'm here because I don't want to be the last to know what really happened."

"You know what happened," Doug protested. "That insane police chief is on a vendetta against me because his daughter was exposed for the liar that she is."

"Are you sure she was lying, Doug?" she said.

Doug glanced at her bitterly. "I wondered when you'd turn on me. God knows, it's not easy living with you," he said. "Saint Madeline."

She had the sudden, stunning certainty that her marriage was on the line. For a moment she wanted to walk away and not pursue this any further. A marriage was such a complicated intertwining of lives. She and Doug were woven together by a thousand separate strands of words, time, and memories. If she interrogated him no further, continued to believe in him, maybe the ties that bound them would hold, would not break. There was a desperate voice inside, clamoring for her to hold on to her marriage. Not to light the fuse that would blast her life apart. They had a child, a home, a life. If she stopped questioning him now, maybe . . .

But it was a fleeting thought. How long could she live in the dark? Faith in another person wasn't something you could fake. She had seen things in him lately, ugly depths that frightened her. She had suspicions. More than suspicions. Grave doubts. And all his sarcasm didn't make her feel like forgetting it. If anything, it had the perverse effect of making her want to pursue it.

"You know what your problem is?" he said. "Your problem is that you're frustrated because your boyfriend the priest got away. I shouldn't have interfered. I should have let you two get on with it. You were much nicer when you had him to cuddle up to."

She looked at him and wondered why she had ever thought he was handsome. He looked washed out, featureless, in the fading light. "Insulting me is not going to get you off the hook," she said coldly. "I want to know the truth."

Doug glared at her. "This doesn't come as any surprise to me. I've known for a long time that you didn't believe in me. You've been dying to say it. So, go ahead. Say it."

Was it true? she wondered. Was he right? She had tried to believe him, because she wanted to believe him so much. How many times the image of him entangled in the arms of that sullen schoolgirl had come into her mind and she had willed it away. It was either believe him or face the fact that her marriage was coming unglued. She shook her head. "You're wrong," she said. "I did want to believe you—more than anything."

"Well, wanting to and doing it are two different things," he fumed.

He was looking out over the slope of the hill into the

trees, glowering, his arms folded over his chest. Her own heart was beating furiously, partly from anger, partly from fear. Fear because once these things were said, they would never be taken back; things would never be as they were. She thought of Amy and wondered what she should do for Amy. This was her father. She had a right to be proud of her father. Not to have him trashed by her mother. But it was no use. Maddy had to live with herself.

"I did believe in you. But I'm afraid that was a mistake on my part."

He looked at her, vaguely surprised that his tactic of taking the offense hadn't derailed her anger. She had never seemed particularly tough to him. In fact, he remembered thinking, when he met her, that she was gentle and pliable. He never would have married her if he had known about her steely side. He'd had enough of dominating women with his mother. Enough to last a lifetime. But, sadly, over these years together, he had come to see that Maddy had the same tendencies as all the rest of them.

It was always the same way with women. They started out sweet and eager to please, and in the end they were cold and they never gave way. It was the nature of the beast. They loved nothing better than to punish you.

Standing here now, gazing at his defiant wife, Doug felt a sudden sense of detachment, of release, that he had not expected. It didn't matter what she thought about him. He didn't care whether she believed him or not. None of it really mattered anymore. He had fought it all he was going to.

Maddy frowned at him. "What is it, Doug?"

"Does everyone think the way you do?" he asked. "I

mean, if your own wife sees you that way, doesn't it follow that the whole world will?"

Maddy sighed and shook her head. "I don't know what you're asking, Doug."

He did not reply, but started down the hill toward his car.

"Wait a minute," said Maddy. "You can't just walk away from me."

She rushed after him, stumbling as she made her way down the hill. As she reached the car, he turned around to face her. "Everyone's going to be saying the same thing," he said.

"Douglas Blake," said a voice behind them.

They both turned around at once. It was Chief Cameron, flanked by three other officers.

Maddy and Doug looked at each other.

"Well, you didn't think we believed that corny old ploy about picking up your daughter," said the chief. "I wasn't born yesterday, you know."

# Chapter Thirty-three

*M*addy stared in disbelief as the police chief yanked Doug by the arm toward the police cruiser.

Doug looked back at Maddy ruefully. "What did you do? Leave a trail of crumbs? Thanks a lot."

Her face flamed at his accusation. "I didn't tell them anything. Doug . . ."

"She tried the little ploy about talking to the baby-sitter," said Frank Cameron. "You don't really think we're that stupid, do you?"

"Good work, Maddy," Doug said tiredly.

Frank Cameron, who still had Doug by the arm, gave him a teeth-rattling shake. "Shut up, you asshole," he cried.

"Easy, Frank," Pete said in a soothing voice, looking around the empty grounds to make sure they weren't being observed.

"You've got a lot of fucking nerve blaming your wife. She was trying to protect you, you slimy bastard."

"Just take him," said Pete.

"Maddy, call Charles Henson," said Doug. "Tell him the cops are harassing me again."

"Harassing you," Frank cried. He pulled Doug up close to him so that their noses were practically touching.

"That's good," Doug said defiantly. "I want your fingerprints in black and blue all over my arms. It'll prove my point."

Frank Cameron only gripped him harder. "Don't play chicken with me, little boy. You are bound to lose."

"Keep it up," said Doug. "Police brutality. People don't look kindly on that, you know. The man in the street doesn't want to be bullied by cops."

"Frank, he's right," Pete interjected. "Let's not give this slimeball a technicality to walk away on."

"Doesn't my husband have the right to have an attorney present?" Maddy asked, rallying to Doug's defense from long habit.

"How much does she know about you?" Frank demanded. "The good little wife who runs around trying to shield you."

"There's nothing to know," said Doug. "Your daughter's a liar."

"What about Karla Needham? Does she know about Karla Needham? Does she know that you were trying to screw another schoolgirl just this afternoon?"

Doug's face turned pale.

"Who is Karla Needham?" Maddy asked. "Doug?"

"Nobody," Doug said. "He's blowing hot air."

A broad, satisfied smile spread across Frank Cameron's face. "Gotcha, didn't I? You didn't realize you weren't alone this afternoon."

"What's he talking about, Doug?" Maddy demanded.

Doug just shook his head. "Go call Charles Henson. He'll get this pack of wolves off of me."

Frank turned to Maddy. "Do you really want to know? Because I'll be happy to tell you."

Pete took Frank gently by the arm. "Come on, Frank. You know this isn't procedure."

Frank angrily shook off the detective's arm. "This isn't official. It's personal." He looked at Maddy, and his eyes frightened her. They were full of pain and intensity. "He made my daughter look like a liar and a sick, messed-up kid. Now, I haven't been the best father in the world. I admit it. But it hurt me all the same. I felt for my kid, and there was nothing I could do. And you, you wanted to believe him. I could see you were trying not to believe a word that Heather said."

"The judge didn't believe her, either," Maddy reminded him.

"He preys on them. He's a vulture. I think he was preying on Rebecca Starnes. But she wasn't having any of it. I think it made him real mad. Mad enough to kill. I think we'll be able to prove it."

Maddy put her hands over her ears. "He's right," she said. "You are harassing him. This is just more speculation. . . ."

"Yeah, well, Karla Needham isn't speculation," said Frank.

"Who is Karla Needham?"

Frank looked at her almost sympathetically. "Karla Needham and Heather have known each other since kindergarten. Karla and her friend Richie Talbot believed Heather. They knew she wasn't lying. They just wanted to prove it."

"Don't listen to him, Maddy," Doug pleaded.

Maddy stared at the chief, wondering what was coming. "How could they prove it? It was your daughter's word against Doug's."

Frank shook his head. "Not anymore," he said. "Now we've got it on a videotape. This afternoon, your husband was looking for somebody new, somebody young, to make him forget his troubles. Karla Needham was there."

"You're lying," Doug cried.

Frank turned and stared at him. "They brought us the tape. That Richie Talbot makes a pretty good photographer. You look like a regular movie star, with your paws all over her, up her skirt, under her blouse."

Doug's eyes narrowed. "You can't use it in court. I was entrapped. . . . Maddy, call Charles and tell him they are holding me without any legally obtained evidence. . . ."

Maddy backed away from him. "You admit it. . . ."

"Actually, I can," said Frank. "You see, it's admissible in court, as long as the police didn't make the tape."

"You're lying," Doug cried. "You've got no right to take me in."

"We're not here about the tape. You see, we have a witness," said Frank, "who saw you involved in a conversation with Rebecca Starnes just before she died. You know, the day you were nowhere near the park. The witness is a baseball fan. He remembered you from your days in the majors."

Doug's face was an expressionless mask as he absorbed this news.

Frank smacked Doug so hard against his shoulder that he lost his balance. "So where's the baby, asshole? What happened to the baby?"

"The baby?" Maddy cried. "No, wait. That's impossible."

Frank pushed Doug again, so that he banged into the car. "What did you do to the baby? His mother can't stand up much longer under the strain," Frank told him through clenched teeth.

Maddy stared at her husband.

"Don't just stand there, Maddy," Doug cried. "Call Charles."

"Doug," she said. "You didn't . . . you wouldn't have." A horrible thought dawned on her. "Do you know where that baby is?"

"You bitch," said Doug. "Just call my lawyer."

Frank raised his fist and Pete Millard grabbed his arm to prevent him from smacking Doug across the face. "Don't do it, Chief," he whispered urgently. "You've said too much already. Don't give him any more ammunition."

Maddy turned away from them and doubled over, wrapping her arms around her waist.

Frank nodded to Pete. "Put him in the car."

Frank planted himself in front of her and waited until she looked at him. "You're not going to get him back until I find out what happened to Justin Wallace."

"I don't want him back," Maddy said dully.

"I won't lie to you and say I'm sorry to be the one to tell you," said Frank.

"No," Maddy mumbled. "I'm sure you're not."

"You have a daughter. Maybe you can understand. . . ."

"He wouldn't have harmed that baby," Maddy whispered.

"You don't know him like you think. You don't know what he'd do," said Frank.

"You're not lying about this tape," she said.

"You're welcome to look at it, if you want to. You

know, according to Heather's shrink, guys like your husband have a compulsion. In a way, they want to be caught. They like the danger. I mean, this was more than a stupid chance he took with Karla Needham. It was his very first day back at school. It was like he was trying to get caught. Maybe so he could be punished."

Maddy nodded numbly.

"I'm going to be glad to be the one to punish him. Do you want someone to drive you home? You look a little shaky."

"I can do it," said Maddy. She walked over to her car and opened the door.

"It might be safer if one of us drove you," Frank said.

"I can manage on my own," said Maddy. "I'm going to have to."

Frank shrugged, acknowledging the truth of her words. He walked over to the police car, where the others were waiting for him, and got inside. In a few moments the two cars pulled away. Maddy fell to her knees on the ground, the dirt and pebbles gouging into her knees. For a while she knelt there without moving, staring unseeing at the bleak landscape around her.

# *Chapter Thirty-four*

"*M*ommy!"

Amy came barreling toward her mother, her chubby little legs pumping. She was wearing Ginny's Halloween costume, a blue taffeta princess dress, over her clothes.

Maddy scooped her up into her arms and buried her face into her soft hair. "Hello, sweetheart," she said, trying to keep her voice from quavering. "Time to go home." She looked up at Ruth Crandall, who was setting the table in her kitchen. "I'm sorry to be so late, Ruth. Was she good?"

"Good as gold," said Ruth. "There were three of them today. Sara Harrison was here, too. They all had a lot of fun together."

Maddy looked sadly at her daughter's beautiful, untroubled face, her tousled hair, the silly outfit, and felt a terrible sadness. Amy's life as she had known it was about to end. Her father's legal fate was now in doubt, but Maddy knew their life as a family was over. The problems of her marriage would never be resolved. I never meant for this to happen to you, she thought. I meant for you to have a happy life, with two loving parents who stayed together. I feel as if I have made a mess of your life.

"Whatsa matter, Mommy?" Amy asked, her face crumpling into a pout as she mimicked the sad expression her mother wore. Kids could always tell.

"Never mind. Go on now, and take off Ginny's costume and put it back in her room."

Amy obediently ran off down the hallway, calling out to her friend. Ruth stopped, still clutching a handful of silverware, and frowned at Maddy. "Is something wrong, Maddy?" she asked. "You do look terrible."

Maddy shook her head. It was impossible to put on a cheerful front. She and Ruth were not close friends, but they had spent a lot of time caring for one another's children, which was a uniquely trusting relationship. Maddy was ashamed to tell Ruth about what had happened. She was vaguely afraid that Ruth wouldn't want Ginny to play with Amy anymore, although Ruth did not seem like that sort of person. Besides, she would soon know, anyway. Everyone in town would know.

"I'm afraid so," said Maddy. "Doug . . ."

"What about him?" Ruth asked, and her disapproving tone made Maddy look at her in surprise.

"More trouble?" Ruth asked.

Maddy nodded. "Serious trouble," she said.

The two women looked at one another. Ruth sighed and resumed setting the table. "I'm sorry, Maddy," she said.

"You don't seem surprised."

Ruth shrugged. "I don't know what kind of trouble he's in. But that thing with the chief's daughter . . ."

"He was cleared of that," Maddy protested.

Ruth looked at her sympathetically. "Well . . . officially," she said.

"What do you mean?" Maddy asked. "Am I missing something?"

"I have teenagers," said Ruth, indicating the place settings that crowded the table. "They talk."

"You mean they talk about Doug?" Maddy cried.

Ruth looked pained. "The wife is always the last to know."

"No," said Maddy, shaking her head against it. Then she looked up at Ruth. "You never said anything. You didn't seem to mind Amy playing with Ginny. You even came to the hospital to get her."

"I love Amy. It's not her fault. It's not your fault, either."

Maddy sat there, stunned by this conversation. "How can I have been so blind?" she muttered.

Ruth shrugged. "We always keep hoping things will be okay."

"Things will never be okay again," Maddy said.

Ruth came over and put an arm around Maddy's slumped shoulders. "Now, now," she said. "Take it easy. You'll be all right. You have a beautiful daughter, you're very talented, and you'll manage. Somehow you'll manage. . . ."

"I'm so ashamed," said Maddy. "I feel as if the whole world knew what was going on but me."

"Hey, the court exonerated him. You believed in him. There's no shame in that. That's what you were supposed to do."

"While the local schoolchildren all knew better," Maddy cried.

"Don't waste time thinking about that," Ruth advised.

"Just take Amy home, curl up together, and try to get some rest. Unplug the phone and lock the door. Things will look better in the morning."

As Maddy tried to process this advice, she thought of Terry and Bonnie, still at her house. Maybe they'd be gone by now. Maybe they just left a note and took off. Oh God, I hope so, she thought. I just want to be alone.

Amy came back into the kitchen, minus the costume, followed by Donny, Ruth's eldest son. Maddy could not even look him in the eye. He was a teenager. He went to the high school. Was he looking at her pityingly, knowing that her husband tried to seduce the female students at his school?

"Come on, Amy," Maddy muttered. She lifted the child in her arms and carried her to the door.

Ruth held it open. "Remember," she said, "Amy is always welcome here. Always. And so are you."

Maddy did not reply because she was afraid she was going to cry. She held Amy tightly and carried her out to the car.

As Maddy pulled into the driveway she saw, with a sense of relief, that the Lewises' car was not there. Oh, thank God, maybe they're gone, she thought. Bonnie couldn't have been shopping all that time. Maybe they just packed up and left. Oh, please, God, she thought. She didn't want any thanks or long good-byes. She just wanted to have her house to herself, so that she could mourn this disaster in peace.

She opened the car door for Amy and lifted her out. "Is Dada home?" Amy asked, and Maddy felt her heart aching. What could she say—that the police suspected her daddy of being a murderer? Maddy couldn't believe it, but then again, she knew Doug so little. He might be right—that this was Chief Cameron's revenge for finally having the truth about Heather. Maybe the videotape of Doug with this Karla girl did not prove anything. Maybe the new witness was mistaken. Maybe, maybe, maybe. She would have to wait and see, like everyone else. She was through with being loyal. There was nothing to be loyal to. The man she thought she was married to didn't exist. Whether he'd killed Rebecca Starnes or not, this marriage was just as dead, Maddy thought.

It wasn't just the betrayal and the lies. It was those girls. What he had done was more than infidelity. It was vile. They were only schoolgirls. Someday Amy would be like them—vulnerable and insecure and attractive to men. Girls that age were supposed to be able to trust their teachers. Instead of being a role model, her husband had been a predator.

Maddy thought again of her own father. She could remember the response she would get from people when she identified herself as his daughter. Former students, men and women both, would tell her what a positive influence he had been on their lives. Tell her she was fortunate to be his daughter. Maddy looked at Amy and felt sad. No one would say that to her. To be Douglas Blake's daughter would be a source of shame. Maddy felt a hatred for him rise up, but she didn't want Amy to see it. Not Amy. To Amy she had to appear normal.

"Dada's not here," Maddy said. "Let's go in the house."

The child was satisfied with this foggy response and led the way to the front door. Maddy sighed when she closed the door behind her. She was glad to have a retreat from the world. The first thing she did was go directly to the phone and take it off the hook as Ruth had suggested. She had called Charles Henson on her way to Ruth Crandall's, and that was all she intended to do. Charles Henson had sounded a little distracted on the phone but agreed to meet Doug at the police station.

Maddy wondered if Charles Henson had known Doug was guilty when he'd defended him so ably before the administrative law judge. He seemed too honorable for that, but lawyers were widely regarded as sharks these days, and perhaps, behind his patrician exterior, Charles Henson was no exception. Maddy shook her head, as if to put the question out of her mind. It didn't matter anymore who believed Doug and who didn't. She didn't, and that was all that mattered.

Maddy took off her shoes, picked up the mail, and sat down to look at it. Amy had come in and immediately started playing with some of her toys in the living room. The house was quiet. Thank God they're gone, she thought again.

"I want Big Bird," Amy announced, sticking out her lower lip.

Maddy sighed and looked around the room. It wasn't there. "Sean probably left it upstairs," Maddy said. "We'll look later." She fervently hoped that Bonnie had not let the child take Amy's toy with him, or Amy would be inconsolable. Even as she thought it, she doubted it. Bonnie was meticulous. She would have left everything as she'd found it.

"I look now," Amy announced.

"Okay," Maddy said absently. "You go look."

Amy toddled resolutely toward the staircase as Maddy frowned at the windowed envelopes in her hands. Bills and more bills. They hadn't yet paid off their debts from

Doug's suspension. Now it would be just impossible. She felt oppressed and, for the first time, afraid. No, she thought. Don't allow yourself to think about it. If you think about the whole thing, it'll drive you mad. You'll just handle each problem as it comes along. What else, she wondered, can you do?

She put down the bills and tried to leaf through a children's clothing catalog, but immediately put that down, too. There would be no extra money for clothes or anything else. Looking at the prettily dressed children in those pictures only made her feel worse for her daughter. For herself.

"Mommy, come!" Amy's little voice cried out from the top of the stairs, terror in her tone. Maddy jumped up from her seat and ran to the stairs. Amy pointed down the hallway. "Mommy, come quick!" she shrieked.

Maddy did not stop to ask why. She could tell from the look on her child's face, the tone of her cry, that it was serious. She took the stairs two at a time, with a force she didn't realize she had in her, and scooped up Amy at the top of the stairs. "What is it, baby? Are you hurt?"

"Sean's dada," she cried.

Sean's dada. What in the world? Were they still here? There was no car. What was going on? She rushed down the hall to the guest room and stopped in the doorway. Sean was seated on the floor, wearing only a shirt, jangling a rattle that must have rolled under the crib. Beside him, sprawled on the floor, lay Terry Lewis, clutching at his stomach. His face was gray, and his eyes were half-open and rolled back in his head. A wet diaper lay open on the floor beside him.

Maddy put Amy down and fell to her knees on the floor beside him. She lifted his head with her forearm.

"What happened? Where's Bonnie? What are you doing up here?" She looked around frantically, trying to figure out what was wrong with him. There was no blood anywhere, but he looked dangerously ill.

"She didn't come back yet," he breathed. "Sean was crying. . . ." His voice was weak, only a whisper.

"Oh, my God," said Maddy, realizing what had occurred. "So you came up the stairs. Did you lift him? Out of the crib?"

Terry nodded slightly against her arm.

"Oh, God, I'm sorry. I forgot when I left you here . . ." She thought of how she had rushed out of the house, trying to flee from the police, trying to get to Doug before the cops did. "I'm so sorry."

She reached for a pillow from the bed and put it under his head. "Don't move now. I'm going to call 911," she said. "You're in bad shape."

The man on the floor did not protest. As Maddy scrambled to her feet, she heard a cry behind her. She turned around and saw Bonnie, standing in the doorway to the guest room, her face ashen. Her mouth had dropped open as she stared at her husband on the floor.

"Terry, oh, Terry," she cried. "What happened?"

"It's my fault," said Maddy. "I thought you'd be right back."

Bonnie did not hear a word that Maddy said. "Oh, my darling," she wailed. She fell to her knees and crawled to her husband's side, lifting his head and cradling him against her breast. "What happened, my darling?"

Maddy bent down and cupped a comforting hand around Sean's little shoulders. "Apparently Terry heard Sean crying for him, came up, and lifted him out of the crib. I'm calling an ambulance. He doesn't look good," she said.

Terry looked up into his wife's anguished eyes. "He kept calling for Dada," he whispered. There was a smile on his own gray countenance that was half grimace, half bliss.

"Oh, you fool," Bonnie cried. "You silly fool. You did this for that brat? He's not even ours. Now look what's happened."

Maddy stared at the woman bent over her husband. She looked at Sean, who sat unnoticed by the foot of the crib. She thought for a moment that she had heard her wrong. But she knew by the sick, awful churning in her stomach that she had not.

In that same instant, Bonnie's back straightened, and she seemed to freeze. Terry was regarding her dazedly through a fog of pain. When Bonnie turned, Maddy thought she had never seen such coldness on a human face.

Maddy tried to pretend she hadn't heard it, but it was no use. Bonnie had instantly realized her mistake, and both women knew what it meant.

"My son," Terry whispered plaintively. Maddy and Bonnie just stared into each other's eyes.

# Chapter Thirty-five

*T*he duet from the second act of *Manon* was announced on the classical station that Nick had playing on his car radio. The duet was one of his favorites, and the cut they were about to play, with Placído Domingo and Montserrat Caballé, was, to his mind, the most stunning version of it. The angry recriminations of Des Grieux against the vain, shallow Manon, who has chosen wealth and ease over his love, and her anguished pleas for him to give her another chance, never failed to move him. The heady, passionate splendor of their mutual confession of love blew him away every time. Yet he was tempted to turn it off. It was only a fantasy, he thought bitterly. In real life people didn't give up luxury for love. People lived with their choices, hardly ever admitted their mistakes. His hand hovered over the dial, and then he drew it back and clamped it on the wheel. He could not resist the beauty of it. He was willing to feel the ache.

The glorious voices spiraled up, filling the car with their golden sound. Nick let it flow over him, washing away his momentary cynicism. Since when did I become so bitter? he thought as the lovers' last notes hung in the air. He had seen plenty of faithlessness and deceit between couples who came to him complaining of the empty shell their lives together had become. But in his years as a priest, he had also witnessed supreme devotion between lovers. He had seen couples stand by one another through sickness, despair, and disaster. He knew perfectly well that there was such a thing as true and lasting love—a steady flame that could not be extinguished by the sorrows of life. It's just my own love that was unrequited, he thought. No need to tar the world with that brush. He was glad he had listened to the duet. Just because he would never have his love was no reason to try to stop feeling.

He drove along in the gathering twilight, feeling weary and looking for a place to stop for the night. The days were short now, and he was unused to driving for hours at a time. As if in answer to this idle thought, a road sign announced that the town called Gravesport was ten miles away. It took him a minute to recognize the name, and then it occurred to him. That was the town where Bonnie Lewis had been a librarian. He thought about Bonnie and Terry. Theirs was an unlikely love story, but they had a life together. There could be no more devoted lover than Bonnie. Making all those trips, standing by Terry despite the fact that she must have met with universal disapproval for her choice. Admittedly it was a weird way to meet someone, but they had met, and found one another, and now they had a family.

Still, it was unfortunate that on the eve of Terry's freedom they had been in an auto accident. If you had to bump into someone, you were lucky to bump into Maddy, he thought. But still, it seemed as if they were so alone. Bonnie was too proud to admit that she needed anything. He wondered if anyone knew of their difficulties or might be willing to help them. Maybe I'll stop there, he thought. I could ask around and find out if someone who knows Bonnie might be concerned enough to lend the family a helping hand.

In a few minutes he reached the Gravesport exit, grateful to be off the highway at last. He drove to the center of town and cruised slowly down the main street. A sign on an ancient brick building at the end of the street read "Hotel." He parked in front and went inside.

The lobby was dimly lit and devoid of decoration except for the boldly patterned wallpaper of fire engines and old cars in burnt umber on a sallow gold background. By the front window stood two captain's chairs pulled up around a low table bearing a dusty plastic flower arrangement and an assortment of *Yankee* and *Reader's Digest* magazines. Nick walked up to the front desk and looked around. No one was in sight. The only indication that this was indeed a hotel was the crosshatched cabinet behind the desk with keys hanging out of the various pigeonholes.

"Hello," Nick called out. "Anybody here?"

A heavyset old woman with an uncombed thatch of gray hair shuffled out from behind a curtained doorway and stared suspiciously at the would-be customer.

"Could I get a room?" Nick asked.

With a nod the woman turned the guest book around and handed him a pen. Nick signed on the first empty line while the woman turned to the pigeonholes, found a key, and handed it to him. Nick knew that Maine natives had the reputation of being laconic, but this woman set a new standard, he thought.

She turned the book around, studied his signature, and said, "How long you staying?"

"Just the night," he said.

"Twenty-five dollars. Pay now."

Nick counted out the money and handed it to her. "Anywhere good to eat around here?" he asked.

"There's a café, on the corner," she said.

"Thanks," he said.

"Room one."

I wonder if I'm the only one here, he thought as he carried his overnight bag up the stairs. Do they ever have enough customers to fill up to room two? he wondered. He unlocked the door, pushed it open, and steeled himself. But the room was perfectly clean and comfortable, although, as in the lobby, no effort had been wasted on frivolity. There was a slightly sagging double bed with a green bedspread, a small bathroom with ancient fixtures, and two paint-by-number seascapes, each hanging in splendid isolation, one over the bed and one on the opposite wall. This'll be all right, he thought. He turned on the bedside lamp and decided to go out and face the café.

When he went back down the stairs, the proprietor had disappeared again. He went out into the quiet street and looked around. The café had a lighted sign, and he headed toward it. As he came around the curving corner of the main street, he saw that the public library, a small white clapboard building across the street, was still open. He hesitated for a moment, then crossed the street and went in.

The library was of a pretty good size for a town like

this, and he tried to imagine Bonnie working here day after day. Nick browsed through the stacks, more interested in the place than in the books. A couple of teenage girls sat together at a library table and giggled. Otherwise the library was empty. Behind the library desk sat a wiry old woman who looked as if she would crumble into dust if you touched her. Occasionally she looked up and glared at the girls, who stopped their giggling for a moment and then resumed. Nick walked up to the desk and smiled, but the woman did not return his smile. "Yes?" she asked.

"Hi," he said. "I'm . . . uh . . . I'm just in town for the night. I have a . . . friend who used to work here in the library. Bonnie Lewis. Her name used to be—"

"Nolan," the woman said flatly. She did not seem in the least surprised by, or interested in, his query. She didn't inquire after Bonnie's well-being. Obviously this was not a person who would be interested in helping out.

"Nolan, right," said Nick. "I was wondering . . . does she have family still living here in town?"

The woman pondered this question. "Bonnie. No. Not anymore. She lived with her mother until her mother died. That was a few years back."

"Oh," said Nick. "Was there nobody else?"

The woman glanced over at the girls, who were at it again. "Girls," she said. "You're in the library."

"Sorry, Miss Carr," said one of the girls, and bent her head over her book.

The woman shook her head. "She took a room in a house over on Maple Street. Do you want me to look up the address?"

"Would you?" asked Nick. "That would be very nice."

"Certainly," said Miss Carr in a tone of voice that said

"Looking things up is my business." She began to page neatly through a folder on her desk. No wonder Bonnie left here, Nick thought. Not so much as a "How's she doing? How's the baby?" These people must have been scandalized when Bonnie up and married a lifer in a prison and had a baby by him. There wasn't any liberal-minded, big city–type tolerance in a place like this.

Miss Carr handed him an address written on a three-by-five card in a flawless cursive hand. "There you are," she said crisply. She looked at her watch. "Fifteen minutes, girls," she said.

"Well, thank you," said Nick, holding the card aloft.

"You're welcome," said Miss Carr, turning back to her work.

Nick waited a moment for her to say something, anything. Clearly she was finished with him, their business concluded. Nick was glad to get back out onto the street. He looked at the address in the light of the lanterns on either side of the library door. It read "Bonnie Nolan," and then the "Nolan" was crossed out, and "Lewis" was typed above it. Then it said "c/o Hartwell, 12 Maple Street."

Nick sighed. He doubted he would have much luck at this house. It wasn't a family member—just someone she had roomed with. If Miss Carr was any indication, Bonnie wasn't much missed around here. He decided to eat first before he called on the Hartwells. He put the card in his pocket and crossed the street to the café.

# Chapter Thirty-six

$\mathcal{D}$oug smoothed back his hair and followed Charles Henson out of the elevator and through the lobby of the Taylorsville Courthouse. When they reached the sidewalk outside, Doug finally caught up with his attorney. The walkway to the courthouse was lined with gas lamps that exuded a pale glow in the autumn evening.

"Charles," he said, extending his hand to him. "You did a great job for me in there." They had just met with the district attorney, who had tried to convince them to accept a plea on a lesser charge than murder in the death of Rebecca Starnes; but Charles had rejected their offer and insisted that they didn't have enough evidence even to indict Doug, much less win at trial. "How about stopping somewhere for a drink?" Doug suggested.

Charles Henson turned and clasped the handle of his briefcase in front of him with both hands in an obvious effort to avoid the handshake. "I want to get home to my wife," he said. "It's a very important night for us. Frankly, I hesitated to come here tonight, but for the seriousness of the charges . . ."

Doug did not inquire what the Hensons' occasion was. He was far too absorbed in his own situation. "Well, maybe another time," he said.

Charles looked coolly at Doug. "This fight is just beginning, Doug. You understand that, don't you? You won this round, but the fight is far from over."

"Well, I have confidence in you," said Doug.

"Doug," he said, "you're entitled to the best possible legal representation. I don't think I'm that man anymore."

Doug stared at him in disbelief. "Wait a minute. You mean you're dropping my case? Are you worried that I'm not going to pay you? 'Cause if that's it . . ."

Charles shook his head. "I can recommend any number of people. . . ."

"I don't want any number of people," said Doug. "I want you!"

"That's impossible," said Charles. "I made up my mind while I was in there. Look, this case is going to take a lot of extra time. They're not just going to let it drop. Chief Cameron will not rest until you are in jail for this crime. This is going to take all the time and cunning of a good attorney, and right now I have more pressing matters in my personal life. I can't get involved in this. I'm going to be cutting back on my practice, not taking on something so demanding. . . ."

"But I am innocent," said Doug. "I never killed that Starnes girl. And I certainly don't know anything about a missing baby. It's absurd. They can't prove I did it, because I didn't do it. But I need you to defend me."

Charles peered at him through the lamplit darkness of the evening with thinly veiled contempt. "Are you innocent, Doug?"

"Of course I am, what do you mean?" Doug said.

Charles shook his head. "After viewing that tape in the DA's office, I think it is fatuous of you to call yourself innocent."

"All you're supposed to be concerned with is the crime itself, isn't that right?"

Charles glanced at the clock set into the courthouse cupola. Then he turned back to Doug. "Sometimes . . . things that happen in your life remind you that there are absolutes that have nothing to do with the law. It's important to me, right now, to stay on the side of the angels."

"How dare you be so high and mighty? You're just a hired gun. You're not supposed to be judging me!" Doug cried indignantly.

"You're right," said Charles. "That is not up to me. You can think of this like a peremptory challenge. No reason given. No further debate possible. Good night."

Without waiting for a reply, Charles turned and headed off to his car in the parking lot. Doug watched him go, feeling paralyzed. It had taken all the indignation he could muster to try to convince Charles Henson to stay with him. And it hadn't worked.

When he could make his legs move again, Doug started to walk. He walked to his car, got in, and turned on the engine. Automatically he put the car in gear and drove slowly through the parking lot. But when he reached the entrance to the parking lot, he hesitated. Which way to go?

He tried to imagine himself driving home to Maddy, but the look on her face this afternoon made him cringe inside. She had probably changed the locks on the house by now. Amy, of course, would be glad to see him, but he could not face her demands for attention. Kids were exhausting. He knew that Maddy wanted more of them, but he couldn't figure out why. Their demands were relentless. No, he thought, he couldn't face it right now.

He turned the car in the other direction and started to drive. He tried to think of a friend he could go to, but try as he might, there was no one. He wondered when he had become so alone. He thought about going to a bar. Much as he would enjoy the oblivion of a few drinks in quick succession, he did not want to get into some inane conversation with a stranger.

If he could be sure that he wouldn't see anyone he knew, and that the subject would stay strictly on football or hockey, that would be okay. But what if some woman perched on the barstool beside him? Women always wanted to talk about personal things. What would he say when she asked him about his life? That he was a man who had once tasted fame and fortune? That now he was a man with no money, in debt over his head to an attorney? A man who was about to lose his job over a stupid rule about students and teachers, and who was suspected of murder to boot? Yeah, that would clear out the surrounding barstools pretty quick. Still, the idea of a drink was appealing. A few drinks. He drove to a nearby liquor store, parked, and went inside.

The brightly lit store wasn't bustling, but it wasn't empty, either. Doug debated for a few moments, then picked out a bottle of vodka. The clerk put it into a brown bag, and Doug carried it out to his car. Now what? he thought. A cloud of despair enveloped him as he sat there, staring at the bag beside him on the seat. His passenger. His companion. Where could a man go to drink in peace? He thought of Binney Park but shook his head. That was all he needed, to be reminded of everything that had happened to him, just because he sat on a park bench and passed the time of day with a pretty girl. What kind of a world was it where that was a crime? They'd had a conversation and shared a package of crackers, and then she'd got up and left with the baby. All right, he had put his arm across the back of the bench and touched her shoulder. That was all he did, just touched her shoulder. Was it his fault she had ended up dead? If she hadn't been so jumpy when he touched her, she might still be alive. But no, she'd hopped off that bench like it was on fire and left him there feeling embarrassed. All he'd wanted was a little conversation, a little human warmth.

Doug turned on the engine. No, Binney Park was out of the question. Maybe the fort. He could go back up there. He'd have the place to himself at night. Sometimes kids went there to park, but they wouldn't bother with him. It wasn't much of a plan, but it was all he could think of.

Doug turned on the radio and set out. He had planned to wait to have a drink until he got to his destination, but he had a clawing thirst that he didn't normally feel. He wasn't much of a drinker, but tonight he craved oblivion. He hesitated for a moment and thought again of going home to Maddy. To try to get her back on his side. To try to make amends. But the thought was almost laughable. Even if she forgave him for one thing, there was another right behind it. Dammit, he didn't feel like getting down on his knees to her.

In a way, it was her fault, too. Not about the insurance, he admitted. He'd screwed up there, but all he was trying to do was coast for a while, save a little money. That could have happened to anyone. If she insisted on believing he was a murderer, that said more about her than it did about him. A woman was supposed to believe in her husband. The only reason he'd had to turn to young girls in the first place was because she had lost all her appeal. It had happened gradually, after the baby was born. She was so . . . maternal. She seemed old and serious and full of questions about the future. He needed someone to help him forget all that, not an overbearing female who wanted to put him in a cage and keep him there. Buy a house, have more kids, join the PTA. If sex couldn't be fun and its own kind of oblivion, what was it for?

Doug shook his head. She had never understood him. Never. He could not remember why he had thought it would be a good idea to get married and have a family. Probably just because he felt the pressure of society. Pressure, pressure, pressure. He was so sick of it. He reached for the brown paper bag, unscrewed the top of the bottle, looked around to be sure that no one was watching him, and then took a swig.

The liquid poured down his throat like a warm sedative, and he immediately felt the pressure on his chest start to lift. He'd never liked the taste of alcohol, but there was no denying the relief it provided. That's better, he thought. God, that feels better.

He drove in the direction of the fort.

# Chapter Thirty-seven

$\mathcal{I}$t was funny, Maddy thought, how some moments seemed to last for a long time, words hanging suspended in the air, as a person instantly, like a computer, ran through the possibilities, tried to assess the impact of each possible response and which would give them the best chance for survival. Like someone caught in an avalanche, or sucked into a riptide, the adrenaline surged through her. She needed to make the right choice, and make it instantly. The process took place in only a moment, but it seemed infinite, a lifetime in slow motion.

My best chance, she thought, is to pretend I didn't hear it. Tell myself I didn't hear it, or maybe I misheard it. Whatever. Make her believe it.

Maddy tried to force her body to follow her thoughts, not her feelings. Keep her expression impassive, keep her hands from trembling, keep her voice calm. She attempted to look at Bonnie sympathetically. "I'm calling an ambulance. He needs help right away," she said.

Bonnie clambered to her feet and grabbed Maddy's arm

in a viselike grip as she tried to turn away. "Oh no you don't," said Bonnie. "You're not calling anybody."

"Let go of my mommy," Amy cried.

"You shut up," said Bonnie.

"Mommy, why is she holding you?"

"It's all right, Amy," Maddy said. She felt the fear thundering through her. But she couldn't show it. For Amy's sake, for her own, for the baby's. She couldn't. "Let me go," she said to Bonnie. "You're scaring Amy."

"I don't care," Bonnie said defiantly. "You're all going to do what I say."

Maddy glanced at Sean, sitting on the floor, whimpering. "Bonnie, I don't know why you're doing this."

"Please. Don't play stupid," Bonnie stated. "I know you heard me."

"Heard you what?" Maddy cried. "What are you talking about?"

"You're making me angry," said Bonnie, but she seemed to waver a little. Bonnie tried to size up the situation, wanting to believe, as much as Maddy wanted her to, that her secret was safe. Sean began to wail on the floor, and Maddy looked over at him. Bonnie kept her gaze trained on Maddy.

"Don't you think you'd better see to him?" Maddy asked.

"Stop telling me how to take care of my kid," Bonnie said, and Maddy felt a flicker of hope. It was working. Bonnie was resuming the fiction.

"I'm sorry," said Maddy, keeping her tone unconcerned. "I do that, don't I? It's a bad habit of mine."

Suddenly, from the direction of the floor, a weak voice said, "Bonnie, why did you say that? Why did you say he wasn't ours?"

Both women turned and looked at the man who had pulled himself up to a sitting position on the floor, his back against a bureau drawer. Maddy felt all the hope drain out of her as Bonnie stared at her husband. It was no use, she realized. Bonnie was not an actress. She was not subtle. She was a heavy-handed person. She must have applied that heavy hand to the head of Rebecca Starnes to get this baby. Maddy flinched at the thought of that innocent young girl, doing a little baby-sitting for some pocket money, never having a reason to suspect that it would lead her to her death.

Then again, why was Terry asking these questions? Hadn't he been in on it? Maddy's mind raced. She could see that Terry really thought the baby was his. Suddenly Maddy remembered Father Nick's words, the words that had convinced her that the Lewises were on the up and up. He had baptized Sean. Father Nick would never lie about that.

Well then, it couldn't be Justin Wallace, could it? Hope returned once again. Maddy's mind bounced around other possibilities. Maybe Bonnie had adopted the baby and not told Terry. That wasn't the worst thing in the world. Maybe they would quarrel over it, but it was no cause for mayhem.

"Bonnie?" Terry asked again, then he grimaced and let out a yelp of pain. But he was determined to get an answer. "Why did you say it? Sean is our baby."

Bonnie stared at her husband, her eyes large and the whites showing behind her glasses. "I didn't mean it," she said.

Suddenly Terry tried to get to his feet. "Did you sleep with someone else?" he demanded.

Bonnie shook her head fearfully. "No. No. Never," she

pleaded. "Only you." She let go of Maddy and rushed to his side. "Believe me, darling. I would never."

"Then why did you say it?" he whispered.

"It was a mistake," Bonnie said miserably. "I don't know why I said it."

Maddy rubbed her arm where Bonnie had gripped it. She was sure that Bonnie was lying. No mother, no matter how indifferent, would deny her child. There was no mistake, but there was something that Terry didn't know.

"Don't lie to me," Terry threatened her. Maddy saw a menacing hint of the man who had weathered years in prison. "I heard what you said."

"Bonnie," Maddy tried to say as gently as possible, "did you adopt Sean? Is he a foster child?"

Bonnie whirled around and glared at her. "You keep out of this!" she shouted. Sean was crying loudly now, and Maddy had to resist the urge to go and pick him up. Amy clung to her leg, pale and silent.

Terry shook his head. "She was pregnant," he insisted. "That's why we got married."

"That's not the only reason," Bonnie protested.

"Save your strength," Maddy interrupted, trying to derail his insistent curiosity. She didn't want to hear any more. The more she heard, the deeper into danger she would slip. "You need to get to a hospital right away. You can talk about this later."

Terry stared at his wife. "You told me you were pregnant. And I figured it was God's will and his plan that I marry the woman who was bearing my son."

"Don't say it like that. We were in love," Bonnie said. There were tears in her eyes.

"Bonnie, you're being childish," he chided her. "You

knew my feelings. I wrote you many letters about it. About my new purpose—about doing God's will."

"But you signed them 'love,' " Bonnie whimpered.

"Now you're telling me," he breathed, his eyes closing in pain, "that this is not my son."

Maddy knew he was right, that Bonnie was lying about something, but she didn't know or care what. All she wanted was to get these people out of here. Now. And here was her chance. "Bonnie," she said sternly, "can't this wait? Terry needs help, right now."

Bonnie did not look up or even seem to hear her. She gripped her husband's arm and began to shake him. "You said you loved me. You told me so. You said we would be together forever. That wasn't just because of the baby. That was because you loved me. Only me. I know you did."

Terry did not open his eyes. "If he is not my son, then you are not my wife," he muttered. He leaned against the bureau and backed down to a sitting position.

Bonnie began to sob. "That's not fair."

Maddy almost felt sorry for her, so complete was her misery. This plain, lonely woman had wanted to believe in her Cinderella story. She had clung to it, and now the truth was being slapped in front of her.

Amy tugged at her mother's trouser leg. "Why is she crying, Mom?" she asked.

"She's upset, honey," said Maddy. "You go to your room."

"Why is Sean crying?"

"They have to leave," said Maddy, trying to think of something quickly. "He doesn't want to leave."

"Can't take Big Bird," said Amy with determination.

"No, no, he won't," Maddy said absently.

"He will. It's in the bag. I saw him. He's taking it."

"Amy, stop it," Maddy cried.

"He can't take it," the child insisted, stomping her feet. "I'm getting it. It's in there. I'm getting it."

The diaper bag that Bonnie always carried sat on the floor beside her where she had set it down when she walked in. Big Bird's foot was visible, sticking out of the top. Before Maddy realized what Amy was doing, the child marched over to it and rifled through it, trying to free the toy.

"Amy, don't," Maddy scolded, but the child had hold of her stuffed animal's leg and was tugging. As she pulled the fluffy yellow head free from the bottom of the bag, a flash of red caught Maddy's eye. She had heard about it before on the news, a hundred times. Whenever they showed those photos of the curly-headed Justin they always mentioned that he was wearing a hand-knit red sweater with a Dalmatian embroidered on the front. Amy let out a triumphant crow and embraced Big Bird as Maddy stared at the red sweater, lying in a heap on the floor, the Dalmatian on the pocket looking back at her with a cocked head and a whimsical look in his eye.

Bonnie, seeing the look on Maddy's face, gazed down at the red sweater and the diaper bag she had guarded so carefully. She sighed almost wistfully, then looked back at Maddy. "I should have thrown it away," she said. "But it was in perfect condition."

Maddy tried to pretend that she still did not understand. "I don't think this argument is any of my business. I'm going to take my daughter out of here. I want you two gone when I get back. I don't care where you go or what you do. I just want you gone."

"Oh no you don't," said Bonnie.

"This is your quarrel," Maddy said, trying to sound weary. "It's none of my concern."

"Leave Mrs. Blake alone," Terry ordered from his powerless position on the floor. "None of this is her fault."

"She knows too much," Bonnie retorted.

Maddy felt fear bubble up inside of her. "I don't know anything. I don't care about your personal life."

Streaks of mascara smudged on Bonnie's face, and Maddy was surprised to realize that Bonnie wore makeup. She had never looked closely enough at this woman. Bonnie was the kind of person who was overlooked. Until it was too late.

"You know who he is," Bonnie said flatly, inclining her head toward Sean. "Don't you?"

Of course she did. No matter what Father Nick had said, there was only one possibility. She looked at the baby sitting on the floor of her guest room, wailing, and she knew. That meant that this woman before her in the shapeless turtleneck and the dull gray skirt, streaks of mascara under her eyes, was a killer.

Maddy's breath was coming in short gasps, as if she had been sprinting and come to a halt. As if she had been forced down an alley with no exit. She had to face the facts. Suddenly, as if in a moment of calm in the chaos around her, she knew that she could not deny the baby any longer. She could not deny his wailing, or his identity, or all the horrible things that had happened to him. She didn't think it could save her if she did.

She walked over to the child, who was crying miserably on the floor, his face red, his nose running. It seemed inhuman to deny him, to leave him there uncomforted. None of them was going to get out of this unscathed. At least she could hold him. She bent down and picked him up, cradled him tenderly in her arms. She wiped his nose, and kissed his head, and held him to her chest.

"Don't cry, Justin," she said. The child's wailing stopped, and he lay very still against her, his eyes wide, clutching her with his tiny hands. "Don't cry, baby."

She turned and faced Bonnie, who was standing in front of her holding a gun.

# Chapter Thirty-eight

There had been only three customers in the café, and Nick's meal had been served without the slightest visible curiosity on the part of the server about the identity of the stranger. The atmosphere did not invite one to linger. He had quickly dispatched his Salisbury steak and walked back out onto the deserted streets.

Now he stood in front of Number Twelve Maple Street, a small gray clapboard-sided house that sat on a large untended lot covered with an ankle-high layer of leaves. The front of the house was almost obscured by scraggly evergreens, and even in the gathering darkness Nick could see that the paint on the clapboard was peeling off in large patches. A few lights were on in the windows behind the curtains, but Nick hesitated to intrude. The house was modest and shabby, and it seemed unlikely that anyone within would be able to offer the Lewises any financial support. But maybe there was someone who really did care about Bonnie. Moral support could be just as valuable. It couldn't do any harm to try, he reasoned. The worst he could meet was a short rebuff, which seemed standard in this part of the world. That didn't bother him.

He walked up to the front step and rang the doorbell. He was a little surprised to hear it chime inside the house. He had kind of figured that the doorbell would be broken, too. Everything else about the house was in such a state of disrepair. He noticed, as he stood waiting for someone to come, that one of the shutters had fallen off the front window and was resting up against the house, as if waiting for someone to come and fix it.

He heard footsteps approaching. For a moment he felt a tiny surge of apprehension. The house was so run-down and gloomy, he half expected a ghoulish figure to open the door and glare at him. To his surprise and relief, the door opened, and inside stood a pretty young girl in her early twenties, in bare feet, jeans, and a cheerful flowered shirt. Her gaze was guileless, and her bright smile lit up the gloomy foyer.

"Hello," she said pleasantly, throwing the door open wide.

"Miss . . . Hartwell?" he asked.

"Mrs. Hartwell," she said, beaming at him. "Colleen, actually."

This girl isn't from around here, Nick thought. He could hardly believe she belonged in this town, where he hadn't seen a smile since he arrived. "Um . . . my name is Nick Rylander. I'm a Catholic priest, actually, and I . . . uh, I have a friend who used to live here."

"In Gravesport, you mean?"

Nick glanced down at the card. "Yes, well, actually, here, in this house. I believe she rented a room from you. Bonnie . . . Bonnie Lewis?"

"Oh," she said, reaching out her hand across the

threshold and shaking his vigorously. "You're a friend of Bonnie's? Well, that's okay, then. Come in, Father. Come on in."

Surprised but pleased by this reception, Nick stepped into the gloomy foyer.

"I'm sorry it's so dark in here," she said. "The light bulb's burned out, and I can't reach it without a ladder. I'm waiting for my husband to come home, so he can fix it," she explained, motioning for him to follow her into the considerably brighter rooms of the house.

"Is he working late tonight?" asked Nick.

Colleen laughed as if he were being incredibly witty. "Oh no. I must have given you the wrong impression. He's a fisherman. He's out for weeks at a time. That's why the place gets so run-down. He's not around to keep it up." Colleen's placid expression radiated kindness, if not intelligence. "I try to keep up with it, but it's impossible."

Looking around her house, Nick wondered how hard she tried to keep up with anything. The house was a mess, every surface piled high with junk, and it looked as though no one had tried to pick up in weeks.

Colleen removed some newspapers, comic books, and a few pairs of worn socks from the corner seat on the sofa and tossed them onto an end table. "Sit down, why don't you?" she asked pleasantly. "Can I get you something? A cup of tea?"

He said yes before he stopped to consider the condition of her kitchen. Well, tea was only herbs and boiling water. How bad could it be?

"I was just having one myself," she said. She went into the kitchen, switched off the little TV on the counter, then stuck her head back in the living room. "What do you take in it?" she asked.

"Just sugar," he said.

She emerged in a few moments with two teacups in chipped saucers. She handed him one, made a space on the coffee table for her own, and cleared a teddy bear, some laundry, and a pile of catalogs off a chair so that she could sit, too.

She carefully tucked a long, shiny curl behind her ear, took a sip of tea, and gave him, once again, her warm, un-ruffled smile. "So," she said, "what brings you to Graves-port? It's nice to have a visitor. We're alone here so much with Georgie out to sea all the time."

"I'm passing through," said Nick. "I'm on my way to Canada. Nova Scotia, actually."

"Vacation?" she asked.

"No. I'm . . . working up there. At a monastery. Doing some art restoration."

She nodded, as if thinking this over carefully, but her expression told him that she didn't have a clue what he might be talking about. "And how do you know Bonnie?"

Nick looked at her narrowly. She didn't seem the judg-mental type, but he wondered how much she actually knew about Bonnie's life. He tried to phrase it carefully. "I actually knew her husband before I met Bonnie," he said.

"Terry!" she exclaimed. "Did you know him before he went to jail?" Her tone was absolutely without reproof. Nick congratulated himself on having come here. This woman might not be able to do much to help. She hardly seemed able to do much for herself. But she would cer-tainly care.

"I met Terry while he was in jail," said Nick. "We

spent a lot of time talking. I performed their wedding, actually."

"You did!" she exclaimed. "That is wonderful. Bonnie told me about the wedding. She can describe something and make it seem real. I think that's 'cause she reads a lot of books, you know. I don't read much," she admitted. "But Bonnie, she's different that way."

"I remember Terry telling me that he had sent out an ad asking for books, and she had sent him some," Father Nick recalled.

Colleen appeared delighted at this. "I always thought that was the sweetest romance, you know. Bonnie was so lonely, and they were penpals. There was something . . . I don't know, kind of old-fashioned about it, if you know what I mean. She used to wait for those letters. She would really and truly wait by the mailbox. Then rush up to her room when they came, just like a teenager."

Nick smiled and sipped tea. "It was good for both of them."

"Of course I never thought he'd get out of that jail. I used to say to her, 'Bonnie, he can never be a real husband to you.' It was a hopeless situation. But she didn't worry too much about it. She loved him, and that was that. Then, all of a sudden, that other guy confessed. Wasn't that great?" she enthused.

Nick nodded. "I was happy for him. For both of them."

Colleen nodded thoughtfully. "It was just like a miracle. I don't see how some people have no belief in miracles. I mean, that was one, right there."

"I agree," he said.

"Well, you would, wouldn't you, being a priest and all. I mean, poor Bonnie. No one in this town ever thought she'd find someone. She is a little . . ." Colleen tried to think of an apt phrase. She waggled her hand in front of her. "A little . . . stiff. But when you get to know her . . ."

"You knew her pretty well?" he said.

"As well as anyone, I guess. She wasn't one to confide in people. But we got along. Poor Bonnie had it rough, you know," Colleen confided, turning sad at the memory. "Her mother was terrible. Very mean to her. She was a pretty woman. Didn't look at all like Bonnie. She treated Bonnie like a slave, I hear, and I don't think she ever gave her any love. I think Bonnie just escaped into those books of hers. Nobody shed a tear around here when that lady died, I can tell you."

Nick nodded. It confirmed what he had suspected.

"Not to be un-Christian," Colleen added hastily, remembering that her visitor was a priest. "I mean, I know we're all supposed to love our neighbor and all . . ."

"Some people make it difficult, don't they," Nick said with a smile.

Colleen sighed and sank back into her chair. "I don't mind telling you, I miss having Bonnie around here. She's only been gone a week or so, and look at this mess. When she was here, this place was shipshape. I felt guilty even charging her rent, the way she took care of everything. The house was always picked up, and she'd do the shopping." Colleen leaned forward. "Now, don't get me wrong. I tried never to take advantage of her. Poor Bonnie'd been taken advantage enough of in her life by that witch of a mother. Oh no, I was always telling her, Don't work so hard. You don't have to do all that. But Bonnie hated a mess. Me, I don't even notice it," she admitted.

Nick stifled an urge to smile. It was pretty obvious that she didn't notice it. But she had a quality of goodness about her that made her appealing.

"So," said Colleen, "how're they doing now, anyway?"

Nick set down his teacup and leaned forward, clasping his hands. "That's actually what I came to talk to you about. I mean, I didn't know if Bonnie had any family in town. . . ."

Colleen shook her head. "I'm about as close as it gets."

"Well, I can see that," Nick said. "The truth is—"

A baby's thin wail pierced the air, emerging from a room down the darkened hallway. Colleen threw up her hands. "I'm sorry, Father, just a minute. I'll be right back."

She started down the hall, calling out, "Coming, angel. Coming, my little sweetpea."

He heard her murmuring, and the crying stopped immediately. In a few minutes she came back into the living room, carrying a big fat baby in her arms. He was wearing a stained sweatshirt and pants, but he was cooing happily in his mother's arms. "This is George junior," she said proudly.

"Very handsome lad," said Nick.

Colleen walked back to the kitchen, one arm wrapped securely around her baby, and got a bottle of milk from the refrigerator. She brought it back into the living room, sat down, settled the baby in her lap, and gave him the bottle. He began to suck on it contentedly. Colleen gazed at him in complete adoration and then forced herself to give her attention back to her guest.

"How old is he?" Nick asked politely.

"Eight months," Colleen answered. "He's full of mischief. Just like his dad. But he's good-natured like his dad, too. Bonnie used to take care of him sometimes. It was great having a built-in baby-sitter." She sighed, remembering. "One weekend I knew George senior was coming into port up the line, and I wanted to go up there and surprise him. I knew I couldn't because of Georgie here, but Bonnie insisted that I go. She wouldn't take no for an answer. So I just left Georgie with her, packed up my laciest things, and off I went. George was so surprised. It was like being honeymooners all over again. We had the whole weekend, alone together."

"I think Bonnie likes to be helpful," said Nick. "Although right now she's the one who needs a little help."

"Now, don't get the wrong idea. I didn't ask her to do it. She volunteered. She practically begged me," Colleen protested. "Anyway, you were telling me that she's in some kind of jam. What happened that she needs help?"

"Well, it seems that no sooner had Terry gotten out of prison than they were involved in a car accident."

"Oh no," Colleen exclaimed. "Not another one."

"Another one?" he asked.

"Well, that's how her mother died. Bonnie was driving her to a church fashion show or something, and she lost control of the car. Drove right into a tree. She was okay, but her mom never had a chance. She was in the death seat, and she was from the old school—didn't wear seat belts. The police said she never knew what hit her."

Nick winced. "Bonnie never mentioned it to me," he said.

"It happened a couple of years ago. I don't think she likes to talk about it," said Colleen. "That's just so sad about the accident. Just as they were really getting started, you know."

"I know," said Nick. "Luckily, there was a very nice person involved in the accident who took them in while Terry had surgery for a ruptured spleen."

"Them?" she asked, wiping a little milk off Georgie's chin with the tail of her shirt.

"Bonnie and Sean."

She looked up at him with a pleasant but blank look in her eye. "Who's Sean?" she asked.

Nick felt a ripple of anxiety. "Bonnie's baby," he said. "Her son."

"Baby? Bonnie doesn't have a baby."

Nick stifled a gasp, as if he had been hit with a bucket of cold water. Images were flooding in, confusing him. He tried to organize his thoughts. "Sure she does. Sean," he said. "Her baby with Terry. I baptized him."

Georgie chortled contentedly. Colleen wrapped him up closely in her arms and drew back a little as if Nick suddenly seemed menacing to her. "Are we talking about the same Bonnie?" she said.

"I don't know," said Nick. But suddenly he did.

# Chapter Thirty-nine

Terry struggled up to a sitting position, holding his stomach, and stared at his wife, who had the gun trained on Maddy and Justin Wallace. "Bonnie, what in hell are you doing?"

"I don't know," she said. "None of this was supposed to happen."

"Where did you get the gun? Why did she call Sean . . . whatever that name was."

"Justin," said Maddy. She rubbed the baby's head gently. "This is Justin Wallace. He was kidnapped a few days ago. And his baby-sitter was murdered."

"You're lying," Terry said flatly.

"Tell him, Bonnie. He's your husband. He has a right to know," said Maddy.

"Bonnie, is she telling the truth?" Terry pleaded. "Sweet Jesus, tell me this ain't the truth."

Bonnie turned on him angrily, the gun wavering away from Maddy. For a moment Maddy didn't know whether or not to lunge, to try to run. It was impossible to get away in this small room, with Terry splayed out on the floor. And she was holding the baby. She wasn't about to let him go. He was trembling in her arms, as if he knew there was danger in the air.

Bonnie glared at her husband. "I wrote to you when you were in prison. I called you, and came to visit when everybody thought you were a murderer. I never once said anything about what crimes you'd done. I didn't care. I loved you for yourself and I didn't care. I wasn't ashamed to marry a murderer. So why are you suddenly so high and mighty about me?"

"Because I don't wanna go back there," he shouted, and then doubled over, his face contorted with pain. "For something I didn't even do," he whispered. "But they'll think I did."

"I did it for you," Bonnie explained. "You wanted a baby so much."

Terry looked up at her with pure, black hatred. "For me?" he said.

"For you and me," she said petulantly. "For us."

"You killed a woman and kidnapped a baby for me?" He laughed, but his eyes were desperate. "Thanks a lot."

"You were happy about Sean," she protested.

"I thought he was my baby. I thought I was a father. I thought I was going to have a chance to do better by my kid than my old man did by me. That miserable prick." Terry shuddered from pain as he took in a deep breath. "And all the time I didn't even see it. I didn't realize you were a complete wacko. I spent enough time around wackos so that I should have known one when I saw it coming, but no. No. I had to go and marry one. I haven't been able to do anything right in my whole miserable life, but this . . . this is the capper. I marry a raving lunatic

who's a murdering kidnapper and I'll be back in jail before dawn."

"You love me," Bonnie insisted, pointing the gun at
him like an accusing finger.

Terry laughed mirthlessly. "Jesus loves you, babe. I
wish I'd never set eyes on you."

For a moment Bonnie sagged, her mouth hanging open
in disbelief. "You bastard," she breathed. Then she
straightened, regarding him with a pitiless wrath that was
frightening to behold. She did not hesitate. In one fluid
motion she pointed the pistol at his chest, steeled herself,
and fired. Terry's eyes opened wide in surprise as his
hand reached for the spot where the bullet went in. Blood
began to appear around his fingers and spread across his
shirt.

Maddy screamed and then jumped back as Bonnie
turned on her. Tendrils of smoke rose from the metal gun
barrel, and the acrid smell of gunpowder filled the room.
Until this moment, Maddy had never realized that guns
actually smoked when they were fired. "You shot him,"
she said helplessly. At that moment Amy appeared in the
doorway, frightened by the noise and crying for her
mother.

Maddy watched Terry slide back down onto the floor,
his eyes rolling back in his head.

"What is the matter with you?" Maddy asked, but there
was really no need for an answer.

Bonnie was shaking, looking at her bleeding husband
with horror. "I killed him. I killed the only one who ever
loved me." Then she shook her head. "No, he didn't love
me. He never did. Oh my God, oh my God!"

"Mommy," Amy cried, seeing the bleeding man on the
floor, the gun in Bonnie's hand.

Maddy did not hesitate. Still clutching Justin, she reached out and tried to grab the gun from Bonnie's hand. For a moment she felt the hot metal in her fingers, and then Bonnie jerked it up and wrested it away. "Get away!" Bonnie shrieked. "Get away or I'll kill you."

Maddy knelt beside her daughter, trying to avert her eyes from the scene and shield both children from Bonnie's madness. She could feel her heart pounding in her chest and she wanted to throw up, but she kept murmuring inanities to the whimpering children.

Bonnie lowered the gun and stared impassively at the man on the floor. "Nothing has worked out like I planned," she said.

Maddy watched her, not knowing what to expect next. Bonnie's mood was careening from hysteria to detachment. Now she looked out the window at the darkness, the bare branches of the trees in the moonlight. For a moment she stood there, lost in thought, seeming oblivious of her husband, who lay bleeding at her feet. Then she turned to Maddy. "Come on," she said. "We're going."

Maddy looked up at her, horrified. "Going where?"

"I don't know, but we have to get out of here," said Bonnie.

"Please, Bonnie," Maddy pleaded. "Just take the car and go. Leave us here. Please leave us. I won't call the police, I promise. You can pull out the phone lines. I don't care. Just leave us and go. You can disappear and no one will ever know who you are. You could start over somewhere. Just please, not the children. Why do they have to suffer?"

Bonnie's eyes glazed over at Maddy's final question. "I had to suffer," she said. "Why shouldn't they suffer? Come on. Let's get out of here. If you don't do anything wrong, I'll leave you somewhere when I'm finished with you. But right now, I need to take you with me. Come on," she said, waving the gun. "Let's go."

Glancing at Terry's inert form, Maddy did not dare to argue with her. "Come on, Amy," she said. "We have to go with Mrs. Lewis."

"Why? I don't want to go with her."

"Just get your jacket on," she said. She started to ask Bonnie if she could dress Justin, put him in a diaper and pants, but she decided it was better just to do it. She reached into the nearest suitcase, pulled out the first pants she grabbed, then lifted a diaper from the diaper bag. Bonnie did not seem to be paying much attention. She was staring down at Terry, who lay crumpled on the floor at her feet. Maddy set Justin on the bed and quickly put on the diaper and pants.

Bonnie fell to her knees beside Terry and gently pushed his hair back off his clammy forehead with her free hand. "Why couldn't he just have said he loved me?" she said. "I would have done anything for him. I did do everything for him. What does it take?" she asked.

Maddy did not know whether or not to reply. Bonnie's question could have been directed to Maddy or to an indifferent universe. She tried to summon up a sympathy she really didn't feel. "It's not too late," she said. "Let's call an ambulance. He might still be alive."

"It is too late," Bonnie responded.

Maddy forced herself to imagine the turbulence in Bonnie's heart, tried to force herself not to think about poor Rebecca Starnes, and the Wallaces, half out of their minds with fear and grief. She tried to put it all out of her mind and consider her words. Finally she said gingerly, "I know you've been hurt, Bonnie. I know it must be terrible for you. But can't you just leave the children out of this? They're completely innocent. They've never done anything to hurt anybody. Can't you just leave them here?"

"Leave them alone here in the house? What kind of a mother are you?" Bonnie asked impatiently, pushing herself to her feet. "You can't leave children alone in a house. They could get hurt."

"We could call someone to come over here and get them. We'll be long gone by then."

"Don't be ridiculous," said Bonnie. "They're coming with us. Now let's go."

Maddy picked up Justin and prepared to take him on the next step of his journey. Please, God, she thought. Let this not be the last.

# Chapter Forty

The moon was full and low in the sky, crisscrossed by bare tree branches. Ghostly gray clouds wafted past on their way to somewhere else. Doug clutched the neck of the vodka bottle and made a toast to the stationary moon and all the bright stars. He had toasted everything else he could think of. Why not the moon? It was good company. That was more than he could say for most of the people he could think of. He leaned against the wide railing that crowned the uppermost rampart of Fort Wynadot. The only thing higher was the guardhouse beside him. Doug thought about that moon again and wished he had a quarter for the viewer so he could study it like an astronomer. He fumbled in his pockets for change, but his hands were unsteady, and he dropped the coins he pulled out. "Fuck it," he muttered. "I'll climb up there and look." A narrow staircase led up to the guardhouse. At the foot of the stairs was a chain hung between the railings and a sign that read "No Visitors Beyond This Point." "Fuck you," he said. He clutched the bottle under his arm and threw his leg over the chain.

In the parking lot below, Randall Burke and Nina Stefano pulled up, and Randall tried to screen the car under the bare branches of a tree, to give them some privacy. He wished he had somewhere else to take her, but this car, borrowed from his older brother, was the best he could do. So far, she had been agreeable, but Nina was a mercurial girl, and he was like a guy walking through a minefield, trying with all his might not to say or do anything that would piss her off.

They had lots of fights, which only increased his ardor for her. They would be going along just fine, having a great time, laughing and accidentally touching over and over, when suddenly he'd say something and she'd take it the wrong way and boom, the night was ruined. She'd flash those black eyes angrily, toss her silky black hair, and demand to be taken home or she'd walk. More evenings ended that way. Tonight, however, things looked good, Randall thought. His palms were sweaty on the steering wheel, and he could feel a jolt of unbearable anticipation when he glanced at her profile. He parked the car with what he hoped was élan, turned to her, and rubbed one finger down her cheek. "Spooky out here tonight," he said. "With that full moon."

Nina stiffened with the usual irritation. "It's just your imagination," she said. It was not that she didn't like him. She did. And she wanted him, too. He was handsome in that burly, Irish way that was at once foreign and familiar to her. Hadn't she always, ever since she could remember, had crushes on altar boys at Our Lady who looked like him? No, it was just the way he went about it. He was so . . . respectful. For reasons she couldn't understand, that infuriated her.

"Maybe there are ghosts," he said, smiling bravely and

thinking about snaking an arm around her. "It's almost Halloween."

She reached up and swatted his fingers away. "Stop it," she said.

"Nina," he pleaded. "What's the matter?"

She felt the familiar fury rising again. "Nothing," she said.

He leaned across the seat and tried to kiss her cheek, but she turned her head and his kiss landed in her hair, above her ear.

He drew back in confusion. "I thought you wanted to come here," he said.

He did not understand that his only crime was being too timid. That if he wasn't more vehement, he would soon lose her to an older guy who knew enough to take control. She didn't want to have to grant permission. It was against her beliefs, to want to do what he asked of her. She needed to be carried away. She needed him to insist that she throw caution to the wind. The fact that Randall didn't understand this made her furious. Although, to be fair, she didn't understand it, either. So there they sat, side by side, filled with longing and unable to proceed. Nina huddled by the door and stared angrily through the windshield. Randall threw one hand across the steering wheel, shook his head, and sighed. There was no hope with her, he thought. There was just no way.

Suddenly she sat up in her seat. "Randy," she cried in a voice that made him tingle, "what is that?"

He turned to look at her, hope renewed, and saw that she was pointing to the fort.

"Look up there," she said. "It does look like a ghost."

Randy looked where she was pointing. "Jesus Christ,"

he exclaimed. A man was standing on the top step beside the guardhouse, holding on to its door with one hand.

"What's he doing?" she cried.

"I don't know," said Randall. He hesitated for a minute and then opened the car door on his side.

"What are you doing?" she asked.

"I better try to talk to him," he said.

"Be careful," she cried, clutching his forearm, and when he turned to face her in the moonlight, the fear in her eyes made him grab her by the arms and kiss her passionately. She kissed him back with equal fervor. For a moment he thought that he didn't care about the guy on the railing, but then, because he was a decent young man, he reluctantly pulled away from her and pushed open his door with a sigh.

Randall got out of the car and began walking slowly up the hill toward the fort. He made as much noise as he could, whistling, kicking leaves, so he didn't startle the guy. The least little thing and the guy might fall off. Randall kept his eyes on him the whole time as he climbed the hill. The man was weaving slightly from side to side, staring up at the stars. Randall could see he was holding something in one hand. Randall had a pretty good idea of what it was. He'd seen plenty of drunk people in his young life, and if this wasn't one of them, he'd be surprised, he thought. When he reached the walkway surrounding the fort, he made sure he was in a spot where the drunk guy could get a clear view of him in the moonlight.

"Hey, fella," he called up, trying to sound offhand. At the foot of the hill Nina got out of the car to watch, holding her breath.

The man on the guardhouse steps looked down without

surprise. He waved the bottle in Randall's direction. "Hey there," he responded in a dull, slurred voice.

"You know, that's kind of dangerous up there," said the teenager. "You maybe oughta come on down from there."

Douglas Blake peered at the teenager on the walkway below. He felt benign toward the boy. Hell, toward the whole world. He was above it all.

" 'S'nice up here," said Doug. "C'mon up. Have a drink." He gestured widely with the half-empty bottle.

Randall winced. "No thanks," he said.

Doug looked down, irritated by this party pooper. What kind of a kid would turn down having a drink up here on a beautiful night?

"Issa beautiful night," Doug cajoled. "C'mon."

"I think you better come on down," said Randall. "Do you need a hand?"

"I don't need a hand," said Doug. "I don't need nothin'." Unexpectedly he started to cry.

"I think you need a hand," said Randall. "I'm gonna come up there. You just sit tight."

Doug sniffed and wiped his nose as the boy disappeared into the gate of the fort. "I'm not sittin', actually," he said aloud to no one in particular. "I am tight, but I'm not sittin'." This joke amused him tremendously, and he started to laugh.

He didn't feel bad anymore. The tears were gone as quickly as they'd started. His mood seemed to be swinging wildly. He'd been drunk plenty of times, when he was young, when he lived in the frat house. He'd usually passed out, but he'd never much enjoyed it. It had been easy to stop doing that. In recent years he and Maddy never had much more than some wine. He thought about Maddy now, through the haze. For a moment he longed for her. He wished she were here with him. Close, the way they were when they first met.

Doug looked up at the stars and closed his eyes. No. He didn't want her here. She was no fun anymore. She'd never join him. He needed a friend. Like that youngster down there. Doug leaned out to see if the boy was still there. He had forgotten that the boy had come inside, was coming up to him. He looked down and didn't see anyone. Then, in the distance, standing by a car at the foot of the hill, he saw a vision in the moonlight. She was young and lovely, with black, shiny hair and long, shapely legs. She had her hands clasped together against her chest, and her big eyes looked sad. As if she were waiting for him, beckoning to him, wondering why he wasn't coming to her. She is a goddess, he thought, and even in his alcoholic haze he felt the rush of desire. Mine for the taking. He scrambled up on top of the round pipe that formed the railing for the steps, straightening up to get a better look at her. He lifted the bottle to wave at her, and as he did, it slipped from his grasp and hurtled toward the walkway below.

"Hey," he cried indignantly, as if the bottle had jumped from his hand. He reached out and tried to grab it. He felt his feet slip from the round pipe on which he stood. He reached out to grab the wall and caught the air.

Randall, who had rushed to the top level of the ramparts, heard a long, gurgling moan nearby him and the faraway sound of Nina shrieking. Then there was a loud thud. Randall ran to the rampart fence and looked up at the guardhouse. The man was gone. Then he looked out over the railing. The first thing he saw was Nina, screaming his name as she stumbled up the hill. The drunken man was nowhere to be seen. Randall looked straight down.

The man lay sprawled out on the walkway, a dark pool of blood spreading out around him. He was surrounded by the glass splinters of the vodka bottle, which glittered like diamonds in the moonlight.

# Chapter Forty-one

$\mathcal{N}$ick held the receiver to his ear and heard, for what seemed the thousandth time in twenty minutes, the shrill, infuriating buzz of the busy signal. She couldn't be talking on the phone this long, he thought. He clicked off the connection and rang for the operator.

"Still busy?" Colleen asked anxiously. She had been tiptoeing around the first floor of the house as if she were in church, trying to keep the baby quiet while Nick stood at the phone.

He nodded abruptly, then held up a hand as the operator came on. "Operator," he said, "could you cut in on a number for me? It's an emergency."

"What is the number?" the operator asked.

Nick gave her the number and waited, hanging in the empty air. He glanced at his watch, then drummed his fingers on the telephone table. The operator came back on the line.

"There's no one speaking on that line," she said.

"Damn," said Nick. The phone was off the hook. "Is

there any way to signal the person in the house that their phone is off the hook?"

"I'm afraid not, sir," said the operator.

"Well, thank you," said Nick. He hung up the phone and crossed his arms over his chest, frowning.

"No luck?" Colleen asked.

Nick shook his head. "I'm going to call the police," he said.

"Maybe you better," Colleen agreed anxiously.

Nick called information for the number of the Taylorsville Police Department and dialed. A brisk-sounding operator came on the line.

"Taylorsville Police. How may I help you?" she asked.

"Hello. I . . . my name is Nick Rylander and I think I might know something about the Wallace baby. . . ."

Before he could ask to speak to the chief, the operator said, "Please hold and I'll transfer you to the tips hot line. . . ." Nick heard a lot of clicking and then a ringing signal. While he waited impatiently for someone to pick up his call, he thought of Terry Lewis and a wave of guilt and regret broke over him. He was sure, he was absolutely certain, that Terry had been sincere in his belief that Sean was his son. Terry had trusted him, confided in him, and now, with this phone call, Nick would certainly send him back to prison. Even if he hadn't done a thing. After all the years he had spent wrongfully accused.

"Did you get someone?" Colleen whispered.

Nick nodded. "They have a separate line just for this case."

Colleen walked back and forth, patting Georgie, who lay comfortably against her, his thumb in his mouth. "I don't understand why she did it. Why did she tell him she had a baby? Why did she pretend that Georgie was hers?"

Nick shrugged. "She wanted him to marry her. She knew how much he wanted to have a child. Then, after all the lies about being pregnant, she had to come up with a baby."

"But how long did she think she could keep that up? What was she planning on doing when he got out of prison?"

"When they got married, she thought he was never going to get out of prison."

"So what was she going to do? Keep bringing Georgie to see him? What about when he got older and could talk?"

Nick shook his head. "I don't know. Maybe she didn't think that far ahead. Maybe she thought . . ."

"Maybe she was going to try to adopt a kid," Colleen suggested.

"With a husband in prison?" Nick asked. "I doubt it."

"But then Terry got out of prison and Bonnie really needed a baby—and quick."

Nick nodded grimly and put up a finger to his lips as another voice came on the line.

"Tips hot line, Taylorsville Police. How may I help you?"

"I'd really like to speak to the chief," said Nick.

"Are you calling in regard to the Starnes murder and the Wallace kidnapping?"

"Yes," said Nick, "but—"

"Please state your name and give me the information. I'll see that it gets to Chief Cameron."

"My name is Nicholas Rylander. I am a priest who used to be at St. Mary's Church. . . ."

"You're no longer there? Where are you calling from, sir?"

"Actually I'm calling from Maine. I don't see what difference that makes."

"What information do you have, sir?"

Nick refused to let his temper get the best of him. This was too important. "I have reason to believe that a Mrs. Bonnie Lewis may have taken the Wallace baby."

"What makes you think that, sir?"

"Well, I know that she is there in Taylorsville and she is traveling with a baby who is not her own. . . ."

"How do you know that, sir?"

Nick gripped the receiver as if he wanted to break it in exasperation. "Look, I don't want to get into the whole thing. Let me just talk to the chief."

"Sir, every tip we receive will be followed up. But we have hundreds of calls coming in. We will get to your information as soon as possible."

"You don't understand," Nick said furiously. "This is a matter of life and death."

"Oh, we certainly do understand that, sir. And we will check it out. Now, where can we locate this Mrs. Lewis? Do you know where she was staying? Is there a license plate?"

Nick fumed at the sound of the impassive voice. "I don't know her license plate. She's staying at the home of Douglas and Maddy Blake. On Decatur Street. Tell the chief you have to send someone over there. Right away."

The woman on the other end remained calm. "We will see to it, sir, ASAP. Thank you for calling the hot line."

Before he could say another word, she hung up.

Nick sat on the edge of a chair and rubbed his hands together. "Maybe there's some other explanation," he muttered. "You're sure she wasn't pregnant?"

"Not any more than you are. I can't believe she just

took Georgie like that. Passed him off as hers. . . ." Colleen bounced her baby protectively in her arms. "What did they say? Will they go and find her?"

Nick made a steeple of his fingers and pressed his face into the spire. He had done the right thing by alerting the police. Even though it meant betraying Terry and possibly sending him back to that prison. But he knew it wasn't enough. He had to get to Maddy. If she was in danger, wasn't it his fault? He remembered her suspicions, the way she had searched Bonnie's belongings, looking for a clue about the baby. Hadn't he been the one who'd reassured her about Bonnie? Telling her how he had baptized Sean? It was his responsibility, really. Then he shook his head. This wasn't about responsibility. At least be honest with yourself, he thought. His desire to protect her was an ache in his throat. He looked at his watch again. Obviously it would take too long to drive. He needed to get there as fast as he could.

"There's something else," Colleen said anxiously.

Nick waited.

"Well, I was worried about Bonnie traveling by herself and I had this old Colt thirty-two that belonged to my dad. . . ."

"A gun?" he said.

"I'm not even sure it worked. I just told her she could wave it at someone if they bothered her. We were laughing about that before she left."

He thought about calling the police back. Then he stood up. "Where's the nearest airport?" he asked.

# Chapter Forty-two

$\mathcal{M}$addy drove, with Amy buckled into the front seat beside her. In the back, Justin was in the car seat. Bonnie sat behind the driver's seat, with the gun pointed at the nape of Maddy's neck. Maddy's neck was stiff from trying to hold it still. With every slight movement of her head she felt the cold steel brush her flesh, and it gave her a chill. At Bonnie's instructions they were heading north on the state thruway, although Maddy didn't know where. She suspected that Bonnie didn't have a destination in mind. She was just desperate to flee.

Amy seemed to understand that they were in danger. She hardly made a peep, didn't cry or ask for explanations. Justin had a pacifier stuck in his mouth and the motion of the car was lulling him into sleep, so there was at least a temporary, fragile quiet in the car as it hurtled through the night. With every passing mile Maddy felt an increased sense of despair and panic. No one knew where they were. No one would look for them. They were trapped in this car, going nowhere, with a woman who had nothing more to lose. From time to time she could hear Bonnie weeping in the backseat, sniffling and groaning in misery, muttering Terry's name. But the gun barrel never wavered from its position against Maddy's neck.

As she drove, Maddy saw a state trooper coming the other way in pursuit of a speeder on the almost empty highway. In vain she tried to devise a means of signaling him. Hoping to set off the radar and attract the attention of the highway patrol, she pressed her foot more heavily on the gas. In response, Bonnie pressed the gun barrel more deeply into her flesh and warned her to slow down.

Maddy did as she was told. She didn't know if there was any chance of escape, but she was not going to be foolish. Not with the two babies in the car. She slowed down and drove steadily, watching the miles click away, the names of the towns become less familiar.

"You know," said Bonnie, wiping tears from her eyes with her free hand, "no matter what he said, I think he really did love me. . . ."

Maddy marveled at Bonnie's ability to weep about the man she had just shot in cold blood. She would have felt less frightened if Bonnie were cursing her husband and praying for his damnation. That kind of anger was predictable, understandable even. It would be easy to know what to say, how to commiserate. But this . . .

"He wrote me a letter twice a week, for two years. Two years before we even met. Can you imagine that?" she asked. "He told me everything about himself in those letters. He poured out his heart to me. He was just a lonely kid who got into a little trouble.

"We got really close writing those letters. He probably would have married me even if I hadn't said I was pregnant. But I just felt he needed that little extra push, you know. Men can be stubborn about marriage. They don't want to get tied down. You might think that was strange for a lifer in prison, but he was a red-blooded American guy. Just like anybody else."

"Sometimes they do need a little encouragement," Maddy agreed carefully, trying to humor her. "Were you ever . . . were you really pregnant when you got married?"

"I tried to get pregnant, but it's not easy with a guy in prison. You don't see him much, and there are a lot of interruptions when you do try to do it." Bonnie's voice was gaining enthusiasm as she told her story. "But he believed me when I said I was. So, we got married. Then I had to come up with the baby." She was quiet for a minute, thinking things over. "First I just borrowed a friend's baby, and pretended it was mine. I don't know. I didn't plan ahead. I mean, who would have thought that he was ever going to get out. He was supposed to be in for life. I thought I'd have time to figure something out. . . . You know, say the kid drowned or got run over by a car or something."

Maddy stifled a gasp. This was the kind of loony thinking that was impossible to understand. She had to remind herself that it made sense to Bonnie. She could see that the other woman wanted to talk, to explain herself. Maybe if she could get some communication going between them . . . Not seem judgmental.

"So . . . what . . . you just looked for a baby, and then . . . what? The baby-sitter caught you trying to take Justin?"

Bonnie's tone of voice changed when she remembered. Gone were the sniffles and the plaintive tone. Instead her voice was steely as she remembered how she had accomplished her purpose. "I saw them in the park. I had a baby carriage and I was pretending to walk my own baby. It was just a doll, but she couldn't see into the carriage. I stopped and talked to her a minute, about babies, so I could get a look at him. I could see he would be perfect, but she kept her eye on him all the time. So, then I walked away, but I still kept an eye on them. And then some guy started bothering her and she got up and was trying to get away from him. . . ."

Maddy froze, remembering the police drawing, their inferences about her husband. In light of what she now knew . . . "Was it Doug?" she blurted out. "Was it my husband?"

"How would I know?" Bonnie said, annoyed at having her story interrupted. "I didn't look at the guy. I was busy looking at the baby, trying to figure out if this was the best one. Trying to get my courage up to do what I needed to do. It wasn't easy, you know," she said, as if she expected kudos for the feat she had performed.

"I'm sure," Maddy murmured, horrified by this whole recitation. It was like agreeing that the world was flat. Once you accepted the initial premise, anything that followed was possible.

"I saw them leave the park. She was upset about the guy touching her. So I caught up with her where I knew no one would see us. I pretended to be real sympathetic, and I went on about all the creeps these days, bothering women. Then I offered them a ride, you know, to get away from the park. And she took it. That was her mistake," Bonnie announced gleefully, as if recalling an opponent's shortsighted move in a chess game.

Maddy shuddered at the thought of the poor, innocent Rebecca Starnes, trapped by her own righteous desire not to get into any trouble. She did not want to hear any more. It was making her ill to hear it. But Bonnie was warming to her ghoulish reminiscences.

"You might not believe this, but I didn't really plan to kill her. I kept telling myself, I won't kill her if I don't have to." Bonnie chuckled, and Maddy's scalp prickled at the sound. She forced herself to watch the road.

"At first she was too shook up by the pervert to notice anything, but then she started asking questions about my baby. How come he wasn't in a car seat and all? She wanted to see him. She got real pushy about it. Then she wanted me to let her out. She kept saying, 'Pull over, pull over. Let us out, now.' That pissed me off," Bonnie recalled indignantly. "She had no reason to think badly of me. She started yanking on the door handle and kicking at the door, making great big scuff marks on everything. I'd gotten that car all spruced up and shined for Terry's big day. I told her to stop, but she was a pain in the ass. Finally, I pulled out the gun and I shot her. She keeled right over on the dashboard. I had to hightail it out of there, and drag her into the state forest. I didn't know where else to put her.

"I regret it now," Bonnie cried. "I swear I do. I wish I could just take it back. You know, once one of these things starts, it just snowballs. I did everything for him, for Terry, so he could have his son. . . ."

Bonnie's voice trailed off as she remembered how all her efforts had been for nothing because Terry didn't love her after all. Maddy felt a sickening twist in her stomach as she wondered again if it had been Doug there in the park, making a pass at Rebecca Starnes. Obviously he had not killed the girl. She thought that should make her feel more kindly toward him, but all she felt was numb. She looked in the rearview mirror and saw that Bonnie had rested her head on her forearm and was staring blankly out into the darkness, even as she held the gun to Maddy's neck.

She's insane, Maddy thought. She sees nothing wrong in what she did. Murdering that young girl seems to carry about the same amount of moral weight for her as if she had pinched a candy bar from a corner store. You've got to do something, Maddy told herself, do something now. But what could she do that would not endanger the children? She felt useless, unable to find a way out of this mess.

A car sped by her in the other lane, its taillights disappearing into the night. After a few moments she saw the flashing light of a state trooper's car in her rearview mirror and heard the whine of its siren. For a moment her heart lifted with hope, then fell again as the trooper's car whizzed by her in hot pursuit of the speeder. At the sound of the siren Bonnie sprang to attention.

"He was chasing a speeder," Maddy said, but even as she said it, she realized that somewhere up ahead he would catch the speeder and might even be standing by the side of the road. Maybe there was something she could do. Please, God, she thought. Give me a chance.

"Mommy, I'm hungry," Amy whimpered.

"We'll get you something," she said, trying to sound as if she were in control of the situation. "Bonnie," she said hesitantly, "we probably have to think about stopping for the night somewhere."

"Why?" said Bonnie.

"Because I'm going to nod off at the wheel. That's why," said Maddy.

"Just keep driving," said Bonnie. "I don't want to stop."

Bonnie's response did not surprise her. She didn't even know why she had asked. Just to distract her from any thoughts of the trooper, perhaps.

"I'm a widow," Bonnie said incredulously. "I'm a widow now."

Whose fault is that? Maddy wanted to ask. The statement sounded perversely funny to her ears, and she almost wanted to laugh, although she was at that moment very close to tears. All right, she thought, stay calm, pay attention to what is up ahead.

A mile later she saw them. The speeder was pulled over to the side, and the trooper was leaning into the window of the offender's car. Please look up at me, Maddy thought.

"How about a little music?" she said, reaching for the dashboard.

"I don't want any music," Bonnie said. "I need the quiet, to think."

Maddy wasn't really thinking about music. She just wanted an excuse to press the button for the emergency lights. She turned them on and hoped, desperately, that the trooper would look up and see them before Bonnie noticed the flashing on the dashboard. She could not tell what was happening. She did not dare look in the rearview mirror.

At that moment Justin awakened and began to cry, knocking the pacifier out of his mouth. Bonnie picked it up and shoved it back between the fussing child's gums. Thank you, baby, Maddy thought.

It all happened quickly on the highway. Once they were past the trooper Maddy reached out and pushed the button to turn off the flashers. Bonnie did not seem to notice. Maddy drove on, holding her breath and not daring to look behind her.

# Chapter Forty-three

There were five passengers on the commuter plane that Nick Rylander took to the Taylorsville County Airport. Nick usually disliked people who rushed to be first off the plane, but tonight he didn't care whom he offended. He was out of his seat and first to the door, ignoring the reproving look of the stewardess, whose only job on this tiny flight seemed to be informing people of what to do in a disaster. Nick was busy thinking about other disasters.

"Excuse me," he murmured. "Excuse me!" as he rushed past baggage handlers who were approaching the plane on the runway. He had come without even a bag, only his wallet. He'd left the rest in his car at the Maine airport. He'd found a flight that connected from La Guardia to Taylorsville with very little breathing room, and he wasn't going to miss it for the sake of a suitcase. It wasn't important, anyway. Nothing mattered but getting back.

Nick pulled open one of the double glass doors to the terminal and hurried in. He rushed to the rental car desk, only to find it unmanned. He looked around frantically. A ticket agent was walking back to his counter, balancing a paper cup of coffee and a piece of pie.

"Excuse me," said Nick. "Do you know where the rental car person is?"

The fellow nodded pleasantly. "She's over in the coffee shop."

"Thanks," said Nick. He ran across the terminal, found the coffee shop, and went inside. Two women were sitting at the counter, one dressed in a similar uniform to the ticket agent and the other a blond-haired woman in a red blazer with the rental car logo on the pocket.

"Excuse me," he said. "I need to rent a car right away."

The blond woman was visibly annoyed at being summoned on her break, but the anxiety in his pale face softened her attitude. "All right," she said.

"I'm sorry about your break. This is an emergency. It's terribly urgent."

The blonde got up from the counter stool. "Okay, I'm coming," she said. She picked up her cup of Coke to carry with her. "Catch you later," she said to her companion.

The woman walked slowly and deliberately back to her counter. Nick had to grit his teeth not to yell at her to hurry, but once she got behind her desk she was quick and efficient. In only a few minutes Nick was in his compact rental car, driving the dark, twisted roads toward Taylorsville.

He tried turning on the radio, but the music only made him more anxious, so he turned it off. This is probably stupid, he told himself. This is probably insane. He didn't care. He had to get to her and find out for himself what was going on, make sure Maddy was all right. She has a husband, he reminded himself, but that didn't really matter to him, either. Doug Blake was selfish. You could see it in his eyes. If that was what she wanted, well then, all right, but right now Nick believed that he himself had inadvertently put Maddy in harm's way, and it was up to him to help her.

Fortunately the roads back to town were familiar to him, because the drive, especially along the River Road, could be treacherous. He forced himself to slow down as the roads became steeper and more winding. It wouldn't do to hurt someone else in his zeal to protect Maddy.

As well as he knew the roads, he made two wrong turns before he was able to find the way to her house from the direction of the airport. Including yesterday, he had been to her house only twice. Their other meetings had been on his territory one way or the other. He probably could have made excuses to visit her more often, but he disliked the idea of going there, of seeing where she lived and ate and slept with her husband. He didn't want to be reminded that the woman he loved so hopelessly was the wife of another man. Nothing has changed, he reminded himself. Once this nightmare is over, you are going back to Canada. And she is staying here, with Doug. He realized that people would think this impromptu trip back was strange. That it showed an inordinate interest in Maddy's welfare. So what, he thought. You'll be leaving again, and you won't have to deal with the snide remarks and the whispers. And, he thought grimly, if you're right about Bonnie Lewis and the baby, whatever actions you take will be justified by the result.

He recognized Decatur Street and turned in, crawling slowly down the street until he came to Maddy's driveway. A couple of lights were on upstairs inside the house, but the first floor was dim. Maddy's car sat alone in the driveway, and the Lewises' car was gone. Nick sat in the driver's seat, his face aflame. Gone. The Lewises were gone. Oh, this is great, he thought. You are going to look like an ass. She's not going to be fooled for one minute. The first words out of her mouth are going to be, "What are you doing here?" Maybe with her husband right there by her side. And you will stand there looking like a perfect fool and try to explain why you had to personally swoop back into town and save her. He reminded himself that Maddy was not the only reason he had come. An innocent child was involved, a baby who, at the very least, belonged to someone other than the woman claiming to be his mother.

Focus on that, he thought. A person could fly around the world for a child in danger and no one would find it strange. Nick nodded as if in approval of his actions and opened the door of his car. He got out and strode up the walkway to the house. His heart was pounding as he reached the door and knocked, anticipating the sound of her footsteps, the look on her face as she threw the door open.

No one came. He waited a few minutes and knocked again. No one was home. Nick frowned. Maybe Maddy and Amy had gone off with Doug to celebrate once the Lewises were gone. He stood uncertainly on the step, wondering what to do next. It was undeniably anticlimactic to rush back like this, only to find an empty house. He felt a little knot of a headache forming over his left eyebrow. He felt more angry than weary. He stood with his hands on his hips, wondering what to do next. The Lewises may have disappeared, but they still had to be stopped. Regretfully he thought of Terry. Well, he'll have to take his lumps, Nick thought. The child is more important. He'd have to drive to the police station and tell them in person. That was all there was to it.

As he started down the walk, he thought he heard something. A noise that sounded like a moan. He turned around and looked at the house. It must be the wind in the trees, he thought. This time of year was spooky, no matter who you were. Even he, a priest, wouldn't want to walk through a graveyard on the night before Halloween. He hesitated, then started off again. When he heard the noise a second time, he was sure it was not the trees.

Nick walked back to the house and tried the doorknob. Locked. It's locked, he told himself. Nobody home. But he could not bring himself just to walk away. He looked at the door, then at the glass panels that surrounded it. Maddy had put stained glass into them. You've already made a fool of yourself, he thought. You didn't come this far to be fainthearted.

He looked around the doorway. Over in the corner, just beneath and beside the doorsill, were three garden statues of verdigris frogs squatting beside a juniper bush. Nick picked up the largest frog. After a silent apology to the homeowners, the frog, and the window, he hauled off and smashed through the panel nearest the knob.

He replaced the frog on the step, reached carefully through the jagged hole where the glass panel had been, and curved his hand around until he was able to unlock the door. He retracted his hand, turned the knob, and let himself in.

The foyer was dark and gloomy. "Is anybody here?" he called out loudly.

There was no answer. He stepped farther into the house, and then he heard it again. The moan. Nick felt the hair on the back of his neck stand on end. The sound was weak but distinct. It was coming from upstairs.

He took the stairs two at a time. A dim light was on in the upstairs hallway and he called out again. "Is anyone here?"

The moan was more urgent this time, meant to lead him. For a brief instant he thanked God that he had come back. He had not been a fool to come. There was someone in need. Nick saw two rooms had lights on. He walked to the first one and looked in. It was Amy's room, a shambles but empty. It had to be the other.

His mouth was dry, his heart hammering, as he approached the second room. He said a silent prayer and looked in.

The sight was horrible. Terry Lewis lay in a pool of blood on the floor, his skin as gray as cardboard. His eyes glimmered through narrow slits.

"Terry, my God, what's happened?" Nick knelt beside the wounded man. "What's happened to you?" The sight and smell of all the blood was sickening, but Nick forced himself to look. "You've been shot."

Terry nodded ever so slightly.

"Oh, my God," said Nick. Clearly Terry's life was seeping out of him. "You need a doctor right away. Terry, listen," Nick said, searching the other man's feeble gaze, "I'm gonna go call 911. Okay? Then I'll come right back. You need help."

As Nick tried to lower the man's head and get up, Terry raised one large tatooed forearm and gripped Nick's wrist with a strength that was amazing in one so weakened. All the years of weightlifting in the prison yard came to bear on that iron grip in which Terry held his would-be rescuer.

"Terry, let go. I've got to call for help," Nick pleaded.

"Bonnie," Terry whispered. "Kidnap." His voice was so faint that Nick had to put his ear to Terry's mouth to hear it. The words sent a chill through him.

"The baby," said Nick. "She kidnapped the Wallace baby, didn't she?"

Terry's nod was almost imperceptible.

"I know about Sean, Terry. I know he wasn't yours. I'm so sorry."

Terry tried to lick his lips. "Didn't know," he insisted.

"I know you didn't. She fooled everyone. What about Maddy? Is she all right? Are she and Amy with her husband?"

Terry's tongue peeped out from between his cracked lips again. Then he swallowed. He was agitated. "Gone," he whispered.

Nick's heart froze. "Gone where?" he said. "Gone with Bonnie?"

Terry nodded.

Nick felt the man slump with relief in his arms at being understood.

"Okay, listen, Terry," Nick said in a low, urgent voice. As he spoke, he worked to release the iron grip from his arm. "Let me go now, because I have to call the police. I have to alert them to find Bonnie, and I have to get some help for you."

Terry's eyelids fluttered and he shook his head.

"Please, Terry. You need a doctor right away."

Terry wet his lips. Nick wanted to tear free of him, but there was a plea in the man's gaze that held him.

"Twenty . . . third . . . Psalm," Terry whispered.

Tears rose to Nick's eyes. He had forgotten about faith. It might be too late for a doctor, and Terry knew it. But it was not too late for comfort. Nick grasped Terry's rough, hairy hands in his own and held them as tightly as he could. "I'm right here with you, my friend," he said.

The faintest hint of a smile glowed briefly in Terry's eyes. Nick made the sign of the cross, then grasped his hands again. "The Lord is my Shepherd," he began. "I shall not want. . . ."

Suddenly he heard the sounds of car doors slamming and radios crackling in the driveway. Heavy footsteps thundered to the door and voices identifying themselves as police shouted for Mrs. Blake. Nick looked questioningly at Terry, who seemed to be beyond all curiosity. Had they finally decided to respond to his call? Had they figured it out, too? "Up here!" Nick shouted. "We need help."

Terry tugged weakly at the lapel of his jacket, like a child whose favorite story had been interrupted. Nick saw innocence in his rugged, scarred face. "I'm sorry," Nick said with a deep regret for far more than the interruption. He looked sadly at this man, this child of God, who had dreamed righteous dreams of starting his life over.

"Let's begin again," Nick said gently. "The Lord is my Shepherd . . ."

# Chapter Forty-four

*P*olice and lab men swarmed over Maddy's house, collecting evidence and making calls. An ambulance waited outside, lights flashing, as four EMTs lifted Terry Lewis gingerly onto a stretcher, an oxygen mask over his ashen face, and hurried him out. Frank Cameron had put out an APB on Bonnie's car, and Pete Millard had called Donna and Johnny Wallace to tell them that there was news of Justin, that he was still alive and well, and that, with any luck, they would find him soon.

Nick leaned against a counter in the kitchen, having fielded questions from every detective in the house. Frank Cameron hung up the phone and looked at the clergyman's drawn face. "So, Father, why didn't you just call us when you found out about Bonnie Lewis?"

"I did call," said Nick. "Check your hot line tips."

"We're up to our eyebrows," Frank said apologetically.

"I just can't believe Doug Blake is dead," said Nick. That, he had learned, was the reason the police had shown up at Maddy's house in the first place. To tell her about her husband's fatal fall from the fort's tower.

"Good riddance to bad rubbish," Chief Cameron said pitilessly. Then he remembered whom he was talking to. "Sorry, Father. I had a personal grudge against the man. He did a lot of damage to my daughter. I can't say I'm sorry he's gone."

Nick shook his head impatiently. He hated it when people apologized to him for expressing their true feelings, as if he were a professional hypocrite instead of a flesh-and-blood man with less than admirable feelings of his own. "Did he jump?" Nick asked. "Was it deliberate?"

"No. A couple of kids saw him. He'd had too much to drink. He shouldn't have been fooling around up there."

Nick thought of Maddy, out there on the road with a crazy woman. Not even aware of the fact that she was a widow. I'll help her get through it all, he thought. Just bring her back to me safely, he prayed.

The door to Maddy's house burst open and Donna Wallace ran in, trailed by her husband and a uniformed officer who was trying to stop them. "Where's my baby?" Donna cried. Johnny grabbed her shoulders and squeezed them, his face slack from exhaustion.

Frank motioned for her to calm down. "We know where he is. We just don't have him yet."

"He's a hostage, isn't he?" Donna said.

"I don't want to use that word at this point," said Frank. "Hopefully, we will be able to apprehend them without an incident."

"Detective Millard said this woman had him. . . ."

"Mrs. Lewis." Frank nodded. "As far as we know, he's healthy, he's been well taken care of. Now that's good news, right?"

Donna began to sob.

"You better not lose him now," Johnny warned. "You can't do that to us."

Frank hated to hear his worst fear stated out loud. "We're not going to lose him," he barked. "Now I've got work to do. I can't stand here talking to you."

Just then the phone rang again, and Frank picked it up. His face changed as he listened carefully. "All right. That's great," he said. "On our way."

He hung up the phone. "All right, everybody. Listen up. A state trooper just spotted the car. Mrs. Blake gave him some kind of a signal. They're traveling north on the thruway."

Donna shrieked and then clapped her hands over her mouth.

Frank turned to the reinstated Len Wickes. "You drive," he said. "Let's move it."

"Yessir," Len exulted.

"We're coming with you," Donna Wallace said with grim determination.

Frank didn't bother to argue. He immediately decided on the lesser of two evils. "Pete," he said, "bring the Wallaces with you."

"I'm coming, too," said Nick.

"This isn't a fucking parade," Frank exploded.

"I know Bonnie Lewis. Maybe I can talk to her—be of some help."

Frank thought about it for a moment. Len Wickes was jingling his car keys. "All right, goddammit. But don't get in my way."

Nick followed the chief and Len Wickes out to the cruiser.

\* \* \*

Bonnie kept looking behind them, although there were no other cars in sight. She seemed to sense something.

"I'm hungry, Mom," Amy pleaded again.

"Honey, when we stop I'm going to get you something," Maddy promised.

The road seemed to stretch endlessly before her. How long before someone discovered they were missing? Apparently her signal to the trooper had not caught his eye. A sense of hopelessness came over her. At that same moment, she saw something in her rearview mirror that made her heart leap. There was no sound of sirens, but there was a flashing light far in the distance.

"Pull in there," Bonnie commanded.

Had she seen it, too? Maddy wondered. "Where?" she asked, trying to stall for time.

"Right there, where the arrow is. Do it now, or I'll shoot your kid."

Maddy quickly checked the empty lanes around her and veered over to the small sign and arrow that was marked discreetly on the right-hand side. She headed up the ramp, looking back regretfully at the distant flashing light.

"Now park," Bonnie ordered. "We'll go in there."

The one-story brick building was a rest stop and nothing more. It did not contain a business or a restaurant. Over in the far corner, two eighteen-wheel trucks were parked side by side. Maddy wondered, as she pulled into the otherwise deserted parking lot, whether she could somehow let the truck drivers know of her distress. No one was visible in either of the cabs. Maybe they were in the rest rooms. Most likely, judging from the out-of-the-way spot they had chosen to park, the drivers were taking a rest from the road, catching forty winks. She remembered seeing on TV somewhere that they slept in their cabs. They could hear me, she thought. Without pausing to think, she reached in front of her and began to blow the horn, as many loud blasts as she could. She counted about ten before she felt a stunning blow to her head. Bonnie had whacked her as hard as she could with the butt of the gun.

"Mommy's bleeding," Amy cried. "Don't hurt Mommy."

"Next time I'll shoot Mommy," Bonnie said through gritted teeth.

Maddy reached up to her head and looked dazedly at the blood all over her hands. Bonnie reached out and jerked back the seat belt, trying to choke her with it.

"Now get out of the car and do what I tell you."

"Okay, okay," Maddy breathed. She could feel the blood coursing down her face, but she ignored it. She undid her seat belt and reached over to free Amy from hers. In a flash Bonnie was out of the car and had the door open on Amy's side. She pulled Amy roughly from the front seat.

"Stop that. Don't you touch her!" Maddy cried.

"Just get the baby," said Bonnie.

"First you let go of my daughter."

"I need her," said Bonnie. "To make sure you do what I say."

Maddy closed her eyes for a moment. It's true, she thought. As long as you have my child, I will do what you say. She went back to the backseat, lifted Justin out, and held him to her. His diaper was soggy—she could feel it through his clothes. She reached into the diaper bag and sneaked out a diaper to take with her. She looked up at the trucks parked down at the end of the lot. There was no sign of life in them. They must incorporate the sound of horns into their dreams, she thought hopelessly. The baby rubbed his eyes and gave a fussy cry.

"Get inside," said Bonnie.

Maddy hurried to follow Bonnie's order, her eyes fixed on Bonnie's hand, which held Amy roughly by the collar. As Maddy feared, no one else was in the rest room building. The lobby offered a rack of information about tourist spots in the state and two vending machines, one for soda and one for crackers and candy.

"Oh, please, Mom," said Amy, "can I have a drink? Can I have some crackers?"

"Not now," barked Bonnie.

Maddy stiffened. "Please, Bonnie," she said. "She's hungry."

"I said no."

"It will only take a second," said Maddy. "If I don't give them something to eat and drink, they'll be fussing. Making a lot of noise. You know how irritating that is."

Bonnie frowned but relented. "Hurry up."

"I will," said Maddy, rifling in her coat pockets for some change, while she held Justin in the crook of her arm. Bonnie scanned the lobby impatiently while Maddy fed the machine and got Amy a packet of peanut-butter crackers and a Sprite. The child gratefully took the goodies and began to eat.

"Come in here," said Bonnie. "I've gotta go."

"We can wait out here," said Maddy.

"The hell you will," Bonnie snorted. She poked the gun in Amy's back and pushed her toward the ladies' rest room. The soda can slipped from the toddler's hand and started to spill out across the floor. Amy began to shriek. Bonnie ignored her protests, pulling her through the door, and Maddy hurried after them, pleading with Bonnie to be careful, not to hurt Amy.

Once inside the beige-tiled bathroom, Bonnie dragged the protesting child toward the stall with her.

"Mommy, no," Amy protested. She looked at her mother with terror in her eyes.

"Bonnie, for pity's sake," Maddy cried. "Let her wait out here with me. I promise you I won't do anything. I promise."

Bonnie just shook her head and jerked Amy by the arm into the stall. Maddy clenched her fists, her fingernails gouging into her palms as Amy's protesting wails echoed through the tiled bathroom. She turned and caught sight of herself in the bathroom mirror. One side of her face was running with blood from the blow to the side of her head. Her hands, which held Justin, were sticky with it.

The locked beige metal door opened, and Bonnie emerged with a squirming, red-faced Amy. The child wriggled from her grasp and ran to her mother, throwing her arms around her legs and burying her face against Maddy's knees.

Maddy crouched down, with Justin still on her shoulder, and put her arm around Amy. "I'm so sorry, baby," she whispered. She did not look up at Bonnie, afraid for her to see the hatred she felt toward her.

"Come on," said Bonnie.

Maddy stood up and took Amy's hand. Bonnie herded them out of the rest room door. As they entered the lobby, they heard car doors slamming outside. Bonnie's face paled. She ran to the window, resting the barrel of the gun on the sill. "Oh, Jesus!" she cried, looking outside. "Don't try to come in here!" she screamed out the slightly open window. "I've got two kids in here and I've got a gun."

Who is she talking to? Maddy wondered. She could hear the sounds of people outside, the murmur of voices and more doors and car trunks slamming. Then she heard the sound of a man's voice magnified by a bullhorn.

"Mrs. Bonnie Lewis, this is the state police. Come out with your hands up. Do not harm the others and we will treat you fairly. I repeat, come out right now."

Maddy crouched down and put an arm around each of the children. Her heart was pounding wildly. The police had found them. They were almost free. Thank you, God, she thought. She looked up at her captor, who was staring out the window into the brilliant glare of the headlights. "Please, Bonnie," Maddy said softly. "It's all over now. What's the use of staying in here? You can't get away from them."

Bonnie ignored her plea. "I'm going to kill them all," she yelled. "I've got nothing to lose. Listen to this if you don't believe me." She turned back toward the trio huddled on the floor. She pointed a gun in their direction.

"I'll show them," she said.

"No," Maddy cried, ducking her head and pulling the children close as Bonnie fired.

# Chapter Forty-five

$\mathcal{D}$onna struggled in the restraining arms of the police officer. "Let me go," she snarled. "Let go of me."

An hour had passed since they had wheeled into this parking lot outside the rest stop. An hour in which Bonnie had announced she would kill all her hostages, an hour in which they had heard a shot and a scream from inside the building. An officer in a bulletproof vest had tried, at one point, to walk toward the door of the little shelter, but Bonnie had fired a shot out the window, hitting the ground just shy of his feet, and he had rushed back to safety behind the cars.

The waiting was becoming intolerable. Donna Wallace had managed to wait days with less impatience than she felt now. She was becoming frantic at the thought that her child might be shot, might be dying in there. That she was unable to get to him and hold him. Johnny kept trying to soothe her with agitated optimism, but it was no use. She kept thinking about that insane woman in there with the gun, and she felt as if she were cracking, as if every moment were more unendurable than the last.

Breaking free from the officer, she rushed up to Frank Cameron, who was conferring with a state police officer. "Why can't you make her come out?" Donna demanded. "Why can't you do something? Tear gas or something. Make her come out. I want my baby back."

Frank made a face. "We're doing everything possible. But we can't just rush in there. She's already shot one man. She may have shot Mrs. Blake," he said. "She fired at a police officer just now. You've got to realize that she is extremely disturbed and dangerous. Please, stay out of the way. We're trying to get these people out of there alive."

Donna glared at him, but Frank was impervious to her anger. She did not seem to realize that this situation could end in a massacre. The Lewis woman was coming unstrung. Any abrupt move on their part might drive her right over the edge.

He turned his back on Donna, who felt the impotence of her situation boil up and bubble over inside of her. She marched up to Pete Millard, who was studying some SWAT team guidelines, the bullhorn resting on the hood of the cruiser beside him. Donna grabbed the bullhorn, picked it up, and examined it. There was a switch that turned it on. She flipped the switch, held the bullhorn to her mouth, and began to yell.

"Listen, you crazy . . . This is Donna Wallace. I am Justin's mother and I need my baby back." Her furious shout turned to a sob. "Please, come out and give him back to me. . . ."

Before she could get any further, Pete Millard snatched the bullhorn and began to chide her. "Stay out of this, Mrs. Wallace," he commanded. "We have experts who can handle this situation." Frank Cameron came rushing over.

"Well, they're not handling it very well, are they?"

Donna cried, collapsing into her husband's arms. "I want to hold my baby. He's right inside there. Isn't there something you can do? My God. I can't take any more of this."

"We're doing everything we can," Pete said soothingly.

"Get her out of here," barked Frank. "Mrs. Wallace, if you can't control yourself, I'm going to have you escorted out of here. Do you get it?"

"Stop yelling at her," said Johnny Wallace. "Jesus Christ, this is just a job to you. She's his mother."

"Okay, all right," Frank said irritably. "Just shut up. All of you. These situations take time."

Nick, who had been pacing back and forth frantically ever since they heard the shot from inside the building, waited until the distraught parents were led away. Then he approached a frowning Frank Cameron.

"Chief, I realize you have your own way of handling these things, but I'd really like to have a chance to talk to her. To Bonnie Lewis. I married her to her husband. I . . . I baptized the baby. . . . She might trust me. She might listen to me."

Frank sighed. "I wish we could get that goddamn phone in there working." The pay phone on the wall of the lobby was out of order. The phone company, at the behest of the police, was working diligently to see if it was something in the lines that could be fixed from outside.

Nick raked his hands through his hair as if to tear it out of his head. "I was thinking . . . maybe I could go inside. . . ."

"Are you crazy? Absolutely not. Do you want to get yourself killed?"

"If I went in unarmed . . . I'm sure she'd let me come in."

"Don't be an idiot," Frank snorted. "You saw what she did to her husband. We'll just wait it out. She can't last forever. Eventually, if nothing else, she's got to sleep. We don't rush these situations."

"The thing is . . . Mrs. Blake is in there with her . . . and the two children. And you know how children are. They might start getting on her nerves. They're probably crying and complaining. . . . I mean, in her state of mind . . ."

"What do you know about children?" said Frank.

"I'm afraid I don't know much about them at all," Nick admitted. "But, like you, in my job, I've seen a lot of people, a lot of families under stress. . . ."

Frank nodded, silently acknowledging the truth of what the priest said.

"Couldn't we just ask her if I could come in and talk to her?"

"I don't know," Frank said gruffly. "I'll think about it."

He walked off to confer with some other officers. Nick stood in the darkness behind the headlights that illuminated the grass, staring at the little building where Maddy was a captive. He knew what the police thought. There was an even chance that none of them was coming out of that building alive. The thought of it made his stomach lurch, so he put the thought away.

Think about what you'd say to Bonnie, he told himself. Imagine that you have a chance to try to reason with her. He tried to think, but the thoughts wouldn't get organized in his mind. He kept thinking of the Twenty-third Psalm, and of Maddy's face, looking down at him from a ladder in the chapel, her soft dark hair falling over her shoulder. Give me a chance, he thought, and he was not really sure to whom he was addressing the thought.

Frank Cameron returned and gave him a quick nod of acknowledgment. The truth was that Frank had never been called upon to negotiate a hostage release in his long career, and he was relying on the judgment of some of the more experienced troopers who were standing by. He had quickly conferred with them, and they had approved a plan to at least offer to send in the priest. "Okay," said Frank. "We're gonna ask her. If she says okay, are you ready to go in? You have to go in unarmed. No heroics."

Nick straightened up, his heart pounding. She might shoot him as he walked through the door, just to show that she meant business. It was entirely possible. "Yes, I'm ready," he said.

"All right," said Frank. "Here goes nothing. . . ."

He walked over to Pete Millard, who had been manning the bullhorn, and explained the latest decision to him. Pete nodded, switched on the horn, and held it up to his lips.

"Mrs. Lewis," he said politely, "Father Nick Rylander is here, and he wants to come in and talk to you. He says he's a friend of yours and your husband's. He's going to come in unarmed, if it's okay with you."

There was no immediate response from the little brick station.

Come on, Nick thought. Let me come in. Please, please. Give me a chance.

The cops looked at one another. "Is this a yes or a no?" Frank asked.

The state trooper in charge shrugged. "Hard to say."

"If it's okay with you," Pete said, reiterating a signal that, so far, Bonnie had not acknowledged in their negotiations, "open and close the blinds."

They waited, watching the window. Holding their collective breath. Suddenly there was a movement at the window. The blinds slid open and shut. Only once. But they had all seen it.

"All right," said Pete, smiling. "All right."

Now that it was a go, Nick's stomach churned. He tried to put the image of Terry Lewis, lying in a pool of blood, out of his mind.

"You ready, Father?" asked Frank.

Nick nodded.

"Now all we want you to do is talk to her," said the trooper. "Don't try anything fancy. You could jeopardize the lives of all the others. Forget James Bond. Just stick to the religious stuff, and try to downplay the consequences. I don't want you making her any promises like she won't be prosecuted for this. . . ."

Pete Millard laughed derisively. "Not much," he said.

"But," continued the trooper, "try to be reassuring. No such thing as a hopeless situation . . . blah, blah, blah . . . It's very important not to get her any more agitated than she already is."

"I understand," said Nick. His stomach was doing a roller-coaster turn.

"You got no safety net here," Frank warned him.

Nick nodded again, not trusting his voice.

"Raise your hands over your head," the state trooper advised.

Nick did what he was told. He said a silent prayer and stepped out in front of the headlights of the assembled police cars, the cordoned-off spectators, and the news organization vans.

Frank Cameron shook his head. "Are they sure about this? I don't like it," he said.

"Sometimes these nuts will listen to a priest when they won't listen to anybody else. I've seen it happen before."

Frank curled his lip. "She's too far gone. He could end up a hostage, too. Or worse. I wouldn't risk my life to walk in there."

The trooper shrugged and watched the man walk, arms uplifted in a gesture of surrender, toward the comfort station. "It's his funeral," he said.

"Let's hope not," said Pete.

# Chapter Forty-six

$\mathcal{M}$addy winced as she laid her coat out on the floor as a pallet for the children. "Why don't you lie down on this," she urged Amy, who had been weeping and clinging to her ever since the bullet struck her mother's side.

"It's all bloody," Amy cried.

"I know, honey," Maddy whispered, "but Mommy needs your help. Maybe if you lie down, Justin will lie down, too, and rest with you."

Amy wiped her tears and looked at the baby, propped up beside her mother, with renewed interest. This would be better than sleeping with a teddy bear. To have a real live baby sleeping beside you. She got busy arranging herself on the coat.

Maddy shivered and pulled her sweater tightly around her midriff, trying to deaden the pain she felt where the bullet entered. After the first searing shock of it, the pain diminished, and sharpened only when she moved around. All she had on now in the unheated building was a thin cotton shirt, blood-soaked under the arm down one side.

All in all, there had been less blood from the bullet wound than from the blow she had received on her head. But she wondered what damage it had done or was still doing. When she'd first realized that Bonnie had shot her, there was a moment where the room had begun to blacken into a pinpoint, and her teeth had begun chattering madly. Maddy recognized that she might be going into shock and willed herself not to succumb. She couldn't leave Amy and Justin to fend for themselves. She tried not to let the children see how much it hurt. They were frightened enough as it was, and at one point both of them had been sobbing. Bonnie had brandished the gun near them, warning them to shut up. Maddy had managed to calm them both down, managed not to shriek, but she felt as if her whole body were tensed up against the cold, the terror, and the exhaustion.

"Okay, I'm ready for him," Amy announced, extending her arms for the baby.

Maddy knew it wasn't going to be that easy. Justin was not a teddy bear, but a hungry, frustrated little baby. She wondered if she could even lift him onto the outspread coat. She took a deep breath and used her arm muscles. She moved him as quickly as she could, and Amy began to coo at him to lie down with her and go to sleep. Maddy was trying to muster enough breath to croon them a lullaby when suddenly she heard the bullhorn announcement that Father Rylander was outside and wanted to come in.

Father Rylander? It took her a few moments to realize that they were talking about Nick. Nick, she thought. What in the world was he doing here? Her heart welled up with a kind of giddy hope. She didn't care. He was here. That was all that mattered. And he was willing to come into this lion's den. She glanced at Bonnie, wondering how she was going to react to this suggestion. Bonnie stood staring blankly at the window, tapping the gun on the windowsill. Maddy didn't dare ask. She resumed singing softly to the children and waited.

"What does he want?" Bonnie muttered.

Maddy wasn't sure it was a question. She hesitated to speak. Bonnie turned and peered at her. "What do you think he wants?" she asked.

Maddy patted Justin and Amy, curled up together in her coat. She knew better than to antagonize her captor. She shook her head. "I don't know," she said. "I guess he wants to help."

"Speak up," Bonnie demanded.

"To help," Maddy said louder. "He wants to help."

"He wants to help you, maybe," Bonnie scoffed.

"I don't know how he ended up here," Maddy admitted. "He was on his way to Canada."

Bonnie shook her head. "I wonder if he knows about Terry." She caught Maddy's unwilling eye. "He knew Terry really loved me."

Maddy nodded, taking some encouragement from Bonnie's pensive tone of voice. "He told me about you and Terry," she said carefully. "He told me all about your love story, and how much you two meant to each other."

"See," Bonnie exclaimed.

"That's what he said to me," Maddy agreed.

Bonnie looked out the window again, toward the sea of cars and police and the certain doom that awaited her outside this building. "What good can he do?" she said hopelessly, but a querulous note hung in the air.

She needs a way out, Maddy realized. Maybe she wants me to convince her to let him in. "He might know something that will help," she said, casting about for the right words. She felt as if she were tiptoeing through a den of rattlers. It was important to get her mind off the pain and focus on finding the right words. "He's a priest, Bonnie. He won't lie to you. You know that, at least. And he's on your side. You know how much he cares for you and Terry."

Bonnie turned and gazed at Maddy and the children. "I should put an end to this whole thing right now," she said in a weary voice. She pointed the gun at them.

Maddy flinched, knowing that Bonnie was all too ready to shoot. She was not toying with them. Her desperation was genuine. Genuine and very dangerous.

"Why put an end to it," said Maddy, forcing herself to sound calm, "until you hear what he has to say? There's no hurry, is there? I mean, they can't get to you while we're in here. It might help to talk to someone who really understands. . . ."

Bonnie sighed. "All right." She turned and pulled the cord on the blind up and down. Maddy felt as if she had been punched in the chest. She nearly doubled over with relief and surprise. She knelt by her daughter's side, waiting, not looking up, as Bonnie watched from the window. After what seemed like an hour, although it was only minutes, she heard Bonnie walk to the door and open it.

Maddy felt the breeze that came for a brief moment through the open door. She looked up and saw him as the door closed behind him. He was wearing street clothes, a gray sweater, and his face was grim with worry. He looked at her, saw the blood caking on her face, staining her side, and it was all he could do not to cry out. Their eyes locked together for a moment, and Maddy sent him an unspoken warning. She said nothing and did not even smile. He understood and tore his gaze from her wounds, from her face.

Nick turned to Bonnie. He knew what she was now—a killer, a kidnapper, a person who savaged the laws of man and God. She had killed an innocent schoolgirl, shot her own husband, and now had spilled the blood of the woman he was in love with. She backed away, pointing the gun at him.

"What do you want?" she said.

"To help you," he said sincerely. Her gun did not frighten him. He belonged here. He had been thinking of the words in Matthew 9:12: "They that be whole need not a physician, but they that are sick."

"You can't help me," she said scornfully. "I think I'll kill you, too."

"I've seen Terry," he said, ignoring her threat. "I've talked to him. He's not dead, Bonnie. Did you know that? Did you know he's still alive?"

The police had shouted to them that Terry was alive, through the bullhorn, but Bonnie had dismissed this information as a tactic. "You're just saying that, right? Just to get me to leave. He was bleeding all over the floor."

Nick shook his head. "He wanted me to say the Twenty-third Psalm for him. He held my hand so tight, I thought he'd break it."

"He is strong," Bonnie said eagerly. Now she studied Nick's face and decided he was telling the truth. Her eyes lit up. Her slumped shoulders rose, then fell again. "I didn't believe them. I thought for sure he was dead," she said.

Nick ignored Maddy and the children on the floor, though he ached to rush to them. How badly was she hurt? he wondered. He had to free her, to get her to the doctor outside. He realized that Maddy didn't even know about Doug. Didn't know that her own husband was dead. But he was not about to say anything to her. Only one thing was important now. Everything else could wait. If he didn't get Bonnie through this, none of it mattered. "I know, Bonnie. But he's not dead. He's not. I swear it. I'm not saying he's in good shape. You know better. But he's a stubborn guy. You know that. He's a fighter. He doesn't quit."

Nick smiled at her, and she smiled back. For a moment her plain, angular face was suffused with love. Maddy felt as if she had seen a glimpse of Bonnie's soul, the corner of it that was pure. The corner that Terry Lewis had touched. Nick, Maddy realized, was able to pierce right through to that part of her—maybe because he was the one person who had known them, not doubted or criticized, and could testify that they had loved. Or perhaps because he radiated understanding, acceptance.

No wonder she let him in, Maddy thought. She felt as if Bonnie's hatred were beginning to seep away with Nick's words. She hesitated before she spoke, glancing at him for his approval. He nodded slightly.

"Bonnie," Maddy said gently, "maybe everything isn't as bad as you thought."

"He is a fighter, isn't he?" Bonnie said, beaming at Nick.

"He's a tough guy. But there's a good heart in him," Nick agreed.

The light suddenly went out in her, and Bonnie was gray and bitter again. "It doesn't matter," she said. "Even if he gets well, he'll hate me. . . ."

Maddy looked anxiously at Nick. "That's not true," she said. "It was a quarrel that got out of hand. Everyone has quarrels. My husband and I have them all the time. It's not the end of the world." As she spoke, Nick avoided her gaze, and Maddy had the sudden conviction that he already knew about Doug's latest disgrace. Her face flamed at the thought.

"How did this happen? I know how much you love Terry," Nick said gently.

Bonnie's face sagged, and she had to stifle an impulse to reach out and clutch at his arms. "He found out about the baby. He said he didn't love me. He said he never did, Father. She can tell you. She heard him."

Nick knew that Bonnie was referring to Maddy, but he did not allow his gaze to move from Bonnie's face. "He might have said something in anger that he didn't mean."

Bonnie drew back again, hardening, remembering the sting, the welt, of her husband's words. "He doesn't want me. I have nothing left to live for," she said.

"He felt betrayed about the baby. You can't blame him for that. You would have felt the same way. But Maddy's right. You're not the first lovers who ever quarreled."

"No," she agreed in a small voice. Then, remembering the enormity of her action, she shook her head. "But most people don't shoot each other."

Maddy saw real compassion for Bonnie in Nick's face, in his eyes. "There is such a thing as forgiveness," he said. "Terry has it within him. I know he does. He has the capacity to forgive you, and maybe you two could find your way back to one another."

Bonnie suddenly jerked herself out of the reverie of a happy reunion. "What do you know about it? You're a priest. You don't know anything about love. And don't give me a lot of God and Jesus talk. I'm warning you. I'm not like Terry. I don't believe in all that. I didn't let you in here for that. I don't know why I did let you in here."

Maddy stifled a gasp as pain stitched into her again. Bonnie was so erratic, it was hard to know which way she would turn. Nick remained calm.

"I think you needed to talk to somebody. Somebody who knows you. Knows what you've been through."

"Knows that I have nothing left," she said.

"What about Sean?" he asked.

Maddy's head jerked up; she could hardly believe her ears. Sean? she thought. Doesn't he know? Don't they know about Justin Wallace? What the hell is going on here? Does he think she's insane? She's not out of touch with reality. She knows perfectly well that she's a kidnapper and a killer. Is he trying to get her to shoot us? Maddy was furious. It was as if he had been walking surefootedly along, carrying them all on his shoulders, and had suddenly decided to make a preposterous leap. Nick caught her horrified expression and threw her a glance that said "Trust me."

Bonnie reacted in exactly the same way as Maddy. "Sean?" she cried. "Don't you know who he is?" she demanded, waving the gun at the baby. "I . . . kidnapped him. I killed the girl. Don't you know anything?" she screamed at him. "There is no Sean."

Nick gazed at her keenly and didn't flinch. "Of course there's a Sean," he said.

Bonnie started to tremble. "No. You're crazy," she said.

"I know this boy is Justin Wallace. I know that," Nick said softly. "But there is a Sean. Sean was a dream you had. The dream of a life that you wanted to have with Terry. I went to Maine, Bonnie. I went to the house where you used to live, and I met Colleen. I went there to see if there was someone who could help you out. You know, after the accident and all. You and Terry were trying to make a new start, and everything seemed to be going wrong.

"Colleen told me a lot about you. She told me about your mother, and what a hard life you had with her. Colleen said nobody deserved to be loved more than you."

Bonnie snorted. "She doesn't know about my mother. Nobody knows about that. Or about the accident, and what really happened. I'm sure she wouldn't be saying nice things about me if she knew that."

Nick tried to ignore her words, though they fed his suspicions about the "accidental" demise of Bonnie's mother. He tried not to think about it. He had to concentrate on convincing her. "Colleen told me about what a good friend you were to her. How much you helped her, and how she missed you when you left."

"I took her baby, too," Bonnie said defiantly. But her voice quivered. "I'll bet she didn't tell you that. Because she doesn't know that. I pretended he was Sean. That day of the baptism. I told her I would take care of him and then I brought him here, and said he was Sean. But there never was any Sean. Don't you see?"

"I know," he said quietly. "I know it was her son I baptized that day. George junior. But I also know that to you, it really was Sean. Wasn't it?"

Bonnie looked at him aghast. "Aren't you mad at me?" she asked, and her voice burbled, sounding like that of a small child.

Nick opened his hands wide. "You had your dreams. Sean—he was your dream. Of the life you wanted. Of a family to love. It wasn't so much to ask," he said. "Something you had never known. You made him real to Terry. And he was real to you. He lived in your mind and in your heart."

Bonnie turned away from him, and Maddy, holding her breath, braced herself against the wall and started to rise unsteadily to her feet. Bonnie shook her head, trying to reject this added burden he had put on her. She found his understanding unbearable. She was used to criticism and neglect. She had a vast tolerance for it. But her weary psyche started to crumble under the repeated blows of his compassion.

"All right," she said. In a warning voice she asked, "Just tell me this. Did Terry say he still loved me? Did he tell you that?"

Nick hesitated, knowing what she wanted to hear and knowing it wasn't true. Maddy, from where she was now standing, saw the fatal unwillingness to lie written on his face. Bonnie read his hesitation and immediately recognized the truth.

"You tried to trick me," she cried. "I knew it." She raised the gun at him and let out a howl. Maddy lunged forward, propelling herself off the wall, and clawed at Bonnie's face, knocking her glasses askew and throwing her off-balance. This time Nick did not hesitate. He grabbed Bonnie's arm and pinned it behind her. After prying the gun from her fingers with his free hand, he held the weapon out to Maddy, who reached for it, seized it.

Briefly Bonnie thrashed like a demon, and then, suddenly defeated, she slumped to her knees and began to weep. Nick lifted her gently, as if she were a balky child. Maddy edged toward the door, her gaze fixed on Bonnie as if she were a tiger at rest who might turn, at any moment, and pounce. But Bonnie was in another place. She didn't even notice.

Maddy went to the door, opened it, and threw the gun out onto the lawn. As it left her hand and sailed into the darkness, her heart finally lifted. She hardly felt the pain in her side. Turning back to the children, who were timidly lifting their faces from the folds of her coat on the floor, she opened her arms to them.

The gun lay there in the glare of the headlights. The police began to walk toward it gingerly, as if it were a meteor that had just fallen to earth. "It's a gun," someone yelled, and the people gathered outside gradually began to realize that the siege was over.

Donna Wallace was the first to act. Ignoring the warnings of her husband and the police, she bolted past the yellow sawhorses that formed a barricade. She dashed across the spotlit lawn toward the little brick building, her uncombed hair flying, her disheveled clothes flapping around her. She ran wildly, her lungs bursting. Maddy met her in the doorway, holding Justin in her arms.

# Chapter Forty-seven

*A*my pressed her nose against the oblong window and looked out in wonderment at the endless sky. She held up her doll, Loulou, to the window and pointed out the shapes of elephants in the clouds below. A stewardess stopped her rolling cart by their seats, offering a drink and some peanuts.

"Do you want some juice, honey?" Maddy asked.

Amy tore her gaze away from the view. "Yes, please," she caroled.

"Apple juice," said Maddy. "Nothing for me, thanks."

Maddy lowered Amy's tray, and the child accepted the cup of juice with both hands and began to slurp. Then she turned her attention back to the clouds.

Maddy looked at her daughter with tenderness. She was often fearful, wondering what scars the experiences of the last year might have left on her. But Amy had that fascination with the day-to-day that was the great joy and balm of childhood, and Maddy had hopes, only hopes, that she had survived without too much psychic damage.

The great elation of their release from Bonnie's captivity had immediately been tempered by the news of Doug's fall. Between his shocking death and her surgery for the bullet wound, Maddy could scarcely remember the days that followed. She remembered that certain people had been kind to her—Charles Henson, and Ruth Crandall, and most of all, of course, Nick. Still, it was a blur of the worst days of her life. The newspapers had taken a lurid delight in detailing Doug's sins, implying that his death had been an effort to escape punishment. The nice young couple who had seen it happen made a special trip by the house to tell her it wasn't so. He didn't jump. They thought it would help for her to know that, and it had. A little bit.

The stewardess stopped by again and picked up the cup. "You'll have to put up your tray now," she said kindly to Amy. "We'll be landing in a few minutes."

Maddy showed Amy how to lock the tray in place. They began their descent through the clouds.

"We won't get lost when the clouds wrap all around us, will we?" Amy asked.

"No." Maddy smiled and rubbed the back of her pudgy hand.

"Mommy, my ears hurt," Amy complained.

"I've got just the thing," said Maddy. She picked up her purse off the floor and rummaged around in it. She pulled out a stick of gum, unwrapped it, and handed it to Amy. "Here you go. Chew this and it will help your ears not to hurt."

Amy looked at her in amazement, wondering why her mother would ever think such a silly thing, but she liked gum and was perfectly content to chew it.

Maddy went to zip up her purse and saw the open envelope sticking up, the Canadian stamp in the corner. She pulled it out and removed the letter. She unfolded it and read it again. She had read it so many times, pondered it so often, she practically knew it by heart.

"Dear Maddy," it began. "It was good to talk to you the other night. My eyes were weary from looking at slides when you called. Teaching these art history courses makes me realize how much I have forgotten since I was in school. Fortunately the department head is patient and seems to want to keep me around.

"Good news about the Henson baby. I'm sure Charles must have been extremely worried about his wife giving birth, even with all the wonders of modern medicine. He must be breathing a sigh of relief, not to mention being deliriously happy, now that Katherine is safely here. I know what a help Charles has been to you in this last year. He seems like a good man to me, and I am really happy for both of them.

"I received another letter from Bonnie today. She is very depressed, of course, trying to come to grips with the reality of facing a lifetime in prison. That she deserves to be there doesn't seem to register. I'll answer her letter. I hope that doesn't make you angry with me. After all that has happened, I feel as if I have to. I'm only grateful that she pled out her case and spared everybody the agony of a trial. There was no chance she would get off, anyway. She told me that she got a letter from Terry the other day. Now he is writing to her in prison. Life is strange, isn't it?

"I have been thinking a lot about what you said on the phone. I want to make something very clear. I did not leave the priesthood because I expected you to marry me. I left because I knew that I couldn't keep my vows. I left because I didn't have any other choice. I don't know how to make you believe that. I know your trust in men and marriage has taken a pounding.

"I've tried to have optimism enough for both of us. But I also don't want you to get the wrong idea about me. I am no plaster saint. I'm in love with you. You know that. I told you so that night, in that most romantic of settings, a highway rest stop. That night, as I saw you crouching there with the children, all of us in fear for our lives, I promised myself that if the good Lord got us out alive, I would tell you how I felt, and damn the consequences.

"Just for the record, I'll say it again. I love you, Maddy. I want to marry you. I want you and me and Amy to be a family and for us to have more kids. I guess I've never made any secret of it since that terrible night.

"You, on the other hand, have not made any such pronouncements. While this is not an ultimatum, there are some things I need to know. Enclosed are two tickets to Montreal for next Friday afternoon. I want you and Amy to come up here, to see my little house in the woods (desperate for a woman's touch) and the university where I teach, and try on my world for size. I know you are afraid, but every love requires a leap of faith.

"You don't have to call me back. I will be at the airport to meet the plane, heart in hand. If you're not on it, I'll suffer. I'm willing to have my hopes dashed, to be publicly humiliated. I can see it in my mind's eye—a grown man trying to climb over a chain-link fence, screaming, 'Let me look on the plane myself. They've got to be there.' "

Maddy smiled again when she read his words.

"Please be there. Love, Nick."

She put her head back against the seat and sighed. She didn't blame him for wanting her to choose. His love, once he admitted to it, was ardent. She had never expected it, never suspected it. He had protected her fiercely this last year. From the very first, he had wanted her to leave Taylorsville and come with him, but she couldn't contemplate such a thing a year ago. When he left the priesthood she had warned him, angrily, not to do it on her behalf, that she could make no promises.

Maddy looked over at Amy as the engines roared and the plane bounced along the runway. The child was filled with delight at the bumps of the landing.

"Please remain seated until we come to a full stop," said the voice on the PA system as people immediately stood up and began to seize their luggage.

"This is us," said Maddy.

"Will Nick be here to get us?"

"Oh yes," Maddy said. She was certain of it, although she would never recover from the deceptions that Doug had put her through. She looked at Amy and wondered if she would ever tell her the truth about her father. She had tried not to let her bitterness taint the grieving process. Together they had mourned Doug's death, and Maddy thought perhaps she would just leave it at that. Someday, if she asked about her father . . . Well, who knows, Maddy thought. She may not even remember him. He will just be a shadowy figure, somewhere in her unconscious. He had never hurt Amy in any way. When she began to feel bitter she reminded herself of that.

She leaned over and unbuckled Amy's belt. "Don't forget Loulou," said Maddy.

Amy clutched the doll to her chest. "We're going to the woods," she told the doll seriously. "And have campfires."

They stood up and shuffled down the aisle of the plane.

Amy gave the stewardess a big good-bye as they reached the door. The stewardess returned the farewell enthusiastically. Maddy could feel her heart pounding as they walked through the tunnel to the gate. People were spilling out of the door around them, into the arms of waiting loved ones. She scanned the lounge, looking for him, and for a moment she was afraid. Little by little she had admitted to herself that she loved him. But how would she feel, here in his world, admitting it to him?

And then she saw him. He was coming toward them, and the worried look in his eyes was turning to joy at the sight of them. He was handsome and brave, and he loved her. She felt her doubts rise up into the air, like bubbles, and drift away. Amy darted away from her and ran into his arms. He lifted her up with a laugh. Mine, thought Maddy, watching them. She felt herself floating toward them, joining them. They were falling together, though they were standing still.

"I knew you'd come," he lied.

She knew it was a lie. No amount of faith could guarantee that a lover would love you back. But there were lies you had to tell yourself, to keep going. I know they will come. I know we will be together. I'm sure we will live happily ever after. It wasn't really a lie. It was hope.

"I love you," she whispered.

She felt him shudder and tighten his arms around her. "Say it again," he said.

And she did.